CROOKED LOVE

"You are honorable to tell me you won't stay. So that I don't engage in frivolous dreams." Miren tried to keep her voice steady, but she couldn't deny a pang of regret; better never to think of it than to be disappointed. "I will remain focused on my own task." She straightened her back. "My sheep. I'll need a new ram. Are you still planning to secure a shearing opportunity?"

Nathan laughed. "You're a practical little wolf, aren't you?"

Miren's eyes narrowed to slits. "What do you mean, 'wolf'?"

"You've got a way of targeting opponents and going in for the kill."

"I do not." Miren liked the comparison. A rakish smile grew on her lips as she imagined herself in that role. "Perhaps I do. Be that as it may, I must plan for the future."

"As a matter of fact, part of Simon's task in Aberfoyle is to secure a shepherd to aid your progress."

Miren brightened with excitement. "Truly? As long as he remembers that I am boss."

"No man is likely to forget that."

Miren frowned, but her glee didn't abate. "They are *my* sheep, after all."

"Maybe I can convince you that a night of fulfilled desire is worth a lifetime of dreams."

Nathan's voice changed, growing low and softly teasing. Miren peeked at him from the corner of her eye. "That seems unlikely." She paused. "How?"

Other *Love Spell* books by Stobie Piel:
THE DAWN STAR

STOBIE PIEL

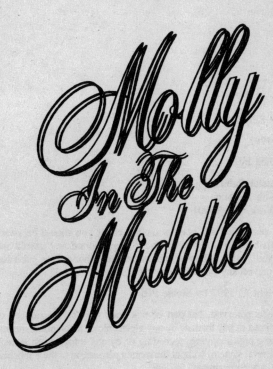

Molly In The Middle

LOVE SPELL **NEW YORK CITY**

LOVE SPELL®

April 1997

Published by

Dorchester Publishing Co., Inc.
276 Fifth Avenue
New York, NY 10001

Printed in the United States of America.

Dedicated to my sister, Lila Haghkerdar, in memory of our childhood with Border collies and Katahdin sheep. I am grateful and proud to share those memories with you.

To Joanna Cagan, who loves soft, squishy Border collie puppies and fat, stubborn sheep, too.

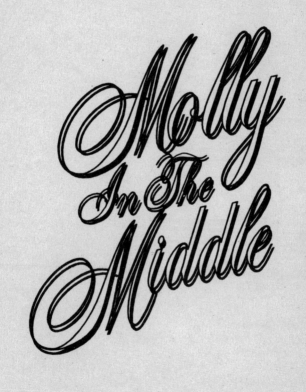

Chapter One

Argyll, Scotland
Spring, 1872

I don't like sheep. They are witless and silly, stubborn at times, and their rules of conduct are an insult to a thinking animal. Yet here I am, sitting beside my mistress, surveying the horizon, and what do I see? Sheep. Everywhere.

This task of "herding" is a strain to me, and one I hope to escape. I will escape! At all costs.

Miren Lindsay sat cross-legged on a crop of heather. Her tartan blanket provided some comfort against scratched legs, but the icy wind racing west over Loch Fyne made the issue a sorry bargain. She gazed across the rolling horizon of Argyll, watching as her flock grazed.

The finest flock in all Scotland. Every ewe looked fat and healthy. Her old ram appeared . . . proud. Stoic and noble and *proud*. A tiny smile grew on Miren's face. Her flock. It was all she had left since her father died. All that remained for her since being driven from her family's land in Kilmartin.

Since that time, a year's time, she and Molly had herded the flock through Argyll. Miren's thoughts halted. More accurately, the flock had moved through Argyll, and she and Molly had followed.

Through autumn and into winter the flock headed slowly south nearly to Kintyre. They situated themselves through the cold months on a windswept crag of land, eking out a feeble existence on heather. Spring came, and they moved north toward the Sound of Bute. They spent a few weeks grazing their way through the ancient burial cairns of Dunadd.

Apparently they found the ancient site tiresome, because they progressed onward until they reached the shores of Loch Fyne. They grazed awhile, then aimed north again. Miren had a worn map. They passed Lochgair, where they offended several farmers. Farther north, an irate gamekeeper demanded that Miren move her flock lest the local deer population be disturbed. Miren had learned during her tenure as shepherd that deer were held in much greater esteem than sheep.

The past week had seen the sheep moving ever closer to the town of Inveraray. Perhaps they'd stay long enough for her to purchase supplies. Maybe even a new dress.

After that, there was no telling. North into the highlands, west toward the sea . . . Miren couldn't guess, but her hopes that the flock would return to Kilmartin were long dashed.

Miren peered down at her dog. An exquisite Border collie, just over a year old. Her coat was black and shiny, because Miren brushed her often. Molly had an attractive narrow stripe down her nose. Her full, bushy tail wagged easily.

Except at sheep. Molly lay beside Miren. Not at attention as a Border collie should be, but comfortably on her side. Her head tilted away as if the sight of sheep pained her. As their months together progressed, Miren became more and more convinced that her cherished companion hated sheep.

Miren banished the thought and patted Molly's head. Molly

tilted her ear for better scratching. Miren complied. "We won't be at this forever, Molly. I promise. After a few more seasons, we'll have accumulated enough money from selling all this wool . . ."

Miren paused and eyed her sheep. They were Highland Blackface sheep. Their wool wasn't particularly salable. They could be sold for mutton, but Miren refused. She had become attached to her flock. Their lives were her responsibility. They wouldn't end up in someone's larder.

No need to think about their shortcomings now. Miren had plans. "When we've gotten them into shape, we'll sell the entire flock—to a worthy buyer, of course—and we'll purchase a ticket to America."

Miren's chin firmed as she ran over her much-considered plans. It sounded good. Easy. "We'll take a ship to America, and my Uncle Robert will take us in, and you'll have a bed of silk beside mine. We'll need more sheep, but more lambs are coming."

Molly's dark brown eyes tilted upward as if weighing the alternatives.

"Of course, I'm not entirely sure how we'll get them to market, or into a shearing situation that might profit us." Miren frowned. "If you would cooperate and *herd*, as Mr. Fergus assured me you would . . . that day might come sooner."

Molly looked away. Apparently, no promise was worth the effort of herding sheep.

"They seem to be on the move again, Molly." Miren sighed heavily and rose to her feet. She collected her tartan blanket and pleated it carefully. The plaid came from her father's Lindsay heritage, green crossed with burgundy. She used it as a blanket, as a dress, and as her only possession from the past.

Miren pinned the tartan over her shoulder with her silver brooch. When she purchased her puppy a year ago, with her last shillings, Mr. Fergus had given her a brooch to clasp her

11

tartan. Almost as if he endured a pang of guilt.

Miren glanced at her dog. Maybe Mr. Fergus knew, even then, that his prettiest puppy hated sheep.

Miren watched her flock plod across the slope. "I suppose we'll have to see where they're heading."

Or we could just let them amble off on their own . . . Molly eyed the sheep with distaste. Yes, the fat fools were ambling off again. Naturally. Sheep move at sunset.

Molly glanced up at her young mistress's face. Small, square chin firm. Eyes narrow and sure. Sure of what, Molly couldn't guess. Sure of aimless wandering that led nowhere, most likely.

A lesser dog might desert her post for a finer kind of scavenging. Perhaps to become a pet. Yes, a house pet. That was Molly's fondest dream. To be carried about in a coach, with livery and several horses. Humans in dutiful attendance.

She had seen a dog in these circumstances before. A small, foolish white dog with curling, ridiculous fur and pointy ears. A dog with a red bow atop its frivolous head. Molly pondered that bow, and decided she would do without that when the time came.

And the time would come. The young mistress was a kind owner, a generous feeder, but she had no skill with sheep. Instead, the girl followed the sheep with dedicated persistence, praised them lavishly, and tried very hard to enjoy their company.

Unfortunately, Molly was fond of the girl. She had bonded. She would stick to Miren Lindsay to the end. So if Molly was to secure a lavish position, it was necessary that Miren secure one, too.

The sheep aimed for a new field of tall grain. Miren trudged after them, but Molly pretended not to notice their direction and eased off the path.

"Molly! You're going the wrong way. Come!"

Molly returned to the path and forced herself into a reluctant jog to catch up. There was just no losing them. The entire flock spread across a wide field. Only their backs showed because the tall grass nearly covered their chubby bodies. Molly turned her back to the flock and gazed at a high-flying bird.

Miren patted her head and directed her attention back to the flock. "Good dog. *Good sheep*. Dogs *herd* sheep."

Only if a cliff was in sight . . . Molly eyed the sheep in intense dislike. They'd moved all night. Just when they seemed to settle, something startled them, and they moved off again. Molly's legs felt stiff. Her tail drooped.

The sheep lay in fat bunches now, chewing their cuds and looking unconcerned. One fat ewe—the one called, foolishly, Blossom—actually had the nerve to seize sprigs of grass while lying down. A low snarl grew in Molly's throat.

"Molly . . ." The warning voice. It never was followed by anything resembling punishment, so Molly growled again.

Miren patted her head again and slipped her a dried cookie. Molly took it, but her gaze fixed on Blossom. If the old ewe happened to die, and Miren could bring herself to cook it . . . One could always hope.

"They look content, don't they?" Miren sighed. "We can sleep here for a while."

Molly glared at the flock in disgust. *Don't count on it.*

"I am Nathan MacCallum." Nathan paused as his hosts turned pale. His gaze flicked from Lady MacCallum to her son. The son recovered first.

"That's impossible."

Nathan allowed himself to smile. He felt like a wolf cornering prey. "Surely you knew that my father was searching for me?" He spoke innocently, his eyes wide. Irene MacCallum just stared, her narrow, aristocratic face devoid of expression. Her son showed more anger.

"We understood there was an accident during my stepfather's visit to America." Brent Edgington placed his hand on his mother's shoulder. "Kenneth MacCallum, my stepfather, was killed in a fire . . . With his son."

Nathan furrowed his brow as if in grief. "Part of that story is indeed true. Kenneth MacCallum is dead." Nathan glanced around the sitting room. The seats were stiff, upholstered in silk damask. Useless armaments hung on the wall, claymores with their basket hilts, sgian-dhus, ancient dirks. A strange and adversarial meeting place. Nathan considered it an appropriate setting.

"Please, be seated, and I will explain the story as it occurred." Nathan spoke as if he owned the manor. Which, by law, he did. "I'm certain it will ease your hearts to know the details of his ending."

Lady MacCallum still hadn't spoken. Brent helped her into a high-backed chair and held her hand. A small reddish-brown dog scurried into the room. It resembled a tiny sled dog, but fiercer. It growled and yipped, backing toward its mistress in both fright and anger. Lady MacCallum took it onto her lap. "Hush, Muffin." She stroked the creature's back, and it softened into a lump.

Irene MacCallum wasn't as old as she looked. Her tense, overly poised manner made her seem elderly, but her age was forty-four, according to Simon. She kept her chin elevated as she spoke, her lips curled in perpetual disdain.

"Muffin is a Pomeranian. Queen Victoria has several, as her most cherished pets. They are of German origin. Muffin's breeding is, of course, impeccable. She is related by both sire and dam to the queen's own Skiffy."

Nathan glanced at the little dog, wondering why anyone would go out of their way to breed such a feeble creature.

"Mother's pride and joy." Brent chuckled, but the effect was strained. "Your arrival is a surprise, naturally. When we received Simon's message, we had no idea that you were with him." Brent was trying to sound calm. He even smiled. But Nathan saw the faint sheen of perspiration on the young man's face. It told far more than words.

14

Simon MacTavish stood beside Nathan, holding his seaman's cap in his hands. For the first time in Nathan's experience, Simon appeared deferential. He even held himself in a slightly bowed stance. It wasn't the Scotsman's normal attitude.

"Young Nathan suggested sending a message by post, but I felt it was better for Madam to receive this news in person. As you may remember, it was I who discovered the existence of your husband's wee bairn . . ." Simon cast a sidelong glance Nathan's way. Nathan repressed a groan. Wee bairn, indeed. "As I verified in America two years ago, Nathan is the only offspring of Kenneth's first marriage to poor, fragile Glenna Reid."

Brent straightened, his expression revealing offense. "We know, of course, that Kenneth had a previous marriage, and that it ended in tragedy when they went to America. We understood, however, that she died before giving birth."

"Just as poor Kenneth believed for all those years." Simon paused and sighed. "But in fact, his wife survived long enough to bear his son. The proof of this was submitted to Kenneth when I revealed his son's whereabouts in the spring of last year."

"We remember." Irene's voice revealed no anger, just controlled poise. "And naturally, Kenneth was ecstatic to learn he had a son. Naturally. Laird MacCallum and I were both widowed, burdened by grief. Our union was blessed with much devotion. I couldn't have been happier to learn that his first, tragic wife bore him a son."

Irene patted her son's hand and gazed up at him with an expression of maternal pride. Nathan considered the effect theatrical. "I understand that my father was ill. Perhaps this explains his wish to find his heir."

Irene sighed and nodded. "He was ill. Very ill. Our physician, Dr. Patterson, felt that his intention to travel was unwise. For this reason, he insisted on accompanying Laird MacCallum to America. He confessed to me prior to their

15

departure that he feared Kenneth's years would be short.''

Irene paused as if regaining control of her emotions, but Nathan's jaw set hard. ''He should know.''

Simon cast him a quick, warning glance. ''I met your husband and Dr. Patterson when they arrived in Philadelphia. I took them to the agreed meeting place, where Nathan was waiting in eager readiness to meet his long-lost father. The reunion was tender, I assure you, but cut short by tragedy.''

Brent's chin elevated slightly, as if he attempted to contain emotion. ''We have heard the sad tale, Simon. A fire broke out, killing all.''

''Not all, Mr. Edgington. When the fire broke out, Nathan and I were''—Simon paused as if a delicate matter were broached—'' 'checking the weather.' In our own respective spots.''

Nathan cast a dark glance Simon's way. Only Simon would resort to this excuse. ''Unfortunately, your stepfather and Dr. Patterson perished in the blaze before it could be contained.''

Irene dabbed at her eyes with a lace-edged handkerchief. Her dog growled. With her free hand, Irene squeezed it into silence. ''A tragedy.'' She sniffed, then drew a pained breath. Her gaze shifted to Nathan, her expression more clinical than distraught. ''We were never told your name. I assume you have proof of your identity?''

Nathan affected confusion. ''Do I need proof beyond Simon MacTavish's word?''

''No. No, of course not.'' Irene shook her head. ''Forgive me. There are so many shiftless persons in this day and age. Simon is, of course, perfectly trustworthy.''

''I have proof.'' Nathan reached into his vest and withdrew an ancient silver brooch. In ages past, it had been used to pin a tartan over the shoulder of a mighty chieftain. Kenneth MacCallum kept it as a badge of heritage.

Irene's eyes widened into pale blue pools as she studied the brooch. ''It is the MacCallum badge!''

Simon nodded. ''Your late husband gave this badge to his

son only an hour before his death. Its value is priceless, due to its antiquity and fine craftsmanship. As you know, Lady MacCallum, Kenneth never let anyone touch this badge.''

Irene sat back in her seat. Brent's hand slid from his mother's shoulder and hung limp at his side. ''Then you are indeed Kenneth MacCallum's son.'' Brent drew a tight breath, then affected the most inappropriate, inauthentic smile Nathan had ever seen. ''Laird MacCallum, allow me to be the first to welcome you to Scotland.''

Miren lay on her back, staring at the blue sky. Fat clouds hung above her, changing shapes in gradual precision to look like . . . sheep. One broke away from the mother cloud. Lambing season approached. Or would approach, if her ram hadn't lost interest in servicing the ewes.

After two weeks of wandering, her flock had finally settled in a lush pasture. A stream raced along the western edge, and Loch Fyne lay concealed to the east. Unfortunately, Miren detected a wheat field just north. That could be trouble, should a farmer discover her sheep trespassing.

Miren had scouted the area beyond, too. Only a narrow road leading north, between a rocky hill and the stream. That should keep them back. Maybe.

Miren shifted her gaze to her flock. ''Just one more set of lambs and we'll have enough to make a profit at shearing season.''

Molly didn't move her head, but her eyes shifted. The impression given was that they had too many sheep already.

Miren folded her arms behind her head. The air felt warm and soft. No rain. Spring gave way to summer, and it promised to be a fine season. The field was covered with bluebells, a bee drew nectar, then flew away. Miren's eyes drifted shut. She would miss this time when she was in America.

But she would be with her family. All that remained of it, anyway. William Lindsay died, and left her alone, but his brother would welcome her. Uncle Robert would understand how her father had suffered. After her mother died, William went into a decline that lasted many years.

His family emigrated to America, and William spoke of following, of new beginnings. As Miren reached adulthood, he gathered his wits again and began planning for her future. The challenge heartened him, and he launched himself whole-heartedly into a new career. Despite the fact he knew nothing about farming, he purchased a flock of Blackface sheep, intending to earn enough money for emigration.

Before a profit could be made, William died, leaving Miren with the flock, and nothing else. After his death, she learned that he had sold their cottage, for a pittance, to pay for the flock. Miren was ordered off the property, and the cottage was destroyed.

Miren refused to surrender the dream of emigration. There had to be a better life in America. Thousands upon thousands of impoverished Scottish families had already gone, as the country turned from farming to industrialization. America offered hope, and Miren needed hope. If only the sheep would cooperate . . .

It hadn't been easy. The worst incident, so far, was when an irate farmer near Lochgair aimed a gun at Miren and threatened to feast on her sheep if she didn't remove them from his pasture. If she shouted loud enough, waved her arms, and blew on her shepherd's whistle, she could get the flock to move. Assuming that Blossom, their leader, moved first.

When held at gunpoint, Blossom had seen the error of remaining in the field, and Miren's sheep were spared. Miren had avoided disaster then, and she would continue to do so. She would go to America, and everything would be all right. Maybe Uncle Robert would be proud that she had survived, on her own, with only her flock as inheritance.

Miren's breath slowed at that comforting thought. The sun warmed her face. Such a lovely pasture. If only they could stay awhile . . .

*   *   *

The last glimpse of white wool disappeared over the pasture's crest. Molly didn't move. She eyed her sleeping mistress, then the empty horizon. Gone! It was a start. A good start. Now if the young mistress could be persuaded not to wake . . .

Molly resisted a small pang of guilt. Miren would be upset. She might even cry. Molly's tail flipped to one side. It was for the young mistress's own good. With the sheep gone, she'd have to find a new vocation.

And take Molly with her.

"You're Nathan MacCallum, boy, and don't you forget it."

Simon MacTavish leaned forward in his seat, glaring. An expression Nathan considered permanent. Nathan gazed out the coach window at a neat, ordered pasture. Scotland was beautiful, perhaps, but he longed for the sea. "I've forgotten nothing."

Simon snorted in derision. "You never had much to remember, but now it matters. You're a laird's son. A laird's son must adhere to social standards *at all times*."

Nathan rolled his eyes, but he didn't respond. Simon tapped his knee. Nathan resisted the impulse to swat the old man's stubby hand away. "Mind my words, boy . . . Another slip-up like this morning . . ." Simon sputtered incoherently, probably in reference to Nathan's refusal of a starched cravat. "You're not in America anymore."

"That much is certain." Nathan turned his gaze to Simon. Simon's blue eyes blazed, at the height of emotion. Nathan drew a calm breath. "Should you refer to me as 'boy' again, indeed our position might be suspect."

The blaze of Simon's eyes intensified. "You're bound to be putting on airs, and I'm bound to follow. Don't you be forgetting who you are, or why we're here."

Nathan held Simon's fiery gaze until Simon twitched and looked away. "I know why we're here. When my brother's death is avenged, and his son secure, I will waste no time returning to 'what I am.' ''

Of all people to be confined with, Simon was the worst. They shared a common goal. They needed each other to restore justice in Scotland, and avenge a bitter wrong. All the more reason to hurry the process and be gone.

"It's been two weeks, and we don't have a speck of an idea why old Dr. Patterson turned murderer."

"We'll find the answer once we know the right question to ask."

"I can't see no reason why he'd want either Kenneth or young David dead." Simon crossed one short leg over the other. "It was a piece of luck he got killed in his own fire, though. He'd have been after the boy next."

"Which is why we must keep the child's existence secret from Irene MacCallum and her son."

Simon nodded. "The Fates act in a circle, boy. Patterson snuffed out two lives in a blaze started by his own hand, then got himself crushed by the door before he could get out. That's the way I'm seeing it. Holding onto the evidence, he was. Pinched the MacCallum badge, and it proved him a murderer."

Nathan retrieved the badge and looked at it. "I find it hard to believe that Patterson's sole purpose was robbery. This badge can't be worth that much."

"It's worth nothing."

Nathan eyed Simon doubtfully. "You said it was priceless."

"To a Scotsman, it is, boy. Something your kind couldn't understand."

"In what way is this worthless badge of value? If it could explain Patterson's greed . . ."

"Only a man of honor would understand. Patterson, he weren't that." Simon seized the badge from Nathan's hands. "It speaks of a time past, before the Jacobite Rebellion, before the atrocities of Culloden. It speaks of a time when clans determined their own fate, when our chieftains spoke with God, and God answered.''

Simon passed the badge back to Nathan and sighed as he looked out the window. He didn't look at the landscape. He looked at the sky. "Time's gone, now. But we don't forget. Scotland bows to English rule, our manor houses serve as hosts to their nobles. A good part of our chieftains now are just those who sided with our enemies in the past, and got themselves rewarded with our land.''

"Kenneth MacCallum remained Scottish."

"He did, boy, and don't you forget it. He weren't a good man. He drank too much, and when he drank, he got mean. Poor little Glenna, she suffered at his hands until she couldn't suffer no more.''

Nathan's jaw hardened, his lip curled in disgust. "That I know.''

"She dinna want her baby to suffer, too. So she ran off, and I helped her do it.''

Nathan studied Simon's craggy face. Beneath the contempt of Nathan's own heritage, beneath the gruff exterior, Simon MacTavish acted on honor. "Yet you admire this man. I've never understood why.''

"Old Kenneth, he held to the Gaelic way. He even spoke the tongue. He dealt with the English, but he never bowed to them.''

"His new wife is English, as is her son."

Simon scoffed. "Kenneth married Irene Edgington to cover his loss of Glenna. He was a widow, she lost her husband off in India. She had a son by that first husband. Mealy boy, he is, but she's devoted to him.''

"Almost as devoted as she is to Muffin."

Simon frowned. "Glad I am to be out of earshot of that dog, and no mistake. Cursed thing bites. But only when the lady isn't in the room. You noticed that, boy?''

"I noticed. Several times."

Simon issued a long sigh, then turned his attention back to

the Scottish sky. Nathan reclined against the coach wall. Time, and reason, would reveal the truth. His investigation moved forward. He'd convinced Irene MacCallum and her son that they were welcome to remain at his manor home. They accepted with grudging, reluctant gratitude, as he knew they would.

Everything worked according to plan. Nothing got in his way. He would set right the bitter wrong, then leave Scotland to memory. His memory would contain little but rain. Today was the first in a week to reveal the blue beyond the clouds.

Nathan closed his eyes and breathed deeply of the late spring air. Fresh, clear. Faintly scented with blossoms. Some sort of livestock animal. Which seemed odd . . .

The coach jerked to one side, a horse snorted. The coach stopped and Simon banged on the door. "What's going on, Grainger? Get moving!"

Nathan sat forward and adjusted the curtain to view the road. At first he saw nothing unusual, though he heard the coachman's muttered curses.

"Can't, sir." The coachman sounded both nervous about Simon's anger and annoyed by whatever circumstance delayed them.

Simon's ruddy face flushed red. "What do you mean, *can't*? What's stopping you?"

"Sheep, sir."

Nathan eyed Simon, then looked out the window. "Sheep?"

"Any amount of them, sir. Everywhere."

Nathan tried to open the coach door. It bumped something. Something both soft and sturdy. He shoved harder. Something grunted, then pushed away. Nathan looked out and down. "Sheep." He bent to look out the door. "Everywhere."

Behind the coach, beside, and before, Blackface sheep mulled. They appeared annoyed, as if they'd been harassed in some way. Some munched at roadside shrubs. None appeared eager to remove itself from the coach's onward path.

Molly in the Middle

Simon peered down from behind Nathan. "Scatter them, Grainger, and move onward."

"No place to scatter them, I'm afraid. We're between rock walls, both east and west. Ran into them at a bad spot, we did."

Nathan scanned the area. A thick, high stone wall ran along the western pasture, overhung with ancient rhododendrons budding with new lavender blossoms. Nathan grit his teeth in annoyance as he stepped down from the coach. A large, fat ewe shoved against him, then wedged herself toward a flowering shrub.

Simon squeezed his stout body from the coach and positioned himself behind Nathan. "This is unacceptable."

"Tell them that." Nathan edged a sheep aside. "I'll move them. We don't have time for this."

Simon trembled with irritation. "You'll do no such thing." He lowered his voice. "A laird's son does *not* tangle with sheep."

"Then the 'laird's son' is stuck."

"Where"—Simon's voice came as a low growl, the Scottish burr intensifying with his anger—"where is the shepherd?"

Grainger held the team's reins in one hand and shaded his eyes. "Looks to be up that way, sir."

Nathan made his way toward the front of his team. The two gray harness-horses looked tense as the sheep mulled around their legs. The narrow road ahead twisted around a bend, and there a woman appeared, a black collie close at her heels. She blew a high-pitched whistle violently. She waved her arms and shouted. The dog did nothing.

Nathan waited. The woman looked up and noticed his coach. Her shoulders slumped. Her head bowed, but she trudged forward, picking her way through the sheep. The dog followed her, but the sheep paid no attention to its presence. In fact, the sheep paid no attention to either mistress or dog. The girl had to wedge between them as they focused on the roadside shrubbery.

"Blossom! Move aside." The girl reached down and pushed the fat ewe out of her way. The dog disappeared beneath a mound of white wool, although Nathan heard occasional growls as they progressed toward him.

Simon stomped through the sheep. "Here she be . . . Wench!"

Nathan seized Simon's arm and met his eyes with a cold expression. "I will handle this."

Simon's bearded lips tightened into a frown, but he didn't argue.

The girl emerged from her flock, dog in tow. Like her sheep and her dog, the girl was a mess. Her hair fell in unkempt, light brown waves halfway down her back. Her dress resembled a sack, and no lady's gown. A worn tartan was tied around her waist, probably to keep the gown from falling off. She carried a pack over one shoulder.

She adjusted a tattered cape, revealing a glimpse of a lace collar around her neck. A touching attempt at fashion. Nathan's temper softened. She stopped in front of him, her head still bowed. She drew a quick breath, then looked up.

For an instant, she said nothing. Her eyes widened as if his appearance surprised her. As if she'd never seen anyone like him in her life. Strange, because no Scotsman so far had noticed anything unusual in his appearance.

"Good morning, sir." A forced and formal smile appeared on her lips.

Nathan couldn't answer. She was dirty, her hair was tangled. She obviously owned only one dress, and had worn it for months. Maybe longer. Her face was delicate and alert, despite her tense expression. Her eyes were dark blue, like a highland loch in a storm, wide and filled with hope.

And he'd never seen so lovely a woman in his life.

She was waiting for his response. Nathan cleared his throat. "Good morning, miss."

Her lips parted in astonishment. "You're American!"

"I am."

A sheep spotted a dandelion beneath the team and shoved its way beneath the lead horse. The horse picked up one hoof gingerly and tensed.

The girl closed her eyes as if in prayer and tried to smile. She seized the sheep by the wool and extracted it from beneath the horse. "Blossom, no!" She faced Nathan, looking pained. "They're not afraid of horses, you see."

"I see. They don't seem afraid of anything." Nathan eyed the Border collie at the girl's side. It waited eagerly, and paid no attention to its flock. Instead, the dog seemed more interested in inspecting his coach.

The girl noticed the direction of Nathan's gaze. "Molly is only a year old, and I haven't finished training her."

Nathan wanted to ask when she expected this "training" to begin, but restrained himself. He had a meeting to keep in Lochgair, where Dr. Patterson had tended an aging baroness. "Miss . . . ?"

"Miren Lindsay, sir." She held out her hand. He took it. It felt small and warm in his. Her fingers were dirty, the nails broken, but still delicate. She shook his hand, then straightened. "And you are called?"

"I am Nathan MacCallum." He waited for the inevitable surprise, the intense, feminine interest when she recognized his name. Everyone in Argyll seemed to know of his arrival and subsequent ascension to MacCallum's estate. But Miss Lindsay didn't react.

"And you own this property?" She gestured to the field of wheat beyond the wall.

"I do now."

Simon uttered a low, warning growl. "Laird MacCallum has recently arrived from America, young woman, which is none of your concern. He is the rightful heir to Kenneth MacCallum, from the laird's first, tragic marriage to Glenna Reid."

Miren glanced at Nathan, who sighed at Simon's rushed disclosures. "This is Mr. Simon MacTavish. My . . . valet."

"I'm pleased to meet you, Mr. MacTavish."

Simon huffed, and Miren turned her attention back to Nathan. "Have you been in Scotland long, Mr. MacCallum?"

"Two weeks, Miss Lindsay."

Simon tapped his cane to the ground between sheep. "And he's in a hurry."

Nathan had been in a hurry. Until now. He had duties, responsibilities. But speaking with Miren Lindsay had its appeal.

"Until recently, I've been aboard a ship."

"You're a sailor?"

"After serving the Northern Army in the Civil War, I gained my own ship, Miss Lindsay. I was captain."

"That sounds honorable." She didn't seem overly impressed by his accomplishments, nor to care whether he had swabbed decks or given orders. "So you're settling in Argyll . . ." She spoke casually, in a conversational tone. As if she'd prefer to chat than to remove her flock. As if chatting were her only option at this point.

"It's pretty land." She gazed around pleasantly, although she looked a little tense. She glanced back at him, biting her lip. "I suppose you own the fields just south of here, too?"

"Why do you ask?"

"No reason!" She bit her lip hard. "We passed in that general direction, by mistake. Wheat can recover from such things as violent storms, deer . . . sheep."

"Sheep."

Simon braced into indignation. "Generally, a shepherd gets permission from a landowner before grazing his, or her, flock on their property."

She sighed, unaffected by Simon's budding wrath. "And I would, but I never know where they're going next." She coughed suddenly. "I mean, I usually get permission, but this was an accident, and I only just caught up with them."

26

Nathan smiled. If Scottish women had Miren's charm, his venture here might be more interesting than he first imagined. "Where are you headed, Miss Lindsay?"

She looked proud. "America."

Nathan's brow angled. A shame that such a beautiful, pleasing girl should be mad. He cleared his throat. "Have you considered the presence of the Atlantic Ocean as an obstacle?"

A frown flickered on her soft lips. "I have." She sighed. "It may take a while." Simon groaned, but Nathan felt uncomfortable. Maybe he should help her. He could arrange for some sort of care . . .

"Why do you want to go to America?"

"My family went there years ago. My Uncle Robert runs a small business in the state of Maine . . . I have spotted its location on a map." Miren sighed wistfully. "So many Scottish people were driven from their rightful land by the English during the Clearances, so Uncle Robert had to start again. People were starving. That couldn't happen in America."

Nathan's mood darkened. "There are some who might disagree."

"Who?"

"The American Indian."

Miren's brow angled doubtfully. "They are a primitive race, aren't they? Small, painted persons, fond of wearing feathers and beads, and little else? Surely their lot has improved under American protection."

Nathan sighed and glanced heavenward. "There's a wider ocean than I thought—"

"Molly! No!"

Nathan turned to see the black dog worming its way into his coach. Its tail wagged cheerfully as Miren Lindsay eased past Nathan. "I'm sorry." She seized the dog and extracted it from the coach. "She's tired of walking, you see."

Nathan looked at the dog hanging in Miren's arms. Its expression was clear. *So close, and yet so far.* Unlike Miren,

Nathan felt sure the dog was sizing up his potential, and possibly his wealth. Its expression altered to determination.

Miren put the dog down, but positioned herself in front of the door. "It is my intention to guide my flock to a suitable shearing station, collect the proceeds from the sale of their wool, and secure passage on a ship." She sighed. "It may take a few seasons."

Simon eyed the flock in distaste. "It may, at that. Blackface dinna give wool worth anything but rug-making and mattress-stuffing."

Miren braced. "You are mistaken, sir. My flock represents a superior faction of the Blackface." Nathan noticed that she addressed both Simon and himself as "sir." Indiscriminately, as if they were both worthy of equal respect, and only a certain amount of it.

Simon shook his head. "You'd be better off selling the whole flock now for mutton than trying to pry any wool off them."

Her small face flushed with indignation. "My sheep are not to be confused with mutton sheep. They are well on their way to producing a fine quality wool, which will make sweaters for babies, wraps for ladies, and possibly hats for gentlemen during the winter months."

"Ha! A Blackface has to be crossed up with a better breed for at least three generations to produce anything resembling salable wool."

Her expression altered. Her face fell. "Truly?" Her shoulders slumped again. "Three generations . . ." She sighed. "And I'd have to get another ram. Huntley is old and doesn't have much interest in ewes anymore. I've sold off his best sons to other flocks to pay for our meals."

For a reason he didn't understand, Nathan didn't want to hear how Miren Lindsay scrounged for meals. He found himself wanting to help her, and this wasn't possible. He had too much to consider already. "Where are you headed, before you embark for America?"

28

"I have no idea..." She caught herself and coughed. "South. Southwest, back to Kilmartin."

Simon huffed again. "Your sheep seem to be heading north, toward the Highlands."

She looked distressed but made no comment.

Simon gestured down the road behind the coach. "You got yourself on a private roadway, girl." He indicated a fork in the road. "Off to the right there is east, and that'll take you smack into Loch Fyne and Laird MacCallum's estate."

"What's the straight path, the north one?"

Simon frowned. "Trouble."

Miren stood on tiptoes to look through the trees. "I can spot a glimpse of Loch Fyne from here. There's quite a meadow." Her voice trailed off, as if this posed a threat to her plans. "I see a rooftop with three gables." She glanced at Nathan. "Is that your house, sir?"

"It is. At the corner of my property is an old abbey. The monks are fond of privacy, so I suggest you avoid the meadow, Miss Lindsay. Farther along the drive, my stepmother is hosting a garden party at my estate house. I doubt she would take kindly to sheep arriving in its midst."

Miren shuddered, as if she visualized the scene too easily. "She's not a farming woman, then?"

"No. She's an Englishwoman..." Nathan meant to explain further, but Miren nodded, as if being English was enough to explain Lady MacCallum's bad temper.

"If she's not your mother, why is she living in your house?"

"Impertinence!" Simon stamped his foot, but Nathan ignored his outburst.

"Lady MacCallum and her son have lived at my father's estate for many years. In fact, no one knew of my existence until recently. Since he had no other heirs, my father saw fit to search me out in America. Unfortunately, he was killed in a fire shortly after our meeting. A fire which I barely escaped myself."

Miren's eyes sparkled with interest, and perhaps in pleasure at the delay. "How horrible!" She paused. "Lady Mac-Callum can't have been pleased at your arrival. How did you convince them you're his real son?"

A shrewd question. Almost too shrewd. Nathan expected another outburst from Simon, but the old man just stood still, mouth agape. Nathan cleared his throat and tried to maintain a casual expression. "Simon managed the American side of MacCall . . . my father's business. Simon knew of my existence, and has verified my authenticity as rightful heir."

Miren's gaze shifted to Simon, then back to Nathan. "You have brown eyes."

"I do . . ." The woman was beautiful, but she was odd.

"If he knew of your existence, why did it take your father so long to find you? You're quite old . . ."

"I'm twenty-seven."

She nodded. "As I said, old. . . . What took him so long?"

Simon issued a choking cough. "None of your business, lass!"

Nathan's patience strained. He'd told this story many times. Each time required thought to keep the details straight. "An unfortunate accident separated my parents when I was born. My father returned to Scotland thinking his wife dead, not knowing she bore his child."

Nathan paused, but Miren waited as if a storyteller's main pitch was to follow. "Go on." For a reason he didn't understand, his uneasiness surpassed what he'd endured when posing his story to Lady MacCallum and her son. "So how did Mr. MacTavish know you existed?"

Simon stomped his foot. "I knew!"

Nathan ignored Simon's burgeoning rage. "Simon discovered my existence some years later, and reported back to my father."

"I see. How very interesting. And here you are."

"Here I am."

"You must resemble your mother."

"Why do you say that?"

"I met your father once. He was fair." She paused. "His eyes were blue. I recall, because they were so pale a color."

"My mother was dark. Very dark."

"I'm sure she was lovely." Miren studied Nathan's face, and she sighed faintly. "Quite beautiful, in fact."

Nathan's pulse quickened. Like most women, Miren Lindsay appreciated his exotic good looks. As long as they didn't know the source of his appeal, women found him attractive, and succumbed easily to his charms. He couldn't offer her much. His stay in Scotland wasn't permanent, and he would soon be gone.

Miren didn't strike him as the sort of girl who would be satisfied with a brief encounter. With Simon fidgeting beside him, Nathan couldn't find out, either. Simon rolled his eyes and groaned.

"Miss Lindsay, as pleasant as it's been to make your acquaintance, Mr. MacTavish and I are expected for"—Nathan paused—"a pressing engagement."

"You avoided your stepmother's guests, I suspect."

Nathan's lips twitched into a smile. "I had more important matters to attend to."

Nathan wondered if she would pry into his "important matters," but Miren nodded, then looked around at her sheep. She fingered the whistle that hung on a rope around her neck. She pursed her lips as if to blow, then cleared her throat. "I suppose you'll be wanting to move on?"

Nathan checked his watch again. "It was my intention to move forward, yes."

"Not back the way you came?" She spoke as if it would be easier to turn the coach around on the narrow roadway than to alter her flock's direction.

"No."

She gulped, then looked around as if desperate to find a new distraction. "Those are fine horses you've got pulling the coach."

31

Nathan's patience strained. "Thank you. Miss Lindsay—"

"What are their names?"

"I don't know!"

Her lips parted. Soft, bowed lips, pink from the sun. Nathan fixed his gaze on her eyes instead.

"You don't know their names?"

Her eyes were well made, too. Wide, angled upward at the corners, framed in thick, black lashes. "Whose?"

"Your harness horses! Sir, that is unacceptable." Indignation rang in her voice. "We share our lives with our creatures. We owe them respect. Names are symbolic of that respect. They must have names."

Nathan glanced at the coachman, who shrugged. "Have they names, Grainger?"

Grainger suppressed a grin. Nathan wondered why he'd allowed the girl to delay him this way. "One and Two, sir."

Miren nodded. "Their names are One and Two."

Nathan drew a calming breath. "Miss Lindsay, I give you my word to use their names at every meeting, if you will remove your sheep from my path."

She looked a little pale. "Of course, your presence is disturbing them. It's *possible* they won't adhere strictly to my commands just now."

Nathan turned his dark gaze to the sheep. "They don't appear 'disturbed.' "

"You don't know them as I do."

His patience crumbled. "Nor is it my desire to know them better. Miss Lindsay, progress your flock on their way."

She looked around as if wondering which way.

"Southwest."

She nodded. "Just so." She sighed, gazed heavenward, then put the whistle to her lips. She blew so hard that her cheeks turned pink and her eyes watered. One sheep looked up. Blossom. The ewe looked more disgusted than inspired to move.

Nathan glanced pertinently at the Border collie. It took his

32

glance as an invitation, and moved to sniff his boots. The small dog looked thoughtful. It turned its attention to Simon, and appeared pleased. Nathan endured the uncomfortable sense that the creature was scheming.

"Molly . . . Speak!"

Here was a command the dog recognized. Molly sat back on her haunches and barked twice. The sheep looked up. Miren beamed with pride and gave the dog a cookie.

Nathan watched in silence. The interlude seemed unreal. It would soon be over, and he would never see this odd young woman again. The world was so much larger than Miren Lindsay, yet he felt curiously drawn to her.

It had to be because she was pretty, and obviously in need. He recognized a dangerous combination. "I'll move them along now," she said, looking strained. "And I'll try my best to avoid your stepmother's garden party."

"That would seem wise."

Simon tapped his cane to the earth between the sheep. "You'd better avoid Garrison Campbell's land, too, lass. He's just north of here." Simon sounded gentler now, as if his sympathies had softened despite himself. "North will land you in trouble and nowhere else. Campbell, he ain't a man with scruples, but he's got enough power to see you tossed up and to Inverness for trespassing."

Miren paled. "North, you say? I'll see what I can do about avoiding his land." Her small face looked tense, as if knowing about possible dangers wasn't enough to prevent them.

Nathan hesitated. He knew he should be gone. He was already late. She looked so vulnerable, and so alone. "Is there anything I can do to assist you, Miss Lindsay?"

She eyed him doubtfully, as if surprised by the change in his voice. Her head tilted to one side as she studied his face, her whistle held poised in one small, dirty hand. The dog looked between them, waiting.

"No, sir. I need nothing. But it was kind of you to inquire."

Nathan considered several things Miss Lindsay needed. Clothes, food. A new dog. Fewer sheep. Possibly a home. He could give her clothes. He might find a new dog, and he could arrange to sell her sheep. But he couldn't give her a home, and that was what she needed most.

Miss Lindsay blew again, then waved her arms. She pulled her tartan blanket from her waist and shook it violently. The sheep reacted. They jolted themselves forward.

And they were moving north.

Chapter Two

So close, and yet so far.

Molly stared down the road, still listening to the coach's grinding wheels. Fine interior. Plush seating, good windows. Ample space for a house pet. The dark human had an even, low voice, the kind Molly preferred. No shouting, no arm-waving such as she'd seen from several irate farmers. He smelled clean. He was well fed, but strong. All fine qualities for the caretaker of a well-tended house pet.

Making matters simpler still, he was male. The young mistress was female. When they spoke, they leaned subtly toward each other. Clear indications of compatibility. The young mistress's attention diverted from her sheep to focus on the male. Molly had sniffed him to be certain he didn't have another mate, and to determine his health. All clear.

Despite all the signs, he'd gone on his way in his coach. Without them. A bitter shame. The young mistress required a mate. Molly wondered where she'd gone wrong. She'd wagged her tail as a signal of friendliness. She'd barked on call. What more could a human male require?

Molly gazed miserably down the road. The sound of the coach disappeared. He wasn't turning back.

Something rammed into her rump, shoving her aside. Molly's legs floundered out to the sides, her stomach scraped the earth before she snapped herself together. She turned with a low growl.

Blossom cast a patronizing glance Molly's way, seized a fern, and began to chew.

"He seemed nice." Miren shaded her eyes against the sun and watched Nathan MacCallum's coach disappear down the twisting road. "But I suppose we'll have to stay away from his stepmother and this Garrison Campbell."

The flock made its way along a steep, rocky embankment. A small waterfall cascaded down toward the road, then whisked south in a fast spring stream. Molly sat at Miren's feet. The dog looked disgruntled.

Miren reached down and scratched Molly's ears. The disgruntled expression remained. "You seemed to like Mr. MacCallum, too. I don't blame you. He was . . . quite something. I'm not sure about his valet, though. They didn't seem to get along very well."

Miren gazed back at the empty road. She liked talking to someone who answered back. Molly might understand— Miren felt sure she did—but she couldn't respond verbally. Nathan MacCallum had a pleasing voice, low and softly accented. She'd heard Americans speak before, but she'd never imagined the sound could be so beautiful.

Something about him didn't fit her image of a laird. Despite his perfect attire, his perfect white cravat and his perfect, shiny boots, his hair was just a little too long, his skin just a little too dark for gentility. His eyes were too soft a brown to be housed in a guarded man. He looked like an ancient Highlander chieftain disguised as a gentleman.

She knew from the moment she met him that he was hiding

something. That he had a plan, and that his mind was working in a methodical, cool rhythm for a purpose. If drawing a sword or wielding a claymore with two hands would work best, Miren felt sure Nathan MacCallum would do just that.

Maybe Simon MacTavish would do it first. He seemed far less controlled than his employer, with a devil-may-care attitude obvious in his stance. Simon seemed an odd choice as Nathan MacCallum's manservant. He wasn't polished, or silent as servants tended to be. He spoke up, without deference to the young laird, his eyes snapping with impatience, his lips curled beneath his gray beard.

Nathan's story piqued her curiosity. His life sounded exciting—fighting in the American Civil War, freeing slaves to live better lives. He even seemed to know something about the American Indian. He'd become a ship's captain, now a laird of a vast estate. He'd have to run it better than Kenneth MacCallum, anyway.

Whoever's son he really was.

"Got a message from Inveraray Jail this morning." Simon spoke idly, as if the information offered nothing to distract Nathan's attention. They were alone in the manor library. Irene MacCallum had gone to Inveraray Castle, and her son had left that morning for a Highlands hunting expedition.

Nathan paced around the library, fingering books that held relevance to nothing. He'd found information on the Clan MacCallum, its branches in Colgin, Glen Etive, and of Kilmartin, but nothing to further his investigation. Kenneth MacCallum had been proud of his heritage. Blue and green plaids hung everywhere. Irene MacCallum had built her entire wardrobe around her husband's tartan, despite being English herself.

"Jail?"

"That's what I said. Jail." Despite his stolid nature, Simon seemed as impatient and restless as Nathan. His short, chunky body moved in a straight line from one library wall to the other. He circled a useless, ornamental desk, then faced Nathan, chunky arms folded over his chest.

"It shouldn't interest you, of course." Simon paused, allowing the suspense to build. Nathan kept his expression impassive, but it wasn't easy. Another day with Simon MacTavish and his mission might prove intolerable.

"A young lady—inmate, as it were—has asked to see you."

Nathan's eyes narrowed, but Simon turned to look out the tall, narrow window. He waited a moment, then glanced back over his shoulder. "It's her. The sheep lass."

"I knew that." Nathan pulled a book from the third shelf and examined it. A history of Inveraray. He replaced it and searched out another. "She's in jail."

From the corner of his eye, Nathan detected Simon's frown of disapproval. "Shouldn't have given her your name."

"I knew that, too." In jail. Nathan abandoned his search. He stared at an open page, but he saw Miren Lindsay's small face instead. He had offered to assist her. She'd turned him down.

"Told her too much, you did."

Nathan's lip curled to one side. He longed to remind Simon who it was that rattled on about family history, but he restrained himself from increasing their mutual antagonism. "I doubt Miss Lindsay poses any threat to our plans."

"You can't know that. Telling her you served in the war . . . now, it may be safe enough. But what if someone goes searching?"

"I did serve in the war."

"Yes, but Kenneth MacCallum's son did not. Expect you just wanted to impress the girl. You weren't no more than a scout."

"A scout who ended as captain of a ship." Nathan couldn't resist the reminder. Simon fancied himself a seaman, and it provided no end of irritation that Nathan had followed suit, with far greater success.

"You got it by default."

Nathan didn't argue. He gazed out the window toward the garden beyond. Rhododendron branches hung low in a soft, steady rain. "Everyone who outranked me died. The first mate panicked. Someone had to take over."

"You were lucky."

Nathan smiled, enough of a response to inspire a flush of red anger beneath Simon's volatile skin.

"The Good Lord didn't design your kind to captain sea vessels."

"My 'kind,' if you recall, is mixed."

"And unholy."

Simon resorted to biblical references only when his more tangible repertoire failed. Nathan took it as a victory. He turned his attention back to the window, to the dismal gray sky beyond. The MacCallum estate sat on the crest of a vale, facing east over Loch Fyne. Every day, the vale was shrouded in rain.

Depressing enough in a luxurious, well-appointed manor house. In jail . . . He hadn't forgotten her, though he wasn't sure why her image stuck in his mind. She infected his dreams, wandering through his memory, out of place and out of time. Looking for something. And when he woke, he thought *he* was looking for something, too.

Nathan set the book aside. "What crime has she committed?"

"I warned the lass, dinna you remember? Complaint against her was issued by Garrison Campbell."

"I suppose her sheep invaded Campbell's property?"

"That's probably the way of it."

"What does she want of me?"

"Message phrases it as 'offering a business proposition.' " Simon shook his head in disgust. "You know what that means. Girl's figuring you're a likely mark, Nathaniel, and don't you forget it. Your position be drawing them like maggots to a dead rat."

Nathan grimaced. "Interesting choice of words."

A slight smile curled Simon's mouth, and he nodded. "Surprised she hasn't tried it before now. Pretty girl, if you washed her up. She'd make money faster than tagging after those ragged sheep of hers."

Nathan didn't answer. Simon referred to prostitution as if it were Miren Lindsay's best option. Apparently, she hadn't thought so. . . . "I suppose I must help her."

Simon thumped his fist on the desktop. "Don't you go near that girl! We've got enough to look after without her."

Nathan drew a brooch from his vest pocket and studied the insignia: the symbol of the Clan MacCallum, a badge with a single tower beneath the words *in ardua tendit*. "He takes on difficulties," Nathan mused aloud.

Simon's expression altered from grumpy indignation to quiet grief. "He does, indeed. Let that be your brother's motto, Nathaniel. Don't you forget it, ever."

Nathan rose from his chair, still staring at the badge. "I never will."

"We've got a job to do, you and I, before our souls rest easy, before we go on our merry ways. That sheep lass, she'll just bog you down."

"I know." Since the war, he'd lived for himself, alone. His choices affected no one but himself. So much rode on his choices now. And Miss Miren Lindsay chose this time to land in jail.

"Girl like that ain't nothing but trouble, mark my words."

"I know." She called to him. She needed him. Nathan guessed she had no one else. He could help her, temporarily. Maybe that was all she wanted.

Simon read his expression. He thumped his fist into his other palm. "Leave her in prison, Nathaniel. It's probably just where she's belonging. You're not responsible for her." Simon stepped closer to Nathan, watching him with a penetrating, dark gaze. "You've got someone waiting on you already, and don't you be forgetting."

"Simon..." Nathan paused to exhale a long, weary breath. "Bring the coach."

Soft rain soaked down from the gray sky, mist rose from the loch as Nathan's coach maneuvered between the white-washed buildings of Inveraray. Every building had been crafted to the same specifications, white walls with black trim, ordered and regular, situated at the northern rim of Loch Fyne.

Nathan's coach passed the entrance to Inveraray Castle, where Lady MacCallum basked in aristocratic elegance as a guest of the Duke of Argyll. While Nathan, the new heir to the MacCallum estate, entered a prison at the behest of a young woman he'd have done better to forget.

The town formed a horseshoe, with Inveraray Jail at its northern curve. Two guards stood at the entrance. As Nathan left the coach, a shrill, woman's cry rang from an upper window. In response, a dog barked, and Nathan's heart ran cold. The woman sounded deranged, but that bark was familiar. He eyed the guards. "Does the Inveraray Jail imprison dogs, also?"

Neither guard met his eyes, but one sighed. "Not until now, sir."

"I'm here to see Miss Miren Lindsay. I understand she is on these premises."

The guard's brow elevated. "You'll have to speak to the warden before seeing that one, sir."

He spoke as if Miren posed a threat. But the girl Nathan remembered couldn't frighten a man. Her innocence and frank manner seemed more likely to make her a victim. The deranged shriek lingered in his mind. Perhaps he'd met her in a rare moment of lucidity. Maybe her lonely life had taken its final toll.

The guard held open the door. "The warden is in his office. Follow me."

Nathan bent to pass the low threshold into the jail. A white-washed corridor led through a row of cells. Dirty hands pro-

41

truded through the bars. A passing guard idly flailed a many-pronged whip, and the hands snapped back. A woman shrieked with laughter. Farther down the hall, someone wept.

Nathan started down the hall, but the guard grabbed his arm. "Not that way, sir."

Nathan fought his revulsion. Enslaved men, even prisoners, turned his blood to instant fire. He lived free, and no freedom seemed wide enough. To live encased in tight walls, devoid of freedom, seemed too bitter to endure. For this reason, Nathan had joined the Union Army at the age of sixteen, despite his father's wishes.

Nathan followed the guard up worn stone stairs. The warden sat in a small, neat office, rummaging through papers. He wore a black suit, and a black cap like a train officer. An iron fireplace warmed the damp air. A low metal bed sat beneath a small window. A shelf above the fireplace held extra blankets and towels, presumably for the prisoners.

The office seemed strangely . . . civilized. A Scottish peculiarity that took Nathan off guard.

"Gentleman to see you, Mr. Burgess."

The warden noticed Nathan, and hopped to his feet. His manner didn't reflect the usual Scottish reticence. He stuck out his hand, an American gesture generally considered vulgar to the British. Nathan shook his hand. "I am Nathan—"

"Laird MacCallum! We are honored to greet you here at our humble facility, designed and continued for the purpose of assuring safety for all of Argyll. Your most honored father supported our efforts and furthered our cause. I don't know if you're aware that the Inveraray Jail sponsors many altruistic endeavors?"

The warden's whole body swayed as he spoke. His enthusiasm seemed genuine, and peculiar in the extreme. Nathan had no idea how to respond.

"Admirable."

The warden drew a delighted breath. "It's good of you to say so." He seized Nathan's arm and directed him to a chair.

"So you're Laird MacCallum's son? We've all heard of your arrival, of course. Glad we are to have a real Scotsman taking the chieftain's seat, and no Sassenach." The warden didn't pause for air, nor for Nathan's response. "Not to be saying there's anything out of order about Mr. Edgington, beyond the usual for an Englishman, anyway."

"I understand." He couldn't think of anything else to say.

It must have been enough, because the warden clapped his hands together. "Now tell me, Laird, what brings you to Inveraray Jail? If you're wishing to inspect the premises, I'd be fully obliged and honored to escort you."

"No. Thank you." Scotland was odd. There was no question. Nathan adjusted his cravat—a discomfort he would never welcome. "I understand you have a young woman jailed here. A Miss Miren Lindsay."

The warden sighed and cast his hands upright to heaven. "Shepherdess, yes."

"May I ask of what crime Miss Lindsay has been accused?"

The warden hopped up again and checked his records, more for the purpose of propriety than to refresh his memory. He clucked his tongue and shook his head. "Caught for trespassing and assault, by the order of Garrison Campbell."

Nathan's brow angled. "Assault?"

"Did him masculine harm, sir. Mr. Campbell won't be walking straight for a good while." The warden looked furtively around and lowered his voice. "Can't say as I blame her. Campbell, he's fathered any amount of wee bairns, then refuses any help for their upbringing. Rumor says more than one of those 'unions' were forced. Hoping I am that Miss Lindsay taught him a lesson."

"If that's so, I see no reason to jail her."

The warden squinted and hedged. "In the eyes of heaven, maybe not. But Campbell, he's got ties, if you take my meaning. Power." The warden winked. "No more than yourself, though."

43

"I see. May I see the girl?"

"Got her out in the exercise run, if I'm not mistaken. Under guard at all times."

Nathan's jaw tensed. "The girl I recall couldn't pose a threat to anyone."

"Not the girl, sir. The dog!"

The warden led Nathan from the jail into a small courtyard. An outdoor cell provided two runs with barred gates for prisoners. Nathan's heart moved slowly as he approached the gate. A tattered man stood in the corner of the first cell. The warden eyed his prisoner in distaste.

"You're out here to move, Maclachlan. So move!"

The prisoner spat, then shuffled forward.

The warden gestured toward the second cell. He stopped a good distance from the entrance. "In there."

Nathan went to the gate. She walked away from him, rain soaking through her prison garb, her long hair plastered around her shoulders. Her head bowed, her arms folded behind her back. She reached the far wall of the cell, stopped, took a breath, and turned. She plodded forward, not noticing his presence.

The dog paced beside her, its head low, too, tail dragging.

Nathan couldn't speak, but his pulse moved in static beats. She came to the gate, and still didn't see him. It hadn't been her desperate cry he'd heard from the upper window. Miren Lindsay hadn't changed since he last saw her. She plodded forward, obedient to jail rules. Her dog plodded forward, too.

Nathan's throat ached. "Miss Lindsay."

She didn't hear his voice, but her dog startled.

The warden tapped Nathan's shoulder. "Better step back, sir. That dog's a menace."

Nathan didn't move. "Miss Lindsay."

Miren looked back, slowly, over her shoulder. The warden hopped back in alarm as the dog bounded toward Nathan. Its long nose protruded eagerly through the bars of the cell, its tail wagged.

"Seems like it knows you, sir." The warden sounded suspicious, but Nathan didn't respond.

Miren Lindsay was as beautiful as he remembered, as she had been in his dreams. Tears welled in her eyes when she recognized him. Nathan couldn't tell if they dropped to her cheeks, because her face was already damp from rain. So much hope sprang into her eyes, so much she needed that he couldn't give.

Nathan forced his gaze from her face to the dog. "Molly."

Molly barked in response. Even the dog looked hopeful, as if Nathan could solve all their problems and make life right again.

Miren Lindsay gathered herself together. She adjusted her damp hair, straightened her slumped shoulders, and came to stand at her gate. She peered over his shoulder toward the warden. "Mr. Burgess, is it permitted for me to stop exercising for a brief while?"

The warden shrugged. "Don't take too much of the laird's time, girl. Guards, keep an eye on that dog."

The warden retreated back into the jail, leaving Nathan with Miren. She took a quick gulp of air, then met his eyes. Her expression looked . . . professional.

"It was kind of you to come, Mr. MacCallum." Her voice quavered, but she held it steady. Nathan wanted to reassure her, but words wouldn't come. "You are, you see, the only person I know in this portion of Scotland. You gave me your name, if you recall." She hesitated, and her expression turned wistful. "It may be that you regret that now."

"No." He couldn't say more. He didn't know why words came so hard. "What do you wish of me, Miss Lindsay?"

"You warned me about Mr. Campbell, and as you can see, I came inadvertently into contact with his premises."

"So I've heard."

"It didn't go well."

45

"I see that, too."

She nodded. "In light of my sentence, my plans have altered. I sent a message to you because I would like to pose a business opportunity for your consideration."

If she offered herself . . . he would take her. "What did you have in mind?"

"My sheep—"

"Your sheep?"

"Molly has been sentenced with me, but my sheep were confiscated. Actually, they tried to confiscate Molly, too. She prevented them. Which is why the guards are somewhat leery of her now. I didn't know she bit. She's never bitten anyone before." Miren's chin quivered, but she didn't cry. "They were going to shoot her, but I convinced them to leave her with me. You see, she bit Mr. Campbell, too."

Nathan reached down and patted Molly's head before he realized what he was doing. He felt a quick, respectful lick. Nathan looked into Miren's eyes. She looked tense, but professional. "What do you want of me, Miss Lindsay?"

Her chin elevated. "I wondered if you might consider seeing my sheep into capable hands, so that they aren't slaughtered for mutton. I do think, given a chance, they will be a fine flock."

Her eyes puddled with tears again, but she kept her expression straight. Nathan opened his mouth to speak, but no words came.

"I know you're not a sheep owner, Mr. MacCallum, but they might profit you in a small way." She paused as if struggling to think of a convincing use for her flock. "They trim fields admirably, will provide wool for fashionable rugs, and"—she bit her lip—"they're scenic when viewed across a majestic landscape such as your property."

"Miss Lindsay. . . ."

She held up her hand, stopping him. "I don't want money for them, sir. I just want to know they'll have a secure position when I go."

"Go?"

She gazed upward, into the soft rain. "To Australia. I'm being deported for my various crimes."

Nathan's jaw dropped. "They can't deport you for a few miscreant sheep!"

She sighed. "Not so much for the sheep as for assaulting Mr. Campbell."

"He deserved it."

"He didn't think so."

"Did he harm you, Miss Lindsay?"

She hesitated, looking uncomfortable. "He issued an unacceptable proposal. I declined."

Miss Lindsay had a gift for understatement. Nathan smiled. "I understand his walk will be hampered for some time."

"He persisted overmuch." She shook her head. "Australia. It's a long way from Australia to America, isn't it? Longer than from Scotland."

Nathan stared. Miren remained focused on her goals. She didn't look back, she didn't rail against the past. She considered Australia a diversion, but she was still determined to reach whatever family remained to her.

He had come to her, thinking she would offer herself as a mistress. He would have taken her. He hadn't really acknowledged it until now, but that had been his intention. He'd considered her a pretty, engaging diversion. And she wanted him to look after her sheep.

A wave of shame eased its way into his heart. Had he grown so old over twenty-seven years, to be so far from innocence?

"You don't want them, do you?"

She'd misread his dark expression. Her small hands clutched the bars of her cell as she fought tears. Nathan placed his hands over hers. "I will do what I can."

She looked at their hands, then into his face. Her expression altered slightly. A faint blush touched her cheeks. Nathan withdrew his hands from hers and turned away. He made no promises, nor offered any reassurance. She didn't call after him, nor beg, nor anything. He looked back from the doorway, but she returned to her exercise, dutifully walking back and forth.

Molly rose up on her hind legs, her front paws against the bars. She barked and whined as the door closed behind him. Nathan watched as Miren patted her head and coerced her from the bars. The two guards poised their rifles in defense, but the dog moved away and resumed pacing beside her mistress.

Chapter Three

*Maybe I don't know humans as well as I thought. I could
have sworn he'd come to rescue us. He gave every sign. Even
laid hands on the young mistress through the bars.*

*This whole disaster was Blossom's doing. The old sow led
the rest of them right onto the front steps of a manor house
because she likes the look of potted plants. Any sensible animal would have known better. But not Blossom.*

*I believe she did it knowing I would be blamed. I had to
fight off an attacker, which I did well enough, until more men
arrived. They stuffed the young mistress into a coach—and
not a lavish one at all—and tried to take her away from me.
I followed, of course. Little did I know where we'd end up.*

*My only comfort is that I'll never see Blossom's round,
woolly body again.*

"My fingers are bleeding." Miren set aside her herring net
and went to the door of her cell. Her door was thick and
metal, and she had to stand on her toes to see out the tiny,

barred window. The man across the hall muttered in Gaelic. From farther down, a woman shouted back.

"Prisoners! Quiet, or you'll be at the wheel!"

Miren frowned. The wheel was an evil device. Hours of mindless labor were spent cranking a wheel which did nothing but occupy the most troublesome prisoners. Others were forced to move a pile of cannonballs from one spot to another, then back. So far, she'd avoided such punishments.

"Excuse me . . . Guard!" A guard sat at the end of the hall, looking bored and irritable. His gaze appeared surly, but he rose from his seat and came to her door. He opened it a crack and scanned her appearance greedily.

"Got that net done yet?"

"Nearly. A problem has arisen. My fingers, you see, are blistering. If you could provide some form of bandage, I would be quicker at my task."

"What'll you give for it?"

Miren's eyes narrowed. "My appreciation."

"With or without clothes?"

She responded with an icy glare.

"You're high up for a peasant wench. Maybe you're thinking that laird will be returning for you?"

Miren said nothing, but a frown twitched at her lips. She shouldn't have contacted Nathan MacCallum. She'd placed him in an unfortunate position, without thinking how her message might be interpreted. He was the only person she knew in Inveraray. He had seemed kind. But it was a lot to ask that he take her flock when she went to Australia.

Maybe she just wanted to see him again. Because she was afraid and lonely. Because he seemed kind and strong. Because she was surrounded with such poverty and ugliness that the sight of his face was the sun.

Molly tensed and growled at the guard. Safe on the other side of the bars, he chuckled.

"I require bandages. If you would alert the surgeon . . ."

"Tie up that dog, and we'll talk. In private. I've got something in need of a wench's care . . .'' The guard adjusted his trousers and arched his brow meaningfully.

Miren grimaced and looked away. She knew what he wanted. The woman in the cell next to hers had obliged him the night before, with loud, slurping noises. Rams were so much more respectful of ewes when mating.

"Never mind.'' Miren returned to her bench and gathered the half-finished herring net again.

"If you change your mind, wench, you know where I am.'' The guard laughed again, locked the steel door, and resumed his position at the end of the hall.

Molly rested her nose on Miren's knee. Waiting. Miren had nothing to give her. No treats, nothing. She shared her meals, because the warden refused to bring extra for a dog. Miren wasn't hungry anyway.

Making her way as a shepherdess was one thing. There was honor in such a vocation. Being shipped to Australia as a criminal was another thing entirely. Uncle Robert wouldn't be pleased about that, even if she could somehow reach America.

Tears filled her eyes, but she kept picking at the net, twisting and tying the harsh ropes. Tears had come too easily since Nathan MacCallum's visit this morning. She felt alone. Since her father died, she'd been without human companionship, but she'd never noticed. Not really. She had Molly, her sheep. She had a purpose.

She wanted a home, and a family. The only family she knew of lived in America. So she had to reach America to reach them. She wanted a good life for the only things in her possession, her sheep and her dog. She believed that a person's worth wasn't dependent on what they owned, or said, or could make other people believe. What mattered was integrity and kindness, to live in accord with what she valued.

As the sky darkened outside her window, Miren felt for the first time that it wasn't enough. She wanted to affect someone's life, to be part of their joys and sorrows. She wanted to know what someone like Nathan MacCallum thought about, felt—what moved his heart. She wondered if he had a wife and children. He hadn't mentioned a wife, but it seemed unlikely that a man like him would remain unattached.

Miren's heart sank, her sore fingers slowed their task. His wife would be beautiful. She would laugh a great deal, and probably tease her stoic young husband. She would know his secrets, and he would be safe in her arms.

Miren suspected that his wife had red hair, with cheerful curls. Maybe he had children. He would be a good father. He would play, he would laugh. He would take them for rides on their fat Shetland ponies. And he would know their ponies' names.

He remembered Molly's name. Miren set aside the herring net and wiped moisture from her cheeks. She hadn't realized she was crying. Because she thought of him, and the life she was sure he had. The life she longed for, too.

A bell rang, signaling the end of the workday. Miren looked out the tiny window above her bench. The hour was past ten, but in the Scottish spring the light remained until nearly midnight, even through the steady rain. The damp weather didn't trouble her. A clear sky, like hope, would be so much harder, when viewed from confinement.

Miren unfolded her thin hammock and strung it between the wall hooks. Inveraray was certainly consistent. Everything whitewashed, with black trim. Even her night basin, white with a black rim.

She straightened her back and looked out the window again. Nathan MacCallum was like a clear sky. He was like hope. Looking at him hurt. She hadn't understood why until now. It was easier to plod through Argyll after her sheep than to look at him and allow herself to dream.

Miren didn't cry, though the dream made her ache inside. Contacting him had been a mistake. She did it to see him again, to involve herself in his life, if only through her sheep. Had she seen the matter clearly, she would have restrained herself, but she had been so afraid.

Don't go wanting what you can't have, lass. Her father gave her that advice when she was a little girl, when he caught her admiring a pretty dress in a tailor's window. Her father was right.

The guard rapped on her door, probably to escort her to the washroom. She would have a brief moment to bathe and see to her teeth, then return to her cell.

"Prisoner, make ready for entrance." The guard spoke without familiarity, so Miren knew the warden must be in the hall, too. The warden wasn't unpleasant. He ran the Inveraray Jail like a strict schoolhouse. Unfortunately, his idealistic approach failed to affect his guards' attitudes.

With the warden present, Miren felt safer bathing. She seized a towel from the shelf, then arranged her hammock. Molly waited by the door. The guard unlocked the door, and Miren gripped Molly's collar. Molly growled anyway.

The warden positioned himself behind the guard, but he smiled in a bright, enthusiastic manner. He held up a dark blue lady's gown. Miren eyed him doubtfully. "What is that?"

"You're to put it on, Miss Lindsay, after you make use of our washroom." The warden spoke like the proprietor of a hotel. He was still smiling.

"It isn't mine."

"It is now, miss. Freshen up, and I'll escort you to your coach."

Miren shook her head. "What coach? I'm not being sent to Australia tonight, am I?"

The warden beamed. "Not to Australia, miss."

"Then where am I going?"

"You're going home."

Nathan MacCallum had come for her. Miren gazed through the coach window as they left Inveraray, then headed south past the castle. Nathan hadn't exactly come for her. He'd sent his coach, and a dress, and had somehow arranged to have her sentence repealed. For a man who had been in Scotland only a few weeks, he had considerable influence.

She wasn't going to Australia, after all. Not yet. Her prison record was erased, and Uncle Robert would never know. Miren considered her good fortune, but a pang of disappointment refused to surrender. Because though he'd sent for her, he hadn't come himself.

Nathan MacCallum was a kind man, a man of duty. A man who took responsibility for others. Miren's disappointment turned to guilt. She had no right to involve him, nor to ask for his help. Then again, she hadn't asked for his help. She'd offered a business proposition, on behalf of her sheep. It never occurred to her that he would see fit to rescue her, or alter her unhappy fate.

Still, she should have known. She'd incited his sympathies, however unintentionally. Miren adjusted her dark blue skirt and crossed her legs at the ankles. She would repay him. As soon as she saw him, she would make her intentions clear. Charity was out of the question.

Molly hopped from one seat to another, as if testing the quality of the cushions. She seemed excited, happy. Miren studied her dog's pert face. *At home.*

Molly placed a paw on a cushion, testing it. She scraped violently, making herself a bed. "Molly . . ." Miren pulled the dog onto her lap. "You mustn't damage anything. It's not ours."

Strange that a dog born and raised outdoors should be so at ease on a cushion. Miren wondered where her sheep were, if they were together, if they were all right. Molly didn't seem upset by their loss, but Miren patted her head in reassurance anyway. Border collies fixated on their sheep, and had to keep the flock in sight at all times.

So even if Molly didn't seem bothered, Miren guessed it troubled her somewhere.

Molly poked her nose into the fattest cushion and went to sleep.

The coach wound its way down twisted roads, past Garrison Campbell's property. Miren winced at the sight of his overturned potted plants. Before they reached the spot where she'd first encountered Nathan, the coach turned left toward Loch Fyne.

They followed a narrow gravel drive which opened on the left to a sloping meadow filled with bluebells. They reached a fork in the road. To the left, a grass path led to a small stone church. Miren noticed a monk bending over as he worked in a small garden.

The straighter drive led farther up the hill. She saw Nathan MacCallum's manor, a brownstone with three gables. It was beautiful, like a jewel on the meadow's brow. The coach stopped at the fork. The coachman got out and opened a gate, then returned to his seat. He headed the team through the gate to a small whitewashed cottage with a heather-thatched roof.

It looked east over Loch Fyne and was surrounded by a stone wall. She couldn't see what was in the pasture, because the coachman led her around the back. A heavy mist crept inward from the loch, spreading around her feet and shrouding the little cottage as if it floated on a cloud.

The coachman lowered the steps and opened the door. Miren hesitated, running through her planned speech to Nathan MacCallum.

Molly didn't wait. She hopped down and bounded from the coach. "I should have taught her 'stay.'" Miren took a short breath and followed her dog.

The coachman stood silently, holding her small pack.

"You're Mr. Grainger, as I recall."

His brow arched in surprise. "I am, at that. Good you are to remember!"

Grainger's accent wasn't Scottish, which surprised her. Few Englishmen traveled to Scotland to work as servants. "Have you worked for Laird MacCallum for a long while?"

Grainger averted his eyes and kicked the grass casually. Miren's attention perked. "I've been working up here for, oh, say twenty years, miss. Lady MacCallum hired me on just after she married the former laird. Needed extra help, what with having her son around and all."

"I see. You're not Scottish."

"No, miss. I'm a Yorkshireman from birth. Been all over Britain, though. London, Bath. May not think it to look at me, but I was a wild youth. Couldn't get enough of life, if you follow me." Grainger sighed. "Times a man's life gets a bit stretched from his control." The coachman straightened, looking proud. "But if he uses his head"—Grainger tapped his skull for emphasis—"he can get himself where he needs to be."

Miren had no idea what he meant, but he looked pleased with himself. "You speak, I think, of redemption."

"That I do, miss. And you're a quick one to see it."

Miren didn't press for further information on Grainger's life. It wasn't her business, and she held to the Scottish value of privacy. Something about him intrigued her, though she wasn't sure what it was. She couldn't guess his age. His hair was gray, but blended with pale blond. His trimmed beard concealed much of his face.

"You were gracious about not running over my sheep. Thank you."

Grainger chuckled. "Didn't have much choice."

"No, but still . . ."

Miren's voice trailed as she looked around. Nathan MacCallum wasn't waiting for her as she expected. The cottage's thatched roof hung low over its white walls. It had a pleasant light blue door and two square windows. A lantern glimmered inside, and Miren saw a small sitting room.

Miren eyed the coachman. "Where are we?"

"We're at the east end of Laird MacCallum's estate, miss. Down by the loch's edge."

Miren turned to the cottage. "Who lives in this little house?"

"You do, miss. Just you and . . . them."

"Them?" Miren looked around. Molly snarled, then flopped to her stomach as if sudden grief overwhelmed her. A bell tinkled. A low, deep "baa" emanated from the darkness. "Sheep!"

"Yes, miss. That they be."

Miren clapped her hands and seized the coachman's arm. "Are they . . . ?" She paused to contain her hope. Hope could be devastating. "My sheep?"

"Counting up as sixty Blackface ewes. One scrawny ram, too."

"Huntley!" Tears swarmed Miren's eyes as her flock came around the corner of the cottage and emerged from the mists. Molly took one look, then aimed at the cottage door. "Molly, drop!" Molly stopped, but didn't crouch at attention. "We don't want to lose them again, *do we*?"

"There's a stone wall runs all about this pasture. They're not going anywhere. Miss Lindsay, these sheep be here to stay."

The sheep circled in, Blossom at the fore. Molly stared in disbelief. Blossom stared back, smug. Chewing her cud.

It didn't seem possible. When Molly saw the coach waiting outside the jail, she'd felt sure their troubles were over. Molly had recognized the plush interior at once. She detected the recent presence of the kind, dark man. Clearly, he had sent for his new mate. Odd that he wasn't here to bring her in, but maybe humans had to enter a mating season before they bonded.

It shouldn't take too long to secure a permanent position. Molly was well on her way to becoming a favored and well-loved house pet. Yes, it had all looked so promising . . . until now.

Until Blossom ambled toward her through the mists, reminding her she was born to be a sheep dog, not a house pet.

That was Blossom's constant message, and why Molly disliked her beyond the other sheep. Huntley, for instance, simply ignored Molly's presence. Blossom aimed for her every time. Molly couldn't count the times she'd been knocked flat by the old ewe.

Molly turned her back on the flock and made her way to the cottage door. The coachman swung it inward, and Molly walked in. She looked left and saw a boxed-in bed, hung with spotted curtains. Two cushions looked inviting, but it wasn't quite as large a bed as Molly conjured in her fondest imaginings.

Near the bed was an inset fireplace, fitted with tools and black pots. A cabinet held plates and pitchers. All good for feeding, but nothing spectacular. A square wooden table sat in the center of the room. It looked . . . used. Molly looked to the right and saw two comfortable chairs for sitting purposes. Adequate, but not grand.

An ominous hall led out from the human quarters. Molly sniffed and recognized a byre for animals, though she detected no recent activity, not even a chicken. Miren came into the cottage, eyes wide, as if she'd entered a far grander dwelling. "It's beautiful!"

Molly eyed her doubtfully, wondering what she was looking at. Miren raced around the cottage, then discovered the byre. She shoved open the byre door to the field, allowing access to the sheep. Molly positioned herself at the door and growled.

"This is their home, too, Molly."

Blossom entered the byre, butted her way past Molly, and aimed for the living quarters. The coachman blocked the entrance to the sitting room, and Molly wagged her tail. Blossom wasn't deterred as she explored the byre. She found an old mound of hay and took a large mouthful, despite the fact she couldn't be hungry.

Molly braced to attack, but Miren took her collar.

"Molly, come."

Molly in the Middle

Miren led her from the byre, back to the human quarters. At least, she wasn't expected to watch the flock at night.

The coachman backed toward the door. "If there's nothing else, miss, I'll be getting back to the manor. You'll find food in the larder and a jug of clean water. Laird MacCallum instructed that I was to deposit you here, see to your needs, and allow you to rest."

Miren nodded, but Molly thought she looked sad. The coachman left, and Miren slumped down into a chair. Molly sat beside her, looking up. She knew the girl's feelings, and they mattered to Molly. When Molly first chose Miren for her companion, it had been the girl's gentle and open manner that attracted her.

Up until Miren came to view the litter, Molly had bitten several rough, work-worn hands. But Miren came into the barn quietly and sat by the litter box. She patted Molly's dam with respect and admiration. She spoke in a sweet voice. She remarked on the beauty of all the puppies. Not once did she ask about their prospects with sheep.

Molly had intended to inspect the girl a bit further before making her selection. Miren wasn't dressed expensively, though she smelled clean. Molly couldn't see if she'd arrived at Fergus's farm in a well-appointed coach. But when Fergus held up one of Molly's sisters, saying she was a natural with sheep, Molly knew she wanted Miren for herself.

She wagged her small tail, she licked Miren's hand. That was all it took. Miren said she was beautiful seven times. She pressed her cheek against Molly's head. And Molly felt a warmth inside she'd never known before.

She loved her young owner. So it was her duty to see to a better life, to direct her away from that useless flock and into better circumstances. She realized, dimly, that circumstances wouldn't change Miren Lindsay. For this reason, more than anything else, Molly intended to see that Miren lived in the finest circumstances life could offer.

*   *   *

The MacCallum manor was set on the hillside, looking down over a field, east over Loch Fyne. Nathan stood by his bedroom window. He could see the thatched roof of Miren's little cottage, but the thick pines and rhododendrons obscured a better view.

He saw the rambling stone wall that circled the hut. He saw the Blackface sheep spread out across the field, grazing. The cottage sat near the edge of Loch Fyne. Probably Miren Lindsay sat on her front steps, her dog beside her, gazing out over the water. A soft breeze from the loch would tumble her long hair . . .

He'd waited three days without going to see her, but he'd thought of nothing else. Nathan shook his head, fighting his imagination. He started to turn away, but Miren appeared in the field, walking amidst her flock. His pulse quickened at the sight of her. He couldn't see her well, she was too far away. Nathan eyed his captain's trunk, then looked out the window again. He should keep an eye on her, after all.

Nathan succumbed, and pried open his trunk. He withdrew his spyglass and returned to the window, adjusting the lens for clear viewing. He found her, and centered his glass upon her as she bent to check a sheep's foot. She tossed something aside. Probably a pebble caught in its cloven hoof. Miren patted the sheep and scratched its ears, then moved on to inspect the others.

Nathan checked for the dog. Odd that it wasn't overseeing its flock. There at the end of the paddock nearest the cottage, he spotted Molly. She lay at rest, her back to the flock. As if pretending they weren't there.

Nathan found Miren again. She was still wearing the dress he had sent for her. It fit well enough, better than her sackcloth garment. Her hair was bound loosely behind her head, falling over one shoulder. He adjusted the glass, but he couldn't bring her face into clearer focus.

"This is pathetic."

Nathan startled and dropped his glass. Simon stood in the

doorway, arms folded over his thick chest. Smug. Nathan's jaw clenched, but he refrained from comment.

Simon stomped into the room as Nathan retrieved his glass. "This is just what I'd expect of your kind. You'll have to resist your instincts, boy. No kidnapping."

The old Scotsman never missed an opportunity to remind Nathan of his true heritage, with an emphasis on those qualities of birth he lacked. "If I fail to resist my 'instincts,' you'll be the first to know." He kept his voice low and dangerous. It worked. Simon paled at the veiled threat, but he didn't depart as Nathan hoped.

"Your people could teach the Vikings new tricks. Mayhem, slaughter . . ."

"My understanding is that Scottish history isn't totally devoid of violence. Wasn't it Tacitus who reported that your ancestors, the Picts, raced into battle, painted, naked . . . with spears? I question the good sense of attacking iron-clad Roman warriors with a spear . . . *naked* . . . And as for the paint . . ."

Nathan tilted his head back, folded his arms, and enjoyed Simon's flush of rage. "You're speaking of centuries past, boy! We're the most civilized race on the Good Lord's green earth."

Biblical references again. Nathan had won easily this time. He drew the MacCallum brooch from his vest and held it up to the sunlight. "Your clan chieftains didn't ascend to power through conversation." He cast a meaningful glance toward an encased collection of sgian-dhus and dirks. "Civilized? I think not."

Simon pointed his stout finger at the window, diverting the conversation. "Lady MacCallum isn't happy about those sheep, Nathaniel. She confided to me her fear that rumors might abound about your relationship with that girl."

"Isn't that expected of a laird?"

Simon hesitated. Whether or not Nathan took a mistress was inconsequential. Even Simon couldn't deny that. "More rumors would start if you didn't . . .'' Simon stopped and shook his head. "Had to bring her here, didn't you? I knew when I enlisted your aid in this endeavor you'd be more trouble than you're worth."

"You enlisted my aid because I'm the only person capable of pulling it off."

"Arrogance . . ." Simon shook his head and clucked his tongue several times. "I'd have more faith if you weren't up here peeping at that sheep lass."

Nathan considered denying the obvious, then decided it was none of Simon's business. He turned his gaze back out the window. Miren clapped her hands, and the black dog came running toward her. It bounced around her feet, then crouched as if inviting play. He couldn't see her face without the glass, but he knew Miren Lindsay was laughing.

"I will see her today."

"If you're thinking of bedding the girl, it's best to go to her at night."

Nathan ignored Simon's suggestion. "Have you told Irene you're leaving for a few days?"

"Mentioned it this morning. Told her I had to head down to Stirling. Dr. Patterson's family is in Aberfoyle, and that's on the way to Stirling, but Lady MacCallum didn't seem suspicious."

Simon paused, looking uncomfortable. "Just what am I looking for when I interview them?"

No wonder Simon seemed uncomfortable. He hated asking Nathan's advice, or putting himself in a position of inferior knowledge. "You're not looking for anything. I want a clear picture of Patterson's history. You bring me the pieces, I will find the whole."

Simon rolled his eyes. "Now you're a detective . . ." He shook his head and left the room grumbling. Nathan heard him stomp down the hall, still grumbling. Something about Nathan's "kind" not being suited to "sleuthing."

Nathan turned his attention back to Miren's cottage. He

wanted her. Simon would be gone, the investigation temporarily out of his hands. She might prove a pleasing diversion. It was expected. His loins felt tight. Congested. He had been long without a woman. He would pose it to her honestly, without pressure. She might long for a man, too.

She didn't care if she never saw him again. True, Nathan MacCallum had been generous in offering his cottage, but his interest in her clearly didn't reach the level of friendship. It was charity. She felt sure her memory had exaggerated his good looks. Probably he wasn't as tall as she remembered, either.

Three days passed, and Miren had seen no one but Grainger. Each day, the coachman brought food, supplies. He'd brought two more dresses, but she left them untouched. She should be grateful. Instead, she felt . . . annoyed.

Miren sat on the front steps of the cottage and glared at the loch. Another sunny day. Three in a row since she arrived. Only fat, puffy clouds in the sky. No doubt everyone at the manor was enjoying the weather. Probably playing croquet on the lawn.

Molly hopped to sudden attention, pricking her ears as if listening. Miren watched her doubtfully. It wasn't her usual posture. Molly rose stealthily to her feet, then crept around the corner of the cottage. She burst into excited barks.

"It's all right, Molly. I've come to see your mistress."

Miren's breath caught at the sound of Nathan MacCallum's low voice. Her heart beat too fast. The reaction doubled her former anger. That she should care . . . She forced a deep breath, then rose from the steps. She brushed dirt off her blue skirt and waited.

He came around the cottage, and her resolve faltered. He was taller than she remembered. He wore a loose white shirt beneath a black vest, with well-fitting black trousers. He looked more like a pirate than a nobleman, but maybe Americans dressed differently, with less attention to detail and more on overall appeal.

His hair was longer than usual for a gentleman, too, hanging to his shoulders. Its softness contrasted with his high, firm cheekbones and his strong, wide forehead. Admirable bone structure, a face the like of which she'd never seen. He didn't wear a beard like most men. It would have been a shame to cover a face like that.

She hadn't exaggerated his good looks. There was no getting around that fact.

He smiled when their eyes met. Miren couldn't breathe. He had the most beautiful eyes, warm and brown. Secrets lay hidden in their depths, secrets that would inspire any woman to closer scrutiny.

"Miss Lindsay, it pleases me to see you well, and free."

For an instant, Miren didn't feel free. She felt trapped. "I'm fine. Thank you." Her voice came too high and too fast. He hadn't made her nervous the first time, but she had waited for three days to see him. Her imagination caused no end of trouble.

His smile deepened. He knew he flustered her. And apparently, it pleased him. Miren tried to remember her planned speech. "I will repay you for your kindness, Mr. MacCallum. Would sixty percent of my proceeds be adequate?"

His smile faded, his brow furrowed. "Sixty percent?"

"Seventy?"

Nathan MacCallum shook his head as if to clear his senses. "Miss Lindsay, what are you talking about?"

"Repayment for your help."

"There's no need—"

"There is. You saved me from the most unfortunate of circumstances. If not for you, I would be bound for Australia now. My sheep would have fallen to ruin. Delivering a percentage of their income to you seems reasonable."

Nathan looked around at her flock, probably sizing up their quality and possible yield. He looked back at her, and his smile returned. "Another option comes to mind, Miss Lindsay."

Something about his expression sent tremors down her spine, into her limbs. Maybe he would proposition her. Men seemed to consider it reasonable for a woman to exchange her virtue for his support.

She swallowed hard. "What option?"

Nathan didn't answer for a long while. He seemed to be studying her. Not for her appearance, but something deeper. He sighed, and his smile turned gentle. "An agreement between us. When you have accrued enough income from your sheeps' wool, you will leave the flock in my care when you depart for America."

Miren's heart expanded with pleasure, then lowered in shame. "I misjudged you, sir. Your suggestion is truly honorable."

"Misjudged me?"

Miren's cheeks soaked with embarrassment. "I thought you . . . wanted more money."

"I wanted you."

Her mouth dropped as he stepped closer and touched her cheek. "But I do not believe such an arrangement would benefit you, after all."

Her mouth was still open. She snapped it shut. It drifted open again, but she couldn't speak. Nathan turned to look out over the loch. "You are beautiful, you know."

The only response Miren could think of was *So are you*, so she restrained herself. He had propositioned her, almost, and she wasn't offended. "Aren't you married?"

He glanced back at her. "No."

Miren's brow knit. "Not to a woman with curly red hair?"

"No. Where did you get that idea?"

Miren shrugged. "It seemed right."

He looked confused. Miren felt confused, too. "Is that why you brought me here?"

Nathan turned to face her, his arms folded over his chest.

He looked casual. He looked strong. What would it mean to become his mistress? To lie in his arms, to do as he wished? Her insides tensed. She drew a quick breath.

"I brought you here because I couldn't think of another way to help you. I couldn't leave you in prison, nor allow you to be sent into further bondage. It troubles me more than I can explain to see people in captivity. So I used my influence to convince Garrison Campbell that dropping his claim against you was in his own best interest. I couldn't leave you to wander around Scotland, could I?"

"I see no reason why not. I was doing well enough on my own."

"Until you landed in jail."

Miren shifted her weight from foot to foot. "There was that."

"You have nothing."

"I have my sheep. I have Molly."

Nathan glanced down at Molly, who sat obediently at his feet, looking back and forth between them as if her own fate hung in the balance. "A more useless animal I've never encountered." He paused. "Other than Muffin."

Anger swept up through Miren, from her belly to her cheeks. "Molly is the best, most true, smartest dog in Scotland." The power and ferocity of her own emotion startled Miren, but her eyes puddled with hot tears of fury. "It may be true that her sheepherding instincts aren't as powerful as some. But she has defended me, she has stayed at my side. You have no idea, because you are favored, and life has handed you good fortune."

Miren found herself stepping toward Nathan, her finger pointed at his face. "Do you know, Mr. MacCallum, that you are not the first to think that my situation might profit from your baser instincts?"

It wasn't a fair accusation. After all, he hadn't really propositioned her. He just said he'd thought of it, and reconsidered. Miren didn't care.

He looked surprised by her sudden anger. His brown eyes widened. Miren detected a trace of humor, and her anger soared. "If you remember, Miss Lindsay—"

Miren waved her finger aggressively. "I remember very well. Everyone wants something, and it's usually at a woman's expense. When my father died, I was so afraid. I had no one, no money, no house, nothing except my sheep. And I didn't know what to do with them. Dr. Patterson said he could help me."

Nathan's expression altered. "Patterson? Drew Patterson?"

Miren hesitated. "Yes. You know him?"

"Not exactly. He was with my father when he died. What do you know of him?"

"He tended my father, in a manner that suggested he didn't care if my father lived or died. And when my father was laid into the ground, Dr. Patterson suggested I become his mistress rather than worrying about how to support myself."

"I take it you declined."

Miren's eyes clouded with tears. "I was more frightened of poverty than that, Mr. MacCallum. I considered his offer. It's not easy to be a lady when you have no food."

Miren was trembling. She had never told another this story. She had tried to forget, but it refused to be silenced. "It seems a good offer, doesn't it? I suppose you were going to offer something similar."

"No. Less." A faint self-mocking smile curved his beautiful mouth. "I thought, since you were here, and I am here, we might find pleasure together, until we go our separate ways."

Miren stared, but a slow smile formed on her lips, too. "That is not less, sir. Your offer places us on equal ground. True, it reveals conceit on your part, but it isn't so much an insult as I thought."

"It wasn't intended as an insult, Miren. Patterson had a wife, didn't he?"

"His wife was ill, near death. He wanted to marry me,

which I believed because he encouraged me to sign a marriage betrothal.''

"Indeed. Why?''

"I'm not sure. He wanted his lust slaked. That was obvious. But he seemed as eager for marriage.''

"It's not so hard to understand, Miren. Perhaps he loved you.''

Miren frowned. "Dr. Patterson was not capable of love. I don't believe he would marry me unless it could profit him in some way. I've never understood how a marriage to a peasant girl could aid his position, but his offer wasn't born of love.''

"Please tell me you didn't become Patterson's mistress.''

Miren turned to gaze across the loch. She didn't answer him at once. She felt the clean breeze in her hair and closed her eyes. What she had done in the past defined her character today. What she did meant far more than any illusion she might portray. When she spoke, her voice came small, as if from far away.

"I waited until darkness filled the sky, and then went to his house as he asked me. His wife was in an asylum near death at the time. I stood outside his door, and I felt as if I stood outside the gates of hell. Fear drove me to that door.''

"Fear, Miss Lindsay, has driven many men to hell.''

"I knew if I went through that door, I would never come back, because my hell would be within. It wouldn't matter if I could reach America. I would carry it with me always. If I acted on fear, fear would be all I'd ever have.''

Miren sighed and drew in the clean air. She looked back at him. He stood watching her, wonder in his warm brown eyes. The sun shone on his dark face, on his black hair. He mirrored the sun, and Miren couldn't look away.

"I had seven shillings in my pocket that night. I left Dr. Patterson waiting, and I walked all night. When the sun rose, I found myself outside a farmhouse. There was a sign that said 'Sheepdog puppies for sale. Inquire within.' So I did.

And I picked Molly. She cost seven shillings.''

Miren waited to see if Nathan dared say she paid too much. He said nothing. He watched her, a strange, sorrowful look in his eyes. "I took her back to my father's cottage to fetch my sheep. Men were there, already tearing our house down. I opened the pasture gate and let the sheep go, and I have followed them ever since.''

Nathan looked down at Molly. She looked up at him, eager. Her tail wagged, as if she were trying to win his affection. "She has stayed with me, and she never asks anything of me. When I think of what I might have been . . .'' Miren stopped and swallowed hard. "I look at Molly and I see goodness, something of value. So I can't allow you to say my dog is useless. She is the best thing in my life.''

Nathan said nothing, but he knelt beside Molly. She placed her front paws on his bent knee, panting happily. He patted her head. He didn't look at Miren for a long while. She sensed he struggled with emotion.

"It seems I was mistaken to doubt your dog's worth. I should know better than anyone that a living thing does what it can, not what it's bred to do. Please forgive me.''

Miren felt odd. As if she'd bled a great deal and the bleeding had stopped, but left her weakened. She didn't understand the meaning behind his cryptic words, but they resonated deep inside her. "It is I who should be sorry.''

Nathan stood up and gazed down into her eyes. "You have nothing to be sorry for, Miren. You deserve all the good things life can bring. I wish I could give them to you. But this home is yours, for as long as you need it. When you're ready to go, I will arrange passage on a ship, and I'll help you locate your family. You owe me nothing in return.''

"I owe you my sheep. We have agreed.''

"I'd forgotten. Your flock is more than enough payment.'' Nathan eyed the roving sheep. "It may be time to have them sheared. Would you allow me to enlist a local shepherd to that task?''

Miren brightened with hope. "Yes! I'm sure the wool will profit us both. Thank you!"

"The money won't be enough to pay your way to America, not yet."

"I know." Miren chewed her lip. "If Mr. MacTavish was right, it will take some work to get my flock into shape. Huntley needs assistance . . . Actually, he needs to retire and allow a younger ram to service the ewes. Perhaps I could buy another ram with the proceeds . . ."

"That seems a good plan."

Miren liked planning. She felt stronger, in control of her destiny. Maybe she wasn't as eager to go to America as she had been a week ago, maybe she wanted to stay near Nathan MacCallum just a little while longer. But it pleased her to think of developing her flock to prime readiness.

"Thank you, Mr. MacCallum." She drew herself up, straight and tall. "You may not believe it, but when I leave this flock to you, they will be the finest in Scotland."

Nathan smiled. "We will work together to assure that outcome." He took her hand in his and kissed it gently. He released her, then started back toward the manor. He stopped and looked back. "I still want you, Miren. But not as an 'agreement' between us. I want you when you're free of all fear. I want you when you need nothing from me but myself."

He didn't wait for an answer. Miren didn't have one anyway. Her heart took quick leaps, her breath came short. His proposition certainly didn't affect her the way Dr. Patterson's had. For one thing, he didn't look at her the same way. It wasn't lust she saw, so much as masculine appreciation.

Miren couldn't deny that she looked at him with an equal measure of female approval.

Chapter Four

This is going to be harder than I thought. Molly watched the dark man cross the pasture. He passed through the wooden gate that led toward the manor, once again, leaving Miren behind. *Nathan.* Molly considered the sound of his name. Much more appropriate to his nature than ''Blossom'' was to the stout ewe.

Just when it seemed certain he had come to claim the young mistress, Miren had flared with anger. Molly had no idea why. Humans were unpredictable, no question.

The road to the manor passed by the field, and Molly kept her eye intently upon it. Since they'd arrived, she'd seen several fine coaches passing to and fro. Lavishly attired humans got in and out, then entered the manor house. Molly itched to see the interior of the mansion. From the outside, it appeared to be ideal house pet accommodations.

Molly looked back at the cottage. It wasn't unpleasant. There was plenty of food. Miren let her sleep on the bed, which was far preferable to the floor. Still, it fell short of

Molly's plan. For one thing, her plan didn't include spending the day watching sheep.

The young mistress had already turned back to her task. Molly wasn't sure what had stopped the young mistress from seizing the obvious mate, but she felt it prudent to be on the lookout for another.

The past three days had taught her that coaches don't stop unless you make them stop. Each day, their passage to the mansion grew more irritating. Molly felt the need to control them. To nip at their front wheels, to hedge the harness horses' onward movement. She understood this came from her innate herding instinct.

Her instinct didn't direct itself at sheep. Why would anyone want to control sheep, let alone keep them together, and nearby? But coaches . . . that was another thing entirely. One could inspect the passengers, check the interior, and possibly gain entrance to the mansion on the hillside.

Molly listened. The coach that came and went daily had left early that morning. It had to return sometime. She cast a furtive glance at Miren, who was hand-feeding Huntley clover blossoms. Painful to see. But at least her attention was diverted. Molly crept closer to the rock wall. An easy leap for an animal who wasn't burdened by wool and fat.

The coach was coming, just as Molly predicted. She heard the horses' hooves plodding, unsuspecting. The wheels kicked up small pebbles on the dirt road. A noise that never failed to incite her aggressions.

The coach came around the bend, and Molly crouched low, quivering. It drew closer, and she could barely contain herself. The horses passed just beyond the stone wall, and Molly jumped, bounced once on the wall, then dove toward the front wheel.

A horse startled, the coachman pulled him in. "Get, you vermin!"

"Molly! Oh . . . Drop! Drop!" Miren raced across the field, breathless as she came to the rock wall. Molly growled and barked at the wheel, knowing time was short.

"I'm so sorry . . . She's never done anything like this before. It's the herding instinct, you understand." Miren paused. Molly abandoned the wheel, hopped to attention, and wagged her tail. Miren seized her collar and drew her back from the coach. "You're supposed to do that to *sheep*."

"Apparently, she finds manor carriages more appealing," a man said as the coach door swung open. Molly scrutinized his appearance. He was tall, although perhaps not as tall as Nathan. His color was much lighter. His hair was nearly as light as Blossom's wool, and some assembled over his lip, too. He paid no attention to Molly. His gaze fixed on Miren.

That might be promising—another male scenting out the young mistress. Good. Molly sat back on her haunches and waited. Miren's face looked unusually pink as she greeted the new male.

"I'm sorry, sir . . ."

"Brent. Brent Edgington. And you must be Miren Lindsay." His gaze ran up and down Miren's entire body. Molly guessed that sight told humans what smell told a dog. He must be sizing her up for breeding purposes. Which meant he couldn't have another mate. Molly eased toward him and sniffed. She detected the presence of another female, but one well past breeding age.

"I am. And I'm pleased to meet you, Mr. Edgington. I hope my presence on your farm isn't too disturbing."

"Not anymore."

Molly decided she preferred Nathan's voice to Brent's. He sounded constricted, as if he hadn't relieved himself in a while. Still, his presence might prove useful. Nothing inspired a male to faster action with a female than the threat of another male.

"I had no idea Nathan's 'guest' was so . . . appealing. Americans have better taste than I realized." Brent spoke in a quieter voice this time, as if he didn't want someone in the coach to overhear his words.

"Mr. MacCallum and I have a business agreement, pursuant to my flock of Blackface sheep." Miren sounded annoyed again. The girl was certainly hard to please where males were concerned.

"Of course. I didn't mean to imply anything untoward."

"Good."

"Brent! What's delaying you, darling?"

Here was a voice Molly never wanted to hear again. Shrill, affected with an annoying lilt, and spoken as if the neck muscles strained over every utterance. Molly's lip curled into a snarl.

"I'm meeting Mr. MacCallum's lovely new charge, Mother."

The woman poked her head out the coach door and scanned Miren as if inspecting a carcass. "Indeed."

Molly detected at once that Brent and this female were related by blood. So there was no way she could allow Miren to bond with that one. She would use him to inspire young Nathan to action, but nothing else.

She turned away and nudged Miren's legs. Something uttered a squeak that almost resembled . . . a bark. Before Molly knew what happened, that *something* landed on her head and bit hard.

"Muffin! Get that dog off poor Muffin! Brent, shoot it!"

Molly squealed in fright, with no idea what had attacked her. She whirled and spun, but the thing clung to her neck. Nothing had ever terrified Molly more. Miren called desperately to her, but Molly was too frightened to listen.

Molly jumped, dove, and spun around. The evil creature knocked her off balance, and she fell to her side. Molly rolled to her back, and the creature came loose. A torrent of squeak-like yips followed. Molly righted herself, and the thing squealed as if *she'd* attacked *it*.

Which was just what Molly planned to do.

She turned with a growl to see her enemy. The creature before her defied imagining. It couldn't be a dog. It was smaller than a newborn lamb. Smaller than a barn cat, and far more horrid. It had pointy ears and a pointy nose, now curled in a growl. Its little bushy tail curled over its back. It bristled for the sake of bristling.

The creature didn't maintain a defensive posture as most dogs, by a code of honor, did. It attacked for the sake of attacking. It attacked to kill.

Molly had no idea how to deal with a dog who didn't respect the code. Her instinct to fight back abated, and fear filled her heart. The little menace recognized her fear. Its lip curled into an evil snarl.

Miren fell to her knees beside Molly and scooped her into her arms. Molly shook all over. Miren was crying. She was shaking, too. Molly licked her face in reassurance. As long as Miren held her, she was safe.

An odd sound came from Brent. It sounded like awkward, controlled, congested laughter. "Muffin doesn't know her own size."

The woman removed herself from the coach and picked Muffin up. She cooed and reassured the wretched pest as if she'd been the victim. "Poor dear, poor Muffin."

"Poor Muffin?" Good, the young mistress was rising in defense. " 'Muffin' just attacked my dog, from behind . . . above . . . A creature like that should be kept on a leash!"

Brent coughed and placed himself between the two women. He held out his arms to both. "Now, now . . . Ladies, I know these little friends mean a lot to you, but let's not—"

"Young woman, are you aware to whom you are speaking?"

"I assume you're Lady MacCallum." Miren spoke without deference. "I am Miren Lindsay. I'm sorry my dog stopped your coach. She won't do it again. But I won't have her threatened because she defended herself against that . . . that little hornet."

"How dare you! Muffin's breeding places her so far above that farmer's mutt. Young woman, you may have wormed your way into Nathan MacCallum's bed, but your place is no higher in society than your dog's. Stay here as a rich man's tart. You're not the first, and you certainly won't be the last. But I warn you, keep away from the manor house, or I'll see that vicious hound of yours shot!''

"Mother, please—"

"Brent, resume the coach." The woman embraced Muffin close to her chest, tossed her head back at a prideful angle, and retreated into the coach. Brent hesitated, and cast a final glance Miren's way.

"Not the best first meeting with your new hosts, I'm afraid. But don't let it upset you, Miss Lindsay. Muffin is Mother's pride and joy." Brent lowered his voice. "Can't stand the little rodent myself, but you understand." He chuckled again, that same forced laughter, then followed his mother into the coach.

The coachman sighed heavily, cast his eyes heavenward, and urged his team forward. Molly took a long look at the wheels and decided that no temptation was worth another entanglement with Muffin.

"Well, you've certainly distinguished yourself."

Miren jumped, gasped, and whirled around to see Nathan MacCallum standing in her doorway, grinning. His brown eyes sparkled. "Mr. MacCallum . . . What are you doing here?"

Molly sat on the wooden table, waiting patiently as Miren tended her wound. Miren wrung out her cloth, then dried the area around the cut. She tried to behave casually, as if Nathan's arrival didn't disturb her senses in any way. "I'm sorry. You startled me."

"Forgive me." He entered the cottage, glanced around, then turned his attention to Molly's neck. "I understand Molly had a run-in with Muffin. I'm sorry I missed it. Molly holding Muffin by the neck, shaking her . . ." Nathan shook his head and issued a "tsk" noise.

Miren braced. "That was *not* the way it happened. That wretched mite jumped out of the coach, landed on Molly's head, and bit her. And she wouldn't let go, either. I suppose Lady MacCallum said Molly did the dirty work."

"She described a hound from hell, yes. But since your version resembles quite closely what Muffin did to Simon two days ago, I'm forced to believe you." He was still smiling. Miren relented, and smiled, too.

"That creature is obviously inbred."

"And with the queen's own Skiffy." Nathan's voice took on a lilting, silly tone, like a pretentious old lady. Molly quirked one ear and looked uneasy.

"Skiffy?" A bubble of laughter threatened to erupt. Miren poked her tongue into her cheek to stop herself.

Nathan's brow arched. Miren looked away. She liked him. She liked having him around, she liked speaking with him. It had been a long while since someone made her laugh.

"So what did you think of Lady MacCallum and her son?"

Miren dabbed warm water on Molly's wound, proud that Molly didn't flinch or whine. "Lady MacCallum and I aren't likely to end up as friends, that much is certain. But I liked her son well enough."

"Brent seemed to like you, too. He seemed intensely interested in the nature of our relationship. You, Miss Lindsay, have a way of attracting male attention."

"That wasn't my intention." She glanced down at her dress. It was splattered with mud from carrying Molly. Her hair hung over one shoulder, clean but hardly coiffed like a lady's. "One look at me should tell you I'm not dressed for the purpose of attracting anyone."

"One look at you tells me you don't have to be."

His voice sent pulses through her nerves. Miren kept her eye on her job. Molly's skin was broken in two places. Small but deep, the effort of Muffin's sharp teeth. "I can't believe that little monster did this," she said. "Attacking a dog twice her size. No sense whatsoever."

"Maybe she thinks her breeding makes her a warrior."

"Breeding is overrated."

"Tell Muffin that."

Miren bit her lip, but she smiled anyway. She wrapped a cloth around Molly's neck, then set her to the floor. "Why aren't you married?"

Nathan seated himself on her table, bringing them closer to eye level. Miren endured an intense regret at having asked. "I never met anyone I wanted to marry."

Miren dusted the table around him casually. "You must be very picky."

"I've never been in one place long enough to consider it, I suppose."

"And you don't want to pick one woman and settle down."

"Maybe not. To marry, that is to take a woman's life into your hands. And soon after, children. Before I offer that to anyone, I want to know I have something worth giving."

Miren studied his face. "You mean more than money and position, don't you? Because you have that, you know. I suppose you mean you must give a full heart or nothing. That is fair. A woman would want a full heart."

"What do you want of a man, Miss Lindsay?"

Miren shrugged. "I haven't thought about it much. I know young women are supposed to plan for marriage, but that phase of my life passed by while my father was dying. I'm twenty-four now, you know. Most women my age are married."

"You haven't answered my question."

"I don't know what I want." Miren paused, considering. "I suppose I want a friend. A man I can trust, and who values the things that matter to me."

"What matters to you, Miren?"

His voice did peculiar things to her senses, even when she wasn't looking at him. It crept into her and stole a place she'd never exposed to anyone. He crept in and encouraged her . . . to dream.

"Truth, to know a person fully. That matters." Miren noticed that Nathan looked down at the tabletop. Of course, she'd chosen that quality for a purpose. She knew he kept much to himself. She knew truth wasn't paramount in his sojourn in Scotland. She had no right to ferret out the truth, but it still intrigued her.

"Truth is sometimes disappointing. You might find the prince is only a frog."

"I always liked that story. Because I thought if the prince had been a frog, if only for a while, he would be a better person when he became king."

Nathan eyed her doubtfully, one dark brow angled. "Unusual interpretation."

Miren met his eyes and smiled. "I always liked frogs. They're so innocent, so vulnerable."

Nathan laughed. "You have a strange relationship to the animal world. I'm surprised you haven't deified them."

"The Celts deified many creatures. Trees, too. It is, I know, offensive to the Church's current teachings, but I thought perhaps it was symbolic."

"That is true of the native tribes in America."

"Do you mean the Indians?" Miren watched him intently. He looked overly casual. "What do they believe?"

"It depends on which tribe you address. The native peoples of eastern America are different from those in the West or the Plains."

"You know quite a lot about Indians. Have you ever met one?"

"One or two." Nathan looked uncomfortable now. Miren wondered why.

"Where did you spend your childhood, before Laird MacCallum found you?"

"Western New York." Nathan was looking around her cottage. He picked up the towel she used to dress Molly's wound, and fidgeted. "And you, Miss Lindsay . . ."

"I have a map."

"What?"

"A map of the United States of America." Miren pulled her old pack from her dressing table and spilled the contents onto the table. She fished through her gear and pulled.out the worn map. Nathan watched as she spread the map out beside him. "Here is New York." She set her finger near the Great Lakes. "Where was your home?"

He swallowed, rather hard. Miren kept her eyes on him as he affected a casual expression. "Oh . . ." He ran his finger around the state of New York, then tapped once just below a large lake. "About here." He withdrew his finger and eased from the table.

Miren scrutinized the map, bending over it to make out the small words. "Here I see the Genesee River. Were you near that?"

"It was around somewhere, as I recall."

"What is this?" Miren squinted. "Canan . . . something lake."

"Canandaigua." His voice altered, the accent shifted.

"You said that very well."

"I've heard it before."

"What is the land like there?"

"It reminds me of southern Scotland, actually. Valleys of rich soil, highlands, many lakes. And yourself, miss . . . ?"

"Where did the Indians live?"

Nathan sighed, probably at the intensity of her persistence. "The Iroquois nation tribes are spread along the lakes through New York. Most are on reservations now."

"Nations? What nations? I didn't know Indians had nations."

"The Iroquois Confederation was composed of many tribes, the Mohawk, Onondaga . . . the Seneca. It was a great and successful union, which might be said to precede the current government in America. Naturally, they are given no credit for ingenuity."

"As I said before, your knowledge is impressive."

"I grew up in close proximity to the Seneca. Does that satisfy your curiosity?"

"Not entirely. What do they look like?"

"Who?"

"The Indians. These Seneca persons."

Nathan shrugged. He looked impatient now. Perhaps annoyed. "They look like people. What do you mean, 'what do they look like?' The men look like men, the women like women."

"Is their skin dark?"

"Darkish."

"Do they wear beads and feathers?"

"Some do—"

"Earrings?"

"It's not uncommon . . ."

Nathan began to pace. Miren felt a warm rush of satisfaction. "Well, well."

He eyed her suspiciously. "If we might conclude your instruction in native peoples, there is something I need to know."

Miren angled her brow, to make it clear to him that she knew he had deliberately altered the subject. "What?"

"Dr. Patterson . . . What do you know of him, other than his lecherous tendencies?"

"Why do you want to know?"

"There remains an unsettled matter concerning my father's death."

"What?"

Nathan drew a strained breath, fighting for patience. Miren smiled. She'd never enjoyed antagonizing someone before. It provided untold delight now. "Do you really need to know?"

"I do. Dr. Patterson accompanied your father when they went to America to find you. They died in a fire. I see nothing unusual about that."

Nathan's eyes flashed from brown to black. "Patterson didn't just die in the fire that killed my father. He caused it."

81

Miren's mouth opened. "Truly? How do you know?"

"Simon . . . I was there, remember?"

"Umm. So you want to know why he would do such a thing, is that it?"

Nathan hesitated. "Yes."

"Is that why you came to Scotland?"

"I came to Scotland to establish my inheritance."

"So you say." Miren resumed dusting, and added a calculated hum. "Of course, several times you've referenced leaving, that your stay is temporary. So I can only conclude that you plan to leave at some point." She stopped dusting and fixed her gaze upon him. "When, for instance, Kenneth MacCallum's murder is explained?"

Nathan's mouth was open. He looked stunned. Miren had never known such satisfaction. He tried to speak, failed, then shook his head.

"If you were honest with me, I might be able to help you."

Nathan stood facing her, his expression dark. He was tall, and his shoulders were broad. Miren felt smaller than usual. She straightened her back and lifted her chin.

"Miss Lindsay, your curiosity isn't in your best interest. The circumstances of my arrival in Scotland are, by necessity, a private matter."

"What do you think I'm going to do? Trot up to Lady MacCallum, nudge Muffin from her lap, and say, 'Oh, by the way, did you know your handsome usurper is fishing around to find out why your husband died?' "

"My experience with the Scottish people proves that nothing, however odd, is beyond them." Nathan paused, his eyes narrowed. "Handsome?"

b   "You know . . ." Miren refused to allow her slip to set her off course. She seated herself on a stool, crossed her legs, and folded her hands over her knee. "I will tell you what I know about Dr. Patterson, for a start." She didn't wait for his approval. "He is . . . was an Englishman, from Yorkshire. He served the British Army in India, where he became a surgeon. He came to Scotland only a few years ago—I'm not sure why. He fancied himself a practitioner to the upper classes here, but he also took smaller jobs. Tending my father, for instance.''

"Did you like him?"

"What has that to do with your investigation?"

Nathan smiled. "Not much. Go on."

"Well, then . . . No, I didn't like him particularly. He made me uncomfortable, though I wasn't sure why at the time. He wasn't unattractive, and he had worldly experience, which I know because he mentioned it often."

"Boasting to impress you."

"I was not so very impressed, because all his good fortune seems to have come by his ability to manipulate situations and people. He never acted from conviction, but from how it might profit him."

"Those seem qualities likely in a murderer."

"He must have thought killing your father would profit him in some way, but it is a big risk to take. Dr. Patterson had no lack of money. That is another thing. Dr. Patterson wasn't a man of courage. He became a surgeon because he feared becoming a soldier, not for a desire to help others."

"A noble man."

"He presented himself as noble, but his actions didn't bear this out."

"You don't seem distracted by surfaces, Miss Lindsay."

Miren rose from her stool and studied Nathan's face. "No, I'm not." She paused, allowing her gaze to penetrate his until he squirmed in discomfort. "Which is why I know you're not who you say you are."

Nathan's jaw dropped, his eyes grew wide. Miren smiled her sweetest smile, and aimed for the doorway. She positioned herself on the stairs and waited.

Nathan stared at Miren Lindsay's small, straight back as if she'd come from another world. Which was probably the case. A gust of soft wind sped from the loch to ripple her loosely bound hair. Even the wind seemed her ally.

Nathan looked around her cottage—everything neat and tidy. Charming. Simple. As he first imagined Miren Lindsay to be. "Where did I ever get the idea that woman was simple?"

She was waiting, there on the steps. Knowing he couldn't ignore her shrewd comment, yet content for him to crumble first. She wouldn't press. She'd just look at him with those too-knowing, dark blue eyes. Her lips would curve in that half-smile that sent his pulse racing. Maybe she knew that, too.

Miren Lindsay was like a wolf. She smelled prey, and she went after it with single-minded glee. Indians . . . "Where do they live?" "What do they look like?" "Do you know any?"

Nathan reflected on where he'd gone wrong. He was led by his lust. He considered her a lively and beautiful diversion. A distraction from more important matters. He wouldn't coerce her, as Drew Patterson tried to do. He would seduce her.

And she'd eke her way into his heart, learn all his secrets, and turn him into a fool.

It seemed a strong reaction. She might be innocent. Just perceptive. Because she wasn't "distracted by surfaces." Nathan fixed his gaze on her back. She hadn't turned, not even to glance his way. Still waiting.

The solution was simple enough. He'd tell her she was crazy, presumptuous. Rude. No, that would incite further suspicions. He'd laugh, and make her look silly.

Miren's sheepdog hopped down from its position on Miren's bed and surveyed Nathan with calm, thoughtful attention. It glanced Miren's way, as if debating the wisest action. Nathan didn't suspect anymore. He *knew* that dog was scheming. He had no idea what it wanted, especially from him, but it wanted something.

"So, tangled with Muffin, did you?"

The dog's eyes actually narrowed. It knew Muffin's name.

"Enemies come in unexpected places, don't they?"

Nathan's gaze shifted back to Miren. Annoying, how she stood so perfectly still. So confident that he would cave at any moment and offer some weak explanation, some tactic to lead her from the truth.

The dog looked at Miren, too. It went out to sit beside her. She spoke gently, but still didn't turn. The dog glanced back at Nathan. It hopped up, entered the cottage again, and nudged his leg with its long nose.

Nathan stared, aghast. "You're not a dog . . . you're a familiar." A creature as knowing as this one could only be a witch's companion. "No wonder you don't herd sheep."

The dog sighed. Sighed. A cool chill swept down Nathan's spine. Maybe he wasn't so far off. The Scots were obviously capable of magic, and dark arts, too. Molly. Probably a vastly powerful, supernatural being.

Molly cast him a pertinent glance, walked halfway to Miren, and seated herself between them. *Get moving. Now!*

"All right, all right. I'll handle it."

Nathan spoke aloud, answering a dog's imagined command. He clasped his hand to his forehead. "I have lost my mind."

He filled his lungs with air, exhaled, and joined Miren on the steps. He glanced down at her. Yes, the faint smile remained. She gazed calmly, sweetly, out over the loch. Her eyelids drifted shut as the breeze caressed her soft, exquisite face.

He wanted her.

Molly took a position on Miren's other side and sat down. Molly's eyelids drifted shut, too.

"I knew, of course, because you have brown eyes." Miren spoke casually, pleased with herself.

Nathan attempted to seem casual, too. "Brown eyes? Why would that tell you anything?"

She peered up at him, still casual. Maybe a little condescending. "Two blue-eyed persons cannot have a brown-eyed child. I saw Kenneth MacCallum once. He had pale blue eyes.''

Perfect. An old wives' tale threatened his entire plan. "My mother might have brown eyes."

Miren's chin angled in superiority as she turned her gaze back to the water. "Yes, but she didn't."

That smug little voice with its rich, Scottish burr began to annoy him. "How . . ." His own voice came too low, threatening to rumble with anger. That betrayed too much. He forced a smile, and controlled his voice with inhuman effort. "How do you know what my mother looks like?"

She turned to face him. Nathan had never seen, on anyone, so superior an expression. "You have just revealed two things. First, that she is your mother, and second, that she is alive. I wondered about that." She didn't let him respond. "I know what she looks like, Mr. 'MacCallum,' because Scotland is small. Argyll in particular."

"That clarifies everything."

"My father spoke of Kenneth MacCallum's wife often. You see, she and my mother were friends."

Nathan sighed and turned his gaze heavenward. "Of course."

"My mother was a Malcolm, from Islay."

"And this signifies what?"

"Glenna was a Reid by birth, and they were affiliated with the Malcolms."

Nathan nodded. "All useful information, Miss Lindsay. Bearing relevance to nothing."

"We'll see . . . Your mother and mine were both orphans, and they grew up together on Islay. Anyway, my mother was hand-picked to marry Kenneth MacCallum."

"Your mother?"

"That's right. But she had fallen in love with my father. Glenna wasn't in love with anyone, so she took my mother's place. She could do this because she and my mother looked so much alike. Kenneth had only seen my mother once, when she was fourteen. He had to wait until she was seventeen to marry her. So they switched places.''

Miren paused, waiting for Nathan to absorb the story. ''My mother had blue eyes.''

Nathan sought for a response. None came to mind. ''You could be wrong about my mother's eye color.''

''I'm not.''

Nathan fell silent. He had no idea what to say. If the story contained a single hole, one loose thread, the little wolf would find it and dive in for the kill.

''Is Nathan your real name? I've wondered about that, too.''

''Nathaniel.''

''Close enough.'' The more pleased with herself she became, the more her Scottish accent turned toward a rolling burr. ''Your real father must have been dark. And tall.''

Nathan stood immobile, refusing to answer as Miren scanned his appearance thoughtfully. She tapped her finger to her lip. ''Kenneth MacCallum was fairly short. My mother wasn't tall, either. I gained height from my father.''

''Fascinating.''

''I thought so.''

Nathan glanced at her. She looked impossibly smug. His reaction didn't fit the gravity of the situation. He should threaten her. Lie. Instead, he wanted to pull her into his arms and kiss her.

''You, Miss Lindsay, are entering dangerous waters.''

She nodded as if his remark clarified something. ''I wondered if you might be a pirate.''

Her smug, chipper response had the annoying effect of fueling his arousal. Her long, heavy hair fell over one shoulder, falling just above her left breast. Small, but firm, round.

Nathan affected a dangerous leer. ''Pirate, sea captain. It depends on your point of view.''

Miren wasn't impressed by his display. She just smiled slightly, as if pleased to be right. Her eyes darkened, and

87

Nathan realized with a fiery rush that their exchange aroused her, too. Her sensuality, layered with her smug self-assurance, threatened far more than danger.

"You look more like a pirate."

"I warned you . . ." He couldn't stand it anymore. Her eyes glittered, her lips curved . . . No man could endure this. Her brows arched as he clasped her shoulders. Her lips parted as he cupped her chin in his hand. A small breath of surprise touched his face as he bent to kiss her.

She didn't resist. Nathan brushed his lips over hers, he buried his fingers in her hair and removed the loose tie. He ran his tongue around the line of her soft mouth until her lips parted.

She hesitated, then wrapped her arms around his neck. Her eyes closed, and she kissed him back. It wasn't a simple kiss, but it didn't surprise him. Her soft mouth gently explored his; she found the corner of his mouth and dipped her tongue between his lips.

Nathan deepened the kiss and pulled her close against him. The wanting turned demanding, but she moved back to look into his eyes. For an instant, he thought she saw everything he was, and everything he ever would be. For an instant, he thought he could be anything.

He remembered who he was, a man with no past, a man with nothing to give beyond desire. If he took her, he couldn't promise more than pleasure. She would become his, and he knew too well how easy it was to fail someone's need.

Miren gazed into his face, her arms still around his neck. She didn't seem shy or disturbed after the passion of their kiss. She accepted it as natural. Maybe pleasure was enough for both of them.

"Do you know, Nathaniel . . ." A trace of humor infected her voice when she spoke his name. Nathan realized with a cool shock that it was he who felt shy after their encounter. He who feared disappointing her with reality. "You don't look like anyone I've ever seen. Sometimes I see the Highlander in you. I can see you wielding a claymore, fire in your eyes. But there's something else, too. Something I've never seen before."

"You, little Miren, see too much."

"I do." She traced a line along his cheekbones, down the plain of his face, across his lips. Nathan stood spellbound. He had no idea what she saw. From his mouth, her finger trailed along his jaw, down his neck. She fiddled with his hair and eased it back behind his ear.

Her small probing fingers examined his earlobe, then stopped. Nathan endured her careful inspection with a tremor of apprehension.

"What happened to your ear?"

"My ear?"

"There's a hole in it."

"Is there?"

"I expect you know."

Nathan smiled. There was no hiding from a wolf. "An Indian needs a place to hang his earring."

Chapter Five

Things are finally looking up. The young mistress has her Nathan hovering—quite closely. I have observed an interesting ritual. Rather than scenting each other, they taste each other's mouths to display affection.

We'll be transferred to the mansion on the hill in no time. That poses a bigger problem than I at first imagined, however. Muffin is in residence already. If my life with Blossom has been a trial, sharing an abode with Muffin would be worse. Deadly.

So not only must I secure the young mistress in the manor, but remove Muffin at the same time.

Blossom might come in handy after all . . .

Miren peered up into Nathan MacCallum's face, into his warm, brown eyes. "An Indian." His kiss lingered on her lips, and it affected more than her lips. Her insides tingled in a way that incited further exploration. "Do all Indians kiss when they're cornered?"

Nathan relaxed visibly. Maybe he had worried about her reaction to his revelation. "I can't speak for all native peoples. My blood is but half Seneca." His dark eyes sparkled. "Maybe they do more than just kiss."

"It is your Scottish half that refrains." Miren kept her arms around his neck. She liked the feel of his hair, she liked his nearness. "So you are an Indian . . . pirate"—her smile grew wide as she considered the irony—"Scottish laird."

Nathan smiled, too, but she saw sorrow in his eyes. "I'm none of those, Miren. I'm a half-breed sailor pretending to be something I'm not."

"Why?"

"Why what?"

"Why are you doing this? It's not for yourself, I know. You're doing it for someone. Who?"

Nathan sighed. He released his hold on her waist and seated himself on the top stair. Miren sat beside him. "You'll pry it out of me eventually. True, we might end up in bed afterwards . . ."

Miren's cheeks felt warm. She puffed a quick breath. "You assume much."

He smiled and her insides turned liquid. "I know that when you and I converse it has a substantial effect on us both."

She couldn't argue with that. She liked edging her way inside him, knowing she affected him. "You divert the conversation, Nathaniel." She paused, her brow knit. "Do you have a last name, other than MacCallum?"

"I have a Seneca name, Deganawidah, if it's any help to you."

"Nathan it is." Miren chuckled. She rested her elbows on her knees and watched his face. "Tell me why you're here."

"I'm here to right a wrong."

"That much, I guessed. But it's not Kenneth MacCallum's death, nor Dr. Patterson's. I don't believe you would grieve over those losses."

Nathan turned his gaze to the dark water. "Another died

91

in that fire, Miren. My brother."

Miren closed her eyes. His words echoed deep pain. Pain, and remorse. "Then Kenneth MacCallum did have a son, after all."

"He did. My mother was pregnant with David when she escaped from MacCallum."

"I have heard rumors of MacCallum's abuse. Glenna married him at sixteen. She thought her life would improve, and my mother thought so, too. She told MacCallum the truth about who she was, and that my mother had eloped with my father. He kept her as his wife, but he resented the trick played upon him. My father told me they saw nothing of her after he took her away, but they both heard that he drank too much, and took his vengeance out on her."

"That is true." A dark frown tightened Nathan's lips. "My mother suffered at his hands, beyond measure and endurance. He brought her to America with him, because he refused to let her out of his sight. When he drank, he accused her of taking other men to her bed, and he beat her."

Miren's eyes puddled with tears. "When she didn't come back with him, people here said he'd killed her. It's strange to me that they can believe this, yet still accept him as a laird."

"It's strange to me, too."

"How did she escape?"

"Simon MacTavish took pity on her and helped her reach a place where MacCallum would never find her."

"Simon? Do you mean your manservant?"

"I wish he were my manservant. Then I could fire him. But unfortunately, Simon is more than that."

"Why would you want to fire him?"

"That man and I do not get along."

"I observed that when I first met you. You were both difficult in each other's company."

Nathan braced, and Miren repressed a smile. "Simon is difficult. I am long-suffering."

"He saved your mother. He must be a good man."

" 'Good,' Miss Lindsay, doesn't preclude annoyance."

"The same might be said of 'handsome.' "

Nathan started to frown, recognized a hidden compliment, and smiled instead. "You still admire my looks despite my ignoble heritage."

"Your heritage has nothing to do with your body." Her voice came unusually husky. Miren's cheeks flamed as she realized how brazen this sounded. Nathan's brow rose, but she cleared her throat. "You were telling me how Simon saved your mother. Where did he take her?"

Nathan's brow angled a little more, so she knew that her alteration of the subject hadn't eluded him. "He had dealings with the Iroquois in New York, and became friendly with the Seneca chieftain. Apparently, MacCallum had a terror of Indians, so Simon knew he'd never dare search for her there."

"So she had her baby there?"

"She had a son, David. And there she met the Seneca chieftain's son—"

"Your father."

"My father."

"I expect he was very handsome."

Nathan grinned. "Handsome again. As a matter of fact, I do indeed resemble him."

"His conceit can't possibly have equaled yours."

"My conceit, Miss Lindsay, is well fueled by your attention."

Miren drew a quick breath to clear her senses. Nathan looked kissable in the extreme. "How did Simon escape MacCallum's wrath? They stayed friendly, didn't they?"

"As irritating as he can be, Simon is a quick thinker. He told MacCallum that my mother escaped on her own, that he'd hunted her down on MacCallum's behalf, and that she'd died before giving birth."

"Which wasn't the case. She'd found your father instead." Miren paused. "Were they happy?"

93

"The only darkness between them was the fear that MacCallum would learn of his son, and come for her."

"So you were born. Did you and your brother get along?"

Nathan smiled. "Most of the time. David was much calmer than I, more content. We grew up among the Seneca, though we went to a farmer's school together to learn English. At school, David met a girl, and they married."

"What happened to her?"

"She died."

"In the fire?"

He hesitated, and Miren knew he hid something away. "She died a few years before."

"What did you do after school?"

"David built a small farm for his new wife, near the reservation. My father wanted me to return, but I refused." Nathan sighed, and his voice turned sad. "Instead, I joined the Union army and became a scout on the western front. I ended up on a steamboat going down the Mississippi, transporting supplies. When we reached the Gulf of Mexico, we came under attack by a rebel blockade runner. The ship caught fire, the captain died. The first mate panicked, and I took over."

Miren held her breath as he spoke, her mind filled with images of fiery ships on dark water, cannons roaring, explosions rending a quiet sea. "Did you escape?"

A glimmer of pride lit Nathan's dark eyes. "We did more than escape. We contained the blaze, and crept our vessel in close. The rebels thought we'd all been killed, so they didn't back off to a safe distance. We ran alongside, boarded their vessel, and acquired a fine new ship for our efforts."

Miren beamed with excitement. "What happened to their crew?"

"We tossed a few overboard, but we weren't far from shore. Half their crew consisted of black slaves. It didn't take much persuading to get them to join us. One or two white sailors stayed on, too. Said they didn't care if I was an Indian or a black man or a spider, so long as I could keep a ship afloat that way.''

"Did they stay with you all through the war?''

"They did. We made our way up and around to Virginia. Engaged in a few more battles, but nothing like the first. The war ended, and our reward was to keep the ship we'd stolen. My sailors renamed the ship *Half-breed,* and we went into business for ourselves.''

"As pirates?''

"As merchants, Miss Lindsay.''

Miren tilted her head back and narrowed her eyes. "Merchant, sir, is just another word for pirate.''

Nathan didn't argue. "Those years after the war were enjoyable, I must admit. I thought I'd finally found a place where my lack of heritage didn't matter, a place where I could live free.''

"It sounds good.''

"And while I was sailing free on the water, my brother was sliding into poverty. I wasn't there to help him. Simon MacTavish stepped in and promised to set him up with his real father. Simon had come to us every few years, to check on David and remind me that my existence was a thorn in the side of all decent humanity.''

"No wonder you don't like him.''

"The truth is, Simon loved my mother, and he always had. He was too much a gentleman to take her, but it didn't set well that she'd fallen in love with a seventeen-year-old warrior, either.''

"Your father was young?''

"A good ten years younger than my mother. Didn't hold them back, though. I have four sisters, all living happily with Seneca husbands.''

"Still, I don't see that as reason for Simon to pick on you.''

Nathan hesitated. Miren thought he looked guilty. "Our antagonism was mutual. I left snakes in his cot, poured water in his Scotch . . .'' Nathan sighed, distant pleasure in his brown eyes. "Oh, and put red paint in his hair tonic."

Miren giggled. "That was bad of you."

"Yes . . . You should have seen him. He looked like a carrot, beard and all. Looked a bit as if he'd really been scalped, something he always accused me of doing." Nathan paused. "The temptation was there."

"It's a good thing you didn't need his help."

"He did his best to help David, and maybe it would have worked. David belonged here, in Scotland. His nature wasn't suited to farming. I can imagine him here. He was born to gentility, but he did his best with what he had."

"Like you, Nathan."

"I was lucky."

"Saving a burning ship sounds like more than luck."

Nathan didn't argue, but he didn't look convinced. "I lived for myself, Miren. Even at sea, even in the war. While I was living a boy's thrill, my father lost his farm in New York and was sent to a reservation in Kansas."

Miren's heart expanded with pity. "It's not your fault."

"Not that it happened, no. But I could have helped if I'd been there. My father needed me, but I was gone. He has never forgiven me, and we haven't spoken since. My brother needed me, and I was gone. By the time I returned, he was dead. Simon found me, told me what happened, and we came here."

"What do you expect to find, now that you're here?"

"Patterson didn't act alone, Miren. He had nothing to gain from Kenneth MacCallum's death, but there are some who profit if the old laird died . . . without an heir."

"Lady MacCallum and her son?"

"They are obvious benefactors, yes."

"So accuse them and have done." Miren stopped herself. "I suppose you need proof."

"That would seem wise, yes. Simon is off researching Patterson's life to see if any connection can be found."

"And if you succeed, do you keep the MacCallum estate, Nathaniel?"

"There is another more deserving."

"Your mother?"

"My brother's son."

Miren sat back and nodded. "You have a nephew. And you've given up your freedom to secure his inheritance. You're placing yourself in danger for another. Again. Because you think you failed your father and your brother."

"A good summation. It is my duty. I'd rather not fail again."

Miren slipped her hand onto Nathan's arm. "You won't fail. I'll help you."

Nathan seized her hand and held it in a firm grip. "No, you won't. Miren, if you offer yourself, I'll take you. And you and I can revel in as much bliss as we can steal. But I can't give you anything more, and I won't place you in danger."

Miren withdrew her hand. "I haven't asked for anything." She paused, annoyed. "Including 'bliss.' "

"If you want the use of my body, that's one thing." Miren rolled her eyes, but Nathan didn't stop. "But you can't depend on me, woman. My ship is anchored off Oban. When I've done what I came here to do, I'll leave, and I'll never look back."

"You're going to leave your nephew here by himself? How old is he?"

"Five years."

"Five! You can't leave a five-year-old in a new country all by himself!"

"I'll see that he's well tended."

"He needs a father, a family."

"You need that, too. I can't provide that for either one of you."

Miren tensed in irritation. "I need nothing. True, I would like a family. But I don't require one. A child is different."

"He'll be cared for."

" 'He.' What's his name?"

Nathan hesitated. "Nathaniel."

"So there is a Nathaniel MacCallum. What's he going to think when you leave him?"

"He barely knows me. He's a child. I'm not well equipped to deal with a child, anyway." Nathan paused. "They make me nervous."

"Where is he?"

"Never mind." Miren arched her brow, and Nathan sighed. "On my ship."

"I take it no one knows of his existence?"

"That's right, and no one will until I've ensured his inheritance, and his safety."

"I won't tell anyone."

Nathan smiled. "I know."

"You are honorable to tell me you won't stay. So that I don't engage in frivolous dreams." Miren tried to keep her voice steady, but she couldn't deny a pang of regret; better never to think of it than to be disappointed. "I will remain focused on my own task." She straightened her back. "My sheep. I'll need a new ram. Are you still planning to secure a shearing opportunity?"

Nathan laughed. "You're a practical little wolf, aren't you?"

Miren's eyes narrowed to slits. "What do you mean, 'wolf'?"

"You've got a way of targeting opponents and going in for the kill."

"I do not." Miren liked the comparison. A small, rakish smile grew on her lips as she imagined herself in that role. "Perhaps I do. Be that as it may, I must plan for the future."

"As a matter of fact, part of Simon's task in Aberfoyle is to secure a shepherd to aid your progress."

Miren brightened with excitement. "Truly? As long as he remembers I am boss."

"No man is likely to forget that."

Miren frowned, but her glee didn't abate. "They are *my* sheep, after all."

"Maybe I can convince you that a night of fulfilled desire is worth a lifetime of dreams."

Nathan's voice changed, it grew low and softly teasing. Miren peeked at him from the corner of her eye. "That seems unlikely." She paused. "How?"

He didn't answer. He just smiled. Miren's gaze fixed on his lips. Lips she had kissed in wanton, reckless abandon. Lips she had tasted. He was looking at her lips, too. "Oh, no . . ."

He kissed her before she could move. She considered hopping up and fleeing, but her limbs went wooden, her eyes drifted shut. He didn't touch her, nor hold her in place. He just brushed his sensual mouth over hers. Miren trembled, her fingers tingled, itching to seize him, to touch his hair, his face. She gripped her skirt to stop herself.

He ran his tongue along her closed lips. He probed sweetly. Her teeth parted, allowing him slow entrance. She was afraid of what he might do, but she couldn't stop the desire to find out. His tongue met hers. Not demanding, just teasing.

Miren opened her eyes. His were closed. His long, thick lashes cast a shadow on his cheekbones. A small moan escaped from her throat and she snapped her eyes shut. If she placed her arms around his neck, he would take it as a concession. She wasn't ready to concede. However much she longed to hold him.

His tongue slid over hers, and shivers cascaded down her back, across her chest. Everywhere. Her insides turned molten. She wanted to do the same to him. She caught his tongue between her teeth and sucked.

It worked. A low, harsh groan tore from deep inside him. He caught her shoulders and pulled her closer. He conceded. She could concede, too. Miren sighed happily and wrapped her arms tight around his neck. Kissing provided untold bliss, yet she found herself wanting something more. To be closer, to touch more of him. To get deeper inside him. To have him deeper inside her. That thought stirred another moan. Miren's fingers wound into his hair. She moved to kiss his face, his neck. Nathan drew a harsh breath, ripe with desire, then cupped her face in his hands.

"I warned you . . . Indians settle lots of things with kissing."

She nodded, breathless. They stared at each other for a moment, then kissed again.

"I knew it! I knew it!"

The harsh voice came so loud that Miren screamed, jumped up, and fell back in one moment. Molly squealed, bristled, then burst into barking.

Nathan just groaned.

Simon MacTavish stomped around the corner of the byre, face flushed in anger. "Knew if I'd be leaving you alone, you'd be into more trouble than you're worth."

Nathan sighed. "Simon."

"Aye. Not expecting me, were ye, boy?"

"Shouldn't you be on your way to Aberfoyle?"

"Why? So as you can bed this wench, squeal all yer secrets, and send us all to ruin?"

"How do you know what he told me?" Miren braced before he could answer. "You were listening!"

"Long enough to hear him squealing his blasphemous heritage like as it's something a MacCallum would boast of!"

Nathan took Miren's hand. "Simon feels my heritage is an offense to God."

Simon nodded vigorously. "Told her everything, didn't you?"

Miren met Simon's furious gaze. "He did. I assure you, Mr. MacTavish, I am completely trustworthy—"

"You're a wench! A greedy wench with an eye for a man's purse." Simon cast a disparaging glance Nathan's way. "And his trousers, no doubt."

Miren frowned. "You're upset, I know, because of what

happened with Nathan's mother, but that doesn't give you the right—''

"Hell's bells, boy, is there nothing you didn't squeal? Suppose you told her how you've set up Brent, too?''

Nathan sighed. "I hadn't, no, but she knows now.''

Miren beamed at the disclosure. "You've set him up? How? And I don't think it's completely fair of you to accuse Mr. Edgington. He seems quite nice, in a stuffy sort of way. His mother, on the other hand, is quite capable of any number of crimes.''

"Fegs! Double fegs! The lass is feeling free to give advice!''

"I am, and it's good advice, so you should listen.''

"I say we kill her. Bury her out with her sheep, and pretend this whole disastrous event never happened.''

Nathan didn't react, so Miren guessed that Simon's words weren't to be taken literally.

"Had to get her out of jail, didn't you, boy? Led by your groin, you are.''

Nathan didn't argue, but Miren frowned. "Weren't you supposed to be researching Dr. Patterson in Aberfoyle? Incidentally, you won't find anyone who knows him there. His family mostly died off, and his mother is dotard, living up in Fort William.''

"Which is what I found out when I went asking, lass. Which is why I turned back, not wanting to waste my time.''

Miren's frown tightened. "Then I suppose you didn't secure a shepherd to assist my shearing.''

Simon grumbled incoherently for a moment, then sighed. "Don't need no shepherd.'' He sighed again, more dramatically, then held up a pair of long, flat shears. "I'll be doing that myself.''

"Truly?''

"My sire made his living as a shepherd, and I got stuck shearing until I took up as a sailor. We got enough folks here without adding another, who'd start nosing around where it's none of his, or *her*, business . . .''

Miren chewed her lip. "The only trouble is . . . Molly isn't exactly an experienced sheepdog. She *may* need a little help rounding them up."

"You don't need to tell me that, girl. I've seen her in action. Which is why I spent the day getting . . . this."

Nathan and Miren exchanged a doubtful glance as Simon placed a small whistle in his mouth. He sighed for effect, then blew a shrill note. Molly braced, crouched, then hid behind Miren.

Something black moved stealthily along the far side of the stone wall. Simon blew again. It leapt over the wall, and aimed not for the cottage, but for Miren's sheep.

"It's a dog!" Miren stared in amazement as the black dog stalked her sheep, maneuvered with artful precision around their southern flank, and began edging them into a bunch.

Molly peeked over Miren's shoulder. Her ears pricked, her eyes widened.

Miren chuckled. "Handsome, isn't he?"

Simon blew the whistle again, and the dog dropped. "Name's Flip. His breeding isn't impressive, he's old, but he knows his way around sheep. Got him off a farmer down by Campbell's residence. Had to give up his sheep due to Campbell's saying they drove off his deer. So the old fellow's gone into retirement. Didn't want Flip to retire before his time, so he let me take him. Dog lives to work."

Molly's left ear drooped as if in disappointment.

Flip didn't look their way. He focused on the sheep and nothing else. Molly eased down from the steps and sniffed casually along the cottage wall. She cast a furtive glance Flip's way. He didn't notice.

Miren watched her little dog in surprise and swelling affection. Molly spotted a squirrel racing toward a rowan tree. She barked an alert, then darted after it. Flip cocked one ear, tensed, then resumed watching the sheep.

Miren eyed Simon, who was glaring around at nothing. "Is

there a way to blow that whistle and tell him he's off duty?"

"A sheepdog is always on duty, lass. Keep that in mind and you might get your little slackabout into shape faster."

"Molly isn't a 'slackabout.' And I want to meet our new dog."

"Flip! That'll do, lad. That'll do."

Flip eased up from his crouch, still focused on the sheep. Blossom and the other ewes made their way to the far side of the pasture. Miren rose and clapped her hands. "Flip! Come, Flip!"

The dog trotted toward her. Molly positioned herself between Miren and Flip, but he ignored her and made his way to Miren. He sat in front of her like a small soldier.

Nathan nodded to Molly. "Maybe she'll learn from watching."

Miren glanced at Nathan. He sat on her steps, his long legs stretched out, boots crossed at the ankles. He was so handsome, pure and confident. He had kissed her. Miren took a quick gulp of air and forced her attention back to the dogs.

Miren patted Flip's head. He was bigger than Molly, heavier boned. He wasn't quite as pretty, but he looked stronger. His eyes shifted to the ewes as if he'd prefer duty to human companionship. "He's not exactly chummy, is he?"

Simon huffed. "A sheepdog isn't a pet, lass."

Nathan gestured to Molly. "Tell her that."

"We'll be teaching her, and she'll be following orders as right as rain."

Molly's expression became intensely suspicious. She circled around Flip and positioned herself beside Miren. Flip noticed her now. "Molly, this is Flip. Flip, Molly. Good dogs."

Molly crept forward, low in a posture of submission. Her exchange with Muffin had obviously taught her to take extreme care with new dogs. She sniffed at Flip's nose. He braced, then sniffed her, too. They circled each other. They sniffed each other's tails.

Miren sighed happily. "Romantic, isn't it?"

Nathan rose to his feet and placed his hand on her shoulder. "It reminds me of our first meeting."

Simon issued a long groan of pure disapproval. "Animals, that's in your blood, boy."

Nathan turned his dark gaze on Simon. "Yes, but it works with women, doesn't it?"

Miren shook her head. "Behave." She paused. "Have you two always treated each other this way?"

"The boy gave me grief every time I saw him. Monstrous little savage, and no mistake. He was worse than the other Indian boys by far. And sneaky enough to get past his mama."

"My mother understood that boys are supposed to be active."

"Active! Ha! You were a hell-bound whirlwind of trouble. And poor David being such a mild, respectful lad." Simon issued a series of tongue clucks to indicate the shame of it all.

Miren decided that Simon's dislike of Nathan wasn't as deep as he pretended. It was possible he even enjoyed their banter. "But you still called on him when you needed him, didn't you?"

Simon glowered. "Didn't have no one else."

"You're both seamen."

"I was a sailor. He's nothing but a pirate."

"He has his own ship." Miren's voice took on a sing-song quality. Irritating Simon was proving enjoyable, too.

Molly crouched before Flip, inviting him to play. Her tail wagged vigorously, and she barked in small, happy tones. Flip looked embarrassed. Miren endured a pang of self-consciousness on Molly's behalf.

"I'm afraid he likes work better than play, Molly." Miren sighed. "That'll do, Flip."

Flip took off and darted across the field, then poised himself in watch over the sheep. The ewes looked nervous, as if they sensed that something was up. Blossom in particular appeared peeved. Huntley was old, and probably deaf, so he kept grazing without noticing their new guard.

"We'll start the shearing tomorrow, girl. It's an all-day procedure, if I'm remembering correctly. Figuring it won't get in the way of Lady MacCallum's party."

Molly hedged back and forth between following Flip and remaining with Miren. She ambled casually after Flip, and Miren beamed. "What party?"

Nathan nodded, as if the event had slipped his mind and proved a tiresome bother now that he remembered. "Ah, yes. Lady MacCallum is hosting a garden party for the Duke of Argyll and his mother-in-law."

Miren's mouth opened, shut, and opened again with a gasp. "His mother-in-law? Nathan! The duke's mother-in-law is Queen Victoria!"

Chapter Six

Flip is the most tedious animal alive. Molly sat on her haunches as Flip oversaw the flock. He liked to keep them in a bunch. If one drifted away, he circled it and edged it back with the rest. He was obsessed. No question.

Flip would make a lousy house pet. He paid no attention to people. Just sheep. He didn't even have the sense to notice other dogs. Herself included. Molly contemplated leaving him to his dreary task. But he was a dog, and she occasionally enjoyed the company of other dogs. He smelled good. He was tedious, but he was well-built.

He never relaxed, which probably explained his strength and agility. He was a mature dog, well beyond puppyhood. Which meant he wasn't interested in play. Molly reverted her attention to Miren. Nathan had gone with Simon back to the manor, and Miren was staring after him.

They were well on their way to a mating. The boisterous Simon got in their way, but Molly felt confident that all progressed admirably according to plan. She glanced back at

Flip. There was no real hurry to ascend into the manor. Muffin was still there, after all.

Muffin. Molly's ears pricked. Maybe she, alone, wasn't a match for the little rodent. But with Flip at her side, she stood more than a fighting chance.

"Shearing starts at dawn, lass!"

Miren snapped up in her bed, eyes shocked and wide. She eyed the window and saw only a trickle of light. Molly popped up, too, yawned, then flopped back down by Miren's feet.

Simon rapped on the front door. Miren groaned. "I'm . . . getting dressed."

"Move along, girl!"

Miren slid from her bed and considered what to wear. Not the dresses Nathan had sent for her—they were too clean. Her blue dress was dirty, but it might tear during the shearing procedure. She chose her old sackcloth garment, found her shoes, and tied her worn Lindsay tartan around her waist.

Molly sat on the bed, refusing to move.

"We've got work to do today, Molly."

Molly eased back into the pillow.

"Flip will be there."

Molly's head rose. One ear twitched. She hopped down from the bed and positioned herself by the door. Miren repressed laughter. She'd invited Flip into the cottage for the night, but he preferred to spend the night in the byre, near the sheep. He seemed uncomfortable in human dwellings. Unlike Molly.

Miren opened the door and found Simon and Flip waiting. The ewes spread across the morning field, picking dew-covered grass, their breath visible in the cool air. Miren sighed. The loch surrendered to low tide, birds picked for shellfish. It was a beautiful, peaceful morning.

"A good day for shearing."

Miren peered casually around, but Nathan hadn't accompanied Simon. She'd dreamt of him all night. Of his kisses, of his ship, of the stories he'd told. She'd even dreamt of the distant past—of Highlanders charging their English foes, of bagpipes echoing between the snow-covered hills. The Highlanders in her dreams turned to Indian warriors, black-haired and wild, defending their ancient home against European invaders.

"They're not so different from us, are they?"

Simon fingered his beard. "The sheep?"

"Indians."

Simon snorted. "Sheep be more our kind than *those*, lassie."

"I don't know . . . The Saxons came to Britain, and they drove our people back. But they didn't destroy us—we're still here. They formed their kingdom, but we wouldn't give up our independence or our clans. So they said we were part of England, and they took our land anyway. But it didn't matter. We're still *Scottish*."

Simon's chest filled as Miren spoke. He looked proud. "True words, lass."

"Well, isn't that what happened to the American Indians? Isn't it happening now?"

Simon's chin squashed upward in a vigorous frown. "No. Not at all. The Highlander, he is honorable. The Indian, he's just stubborn."

Miren angled a brow and waited for Simon to cave to the obvious. He shifted his weight and cleared his throat twice.

"Nathan says you were friendly with his grandsire, the Seneca chieftain. Was he 'stubborn,' too?"

Simon didn't answer at once. "The old chieftain, he dealt like an honorable man. I figured Glenna, she'd be safe among his people." Simon glowered in a dark frown. "Didn't take his son into account, though."

"Nathan's father?"

Simon's eyes narrowed to slits. "That miserable savage wore almost no clothes, and he did it a'purpose."

A vision of Nathan without clothes popped into Miren's mind. She drew a quick breath, but her cheeks warmed. Simon glared in disgust. Miren forced a weak smile. "I understand they were very happy."

Simon just huffed. "We got work to do, girl. And don't you be casting your eyes up to the manor, because he ain't coming."

Miren tried not to look disappointed, but the day seemed a little more bleak than she first imagined.

"Lady MacCallum's got her fist on him today, lass. She wants him presentable to Duke and their English queen. He's got a ruse to maintain, after all. It wouldn't look right if he backed out, and headed on down here." Simon's voice gentled as he spoke, as if he understood her disappointment.

Miren met his eyes and she didn't see an enemy. She saw a Scottish man who knew what it felt like to long for something beyond his reach. "It's good to be Scottish. Because we endure, and we are free, no matter what happens on the outside."

Simon held Miren's gaze for a long moment. A slow smile formed on his bearded lips, and he nodded. "Fate, lass, isn't decided by the circumstances you get tossed into, not the good nor the foul." He tapped his chest, and his blue eyes burned. "Fate is decided within."

Shearing wasn't easy. Flip did his best, but the ewes weren't accustomed to anyone directing their activities. Three hours passed as Flip drove them into a corner, Blossom broke free, Flip went after her, and the other ewes scattered.

Flip looked depressed. Simon was furious. Miren sat cross-legged on the grass and cried. Molly chased a squirrel.

Huntley grazed thoughtfully by the stone wall. Miren dried her cheeks and sniffed. "We could catch Huntley."

Simon glared. "A wee bairn could catch Huntley, lass. He ain't worth shearing. His coat's thin as a spider web."

"Yes, but it might reassure the ewes that shearing won't kill them."

Simon rolled his eyes. "They ain't thinking creatures, girl. They ain't reasoning the situation out."

Obviously, Simon didn't know Blossom. Miren struggled to her feet, determined to succeed. Simon drew an exaggerated breath, positioned his whistle, and summoned Flip. Miren had no idea what the whistle blasts signified, but Flip's ears perked, and he took off after poor Huntley.

Huntley didn't notice. He just stood grazing innocently. Miren endured a pang of intense guilt. Catching Huntley had been her scheme, after all.

Flip cornered Huntley. Huntley finally took note of his attacker. He bumped into the stone wall, then tried to reunite with his ewes. Flip darted back and forth, pinning Huntley close to the wall as Simon moved in.

"I'll be needing your help, lass!"

Simon sounded enthused, despite his assessment of Huntley's wool. Miren rose to her feet and hurried across the field. Molly followed from a safe distance.

Simon seized Huntley by the wool and flipped him onto his side. Miren cringed. "Be careful! Huntley is old."

Simon huffed and extracted his shears. Miren sat by Huntley's head and spoke in a soothing voice. "You'll feel much better when we're done here, Huntley. I'm sure all this wool keeps you so hot. You'll feel like a young ram again, I promise."

Simon muttered and cursed under his breath as he clipped Huntley's wool. "When a man's experienced, he gets the whole fleece off in one layer." A portion fell off from the rest, and he grumbled. "That's if the sheep's got real wool, of course."

One side completed, Simon rolled Huntley over. Miren watched as Huntley's other side was bared of wool. "He's a bit thin, isn't he?"

"He's all right. Just old." Simon released Huntley, who just lay stunned. "Up, lad!"

Huntley struggled to his feet, gaped, then backed against the stone wall. Miren tried to smile. Huntley looked more pathetic sheared than ever he had with wool. "You're quite a ram," Simon scoffed and rolled his eyes. "You'll feel much better now, Huntley. My, what magnificent wool!"

Miren picked up Huntley's wool. It hung limp and frail, rather than tight and full. Molly sniffed the wool doubtfully, then cocked one ear. Flip turned his attention to the ewes.

The ewes had watched the procedure from a safe distance. They took one look at Huntley, and Miren knew his death would have been preferable. They scattered, and spread across the field.

"This, missy, is going to be a long day."

Three more hours passed, and not one ewe had been secured and sheared. Flip managed to get pockets of them into corners, but the ewes weren't particularly afraid of dogs, having known Molly, and they broke free every time Simon drew near.

The sun grew hot, and Miren wondered if surrendering to tears again might be her best option. Flip looked tired. Simon stood like a statue, whistle silent in his mouth.

Several coaches proceeded along the road to the manor. Miren brushed her hair from her forehead and watched. Simon shook his head as each one passed. Seven passed by, one large and ornate and glorious. "Must be the old lady."

"Simon! That's the queen."

"Bet she's wearing plaid. Old woman has an affection for Highlanders. Shows it in the silliest way."

"Yes, but the sales of woolen plaid have taken a good turn up."

"Practical little thing, you are."

Miren watched the coaches assemble in front of the manor. "Shouldn't there be a pavilion for the queen?"

"Och, she wanted it 'simple.' Just a pleasant visit between neighbors. Lady MacCallum's been setting this up for months. Word around Inveraray is that the queen is after seeing young Nathan. Word's passed around that he's a bracing lad. They're treating him as if he's some Highlander warrior come up from the grave."

Miren sighed. "That sounds fitting."

"It'll go to his head and no mistake. But the queen's bringing enough young eligibles with her to start twenty weddings."

Miren's heart took an odd twist. "Do you mean she's bringing women for him to meet?"

"That's what I've heard."

Miren tried to appear unconcerned. "He doesn't want a wife."

Simon laid his broad hand on Miren's back. "Is that what he told you? Lass, he don't want a peasant wife. Never known that boy to think of anyone beyond himself. If he gets propositioned by a lady, one who'll give him everything he lacks, he'll take her. He's tossed more than one aside who didn't come up to his standards."

"I don't believe you."

"Ask him."

"He's doing this for his nephew, not himself."

"And if he can set himself up as a nobleman in the process, do you think he's going to turn it down?"

"Yes." Miren felt odd inside. Cold and deflated. *I have nothing to offer him, it's true. I don't know why I thought I did.* Miren turned away from the manor and forced her attention back to her sheep. "I suppose we should try again."

"I suppose we should."

Miren watched Simon stomp after the ewes once more. His words rattled in her mind, but she knew he wasn't trying to hurt her. He was offering a genuine warning. Maybe Simon knew Nathan better than she did. At best, he'd wanted her in bed. Nothing more. He'd been honest about that. But she hadn't considered that he might be searching for another kind of wife or the life of a nobleman.

Well, he was welcome to it. Nobility was far overvalued. If he wanted to spend his nights in a pretentious woman's arms, that was his misfortune. But maybe she wouldn't be pretentious. Maybe she'd be young and sweet, shy. She would be elegant and beautiful, poised.

I have to get out of here. There was only one way. Her sheep needed to turn a profit. To do that, she needed enough money from this shearing to purchase a new ram. So Blossom would have to cooperate, one way or another.

Miren straightened her back. She banished images of Nathan and the queen's beautiful entourage. She beaded her gaze on Blossom, and she marched in.

The young mistress has lost her mind. Molly watched as Miren mirrored Flip's actions. Miren stalked the ewes from one side, and Flip came in from the other. They drove a packet of ewes into a corner. One broke free, and Miren jumped toward it. She missed, and slid onto the wet grass.

She rose again, still determined. Flip seemed to appreciate the assistance. He worked even faster than before. They cornered two more ewes, and Miren moved in, Simon just behind her. Miren seized the ewe, but it bolted. Miren held fast.

The fat ewe bounded across the pasture, dragging Miren with her. "Lass, you let go!"

Molly erupted in a fierce roar, then took off after the panicked ewe. Simon shouted, Flip raced around the far side of the flock, and the ewe hauled Miren toward the wooden gate. It stumbled, rolled, and crashed into the gate. The gate opened, and the ewe charged through.

The other ewes seized the chance to escape. Blossom led, thinking quickly as usual. Even Huntley got caught up in the stampede. Molly couldn't see Miren. The sheep careened through the gate in fat bunches, bumping off each other, issuing hoarse "baas."

Simon swore and shouted, then blew his whistle. Flip reacted, but the sheep were already pounding up the road. They didn't stop at the forked road, or head toward the stone church. They aimed directly for the manor.

"Oh no, oh no!" The last sheep made its way through the gate, and Miren sat up. Trampled, muddy, her dress twisted to one side. Simon knelt beside her.

"Lass, are you all right?"

"I am. They jumped over me, most of them." Miren was crying. "It's my fault. I lost my temper."

"That be your Highlander blood, lass. You had a good hold on her. Might have brought her down. I should've thought to check that gate. Latch was old, that's all."

"Where . . ." Miren sniffed. "Where are they?"

Simon hesitated before answering. "Well, now—"

"Oh, no!" Miren jumped to her feet. The sheep were moving in a large clump up the road, and they were headed for Lady MacCallum's garden party. "Simon . . . Did Lady MacCallum decorate with . . . potted plants?"

"Got 'em everywhere."

"Oh, no!" Miren seized Simon's arm. "We have to stop them. Blossom can't resist a potted plant!"

Miren took off up the hill. Simon blew the whistle, and Flip set off, too. Molly sat a moment. Potted plants. A queen. *This . . . should prove interesting.*

Molly learned that she was faster than Flip. She caught up to him without trouble. Miren ran faster than Simon, so Molly guessed the female of any species held the advantage. Blossom certainly reigned supreme over Huntley.

Elaborate coaches clogged the manor's front entrance. Molly hesitated, tempted to inspect the largest. But the sheep disliked gravel surfaces, and made their way around the manor to the short grass. Blossom stopped to bite off a red flower from a potted plant, but Flip edged up behind her, and she took off.

"Blossom, no! I'm sorry I tried to shear you. Oh, stop!"

Miren raced up behind the ewes, but it was too late. They charged around the corner of the manor, and all was lost. Someone screamed. Something yipped. And a man laughed.

"Brent, do something!"

"These are the elegant Highland Blackface, are they not?" Molly hesitated. She liked this woman's voice. It remained calm despite the clamor. "Now, where might the shepherd be?"

Miren stood at the corner of the manor. She gazed up into the sky. She turned and placed her hands on the manor's ivy-covered wall, then bent forward to rest her forehead. Simon came up, panting, and gave her a firm slap on the back. She straightened, and together they went around the corner.

Molly followed. The sight opening to her came from both her dreams and nightmares. Lavishly attired humans sat beneath parasols, served by other humans. And there, all around, everywhere, swarmed Miren's sheep.

Lady MacCallum stood shrieking. Her son stood beside her, offering reassurance. A fat woman who looked like Blossom sat in a big chair beneath a black parasol. At her feet were several . . . house pets. They were tucked in around her skirts, but not one barked or misbehaved.

Molly ignored the sheep as she studied the large woman's pets. Their situation surpassed a dream. They came in all sizes. Some with scruffy coats and big eyes. One large collie struck Molly's eye. Brown and white, of a similar type to her own, but larger. Fuller coat.

Two on a leash resembled Muffin. But even they didn't bark.

Muffin barked. She hopped up and down beside Lady MacCallum, growling and yipping in a manner that suggested she was, once again, out of control.

Molly growled to alert Flip to the danger. He paid no attention to Muffin as he focused on the sheep. Herding them here wouldn't be easy.

115

"I did understand that it's usual for sheep to be leery of people." The woman who resembled Blossom spoke again, still calm. "Now, this variety seems to have no fear whatsoever."

Her voice held a graceful accent. Quite beautiful, really. Not constipated like Brent's, nor shrill like Lady MacCallum. Molly wanted a better look. She eased through the sheep and made her way toward the woman.

"Your Highness, these beasts will be removed. Brent!"

"The shepherds have arrived, Mother."

All eyes turned toward Miren and Simon. Even the house pets took note of their arrival. Simon stood with his hands on his hips, blowing his whistle. Flip spun around the far side of the ewes and attempted to edge them back. Blossom had no interest in leaving. She'd found a large, elaborate potted plant, and she was feasting.

Huntley, sheared and naked among the others, found green plants on a plate and took a slow, thoughtful bite.

Someone needed to take charge. Flip had more than he could handle. With all the screaming and shrill cries from Lady MacCallum, and high-pitched yips from Muffin, Flip couldn't hear the whistle signals anyway. Molly looked around for Nathan. He stood near a group of females.

Young females. They clustered around him, seeming more afraid of the sheep than the situation warranted. *You'd think a pack of wolves set in.* Molly didn't like the look of Nathan's companions. One light-haired female clutched a tiny white dog as if the sheep might threaten its life. She clung to Nathan in ludicrous fright.

Nathan didn't seem frightened. He just shook his head, but he was smiling. Miren didn't look amused. She looked very small. Her hands clasped in front of her body as if in protection.

Something had to be done. Molly made her way to the center of the party and stood in the middle of the thronging ewes. She nudged Huntley from the gentleman's plate. He

116

complied. She eyed Blossom as the fat ewe made her way between potted plants.

Blossom neared Muffin's position. Molly hesitated. Only Blossom was stupid enough to tangle with that little fiend. Molly barked a quick warning. Muffin braced, then leapt toward Blossom. She growled, snarled, then dove toward the ewe's leg.

Blossom squealed in fright, then spun away. The wretched mosquito hung on, her teeth gouging into Blossom's hind leg, just below the hocks. Anger blazed in Molly's soul. Passion clouded her senses. She bounded through the sheep and guests and house pets, and knocked Muffin from Blossom's leg.

Blossom hobbled away, and Molly set herself to face Muffin.

"Stop her! That vicious hound is after poor Muffin again! Brent, get your gun!"

"Now, it does seem to me that the noble little collie is protecting her flock . . ." Molly caught the soft words. Ridiculous words, but flattering. She held her ground. Muffin snarled.

Something large and black and strong came to her side. Flip. Molly's blood ran faster. He had heroic tendencies, after all. Flip growled. Muffin wasn't stupid. She squealed, tucked her tail down, and fled.

"Well, now. That seems to be settled."

"Your Highness, please forgive—"

The fat woman chuckled, a soft and graceful sound. "There's no need for that, Lady MacCallum. This has been a most interesting interlude."

"Glad I am to hear it, Your Extreme Eminence." Simon sounded cheerful as he approached the queen. "The thing is, you people are getting in the way of our sheep. So if you might, well, pocket yourselves together, we'll just round them up and get them on back to their field."

Lady MacCallum gasped. "Mr. MacTavish, you have exceeded—"

"Of course. What a good suggestion." The queen rose and led the guests to the manor. The young females picked their way through the sheep daintily. Brent assisted his mother.

Nathan followed the others. He positioned himself at the far end of the guests, his arms folded over his chest. Molly had never seen him look happier.

The queen assembled her house pets and nodded to Simon. "Proceed."

Simon took a breath, resumed his whistle, and blew. Flip worked in quick darts. It wasn't easy. Huntley had discovered an abandoned plate of greenery and proved unusually stubborn. The ewes cooperated without much resistance. Blossom limped behind them, shaken by her encounter with Muffin.

The little rat meant to kill Blossom. Molly endured an unexpected surge of sympathy. Blossom had been enjoying herself. She'd found her dream, a field of potted plants. And Muffin turned it into a nightmare.

Molly knew a predator's mind. Now that Muffin knew where the sheep were, she would be a threat. Flip would have to be on his guard. Molly might even lend a hand . . .

Nothing in her evilest dreams had prepared Miren for the devastation of Lady MacCallum's garden party. The Queen of England stood plastered against the manor wall so Simon could collect the sheep. Mercifully, they seemed to be cooperating.

Flip rounded them up and edged them around the manor. They would exit, and Miren would sneak away in the night and pretend this awful series of events had never happened. It had started with jail. No. When she first met Nathan MacCallum.

She didn't dare look at him. She knew he was there. One glance had told her he wore a long black coat and a white shirt. She knew he looked tall and handsome, and that his hair was still too long.

He looked better than a nobleman.

118

Molly in the Middle

A damp glob of dirt dropped from her hair to her eyebrow. Miren smudged it away. Her sackcloth dress was torn from her ankle up to her thigh. Miren tried to pinch it together as she eased back from the party.

"Young woman . . ."

Miren froze. The queen spoke . . . to her. She wondered if beheading was still an option to the English crown.

She turned. The queen was looking at her. "If you don't mind, dear, I would like a word with you."

Miren looked at Simon. He bowed and hurried after the sheep. "I'll move them on back, lass. You just . . . um." He turned and departed, and he didn't look back. No doubt he didn't expect to see her alive again.

Lady MacCallum positioned herself by the queen, clutching Muffin to her breast. She looked evil and triumphant. Brent stood beside her, looking stiff. For the first time, Miren noticed that he wore a Stewart plaid kilt, argyll socks, and an elaborate brooch pinning another tartan over his shoulder.

Miren fought an urge to groan. Her own Lindsay plaid neared black with mud, the red and green had faded. Miren stood motionless. Highland warriors didn't wear pressed kilts. They wrapped blankets around their bodies to stay warm. They chose certain colors to prevent annihilating each other in a raging battle.

She was a Highlander. How many times in Scotland's past did the brave Highlanders face the far greater English legions? Anything less dishonored her ancestors.

Miren took seven steps toward the queen, then stopped. Molly came to her side, and stopped, too. Miren took a tight breath, then curtsied. A girl giggled. Miren cringed.

"You're a Scottish lass, I see."

The queen had moved. She stood right in front of Miren. Miren straightened and looked her in the eye. Queen Victoria wasn't beautiful in pictures, but her presence far exceeded beauty.

She was smaller than Miren, and clothed all in black. The

queen had remained in mourning since her beloved husband, Albert, died in 1861. She wore a white lace cap over her brown hair—a dour image, but the queen didn't look sad. Her eyes twinkled, as if the advent of Miren's sheep had provided enjoyment.

"I am a Scot, yes . . ." Miren had no idea how to address the Queen of England. *Your Extreme Eminence* didn't seem quite right.

Queen Victoria smiled. "You are to call me 'Mam.' "

"Mam."

"You wear the Lindsay plaid. Is it your own?"

Miren's eyes widened in surprise. The queen's interest in Highland customs hadn't been exaggerated. "It is my father's plaid, Mam."

"It's one of my favorites."

If the queen was furious, she concealed it admirably. She seemed maternal, protective. After the utter humiliation and catastrophe of her loose sheep, Miren found Queen Victoria an oddly comforting figure.

Lady MacCallum was far more intimidating. She stood, imperious and outraged, beside the queen, ready to smite Miren from existence. "You are to beg Her Majesty's pardon, young woman, and be gone."

Miren bit her lip. "I am covered in the deepest shame for my actions—"

The queen held up her hand. "You are covered in mud, child, but no shame." She held up a white handkerchief and wiped it over Miren's cheek. The handkerchief came back stained with dark mud and grass. Miren wanted the world to open now and swallow her whole.

The queen wasn't finished. She fiddled with Miren's loose hair and extracted several blades of grass. She plucked a wad of Huntley's wool from her dress. "There. That's better, isn't it? Tell me, child, what were you doing with those fine sheep?"

"Shearing, Mam."

"I hadn't realized the procedure to be quite so . . . lively."

"I expect it isn't, generally."

The queen peered down at Molly. Molly wagged her tail and looked eager. Miren held her breath. Dogs of all sizes waited for their regal mistress. Miren thought of Molly's battle with Muffin. If she tangled with the queen's pack . . .

"What a beautiful little collie you are!"

Miren puffed a breath of relief. "Her name is Molly. She's been with me since she was a wee pup."

"What a good dog! Protecting your flock and your mistress." The queen looked as if she wanted to pat Molly, but the constrictions of feminine undergarments must have held her back. She bent slightly and smacked her lips. Molly hopped up, placed her front paws on the queen's dress, and panted cheerfully.

"Molly, no—"

"Oh, that's all right, my dear. Such a pretty dog." The queen bent enough to pat Molly's head. Lady MacCallum glared.

"Her breeding is uncertain, of course, Your Majesty. A Scots dog is usually mixed."

"Those are the hardiest kind, Lady MacCallum."

Muffin issued a perky yip, but the queen ignored her in favor of Molly. Miren cast a pertinent glance Lady MacCallum's way. She couldn't resist. Lady MacCallum glared back with such hatred that Miren stepped back. The woman wasn't just offended. Like her dog, she had no control within.

The queen didn't notice her hostess's savage temper. She patted Molly again, then turned her attention back to Miren. "The Highland Blackface seems to be an independent sheep variety."

"That is true." Miren's voice came with a small groan.

The queen cast a thoughtful gaze along Miren's smudged, tattered body. "It appears they got the best of you today. But one wonders how you received mud into your hair. Perhaps they are too aggressive for a lovely young lady to handle."

121

Miren gazed upward, beyond the treetops. "It wasn't their fault. I lost my temper and grabbed one of the ewes. Our shearing wasn't going especially well, you see."

"I see."

"I caught one, and I didn't let go, because I was mad that they wouldn't cooperate. She crashed into the gate, and Blossom saw a way to the potted plants—"

"Blossom?"

"The ewe that Muffin bit."

The queen's brow furrowed in disapproval. She clucked her tongue. Queen Victoria—matronly, kind, and polite—stood like a large, soft shield before Miren and made pleasant conversation. Miren didn't like the English, she resented ages of domination like many Scots. But quietly, to herself, she vowed never to forget a widow's kindness.

"Poor ewe. I trust she'll recover admirably."

"I'm sure she will. Blossom is a sturdy ewe."

"So you were helping your father. Admirable . . ."

Miren's brow furrowed. "My father?"

"The gentleman who withdrew the flock."

"Simon isn't my father. He was helping me . . ." Miren's voice trailed off as the queen arched her brow.

"Then who are you?"

Lady MacCallum tensed visibly. Miren suspected they were well on their way to a scandal. She didn't know what to say.

"Miss Lindsay is my fiancée."

The queen turned. Lady MacCallum turned. Muffin growled. Miren's mouth dropped open and stayed there as Nathan walked smoothly to her side. He smiled casually as he slipped his arm over her shoulder.

A sharp hiss escaped Lady MacCallum's parted lips. "No—"

Miren forgot the queen. "Fiancée? Since when?"

Nathan dropped to his knee, seized her hand, and kissed it. "Since you bombarded Lady MacCallum's garden party with your pirate sheep . . . Before I had the chance to make the announcement, my sweet angel."

Miren tried to close her mouth and failed. "You and I need to have a talk."

"Will you marry me or not?"

Miren looked around at Lady MacCallum's astonished guests. The pretty girl who had hovered at Nathan's side dropped her little white dog. Brent stood with his mouth agape, looking pale and fragile in his starched kilt. Lady MacCallum looked more like a flame than a woman. Her long face was white, her lips squeezed and tense.

Queen Victoria beamed. Tears even filled her luminescent eyes. "There is nothing quite so dear as two hearts that finally beat as one. But tell me, Laird MacCallum . . . Why wasn't your fiancée included in the day's festivities?"

A good question. Miren waited for Nathan's answer. Nathan didn't hesitate. He cast a loving glance her way, which she didn't believe for a second. "We thought it wiser to refrain from announcements before my inheritance was officially approved."

"It is approved now."

A cool wash circled inside Miren. Of course. He needed the monarch's backing to fully establish his inheritance. He had it now. An odd way of getting it, true.

The queen clasped her small hands together. "This is the Scottish way, and I am humbled to be a part. But, dear child, you haven't answered your beloved."

He was scheming. Miren knew it. He had no intention of marrying her. She wasn't sure how she knew it, except that Scots were practical, and knew better. She met his eyes evenly. He had the most beautiful eyes she'd ever seen, but they were scheming.

"I should answer him, shouldn't I? I can't imagine why I might say no . . ." The queen sighed, and Nathan started to rise, both taking her words to mean yes. Miren pinched his hand and directed him back to her feet. "Of course, there are a few things we need to establish first."

Nathan looked suspicious. *Good.* "Whatever you ask, my sweet."

"I'll need you to contact my uncle Robert in America, so that he may come to our wedding."

Nathan looked relieved. "That poses no problem. I'll send word to him at once."

He started to release her hand, to rise. Miren squeezed his fingers. "Not so fast."

His suspicions returned, doubled. A satisfying situation, if ever there was one. "Yes, dear angel?"

"Children. I will want several."

He tried to smile. Miren remembered his fear of taking another's life into his hands. "Naturally."

"Seven, at least. Seven little persons who will quite closely resemble yourself." Meaning they would pillage his mansion, disturb his peace, and wreak general havoc. Miren liked Nathan's sudden discomfort. She found herself wishing the image she portrayed were true.

"As many as you desire. What else can I promise you, my darling?" The way he said "promise" revealed quite clearly that it was a promise not to be kept. Miren's lips curved.

"Our wedding date . . ."

His eyes flashed open, revealing a brief surge of panic. He resumed his doting smile. "Tomorrow?"

Good response. She admired the agility of his mind. He'd turned the tactic, and caught her off guard. "Not quite that soon. I need time. A good deal of time."

Those sweet brown eyes glittered. "You'll have it."

They were fencing. Miren began to enjoy the battle. She wasn't flustered or heartsick like a pining, infatuated girl. She recognized his tactics, and joined them. *Because I am a Highlander.*

"One more thing . . ."

He glanced up at her from the corner of his eye. "What would that be?"

"Shearing."

"Shearing?"

"Simon and I are having a small amount of trouble concluding the procedure. As my affianced, and beloved, I'm quite sure you'd be pleased to assist."

"Now?"

"I was thinking that might be desirable, yes."

Nathan's eyes narrowed slightly. She'd caught him right back. "As you wish." He paused as Miren tapped her finger to her lips, waiting for a further display of affection. "My precious . . . angel." He spoke through clenched teeth.

Miren presented her hand for another kiss, which he dutifully accepted. Perhaps with less enthusiasm this time. "Then, yes, *Laird* MacCallum, I shall be honored in the most extreme sense of the word to become your wife."

Queen Victoria applauded, and Lady MacCallum's guests joined in. The queen's companions seemed genuinely enthused. The Duke of Argyll and his wife were laughing, happy, though the young "eligibles" clapped with very small effort. Brent applauded in his usual stiff fashion, but he wasn't smiling.

Lady MacCallum's hands looked like claws, tentacles that resisted touching each other but had to, under severest pressure. Nathan rose from his knee, still clasping Miren's hand. He bent to brush his lips against her cheek.

"This is war, woman."

Miren beamed like a bride. "I know."

Chapter Seven

A happier sight I've never seen. Every young, strong male at Lady MacCallum's garden party is on his way to the sheep pen for the purpose of shearing. It was the queen's idea. To get the real, firsthand view of Scotland.

Some took the suggestion better than others. The Duke of Argyll ripped off his finery and marched down to the pasture as if he'd dreamt of shearing all his life. His wife clapped and cheered. Nathan seemed happy just to be out of his black coat and back to his loose white shirt.

I noticed that the young females seemed happy for him to be out of his coat, too.

Pale young Brent didn't take it so well. Though he didn't object, it's obvious to a dog that he'd rather be dead than working like a shepherd.

"There's nothing quite so glorious as a man at his most elemental task." Queen Victoria's chair had been carried from the manor and positioned outside the sheep pasture's stone wall. Her dogs sat around the hem of her dress, watching Flip at his task.

The queen's rough collie seemed especially interested in the proceedings, but it remained motionless, well-behaved. The terriers sat with imperious expressions on their scruffy faces, as if convinced they could handle the sheep better but considered the task unworthy.

The queen's two Pomeranians sat alert on her lap, both content to have their ears scratched. Miren wondered if one of these was Skiffy, but neither had Muffin's ferocious disposition. They were actually quite pleasant little dogs, which aroused Miren's suspicions. Perhaps Muffin's ruthless tendencies came not from bloodlines, but from her proximity to Lady MacCallum.

Muffin had been retired to the manor, lest the shearing "disturb" her delicate nerves. Miren took it as a victory. Molly sat beside the queen. Muffin had been sent to her room.

Miren stood beside the queen and the Duchess of Argyll, favored unexpectedly above the other guests. She had attempted to rejoin Simon, but the queen had taken her hand and said the fiancée of a laird must leave such tasks as shearing to her future husband.

"I do so love Scotland. The Highlands in particular. Miss Lindsay, you are a lucky child indeed to call this your home."

Miren gazed across the pasture to Loch Fyne. "Do you know, I have spent most of my life dreaming of leaving, of going to America?"

The queen turned in her chair. She shaded her eyes against the high sun as she inspected Miren's face. "You mustn't leave, child. So many have gone already. The Highland regiments are Great Britain's finest, but they have taken their toll. My predecessors perhaps waged unfair tactics upon the Scots, but I will see the honor restored. I believe much is restored already."

Miren nodded, though a faraway longing infected her heart. "Scotland is within. I do believe that wherever a Highlander goes, he carries his homeland with him.''

The queen's bright eyes glistened with tears. Miren realized that despite her vast power, Victoria was a tender and sentimental woman, with a well-developed imagination. She could look at the Scots and imagine what it was to have a Scottish heart beating within.

''My dear Albert loved the Highlands so.'' The queen's voice softened almost to a whisper. Miren's heart stirred. To love so much . . . Miren had endured her own losses with a Scottish practicality. But she had never been in love. Miren's gaze drifted to Nathan.

He stood at the center of the pasture, laughing as the Duke of Argyll pinned a ewe against the fence. He was so handsome, so sure of himself. He was an Indian, a pirate, a Scottish laird. He'd come to Scotland like a detective, to solve a crime and be gone. Miren had no doubt that he would succeed.

And one day she might speak his name the way Queen Victoria spoke of her Albert.

''The young gentlemen are making a pudding of it, aren't they?''

The queen relished the day. Miren suspected she far enjoyed the shearing to Lady MacCallum's garden party. ''Yes, but they're entertaining.''

The queen chuckled. Irene MacCallum uttered a false laugh, but the Duchess of Argyll cackled in glee as her husband dove after the ewe and missed. ''My Louise is happy here.''

''Never so happy as today, Mama.''

Simon MacTavish stood at the far end of the field, whistling instructions to Flip. Nathan shook his head. His long, dark hair glistened in the sun. ''Has anyone considered driving a few of them into the byre and *then* getting hold of them?''

The Duke of Argyll pondered this, then nodded. Simon puckered his entire face. ''That's a fop's solution. A real shepherd takes the task to the pasture.''

Nathan took a deliberate step Simon's way. ''A 'real shepherd' would be done with the 'task' by now and be on to dinner, wouldn't you say?''

Simon braced at the thinly veiled slur. ''If I had better help—''

''You don't.''

''Hell's bells!'' Simon sputtered incoherently for a moment, then held up his shears. ''To the byre!''

Miren frowned. ''Fegs! We won't see what they're doing in there.''

The queen sighed, too. ''But we'll see the results, my dear. That should be engaging in itself.''

The queen was right. Nathan's plan worked relatively well. Flip separated small pockets of ewes and edged them toward the byre. Nathan and the duke blocked them in, then followed Simon to the hidden shearing task. Brent Edgington floundered around the field but didn't appear to have much use. He looked odd, alone in the field, wearing his kilt, his pale face flushed from the sun. Miren felt sorry for him.

Apparently, Irene MacCallum noticed this, too. ''My darling Brent isn't at all suited to such a task. His talents are in the field of diplomacy.''

The Duchess of Argyll turned to Irene. ''Wasn't Brent studying with a physician for a time? Dr. Patterson, wasn't it?''

Miren pretended indifference to the disclosure, while listening carefully for anything that might benefit Nathan's investigation.

Irene appeared a little tense. ''Dr. Patterson was a family friend. His death was a great shock to us all. He and Brent were involved in a business venture. My late husband, Colonel Edgington, and Dr. Patterson were friendly in India.''

The queen eyed Brent without admiration, but maybe with

a little pity. "The young man does seem better suited to office work."

Two ewes emerged from the byre, shorn to the skin. The queen applauded and the duchess cheered. Simon emerged, too, and held up his shears in victory. Miren smiled. Despite his avowed disrespect for the English monarchy, the old Scotsman reveled in the attention.

"We've got two sets of shears going, Your Eminence! Young duke's trying his hand, got Nathaniel pinning her down. You'll be seeing some fine quality wool in no time!"

The queen waved and nodded. Simon directed Flip after three more ewes. "High-strung little man, isn't he?"

Miren sighed. "You have no idea . . ."

The queen turned her attention to Miren. "You, my dear, have had an interesting engagement party. But I think our fine shepherds might be at this task longer than will prove entertaining for the ladies." She paused and eyed Irene. "Lady MacCallum, you have indeed provided a fascinating diversion. I wonder if you might see fit to arrange proper attendance for this dear child?"

Lady MacCallum blanched, but she affected such a rigorous smile that Miren could only stare in astonishment. "It would be my great pleasure, of course. Dear Miren has been a joy and a delight. I would be ecstatic to assist in any way I can."

"I hoped that was the case."

Miren shifted her weight from foot to foot, wondering what the queen meant by "attendance." "I should be getting back to my flock."

The queen seized her daughter's hand and rose to her feet. The dogs positioned themselves like soldiers around her. "Nonsense. Lady MacCallum will provide proper bathing facilities, and we will locate a fitting gown for your use." She looked around at the young ladies. "You, Sarah . . ."

A young blond woman stepped forward and curtsied. She looked apprehensive. Miren recognized the pretty girl who had hovered at Nathan's side, and sighed when he removed his coat. The same who had dropped her white dog when he announced their engagement. "Yes, Mam."

"Your trunks are in the Spottington coach, are they not?"

"They are, Mam."

"You and Miss Lindsay are of a similar size. See to it that the liveryman deposits your wardrobe trunk into Lady MacCallum's dressing room, and Miss Lindsay will select a suitable gown."

Miren chewed the inside of her lip. She knew it was an excruciating request for Sarah. Miren suspected that the queen chose Sarah for a reason, and it wasn't a favorable one. "I have a dress of my own."

The queen cast a too-knowing glance her way. "Is it clean?"

Miren hesitated. "Not entirely."

"You will wear Lady Sarah's gown. Find a color suitable to the Lindsay plaid."

Queen Victoria might be charming and matronly, but she was still queen. Miren curtsied and bowed at once. "Thank you, Mam."

"Ladies, proceed back to the manor. Lady MacCallum, see that your chef produces suitable drinks for the gentlemen." The queen waited until the other ladies began the trek back to the manor, then seized Miren's arm. She lowered her voice conspiratorially, her eyes twinkling with mischievous delight.

"And you, Miss Lindsay, are to bathe and scrub and decorate yourself in such finery as to make Laird MacCallum consider upholding that proposal of his."

It had all started when sheep had surrounded his coach. No. When he had seen Miren Lindsay's small, tense face and decided she needed his "help."

His shirt was torn. His foot hurt because Blossom had stomped on it, deliberately, in an attempt to dissuade him from his final shearing.

Nathan trudged up the dark road to the manor, silent as he plotted vengeance. He had asked her to marry him. In front of Queen Victoria. He had got down on his knees and begged her. And the little squirrel hadn't blushed and accepted with girlish delight.

No. Her dark blue eyes had narrowed, her stubborn little chin had risen . . . And she'd issued a long series of demands before conceding. She knew exactly what she was doing. Because she was Scottish, and the Scots always know. The woman was practical. Devious, but practical.

The sheep had infiltrated Lady MacCallum's tidy garden party for a reason. Driven there by Miren's fiendish familiar, Molly. Miren Lindsay had him just where she wanted him . . .

"What a day! Not much as tiring as sheepshearing, is there?" The Duke of Argyll sounded happy. His hair was tousled, parts of it stood straight up. His shirt and vest were askew, torn and muddy. Wool stuck to his trousers like burdocks. And he was still smiling.

"Anything like this in America, Nathaniel?"

Despite the nobility and genteel ease, Nathan liked the duke. His enthusiasm was infectious. "Not that I've seen, no." Actually, sheepshearing reminded him of the Iroquois sport lacrosse. More than once, he'd been tempted to hurtle a ewe across the field.

"Ought to add it to our Highland Games. Her Majesty has reinstated the ancient tournaments, you know. Caber tossing, hammer throwing. Fascinating history we have here in Scotland. While the bloody English—sorry, Brent, didn't mean to offend—were testing their knights in tournaments—and losing half of them to severed limbs and displaced heads—our Scots were testing the real strength of manhood in the Games."

Nathan nodded, amazed at the duke's abundant energy and continual enthusiasm. "It seems more sensible to challenge strength and skill rather than annihilate it, yes."

"Thought so myself. Her Majesty finds the Games a worthy pursuit. Got a fine tournament coming up in Oban in a week. Ought to be a sight. Join us, will you, Nathaniel?'' The duke glanced back at Brent, who scurried along behind, his pressed kilt in sorry disarray. ''You and your mother, too, Brent.''

Brent seized a breath and tried to bow while walking. ''It would be my great honor and joy, Your Grace—''

''Good, good. Bring your young lady, Nathaniel. Scottish lass like that must be a fine one at the fling. Maybe she'll even compete!''

Nathan eyed him doubtfully. ''The fling?''

''Och, but you've been born abroad! The Highland fling. A dance, mon.'' Away from the queen, the Duke of Argyll reverted to a thick, Scottish burr. *They're all crazy. Nobles, peasants. Every one.* ''There'll be pipers, dancing. I've got to say, it's my greatest joy to attend.''

Nathan liked the idea of Miren dancing. Yes, he would insist. His vengeance started now. ''We will be pleased to attend, Your Grace.''

The duke chuckled. ''Maybe Brent will try his hand at the caber toss.''

A weak moan was the only response.

The doormen were waiting by the entrance to MacCallum Manor. Both repressed grins at the sight of the returning shepherds. They swung open the doors and bowed. Nathan considered it a deliberately exaggerated action.

''Your Grace . . . Laird MacCallum . . .''

The duke stopped and set his hand on a surprised doorman's shoulder. ''You gentlemen shouldn't have missed it! The wool we gathered . . .''

Nathan stopped listening. He'd promised her war. He meant to deliver. His proposal had seemed the best solution at the time. He had several good reasons for issuing it in public, before the queen. First, and unexpectedly, it solidified his claim of inheritance. He needed approval from the English monarchy, and thanks to Miren's charm, he got it.

Second, it removed the trouble of putting off young girls in sight of marriage. From the moment the girls arrived, Nathan realized they were there as prospective brides. If he didn't pay court, it might be seen as suspicious. Yet a woman's flirtatious demands could easily get in his way.

He had other motivations, too. If Brent Edgington was behind Kenneth MacCallum's murder, he would certainly act again. Should Nathan marry, his wife, not MacCallum's former heirs, would inherit the estate. So if Edgington planned to act, he would act faster now.

They weren't excuses. They were valid, legitimate reasons for proposing marriage to Miren Lindsay. In public. They both knew it wasn't his real intention. Not for a moment did Miren believe him. He saw that in her eyes. She didn't want to marry him any more than he wanted to marry . . . anyone. She wanted to go to America. He would help her, and they would be equal.

Something else had influenced his rash declaration *"Miss Lindsay is my fiancée."* She looked so small and so alone, standing in the middle of her sheep, her faithful, slackabout dog at her heels. Facing the queen with all her courage. Mud dripping from her hair, smudging her cheeks. Her sackcloth dress torn from her ankle to her thigh. One glimpse told him those were legs worth closer viewing.

He'd watched her, wreaking havoc as she always did, still innocent. Beguiling. He'd watched her facing the most powerful woman in the world, threatened with imminent scandal because he'd brought her to his estate. He thought of the well-dressed, coiffed, polished young ladies giggling behind their fans because Miren carried half the sheep pasture with her. He saw Brent Edgington's furtive glances at her exposed leg.

And he stepped forward to claim her.

The duke was still chattering to the doormen. Brent was trying to join in, but his face looked strained. Nathan wanted a bath. A hot bath. A benefit of being laird he intended to seize.

He turned his attention to the foyer. Marble floors . . . a ridiculous excess. He heard female laughter. The duke's wife came into the hall and shrieked. Not the mincing tone expected of nobility, but a woman's hearty glee.

"You will walk *behind* the carriage!"

The duke abandoned the doormen and marched to his wife. "I will ride at the fore, my dearest, in honor of returning to the castle."

She kissed his cheek. He laughed. They were happy, the image of wedded bliss. For an instant, the Duke and Duchess of Argyll reminded Nathan of another couple. His parents, laughing and teasing each other on the Seneca Reservation. In such moods, they often sent him and David outside to play. . . . He began to understand why.

Nathan looked around for Miren. She wasn't there, though Lady MacCallum and the queen entered the foyer. The young ladies huddled together, whispering behind their fans. The scene seemed unreal, as if he viewed it from a great distance. As if a theatrical presentation unfolded, and he sat alone in the audience.

He tried to remember who he really was. A half-breed Seneca, captain of a stolen ship, a man bent on vengeance. A man who couldn't wait to go home, and never see Scotland again.

"Saints! What happened to you?"

That sweet, melodious Scottish voice . . . Miren emerged from a side door, her eyes shining with mischief. She leaned forward, clasping her hands in delight.

Nathan just stared. He knew his mouth hung open, but he couldn't close it. She wore a burgundy dress, cinched tight at the waist, slim over her hips, full over her breasts. Her dark hair had been pinned loosely behind her head, allowing wisps of curling hair to frame her little face.

Her refined appearance hadn't changed her devious glee.

135

She sauntered across the foyer as if she owned the manor already, and placed her hands on her hips. She reached out to his shirt and removed a blade of grass. She extracted a tuft of wool from his hair.

"Well, well . . . it must have been a battle."

Nathan glared, though his pulse raced suspiciously. His physical reaction to Miren's appealing presence could be contained. "Only the last."

He'd never seen such delight in anyone. "What happened?"

He narrowed his eyes, darkening at the memory. "Blossom."

Miren burst into demonic giggles. "I trust she left you undamaged."

"That I can't say until I have scraped the mud from my body."

The queen made her way across the foyer. "Laird MacCallum, I trust this day has been as enjoyable for you as for Her Majesty?"

Nathan bowed. "It has been eventful indeed."

"I look forward to news of your wedding."

"As do I, Your Majesty."

The duke waved his arms in excitement. "I've invited Laird MacCallum to join us at the Games in Oban, Your Highness."

The queen smiled. "That should prove interesting. We will be there."

The queen's entourage departed, leaving Miren standing in the foyer with Nathan, while Brent sank into a hard chair and Lady MacCallum waved at the door. She stepped back and the doormen drew in the doors, then exited silently. Nathan didn't like the way Irene MacCallum ran the manor. It seemed stricter than the army.

If he actually planned on remaining, he would do things differently. But he saw no need to disturb the management of the estate now if he soon placed it in other hands.

Molly explored the manor with a critical eye. She entered the sitting room, sniffed around, crossed the foyer, then examined the dining room. She headed for the staircase, but Irene stamped her foot. She seized Molly's collar and dragged her to the door.

"Out!"

Miren braced. "She was very well-behaved."

Irene turned, smiling over clenched teeth. "I think she needed to do her 'duty.' "

Miren was doubtful, but she didn't argue. With the queen gone, she felt less comfortable. She edged back toward the door, casually. "I think I'll just head on back to my cottage, too. Lovely party, Lady MacCallum."

Lady MacCallum smiled again, but her eyes remained black with distaste. The contorted expression made her look inhuman. Nathan found himself moving to Miren's side in protection.

"Her Majesty has favored you, Miss Lindsay. It is inappropriate that you remain in a crofter's hut."

Miren's gaze darted to Nathan. "I want to stay in my cottage."

Nathan took her arm. "And you will, beloved. In fact, I will walk you there."

Irene braced. "That also is inappropriate. You are engaged toward marriage. You mustn't spend any unchaperoned time alone together."

Nathan rolled his eyes. "In America, engaged couples are bundled together." It wasn't entirely true, but it worked. Lady MacCallum blanched as Nathan eased Miren toward the door. "It's necessary"—he opened the door—"so that they know they'll like each other in bed."

Miren gasped, Lady MacCallum gasped louder. Brent sighed. Nathan led Miren outside and closed the door behind them. He offered his arm. She took it, but remained intensely suspicious as they walked down the stairs.

The night was moonless and dark, though stars glittered in

the sky. Molly was waiting at the foot of the stairs, looking offended and hurt.

Miren slapped her thigh. "Come along, Molly."

Nathan glanced down at Miren as she walked beside him. She looked dark and lovely, her hair reflecting the lanterns that circled the estate. Her hand rested on his arm; her stride matched his.

A sensation he'd never experienced grew within him. He felt shy.

"Unusual day." A foolish comment. He wished he'd waited for her to speak first.

"Yes." She didn't sound nervous. She drew a deep breath, as if enjoying the cool night air.

"You seemed to like the queen."

"Yes."

"Another disaster turned to good fortune. The luck of the Scots, perhaps."

Miren stopped, catching Nathan with her. He stumbled, then drew around to face her. "What's the matter?"

"Should you call me 'darling' again, I will strike you." She paused. "That also includes 'my sweet,' 'my precious angel,' or any other such ridiculous endearment."

He wanted to react with anger. Instead, he felt . . . hurt. "Miren, I—"

"You what? Were you expecting me to thank you for this bit of luck you've tossed my way? It's the 'luck of the Irish,' sir, not the Scot. The Scots are long-suffering, and long-enduring. We are independent and stubborn, and we do not give up. I was well on my way to America without your interference."

"Interference?" Good, anger was forming, after all. "I saved you—"

"From what?" Miren Lindsay had to be taught not to interrupt. "From embarrassment? Do you really think it matters to me if I look scandalous to the English nobility? To Lady MacCallum? To *anyone*?" She pointed her finger into his face and shook it. "I can tolerate a moment of embarrassment, sir. I can tolerate laughter because I'm messy, or my hair is wrong, or because my sheep disrupted a noble's gathering. What I cannot tolerate is being used to further your crazy schemes."

Miren snatched her arm from his grasp. "I will walk myself to my cottage, thank you."

Miren started away, leaving Nathan dumbstruck in the road. He was angry and hurt, and had no idea what to do about it. "We need to talk."

She glanced back over her shoulder, more imperious than the queen. "And we will. After I have rested and seen to my wool. Tomorrow."

She hadn't been angry at first. At first, she'd enjoyed the charade. She especially enjoyed Nathan covered in mud and wool, his white shirt torn open at the collar. His beautiful dark hair in careless disarray. His shoulders were broader than other men's, his hair was darker—everything more than other men.

She had entered the manor's foyer and seen him, looking disgruntled and masculine. And she wanted him. She wanted his ruse to be true. Not for the sake of marriage and safety and a family of her own. She wanted him for the purely sensual pleasure of kissing him whenever she wanted, of sharing privacy every night. Of teasing and kissing and looking at each other the way the duke had looked at the duchess. As if they couldn't wait to be alone.

That was when her anger had flared. It hadn't been there when the queen ordered her to bathe. She'd enjoyed Lady MacCallum's tense fury when Queen Victoria ordered her bath made ready—for Miren's use. She'd enjoyed Molly seated on Muffin's tiny cushion while Lady MacCallum clutched the angry pest in white hands. And Queen Victoria again lavished praise on the "noble collie."

Now nothing seemed real beyond her anger. Miren stomped

down the road toward her cottage. Molly trotted along beside her, looking thoughtful. Simon came toward them, returning home after work. He looked happy. He looked Scottish.

Miren forced herself to smile. Simon yanked off his sailor's cap and bowed. "Miss Lindsay, you are now the proud owner of sixty quality fleece. Should bring you enough to purchase a fine ram. Now then, I'm trusting the Englishmen's queen didn't do you much insult after I . . . parted company?"

"She was very nice."

"Good sense on the woman. Sending in the menfolk. I'll be saying, young Nathaniel proved himself at the task. Suppose it's in their blood—manual labor, that is." Simon wiped a dirty handkerchief over his brow. "Fine day. Fine. Forgotten how good it feels to get the job done."

"I'm sorry I missed it."

Simon took note of Miren's new dress. "Garbed ye up, did she?"

Miren nodded. "It was a strange day, in all."

"That it was, lass. That it was. Anything else happen as I was working?"

"I learned that Brent Edgington worked with Dr. Patterson recently and that Irene MacCallum's first husband and the doctor served together in India."

"Is that a fact? Well, well . . . Anything else?"

"Nathan asked me to marry him. I accepted. He will pay."

Miren ignored Simon's shocked expression and headed on toward the cottage. She touched his arm as she passed. "Thank you, Simon. I was lost without you. Good night."

She walked on, and Simon didn't stop her. She heard him grumbling and sputtering as he continued toward the manor. "Red man's got the sense of a pea. But they know their way around women, and no mistake."

He won't get around me. Miren marched on, determination filling her limbs. He'd probably expected to "walk her" straight into bed. To which she would certainly succumb "in gratitude." Ha! Miren fumed as she walked on.

He needed her for any number of purposes. The queen had revealed one. To fully insure his inheritance, he needed the queen's approval. She had given it, thanks to his blatant and disingenuous sentimentality in asking Miren to marry him.

Miren guessed two other reasons why Nathan needed her. He didn't really want to marry anyone, for one thing, and could easily throw her over. And if he was known to be engaged to Miren, it would fend off the hopes of other women, such as the host of "eligibles" that Lady MacCallum had invited to the garden party.

He couldn't waste time with that. Miren guessed he preferred a willing woman in bed, not a blushing would-be bride at a garden party. If one of those lovely young women was apt to his baser attentions, Miren had no doubt he would make love to her instead. He hadn't appeared exactly averse to Sarah's attentions, as it was.

Miren's anger churned as she reached the pasture gate. The latch had been repaired. The ewes lay in solemn bunches, silent in the night. Miren felt guilty. They looked unhappy. As if they'd trusted her, and she betrayed them.

She was feeling overly sentimental. No question. Sheep were meant for producing wool, and mutton, too. They weren't bred for display, or companionship, nor to carry a rider in splendor. Still, their lives were her responsibility. She would treat them with respect, because she believed that all living things were worthy of respect.

"You need something to focus on, a future," she told herself. "Tomorrow I'll search out a new ram, and in a short while you'll have lambs to care for."

Flip was curled up by the cottage door. He moved aside respectfully for Miren to enter, but he wouldn't come in when she invited him. "As you wish, Flip." Molly sniffed Flip, wagging her tail with more dignity than at their first meeting. He seemed pleased, in a restrained way, to see Molly, too.

"Maybe you'd like to stay out here?"

Molly swished past Miren into the cottage, hopped up to

the foot of the bed, and curled up on her pillow. Miren shook her head. She liked the cottage better than the manor. Here, she was free. No requirements, no delicate sculptures to avoid, no elegant crystal too easily shattered.

Miren poured water from the pitcher into her tin cup and drank. She pulled out her hairpins and brushed her hair with her mother's old brush. She extracted herself from Sarah's burgundy dress, hid the borrowed corset in a drawer, and found her own chemise. She'd washed it so often that the fabric was worn spider-thin, but it was comfortable.

Miren sat on the edge of her bed, and she felt lonely. Molly was already sleeping. Exhausted after a long day in privilege. Molly seemed more at ease in finery than Miren. More at ease than the queen herself.

Miren kissed her dog's forehead, then crawled under the farmer's quilt. She pulled her Lindsay tartan over the quilt and lay staring at the wooden ceiling. The bed was set in a cubby, safe and secure, decorated with pink and yellow floral curtains. Miren liked the bed, but she felt lonely.

Some nights, the sheep moved around the pasture making comforting sounds. Bells tinkling as they repositioned themselves. Low "baas" as they conversed in their private tongue. Tonight, there was silence. The ewes were exhausted, too.

I'm engaged. He doesn't really want me. But I'm engaged. Miren wanted to cry. Nothing had really changed. Nathan would see that the circumstances of their eventual "break-up" wouldn't reflect poorly on her reputation. Miren knew that. She could still go to Uncle Robert in America and build a new life.

Scottish people are practical. We accept life as it is, and we go on. Miren lay a long while in darkness. "I will go on."

Chapter Eight

All is not lost. If Nathan can't endure a night without viewing the young mistress, he'll soon be bringing her—and her house pet—to the manor. I'll stay out of it, for now. As long as they're handling things well enough on their own.

Molly kept her eyes closed and feigned sleep.

"We need to talk."

Miren woke, saw a black shadow hovering over her, and screamed. He clamped his hand over her mouth and pinned her to the bed. "Quiet, you little demon."

Nathan. Miren's heart beat so fast that she couldn't catch her breath. She couldn't speak. Molly should have alerted her. Miren twisted her head free. "Where is my dog?"

Nathan gestured to the foot of the bed. "She's sleeping." A small, rumbly snore indicated the truth of his words.

"She didn't bark."

"She didn't wake. Not much of a watchdog, is she?"

Miren struggled to sit up. Her hair fell over her face. She

143

shoved it back, fighting to gather her rattled senses. "She's always woken me before. Even when nothing was there. How did you sneak in here?"

"As Simon mentioned, Iroquois are a sneaky lot."

"He said nothing about Iroquois. He said *you* were sneaky . . . which I have no trouble believing."

Her shock faded, but her heartbeat refused to slow. He was sitting on the edge of her bed, casually. As if he belonged there. "What do you want?"

"I told you. We need to talk."

Miren looked out her window. She saw no trace of light. "It's still night."

Nathan shrugged. "It's maybe two-thirty, but it's morning. This can't wait."

Miren attempted a false yawn. "Why not? I'm tired."

Her yawn fooled him. He looked embarrassed. "Sleep late in the morning."

But not embarrassed enough. Miren sighed. "What do you want to talk about?"

"Our marriage."

"I hope you don't think me such a fool as to believe you really mean to marry me."

"Of course not. But I don't want you thinking I'm using you, either."

"You are."

"Only partly."

Miren laughed despite her anger. She cast her gaze heavenward and sighed. "I stand corrected."

Nathan adjusted his position on her bed, affording himself more comfort. "I was wrong to think you'd be embarrassed."

"True."

"I thought you needed me."

"Oh, please . . ."

"If I have to pay court to someone, it might as well be you."

Miren clasped her hand over her breast. "I am flattered,

144

more deeply than words can say.'' She remembered she wore only her light chemise, and edged her tartan blanket higher.

Nathan's gaze followed her motion. ''I don't have to keep my true purpose in Scotland secret from you.'' His voice sounded huskier than normal. Miren fiddled with her blanket.

''There are times I wish you would. But go on.''

''Ferreting out Edgington will be easier if he thinks I'm about to take a wife.''

Miren nodded. She fought to keep her voice calm and low. ''I see . . . I'm *bait*?'' Her voice came shriller than she intended. ''Because I'm *expendable*?'' Way too shrill this time.

Nathan cupped her face in his hands and looked into her eyes. ''I won't let anything happen to you, Miren. You have my word. Edgington won't act against you. He has to remove me first.''

Nathan obviously intended this as reassurance, but it didn't work. ''So *you're* the bait? So if he shoots you in the dark, or smothers you, or poisons you, your sacred soul will know who did it?''

''I'm smarter and quicker than that.''

''You're not quicker than a bullet!''

''I am.''

''You are the most conceited man alive. It is well you weren't born a nobleman. You'd be ruling the world beneath pure tyranny by now.''

Nathan took her hands in his, easing them from her clasped tartan blanket. ''You're nervous. I understand that. But I've faced worse enemies than Brent Edgington.''

Miren felt exposed. Her tartan slid to her waist. The room was dark. He couldn't really see. Although the moon had risen and shone through her window.

''What makes you think Brent had anything to do with Dr. Patterson's actions?''

'' 'Brent?' You're calling him 'Brent' now?''

Miren arched her brow, trusting the moonlight to reveal her knowing surprise. ''He mentioned that I should.''

"Did he?"

The moon shed enough light to illuminate Nathan's frown. Miren smiled. "He did. When we were walking down to the pasture, before the shearing began."

"A man who would dally with another man's woman is not to be trusted."

"He said nothing about dallying. Just that since we'd be relatives soon, in a sense, we should cease formality."

"Brent hasn't 'ceased formality' with his mother."

"That is a problem for him, I know. Poor thing. She is a domineering person, no question. I do not envy him his childhood."

"His childhood was the best money can buy. He attended the best schools in England, traveled, had positions handed to him . . ."

"You, of all people, should know that the quality of childhood exists beyond money and position."

Nathan didn't respond, so Miren knew her point was made. "I believe you're jealous. Odd for someone as conceited as yourself to be jealous, especially over someone as vulnerable and weak as Brent."

Nathan fiddled with Miren's blanket. "Weak and vulnerable people cause the most damage, Miren. They act and react out of fear. In their minds, that justifies anything."

"Like Muffin. You are right. But I don't think Brent is behind your brother's death, Nathan. He's too eager to please. He's more afraid of being the odd man out than about securing your inheritance."

" 'My' inheritance was directed to Brent, before Kenneth MacCallum went looking for his long-lost son."

"Lady MacCallum is the obvious suspect. Or do you consider women incapable of such crimes?"

"After meeting you, woman, I feel confident a woman can commit any crime, get away with it, and come back to do it again. In your case, the power may well be supernatural."

"I'm not the one who creeps about in the night."

"I was worried about you."

"Why?"

Nathan hesitated. "You seemed angry when we parted. Quarrels disturb women."

"Not as much as men, it seems. I was sleeping comfortably. You, on the other hand, must have tossed and turned a good while before disturbing my peace."

His jaw set hard. Miren's former delight returned, and doubled. "Not at all."

"You were sleeping, then? Just happened to wake up and decide I'd slept long enough? Hmm?"

He twitched. "Miss Lindsay, you are an infuriating woman."

"Not at all." She wasn't sleepy; her voice came chipper as she teased him. "I am practical. Practical persons see reality with greater ease than high-strung, nervous individuals such as yourself." Miren paused, relishing Nathan's obvious tension. "Which is why we practical persons sleep so much better than those tense, worried . . . *lovesick* . . ."

He grabbed her, tossed aside her blanket, and kissed her. Miren pressed her hands against his chest, but he didn't stop. Her fingers softened and curled into his white shirt. His lips parted hers, his tongue found entrance, and he bent her back to her pillow.

"I am not lovesick."

He kissed her again.

"I am not high-strung or worried or . . ."

"Nervous."

"Or nervous. Miss Lindsay, I am enchanted."

He was lying on top of her, his weight supported on his strong arms. His hair fell around his face, his eyes shone. She should be shocked. She wasn't. *Because I am Scottish, and the Scots are practical.* Miren eased her arms around his neck. "This is no way to treat your fiancée."

"My sweet, precious angel, it is the only way."

Miren opened her mouth to speak, but he stopped her words

147

with a kiss. His hair fell around her face, a primeval veil. He kissed the corner of her mouth, her cheek. He bent to kiss her throat, and she closed her eyes and moaned.

Nathan's breath felt unusually hot and moist. The smell wasn't quite so pleasant as she imagined. It smelled like . . . dog food. Miren opened her eyes. "Molly!"

Nathan groaned, rested his forehead on hers, then looked over his shoulder. "Molly. Maybe you'd like to go outside?"

Molly panted happily, wagging her tail. She placed a paw on Nathan's shoulder. Miren blushed. "She thinks you want to play, because we're . . . you know . . ."

"I *do* want to play, but not with her."

Molly hopped down from the bed and whisked to the door. She scratched to go out. Miren eyed Nathan doubtfully. "She knows."

Nathan sighed. "Of course." He left Miren's side and opened the door for Molly. She trotted out to join Flip, and Nathan returned to Miren. "We're alone . . . at last."

Miren took a quick breath. *Alone.* He intended to make love to her. She would be his woman, in body and in her heart. But she wouldn't be his wife. "So we are." Her confidence dwindled. She didn't feel practical anymore. She felt nervous.

I want you. There was no denying her desire. Once, the role of mistress had appalled her. But Dr. Patterson had attempted to coerce her, to manipulate her into his bed. He'd used his power, and preyed upon her fear. Nathan wasn't appealing to fear. He appealed to her senses, and her secret desires.

Nathan settled himself on the bed beside her. He touched her hair and stroked it back from her cheek. "You and I would be extraordinary lovers. And we both know it. Maybe you don't know it from experience, but you know."

Miren took another gulp of air, but she didn't disagree. She couldn't.

Nathan untangled her hair, softening it over her shoulder. "You are beautiful in moonlight."

"Like you." Her voice sounded very small, tense. He smiled, and her heart fluttered.

His hand went to her cheek, grazing her skin gently with his thumb. "The temptation to seduce you grows stronger every time I see you."

Why on earth was he hesitating? He'd won. When she thought, she found reasons to deny herself his company. But when he kissed her, her thoughts fled and left nothing but desire. Nathan sighed, then bent to kiss her cheek.

"If you will promise to refrain from igniting my ardor, I will leave you unscathed this night."

"Why?" She felt relieved, and she felt disappointed.

"Because I came to you." Nathan took her hand and kissed it. "It isn't the Seneca way. A woman goes to a man for her pleasure, not the other way around. Simon informed me that this trait was true of a Scotsman, too. So it comes from both sides of my blood."

"That isn't the reason."

"No, it isn't. For a reason I don't completely understand, I find myself averse to coercing you into anything."

"Other than an engagement."

"That was a question. You answered as you saw fit."

"True." Miren's gaze lingered on his face. "Then you're going back to the manor?"

Nathan huffed, stretched his tall body down on the bed beside her, and pulled the quilt over both of them. "I'm not going anywhere, woman. I haven't slept at all tonight. You have infected my thoughts and my dreams. I wake and find myself worrying about you. If I sleep in proximity, I trust my dreams will allow peace."

He closed his eyes. Miren stared, confused. He didn't move, his breaths came even and deep. "A pleasing admission." She paused, chewing her lip. "As it happens, I dream of you also. So I think your plan is a good one."

He nodded, but he didn't look at her. Miren waited another

moment, but he made no move. "This is scandalous, you know," she said.

"Um."

Miren didn't care. "But since we are both clothed, honor is maintained."

He opened one eye and glanced at the collar of her nightgown. "If you want to call yourself clothed, wearing that flimsy, see-through fabric meant for tantalizing a male and nothing else—"

Miren yanked the quilt to her neck. "It was meant for comfortable sleeping!"

He chuckled, to indicate he considered her explanation weak.

"It is so!"

"Um."

Miren lay fidgeting. Nathan breathed slow and deep. "I had no idea you would burst into my cottage—"

"Quiet, woman. I'm trying to sleep."

She grit her teeth, jammed her head onto her pillow, and forced her eyes shut. She knew he was smirking. "I suppose you ripped off your coat, rolled up the sleeves of your pirate costume, and exposed your bronzed muscles just to keep cool?"

"Yes." His smile grew, but he didn't open his eyes. Miren flushed pink in the night. She'd revealed her close scrutiny of his body, and admitted his appeal. Curses!

"You shocked the young ladies, you know."

"Which is why Lady Sarah asked if I would 'pleasure her to the limit of her endurance'—"

Miren shot up in bed, aghast. "She never did!"

"She said she couldn't allow me 'penetration,' but she knew several other ways to please a man. Her virginity is of paramount concern. Almost as much as her lust."

Miren shook her head. "I don't believe you."

"She punctuated the request with a well-practiced squeeze."

"Squeeze? Where?"

"Where I'd notice it most."

"No, no, no. You are making this up to shock me. It's impossible."

He still hadn't opened his eyes. "You are so innocent."

"You are teasing me. Very funny." Miren lay back down beside him, her hands folded over her breast. Her brow furrowed tight. "Lady Sarah is younger than myself by several years. At most, she is eighteen."

Nathan slid his hand down his side, fished around for something, then held up a glittering object. His eyes stayed shut. He even yawned. Miren took the object. "An earbob." She drew a clearing breath. "Lady Sarah's earbob." She handed it back to him. "How did you get this?"

"She gave it to me"—Nathan yawned again—"in order that I might find cause to return it—at an appropriate time."

"It doesn't make sense. She can't have expected to simply retire with you to a bedroom, without anyone noticing, for an . . . event that must take, well, a bit of time to complete." Miren paused. "Although rams are fairly speedy. True, Huntley hasn't been very active since winter, which is why my ewes had no lambs this spring . . ."

Nathan finally opened his eyes. "I trust you're not comparing me to Huntley, woman."

"No, just speculating . . . I understood couples generally take their affections to a bed." She remembered they were in bed now, and squirmed uncomfortably.

"Lady Sarah mentioned nothing about a bed. For her needs, a wardrobe closet was good enough."

"That is disgusting. One couldn't lie down in a closet."

"I don't believe Lady Sarah's intentions required lying down."

Miren lay very stiff, shocked beyond words as the sordid image throbbed in her brain. When her voice finally returned, it came like a squeak. "Did you . . . did you return the earbob?"

Nathan held up the earbob again as evidence. "No."

Miren started to feel relieved, then remembered the course of the garden party. "Did she make this suggestion before or after my sheep invaded the party?"

"Before, of course. I didn't see her afterwards, and by then I was a betrothed man."

"That wouldn't stop such a female." Miren's lips tightened into a round ball. "Then you didn't deny her."

"I didn't get the chance."

"You were interrupted! And you kept her earbob, which has to mean you *were* going to return it!" Miren wheeled around on the bed, braced her shoulders against the cubby wall, mustered every speck of her strength, and pushed him with her feet.

He wasn't expecting attack. Nathan thumped to the floor with a satisfying grunt.

Miren scrambled to the bedside and leaned over the edge. "You are evil beyond measure to tell me this story. I suspect you did it in vengeance, because you promised 'war.'" Miren pointed down at him. "But the first casualty is mine!"

Nathan sat up. He looked so calm. Innocent. "Oh, no!" He grabbed her in one swift motion and dragged her from the bed. She fell on his lap, ready to fight.

He caught her fists in his hands and kissed her. Miren fought the temptation to kiss him back, and twisted her face away. "You will stop."

He kissed her cheek, then cradled her head on his shoulder. "You care."

"I do not." Miren rested against him, knowing she cared very much. "Why did you tell me this?"

"I don't know." Nathan drew a long breath, then rested his face against the top of her head. "I think because it bothered me."

Miren peeked up at him. "You mean you found her attentions insulting?" She hoped this was the case, and suspected it wasn't.

152

"On the contrary, I should have been flattered. I should have been aroused, and I should have taken her. The pirate that left American shores would have taken her."

"You weren't a pirate, Nathan. You were a sea captain . . . Perhaps you didn't want to engage her innocent heart."

Nathan scoffed. " 'Innocent' is the last term a man would apply to Lady Sarah. And she wasn't looking for marriage, either. She is unofficially promised to an English marquess."

"How foul! She wanted the use of your body, because it's such a strong body and might afford much enjoyment." Miren blanched and buried her head on his shoulder. Nathan chuckled with masculine pride.

"Thank you. Yes, she wanted that. But such women often find less satisfaction in the body's delights than you'd think. I believe they gauge their value from their ability to attract and arouse men—to prove to themselves they have power, that they're more desirable than other women. So they choose the handsomest, strongest male and aim for his weakest spot."

"Your vanity astounds me . . . And I'm sure you're wrong. I think she just wanted you."

"You wouldn't understand, because you *do* just want me." Miren braced, but Nathan continued, unaffected by her potential wrath. "You don't count your value by your ability to control others."

"How do you know so much about women?"

"No man knows much about women. But as it happens, I knew another woman like Lady Sarah."

"Another noblewoman?"

"No. She was Onondaga. Although by their terms, she might be considered nobility. She came to our village with her father, head of the Onondaga Clan of the Deer. She came to me late in the night and—"

Miren held up her hand. "Don't tell me. What happened afterwards?"

"I wasn't her first lover, but the next morning I asked for her hand. She declined."

153

"Why?"

"Another man had asked for her already. His position was greater than mine. He was older, and she considered him a better husband. My attention flattered her, made her superior—in her eyes—to other women."

"Did you love her?"

"I thought so. A boy of sixteen mistakes sex for love easily, my dear. But my reaction was more one of injured pride than the heart's pain. My father told me this, but I wouldn't listen. It was then that I joined the Union Army and left my people. I learned soon enough that women in the white man's world maneuvered to the same standards, although beneath different titles. I learned to keep my heart out of it, and seek pleasure where it was offered."

"Which you offer to me."

"It has its delights, Miren."

Miren sat back on his lap and touched his face. "I can imagine that." Nathan met her eyes steadily, without assuming that her reply meant acquiescence. He looked vulnerable, sweet, sitting on the floor where she'd shoved him. Yet all she longed for glittered in his dark eyes.

"I do not think it wise to desire a man who hides his heart," she said.

"You may be right."

"It's not practical."

"No."

Miren ran her fingers through his hair. "You are desirable. As you know, because you say so often. I couldn't flatter you half as much as you flatter yourself."

Nathan angled his head. He looked ready to fight again. Miren smiled and moved a little closer. He started to speak, but she laid her finger to his lips. "I like you."

His expression changed, gentled. "I like you, too."

"Since we are—temporarily—engaged, that is good."

"It is."

"I will remain practical, and you will remain guarded. If

we know that now, we can save ourselves much grief.''

Nathan nodded slowly. ''You are practical. And you are beautiful, and charming. For that reason, it seems wise that my guard reveal no holes.''

''I've seen no holes.''

Nathan drew her into his arms. ''Woman, I'm here. If that's not a gaping hole, what is?''

''You were worried about me.''

He held her close and kissed her forehead. ''I appreciate your pretending to believe that.''

Miren kissed his cheek. ''I wanted to be near you again, too.''

They left the floor and returned to the bed. Nathan wasn't sure whether she wanted him to stay, but she seemed happy when he lay down beside her. She even adjusted her blanket over his chest.

The whole night confounded him. From the hours in his bedroom, fighting to sleep, to the moment she kissed his cheek and said she wanted him near, he was lost. He couldn't stand to lie in his bed and know Miren was here, angry. He couldn't stand not knowing *how* angry, or exactly what provoked her, or if she meant to call off their pretend marriage.

He'd told himself she was upset. Probably crying. He came to her cottage to reassure her. And found her sleeping comfortably on her back, her snoring dog curled up at the foot of the bed. He should have been satisfied, turned around, and gone back to his own bed, relaxed in the knowledge that their quarrel hadn't devastated her.

Since he didn't know what caused the quarrel in the first place, he'd found himself standing by her bed, then sitting. Then speaking into her ear. Twice.

He wanted to prove to himself that inside, with her innocence jaded, her brain worked like any other woman's. So he told her about Lady Sarah's proposition. She kicked him off the bed as a reward. So much for inciting feminine competitiveness.

What really bothered him was that he'd had no sexual response to a provocative woman's request, but couldn't stop fantasizing about Miren. Miren was prettier, true, but she knew nothing about sex. Still, she managed to stumble into a party, stand in her sackcloth dress among elegant, beautiful women, and make them look like crones.

She was innocent, yet she saw inside him better than anyone ever had. Just when he thought he'd shocked her, she turned the tables and sent him to his knees. Now, he lay awake as the first light of dawn broke in the sky, and she slept peacefully beside him. Her hand found its way to his arm, then his chest. She moved a little closer.

His heart responded with a surging pulse. He placed his hand over hers and tried to content himself. She liked him. He liked her, too. They were friends, first. Maybe they would become lovers. Nathan felt certain they would. But not tonight.

They were already confidants. They trusted each other. That hadn't happened often in Nathan's life. He had been close to David, until their lives took separate paths. He expected the same with Miren. He hoped she would remember him with affection. He knew he'd remember her.

Nathan pressed a gentle kiss on her forehead. She murmured softly and kissed his shoulder. Nathan held himself still. Miren snuggled closer and nuzzled his neck. She tipped her face upward, sighed, and kissed his jaw. He felt her breath as small puffs against his neck. Torture.

"Miren . . . you're arousing me."

She startled into wakefulness, seemed surprised to be so close, and withdrew hastily. "You can't just let me sleep, can you?"

"It's almost morning. If you'd stop your demonic assault, woman, we both might find rest."

"I did nothing."

"You kissed my shoulder, here." He pointed to the spot. "You nuzzled my neck—which was incredibly sensual, I might add. And my face, here." He touched his chin.

"I never did." Miren paused. "You kissed me first."

"I knew it!" Nathan clamped his hand to his forehead. *I sound like Simon.* But he wouldn't let her squirm out of a confession this time. "If you were sleeping, how did you know I kissed you?"

He had her. Yes, the little vixen squirmed, bit her lip, and twisted in bed. Twisted so that her leg brushed against his. "I knew because . . ." Miren puffed an angry breath, rolled herself half on top of him, and kissed his mouth. She drew back, enough for him to see her blazing, moonlit eyes. "I can't sleep, either."

Nathan couldn't speak. He wrapped his arms tight around her and pinned her against him. She didn't struggle. Her feverish little mouth trailed warm kisses over his face, back and forth over his mouth. Her devilish little tongue slipped between his lips and played against his.

"Nathan . . ." She caught her breath. "Such imaginings possess me . . ." She kissed him again. Her fingers gripped his hair as if to hold him in place. "It's partly your looks." Her lips found his neck and centered over his pulse. "In this shirt especially." Her fingers tugged his collar apart and she kissed the base of his throat. "Just when I remind myself that good looks are insignificant, you look at me . . . a certain way. Oh . . ."

Nathan lay weak, his body quivering. She crawled farther on top of him, positioning herself to kiss his mouth. "And just when I think you're the most difficult, annoying man, you tell me you like me . . ." She tasted his lips with vigor, then sucked his bottom lip between her teeth.

His body went tight as a drawn bow, his heart slammed in his chest.

"Miren, we're headed—"

"I know."

"In a direction you might not want to go."

She caught his earlobe between her teeth and bit, then sucked fiercely.

"Then again, you might."

A man can stand only so much. Nathan rolled her over and positioned himself above her. His hands shook as he unbound the tie of her high collar. He could have torn the garment with one finger. He wanted to.

Her heart raced. He felt her swift pulse beneath his fingers as he touched her neck. Her dark hair splayed out across the pillow, her eyes blazed. She was the lover he'd dreamt of, a woman of natural passion.

She smelled warm and feminine, clean and softly scented with something floral, probably from her enforced bath. He tasted her skin, just above her collarbone. She tasted sweet, too. She wrapped her arms around his neck and he bent to kiss her. Her arms tightened, but he drew away and smiled.

Nathan kept his gaze locked with hers as he ran his hands along her sides. He indulged himself in the feel of her skin beneath her thin gown. She watched his face, wide-eyed as he gathered the gown to her hip. He slipped his hand beneath the fabric, touching her hip, her waist. Every muscle drew taut beneath his fingers. Her breath came in small, desperate gasps.

His own pulse raged, sending merciless shocks of fire to his groin. His manhood filled beyond endurance, his whole body ached. She stared up at him, shocked, stunned by intimacy. She had no idea what to expect, but she trusted him.

Nathan moved his hand outside her gown, annoyed with himself for the hesitation. Now wasn't the time to become honorable. He fought his nobler impulses. He would refrain from full penetration. He would seek his release outside her body. Allow only shallow entrance, to fulfill some portion of his fantasies.

Miren didn't know the results of lust, so he couldn't convince himself that lust was her reason for lying beneath him.

Curiosity, perhaps. No, she cared for him. He meant something to her. Maybe their "engagement" meant more to her than he realized. Perhaps only pride made her say otherwise.

She wanted his touch. She wanted him to show her the pleasures of a woman's body. He saw it in her eyes. He wanted that, too. Nathan banished his doubts. He wasn't hurting her. They stood on equal ground. She understood.

His hand slid up from her waist to her ribcage, then moved just beneath her breast. Her heart raced like a captured bird's. He traced one finger around her firm, round breast, examining its shape. A beautiful, maidenly shape. Small, but full. His pulse rang in his ears as he deepened the caress. He circled one breast with his palm, then the other. Her chest rose and fell in quick breaths beneath his touch.

He brushed his palm over one small, taut peak and felt it pebble against his skin. Miren responded well. Too well. He ached to taste her, to drive her deeper into oblivion. He bent to take the little bud into his mouth. Her breath caught in surprise, but when his lips grazed the sensitive tip, she moaned softly and tipped her head back, eyes closed.

Yes, too well. He flicked his tongue over the tip, and she arched her back. He moistened her gown until nothing seemed to remain in his way. He suckled gently, and she whimpered his name. She called him Nathaniel.

No woman ever inflamed his desire this way. His blood pounded, his senses raged. He cupped her ribcage in his hands as he moved his attention from one perfect breast to the other. Were it any other woman, her desire would have reached the point of fulfillment. He wouldn't wait—he would pull up her gown and drive himself within her. He would revel in her muted gasps, her delirious pleasure.

But it was Miren beneath him, and she deserved more. She deserved all he had. And he had so little, beyond desire. Another troublesome thought invaded his pursuit of pleasure. Nathan rested his cheek against her breast, listening to her racing heart. Trying to ignore what he couldn't offer.

Her fingers clutched his shoulders as if she braced herself against the onslaught of pleasure. She trembled. "Miren . . ." He straightened beside her and gathered her into his arms. She molded against him, she kissed his neck, she ran her hands along his back.

Her hands slipped beneath his shirt. She sighed at the feel of his skin. "I've longed to touch you, you know."

"Have you?"

She nodded against his chest. Her hands didn't stop. She stroked the expanse of his shoulder blades, down his spine, to the small of his back. His control wavered. He wanted to seize her small, soft hand and place it over his length, to feel her fingers wrapped tight around his shaft. He couldn't rush her. She would find his desire, she was searching now.

He moved to his back, drawing her with him. Separating their bodies enough for her search to reach a successful conclusion. Her hand wound its way from his chest to his stomach, but there she seemed at a loss. Directing her was too close to coercion. Teaching her by example might be a more enjoyable solution.

He reached down and eased her gown to her waist. Miren stopped her search. "What are you doing?" He heard no suspicion in her breathless voice, just curiosity.

"There are secrets in you, my little Miren. Secrets you don't know yourself."

"There aren't." Still stubborn. Still . . . Scottish.

"Oh no?" Nathan angled his brow, his gaze fixed on hers as his fingers played along her inner thigh. She watched him suspiciously as his touch crept up and inward. His fingers grazed the soft curls at the apex of her thighs, and her eyes widened like saucers.

"You can't touch me there! It's . . ."

Nathan grinned. "Secret?"

She nodded, swallowing hard.

He outlined the soft triangle, then dipped his fingers inward between her legs. He stopped her harsh gasp with a quick kiss. She tried to squirm away, but he touched moisture—warm, liquid desire. Feminine need. She froze, probably wondering if something odd had happened within her.

"Here, you are ready for me. Here, nothing is secret."

His words soothed her, and she relaxed slightly.

"This is . . . normal?"

"This is heaven."

He hadn't prepared himself for the impact of finding her fully aroused, damp and warm and female. His seed burned and demanded release. He explored her petal softness, eased his fingers between the damp folds, and she held her breath.

"Breathe, woman. I won't have you fainting now."

She gulped a mouthful of air and held her breath again.

"Slow and even, Miren. Like this . . ." He showed her, starting in a gentle stroke as he dipped his finger in slightly. Her whole body tensed. Nathan tensed, too. She was tight, her entrance squeezed around the shallow probe, and he thought he would die from wanting.

He withdrew his finger and continued his exploration. Her tiny feminine bud met his touch, alive and pert, demanding beyond her knowledge. He centered his touch there, and her breath came as a shuddering moan. "That . . . was secret."

"No more. Are you sorry, Miren?" He kept the rhythm of his voice in time with his caress. Her hips arched to meet him.

"No."

"Shall I stop?"

"No!"

The first light of dawn inched across the little cottage, revealing her flushed face, her glazed, passion-filled eyes. He wanted to see her in rapture. He increased the pressure of his touch, then lightened it. Faster, then barely moving. Her body quivered and squirmed beneath his direction.

He'd come to Scotland to find justice, to set right a bitter wrong. He'd found enchantment instead. He even heard bagpipes in the distance. Bagpipes. Nathan's brow furrowed, he stopped teasing her and listened. Miren didn't notice at first, but the sound echoed over the loch. "Bagpipes."

Miren took several short breaths. "Bagpipes."

"Is this normal in Scotland? I've never heard bagpipes at dawn."

Miren sat up. "It's not coming from the loch." She adjusted her gown, swung her legs over the edge of the bed, and went to her window. "It's coming from the woods behind the manor."

"Odd." In Scotland, anything was possible. "Spirits of the dead?"

She looked back at him, one brow angled. "Someone is practicing. Perhaps for the Games at Oban." She listened a moment longer. "Whoever it is has great skill." Miren drew a long breath. "I can never hear a piper's music without it piercing my soul. It reminds me of who I am." She paused, and her chin rose. She looked strong and independent. "A Highlander."

She had been on the verge of release. Her first. Now she stood at the window, thinking of ancient clan warfare. *Bagpipes.* Nathan tipped his head back and exhaled a shuddering, painful breath. "Scotland . . . is hell."

Chapter Nine

A problem arises, one I hadn't foreseen. Rather than laying claim to the young mistress and bringing her, with her house pet, to the manor, Nathan has instead come to the cottage.

He's not a usual human. It's not beyond him to take up residence here, in the cottage. Worse, it's not impossible that he take up with the young mistress and end up following the flock, too. Something has to be done to edge them in the right direction.

Now that I've seen the mansion's interior, I'm sure it's the most fitting abode for a house pet. Muffin's cushion, and Muffin, need to be removed, of course. Lady MacCallum must go, too. Twice she snapped at me for examining the furniture. I was testing a long, soft chair, scratching out a spot, and she swatted at me. She seized my neck ornament and tossed me outside.

I look forward to the day when it's Lady MacCallum tossed into the cold, and myself at the door . . .

* * *

"Twenty-five shillings! Just enough for a new ram." Miren held up the small felt bag and jingled the coins. Simon stood beaming with pride.

"Got more for it than I thought, but that's the way of a good bargainer. Got myself up before dawn and headed into Inveraray. Early bird, they say."

"Thank you, Simon. I would have gone myself if you'd told me."

Simon clucked his tongue. "You had a busy day, lass. You needed your sleep."

Miren's face flushed pink. She hadn't slept at all. She'd done things she'd never imagined possible, but she hadn't slept. If not for the far-off bagpipes . . . She drew a quick breath to banish the memory of Nathan's touch. "Did you hear bagpipe music this morning around dawn, Simon?"

Simon's brow furrowed. "Can't say as I did. But I was in Inveraray by the time the sun rose. Why?"

"Someone was playing in the hills beyond the manor. The piper has impressive skill. I wondered if you knew who it was."

"Only a Scot would play afore dawn, and that's a fact. One thing for certain, it weren't Nathaniel."

Miren gulped. Nathan had returned to the manor before the others woke up, leaving her shocked and embarrassed by her wanton behavior. But at least she considered their interlude secret. "Why do you say that?" Her voice came small and very guilty. Simon eyed her doubtfully.

"His kind don't take to music."

"Oh." Prejudice. Good. Simon didn't know just what Nathan's "kind" had been up to in the night. Miren relaxed. "Where will we purchase my new ram?"

"Got a market in Inveraray today. There'll be a fine selection of wool rams."

"I suppose we should go early . . ." Miren glanced toward the manor. "He probably doesn't want to see a sheep again for a long while."

Simon huffed. "I think you can count on it, girl. That boy weren't meant for farming. His kind, they're hunters. They use what's near and easiest, and then move on. Don't you be forgetting it. You're a good Scottish lass. You don't want to tangle up with the likes of that black-eyed—"

"Savage?" Nathan appeared in the doorway, behind Simon. The old man jumped and swore, then spun around, his face flushed with anger.

"Creeping up on me, you were. And not for the first time."

Miren's cheeks warmed, but she fought for her composure. They weren't alone. He wouldn't touch her. They wouldn't kiss. She was safe. "Has he crept up on you before, Simon?"

"Aye. Once in particular, and it being a day I won't forget soon . . ."

Miren peeked around Simon to Nathan. "What did you do to him?"

"Nothing significant. And it caused no harm."

"No harm!" Simon shook his fist. "You snuck up on me whilst I was at fishing, and myself being an honored guest of your grandsire—the only honorable one of the bunch."

Miren's brow knit. "That doesn't sound so bad."

"I were standing on a rock, missy. A slippery rock out in the Genesee River, and it weren't warm, I'll tell ye."

"How do you know how cold . . . ? Oh. I see. You fell in."

"I didn't fall. He pushed me."

Nathan's hands rested on his hips. He looked casual. Superior as he angled one dark brow. "You fell. I never touched you."

Simon straightened like a ramrod. "You crept in, you and those little buggers who followed you. You hid in the bushes, and you all burst out screaming like beansidhes."

"Banshees."

"Same thing." Simon turned his attention to Miren, as if she were judge. "They were waving tomahawks—"

"Sticks, but go on."

"They were carved like tomahawks!"

Nathan scoffed. "A few little nicks and cuts don't make a weapon, Simon."

Miren positioned herself between them, closer to Simon. She held up her hands, separating them. "Now, did Nathaniel actually hit you with his tomahawk—"

"I told you, woman, it wasn't a tomahawk. It was a gnawed-off oak branch."

Miren cast a dark glance Nathan's way. "You were waving it, weren't you? That makes it a weapon. Simon, did he hit you?"

"He meant to."

"I see. But he didn't actually make contact."

"Because I'd already fallen in!"

Nathan looked smug. Simon went red with fury. "Those little red devils stood on the bank howling like wolves."

"We were laughing."

Simon glared, angered beyond words.

"We offered to pull you out."

Simon's jaw bunched into a stubborn ball. "You'd have handed me a snake instead of a rope." He nodded to Miren. "His kind has an affection for the creatures. If that isn't hea- then—"

"As I recall, the snakes preferred you. They kept finding their way to your bed."

"Nathan!" Miren grabbed his arm. Curses! Now she'd touched him. His arm was strong, warm. She eased her hand back to her side. "You're deliberately baiting him. Behave! Simon and I have work to do."

"I know. I'm coming with you."

Simon groaned, but Miren couldn't help a surge of happiness. "If you must."

He smiled. His dark eyes twinkled. "I must."

Inveraray Market was filled with farmers mulling around looking for good buys. The atmosphere was exhilarating. Miren found herself looking at dress fabric and new shoes,

tasting offered sweets and shortbread. She sampled a shortbread biscuit that sandwiched a layer of crisp toffee, topped
with a thin layer of chocolate.

"Good." Miren finished her sweet and licked her fingers.
"I hope I have enough money left over to buy the whole
thing."

"Rams, Miren. We're not here to quench your appetite."
Nathan took her arm and they followed Simon to the rear of
the market. Molly trotted along beside, her tail up, her ears
pricked in excitement. Miren shared her sweets with Molly,
but Molly seemed more interested in a collection of ornate
cushions.

"She wants a cushion."

Nathan rolled his eyes. "That dog of yours wants a coach,
livery, and eight horses, maybe a castle to put it in. Move on,
woman."

Miren reached down and patted Molly's head. "If we have
enough money, I'll buy you a cushion of your own. Like
Muffin's, only bigger."

Simon marched through the crowd like a ship in full sail.
If someone got in his path, he shoved them aside, then doffed
his cap respectfully. Nathan shook his head. "That man
should be at sea. There's not enough room on land for Simon
MacTavish."

Miren scurried along beside Nathan, eager and happy. "I
haven't been to a market since my father died. Maybe you
should buy yourself a shoulder plaid, Nathaniel. Or a sgian-
dhu. Yes, you need a dagger, for protection. See those, with
the jeweled hilts!"

Miren veered from the onward path to study a collection
of Scottish dirks. "There's a nice one!" She pointed to a
small dirk in a glass case. The merchant beamed and nodded.

"That's one for a laird and no mistake, lass."

Nathan placed his firm hand on her shoulder. "I don't want
a dirk, Miren."

"It's a little small." She fixed her gaze on a large empty slot. "What was there?"

"That wasn't much, lass. Big sticking knife, good for butchering hens, maybe a small pig—"

Miren grimaced. "Never mind."

"Told the fellow that bought it he could do better with one of these." The merchant gestured toward the other dirks. "Them as got the fine quality craftsmanship. Everything you're seeing, done by my son and myself."

Nathan nodded without much interest. "They're well made. Miren—"

"Glad I am to hear you say it, sir. Tried to tell that fellow the same, but he just wanted the big knife. Try telling an Englishman anything. Don't know what he wanted with a butchering knife, anyway. He was all set up as a gentleman. Didn't have the muscle to wrestle a hen, let alone a pig."

"How odd! I wonder what he wanted with—"

"Thank you for your time." Nathan seized Miren's arm and drew her aside. "We're here for a ram, woman, not an hour's conversation."

"Oh, very well. It was interesting, I thought."

"Rams, Miren."

Nathan pointed to Simon as he stomped through the crowd. Miren clucked her tongue, but she continued toward the livestock pens. "Men shouldn't be allowed at market. Just get in, get out . . . No time for anything interesting."

"I was just thinking how much faster these transactions would occur if women were left at home."

Miren lifted her chin. "Rams, Nathan."

They found Simon waiting by the sheep pen, examining the offerings. A stocky farmer with a bright red beard and a bald head proudly displayed his rams. His red-haired wife was equally formidable, perhaps more so than her husband. She braced pudgy arms over her immense chest and nodded to Miren.

Miren hesitated, then nodded back. "How do you do, ma-

'am?'' The woman smiled but didn't answer.

The farmer stepped through his rams and set his hands on the railing. "Mrs. MacBain don't speak English, lass. Only the Gaelic." He lowered his voice. "And too much of that."

Mrs. MacBain eyed her husband suspiciously, but he erupted in a broad smile, placating her. Simon caught Miren's eye and winked. "Mr. MacBain here is heading for a sheep station in Australia come summer, so he's selling off the bulk of his stock. Hoping we get a few good bargains."

Mr. MacBain beamed. "That you'll be doing, sir, and no mistake! Got a fine Shetland ram here. They're small, but nothing beats their wool. Romney over there. He'd do in a pinch. I'd say the Cheviot, the one in the corner, that's your best bet."

Miren studied the rams. The Shetland ram was most appealing, with heavy wool and a sweet expression. Miren pictured him faced with Blossom. "He's pretty, but he'd never stand up to Blossom."

Simon nodded. "It would be a stretch for him, attempting to get a leg up on Blossom."

"It might damage his pride."

Miren caught a glance between Simon and Nathan. They both shook their heads. Miren ignored them as she focused attention on the rams. "The Romney looks drab." She eyed the Cheviot. Its ears stuck up, it had a Roman nose, and it looked nervous. Its wool was full and white. "I suppose he's impressive."

"Hell's bells, girl. Cheviots, they're the mainstay of the wool producers. Pick him, and let's move."

Miren sighed. The Cheviot ram skittered back and forth along the farthest wall. "He doesn't look friendly."

"A sheep ain't a pet, girl."

Nathan placed his hand on her back. "Simon is right, Miren. You need something to improve your stock, not a companion. I wouldn't refer to Blossom as a pet, by any means."

"Blossom is good-natured. True, she can be willful . . .''

Both Simon and Nathan issued huffs. Miren frowned.

"But she's sensible. She's not flighty. That Cheviot ram looks flighty."

Nathan shrugged. "Then pick the Romney, and let's go."

Miren started to nod, then spotted another pen. "What's in there?"

Simon glanced at the pen. "They're the mutton rams. You said you weren't breeding for mutton."

"I'm not." Miren aimed for the mutton pen anyway. The rams all looked fat, with shorter wool than the others. None appeared enthusiastic. The ram standing in the center caught her eye. He was fat, with a stodgy face, short legs, and an earnest expression. Miren turned to the farmer.

"I'll take him."

Nathan eyed her doubtfully. "The fat one in the middle?"

Simon set his fists to his hips. "That's a Southdown, missy. They're for mutton."

The farmer nodded. "I'm selling all my mutton stock. Since we're heading off to the outback, don't see the need for meat sheep." He eyed Miren. "You look like a good, strong Scottish lass. Don't suppose you'd consider taking up employment for Mrs. MacBain? She's got something of an achy back. Figuring we need a housemaid, someone to take on the chores as put a strain on her poor back."

Miren smiled politely. "No, thank you. I have family in America." As Miren spoke, her old plans seemed thin, not as definite as they had before she spent a night in Nathan's arms. "I had a close call with Australia already. But thank you for inviting me."

Simon eyed the ram. "What're we looking at here in the way of finances?"

The farmer reverted to business, although he looked a little disappointed. "Southdown's a cull. He's throwing lambs with heavy wool, and not enough fat on their joints."

"What do you mean, 'cull'?" Miren watched the ram. He looked proud.

170

"Means I'll get more selling him for butchering than as a ram."

"No!" Miren seized her purse. "How much do you want for him?"

"Twenty pence. And that's a bargain."

"Twenty pence!" Simon started to argue, but Miren handed the farmer his coins.

"Thank you, sir. I will collect my ram." She paused, feeling proud. "And I will name him Earnest."

I can't believe she got another one. Earnest, indeed! First, she forgot my cushion. Then the young mistress removed my neck ornament and placed it on that pudgy, sluggish ram. Never have I been so offended.

Molly walked at Miren's side, but she wasn't happy. Earnest walked slow, nibbling bits of grass as they led him to Simon's cart. Nathan sat on the driver's seat with Simon, but Miren sat in the back with Earnest. Molly displayed her disapproval by turning her back to the ram, but Earnest didn't care. He just munched on old hay, content with his fate.

He should have been food. Yes, carved up, baked, and fed . . . to a house pet. Molly snarled.

"Molly! We must make Earnest feel welcome. Behave."

The young mistress actually seemed to mean the admonishment. Molly stuck her nose out of the cart and pretended to watch for squirrels.

She saw one squirrel poised on a branch, but it wasn't worth barking at or chasing. Too high. A rider across the field caught her eye instead. The day was hot, but the rider wore a hooded cape. Which seemed odd. He seemed to be following the cart, then eased his horse into the forest beyond.

Molly barked an alert. Miren patted her head. "Hush, Molly. It's just a squirrel. And you're disturbing Earnest."

Nathan stood in the small pasture, watching as Miren introduced Earnest to the ewes. He should have returned to the manor, to keep an eye on Brent Edgington. To ask a few more questions about Patterson. Instead, he hovered near Miren Lindsay like . . . like a lovesick boy.

Nathan's pride had taken a dim turn. He'd returned early to the manor, couldn't sleep, and instead bathed and readied himself for his next meeting with Miren. Pathetic. His only consolation was that Simon had no idea of the depths to which he'd sunk.

He planned for the evening to come. They'd pick up where they left off. On the verge of release. She had to be frustrated. Curious. She cast quick glances at him when she thought he wasn't looking. She tried to pretend that nothing had happened between them. Which only served to heighten the tension.

True, at this moment Miren was fixated on Earnest, but Nathan knew that desire still flooded her sweet body. A body which defied his previous imaginings. Taut and firm, yet soft. The result of following her flock around Argyll, perhaps.

"Nathan, do you think Huntley is troubled by Earnest's presence?"

Nathan eyed the old ram. He stood beneath a willow, his eyes half closed. "He seems to be handling the shock well enough."

"Good. I thought so, too, but I couldn't be sure. You're a man, so I thought you might know better."

"Huntley is deaf, half-blind, and aged, woman. Why would you think I might identify with him?"

"You seem threatened by Brent. He's younger than you are."

Simon chuckled. "Young Brent ain't exactly a strapping lad, but I'd guess he's got something of a way with ladies. Smooth . . ."

Miren nodded. She gazed upward thoughtfully. The most calculated effort Nathan had ever witnessed. "He's polite. And he has quite a pretty face."

She liked to torment him. What annoyed him most was that her attempt worked. He was annoyed. He couldn't help wondering if Brent's attentions pleased her, if she might respond to his overtures.

"Brent is most likely the instigator of murder. His mother mentioned this morning that Brent was almost as grieved over Patterson's death as over his stepfather's. Interesting, wouldn't you say? Afraid, perhaps, that his lackey failed . . . and he might have to do the job himself."

Miren set one hand to her slender hip as she considered Nathan's disclosure. She looked like a detective. "Brent is hiding something. That is easy to see. But I don't think it's murder."

Nathan frowned. "He's probably hiding his latest trip to Glasgow's brothels."

Miren gasped, offended. "That is a foul suggestion. Don't you agree, Simon?"

Simon hesitated, and one side of his face scrunched as he resisted agreement with Nathan. "Well now, lass, I'm not akin to gossip, but from what I've seen, young Brent's hunting expeditions don't seem too likely. I've seen him shoot. Can't hit a barn broadside. And he never comes back with anything, either. Claims to be duck hunting. Now, that takes marksmanship . . ."

Nathan nodded. "What Simon is saying is that I'm right, and a brothel is a much more likely destination."

"You could be right, I suppose. Men have peculiar habits, I know. Spending an evening with an unwashed female seems to have appeal. Still, I can't believe Brent is hiding anything so disgusting."

"He's hiding greed, ambition, and probably murder." Nathan felt unusually stubborn. He couldn't deny that Miren had good instincts about people. Probably because she viewed them the same way she viewed her animals. Not by their breeding, but by what she actually saw in their behavior. She judged creatures not by their credentials or what they claimed, but by actions. "And he's only three years younger than I am."

Both Miren and Simon arched brows, smiled slightly . . . radiating victory. Neither said anything. They exchanged a meaningful glance, and nodded. "If you'll both excuse me, I have a croquet match scheduled . . . with the heroic Brent Edgington," Nathan said.

He headed back to the manor, fuming. Because she'd caught him. Again. It was possible that their night of thwarted passion affected himself more than Miren. She hadn't changed. He, however, was playing the role of doting fool to perfection.

He had to bed her and be done with it. Sex did strange things to a man. She had the upper hand now, because he wanted her, and his desires were strong. She didn't know how good it could be, so it hadn't weakened her to the same extent. Reasonable.

Nathan's anger faded. Tonight he would show her. By morning she would be kneeling at his feet.

Brent Edgington was slick. Five hours after Nathan left Miren's pasture, he found himself returning down the road from the manor, knowing nothing more than he knew before he'd set out.

Brent "liked and respected" Drew Patterson, but they hadn't been close. Yes, Brent had considered a career in medicine, but his mother felt strongly that the professional class was beneath his aspirations. Also, Brent disliked blood.

Brent liked croquet, and he was better at it than Nathan imagined. Nathan played croquet like lacrosse, and found himself going down to defeat because the game required control rather than aggression.

So Brent won, said how happy he was to "bear witness" to Nathan's engagement, and privately wished him well. He said his mother wouldn't tolerate him marrying a commoner, sighed, then implied that a life of free choice must be worth a lot.

Nathan walked toward Miren's cottage in more confusion

than when he left. If Brent arranged for Kenneth MacCallum's murder, he covered it up well. He seemed just as Miren said, the odd man out, eager to please and to be accepted.

Nathan met Simon coming up the road. Good. He would see Miren in private. Simon didn't look at him, he just trudged along, frowning. He reached Nathan, nearly passed him, then stopped. "Hurt that lass, boy, and you'll find yourself in a pickle."

Nathan drew an impatient breath. "That would be my concern, and hers. Not yours."

Simon looked up and met Nathan's eyes. The blue looked cold and hard, unyielding. "I'll tell you again, boy. Leave her be, let her find her own path. Or by my soul, I'll see you in the ground."

Simon didn't wait for Nathan's response. His threat shocked Nathan beyond words anyway. The old Scotsman stomped up the road without looking back. As angry as he'd been in the past, Simon's threats never seemed genuine. But this time, Nathan knew he meant every word.

The gray clouds surrendered, and rain fell as if dropped from a bucket. Nathan was drenched by the time he reached Miren's cottage. She sat on her front porch, ignoring the rain as she gazed across the loch. Molly sat in the threshold, dry but watching over her mistress.

Miren didn't look up as he approached. Nathan hesitated, then sat down beside her. "Miren?"

She looked at him, her expression gloomy. "Will it be the same when I have a real husband?"

Nathan's eyes wandered to one side. "Will what be the same?"

"Will I feel for him what I feel for you?"

Nathan began to understand her line of thinking. She wanted to know that their passion would be equaled in her future relationships. He started to nod, to maintain dignity. His head was shaking instead. "No."

Her brow furrowed. "This is assuming I eventually marry,

of course, which doesn't seem likely. But I thought I might meet someone at a later point in time, a man with interest in a permanent arrangement.''

"No."

"No?"

Nathan drew a calm breath, in an effort to control himself. "I mean, of course, you'll meet someone. And I'm sure you'll marry." He controlled his voice admirably. He sounded mature, wise. "Your relationship will be . . ." He wanted to say wonderful. Fulfilling. Everything a girl could want. ". . . nothing like what we had last night.''

He couldn't stop himself. He turned to face her. "Do you really think this sort of thing happens twice in a lifetime? It doesn't. You and I were drawn to each other from the moment we met.''

Her brow furrowed deeper. "I thought you were handsome, true, but—''

"But nothing, woman. You wanted me, I wanted you. You summoned me from jail, didn't you?''

"I didn't know anyone else.''

"I'm the first person you thought of.'' Nathan paused, knowing his composure was shattered beyond recall. "Just who are you thinking of marrying?''

Miren smiled, tender and sympathetic. He'd reached new lows. "I wasn't thinking of marrying anyone. It occurred to me that I'll always be comparing other men to you. And they won't look very good in comparison.''

She was placating his pride. "Um.''

Miren watched him intently. "Simon says your people are hunters. He says you are, too.''

"What of it?''

"He says you're selfish, that you hunt for what you want, take it, and move on.''

Nathan frowned. He didn't like the description. But it was true. "Yes.''

Miren kept her penetrating gaze fixed on his face. "He says

you've abandoned several women before me.''

"My prior relationships have begun and ended mutually.''

"An evasive answer if ever there was one. So while you expect our relationship to be the height of my romantic life, you will forget all about me.''

"That doesn't seem likely.''

She didn't appear convinced. Nathan took her hand and kissed it. "I've never known a woman like you, Miren. And I never will again. If it matters to you, then yes, you are special to me. I've never developed a friendship with a woman, not this way. It makes our affair inconvenient at times, but I do care.''

"Then I am more than a cheap tart you intend to use and discard?''

He laughed. "Yes.''

"Then are we . . . friends?'' She spoke hesitantly, as if the term might be more than he could accept. Nathan kissed her hand again.

"We are.''

"I see.''

Nathan checked his pocket watch. "I'd forgotten. You've been requested at dinner this evening. If you'd care to don your red dress, we should go.''

"I'm not sure I'll enjoy an evening with Lady Mac-Callum.''

Nathan couldn't argue. "She requested that Molly—actually, she said 'that vicious hound'—be left here.''

Miren frowned. "Perhaps I shall dine here.''

"Bring her some table scraps, woman.''

Miren patted Molly's head. "Very well. Will we work on Brent for information about Dr. Patterson?''

"I spent the afternoon doing just that. And it got me nowhere.''

"Dinner conversation always yields something. I'll help.''

Nathan stood and clasped her shoulder. "Be careful, Miren. If they know what we're delving for—''

"I'm not a fool, Nathan." She angled her head back, then marched into her cottage. Nathan started after her, but she shut the door. "Wait there."

"I'm delighted you could join us, Miren dear." Irene MacCallum stood by the dinner table, dressed in black. Miren considered her attire significant.

"I'm please you invited me, Lady MacCallum." Miren glanced at Nathan, who shrugged.

"Please, everyone be seated." Irene took her place at the head of the table, Brent on her right hand. Nathan sat at her left, Miren beside him. Simon stormed around the table and sat beside Brent. He set his fists to the tabletop, and everything rattled. He didn't seem angry or distressed—it was just his natural way. *A ship in full sail.*

"Do you ever think of going back to the sea, Simon?" Miren asked.

Lady MacCallum leaned slightly forward. "Dear Miren, since you have but recently entered society, I will excuse your lack of formal manners. But all conversation must first be directed to your hostess. Also, addressing Mr. MacTavish as Simon is quite out of the question."

"Sure, I think on it, lass. Think on it, dream on it. The open sea, that's a man's dream. Salty wind in the face, creaking of the timbers . . . She's a paradise, even in a storm. Ain't got no one telling you go this way or that. To step aside being's as it's too crowded. How to 'address' folks."

Irene braced, but Nathan chuckled. "The sea offers unlimited freedom."

Miren ignored Irene and turned to Nathan. "Were you happy there?"

"I was. Although at times I found it cramped and confining."

Brent set aside his wine goblet. "Spent time on the sea, Nathan? I understood from Simon's first report that you were a farmer."

Miren paled and held her breath, but Nathan didn't seem worried. "I tried my hand at farming, yes. A man must seize life in many places."

Brent's brow furrowed as if he considered Nathan's words prophetic. "That may be true. If you're a brave enough man to attempt it."

"From what I've learned of bravery, it comes when it's needed, and not before. It comes when you want something more than you fear its loss."

Brent straightened. "Words to consider."

Miren sat back as footmen attired in white delivered her first course. A low, wide bowl of soup. It smelled good. Simon didn't wait for the others. He dove in with his spoon, slurping with delight. "Turtle soup! Fine broth."

Miren dutifully waited for Irene to begin. "I don't suppose you have those wonderful shortbread cakes for dessert."

Nathan edged her with his elbow. "Do you mean the little pastries you devoured at the market?"

"I only sampled a bite, Nathaniel. You should have tried them. The toffee in the middle was a good touch. And the chocolate . . ."

Irene frowned in distaste. "It sounds Scottish."

Miren glanced up from her soup. "It is Scottish." Maybe Irene needed reminding. "We're in Scotland."

Irene's face tensed, her fingers curled like spiny claws. She didn't rebuke Miren for impertinence, but her dark gaze was more than enough terrorism. "I find that things Scottish have charm, of course. Her Majesty often espouses the virtues of Scotland. I do find it distressing that Englishmen take on Scottish habits."

Brent set aside his spoon. "Scottish habits, Mother?"

"The wearing of plaid, when affiliated with the loyalist clans such as the Stewart, is, of course, perfectly acceptable. Other pursuits, such as engaging in these 'Highland Games' is, I think, questionable."

Miren noticed that Brent appeared downhearted at his

mother's proclamation. "You didn't mention that when the queen invited us all to attend," Miren said.

Irene's fingers twitched. Her lip twitched, too. "Attendance, dear Miren, is one thing. It's expected that the upper classes view sport. Taking part removes one to the level of competitor, which should remain beneath us."

"It's not just sport. There's dancing, piping. In fact, the most prestigious victory is that of solo piper. I wish I knew who was playing the bagpipe last night. He'd win, for certain."

Irene grimaced. "I seem to remember hearing a shrill whining just before dawn. I thought I was dreaming. We must find the offender and see that he respect silence. Brent, did you hear this racket?"

"I heard nothing, Mother. But I will see that the matter is resolved. The bagpipe is indeed a distraction."

"Good. See that it is done."

The footmen arrived to clear the table for the second course, which Miren awaited eagerly. Nathan caught her hopeful expression and grinned. "You certainly appreciate food, my precious beloved."

Miren cast him a reproachful glance, but the footmen delivered a fine sampling of plover's eggs, then renewed the wine. "Life is for living, Nathaniel, not for eating delicately."

Brent eyed her doubtfully, but a forced smile appeared on his lips. "I quite agree, Miss Lindsay. As a matter of fact, I'm headed off tonight to the Highlands to partake in pheasant hunting."

Irene turned to her son. "Tonight?"

"Couldn't be helped, Mother. Have to get an early start on the birds, don't I?" He chuckled, but the effort seemed forced.

"Your hunting companions are, of course, of a suitable society?"

Brent sampled the plover's eggs. "A marquess, a duke's son, and their entourage, Mother. We'll have a time of it."

Miren noticed that he gave no names, but the titles seemed sufficient to placate Lady MacCallum. He was probably heading into Glasgow to visit a brothel, just as Nathan said. Miren shook her head, and beaded in on the plover's eggs.

Dinner progressed without major revelations. Miren felt a little disappointed that she hadn't uncovered something significant, thus proving her worth to Nathan. As they entered the foyer, a German clock rang out ten o'clock, and Miren yawned. Nathan stood close beside her, looking impatient.

Lady MacCallum seized Muffin and went to her room without comment. Brent stood awhile in the foyer, looking hopeful. Miren sensed he wanted to engage in conversation, but wasn't sure how. "Well, good night, all. Miren, your company was a delight. Pleased you could be here."

"Good night, Brent." She wanted to say more. He looked so lost. She didn't know why, or how he could be helped, so she smiled gently. He nodded, bowed, and headed for the stairs.

"Odd duck, he is." Simon clucked his tongue. "Never will understand an Englishman." Simon eased between Miren and Nathan and took her arm. "I'll head you on back to your cottage, lass. Don't want nothing creepy or slimed-up to come after you."

Nathan darkened, stepped in front of Simon, and took her other arm. "I will attend my fiancée, if you don't mind."

Miren looked from one to the other. She'd become the new source of their conflict, and it wasn't a position she enjoyed. Simon had begun to treat her like a daughter, and his protectiveness rose accordingly. She liked the old Scotsman. Maybe because she missed her father. Or because it felt good to matter to someone.

Miren eased toward the door. "I'll walk myself home, thank you both."

Nathan's lip curled into indignation. Simon took it as a

victory and smiled. ''Be watching you from the window, lass.''

''Thank you.''

Miren met Nathan's eyes and allowed a small, suggestive smile. ''And you, my dearest beloved, will infect my dreams''—she opened the door and glanced back over her shoulder—''just as you did last night.''

It was bold. Brazen. And the effect was admirable. He gulped, his dark eyes flamed. His frown curved upward and he nodded once. Miren's heart skipped a beat, then sped forward with glee. He would come to her tonight. She wasn't sure when she'd made the decision. Perhaps just after the footmen removed the turtle soup, when her knee touched his leg by mistake, and he smiled.

Or when he teased her about requesting a second chocolate cream for dessert. She'd lost her purpose and her attention. She thought of his eyes, dark with passion as he kissed her. She remembered his touch, and her nerves tingled.

Nathan kissed her cheek. ''Await me.'' His whisper sent fierce currents through her body. She nodded, though she knew her cheeks turned pink. Simon's eyes narrowed to slits of suspicion as she headed out the door.

''Good night, Simon. Nathan.''

''Sweet dreams, my precious darling.''

''Sleep, lass. And lock that door.''

Chapter Ten

Something is wrong. I feel it, but the young mistress seems cheerful, puttering around our cottage. I sense a threat, but whatever it is doesn't disturb Flip.

So it can't be a threat to the flock, such as a wolf which would prey on sheep. Flip would notice that, and guard them. But what I feel—it is like a wolf. A human wolf.

Nathan waited until midnight. Curse the Scottish spring! Gray light delayed his departure despite the rain. Nathan looked out his window. It was still raining, and raining hard. But it was a walk worth taking.

She had invited him. Which meant she had come to him, as he asked. She knew what she wanted, and he would provide it. And more. His erection hadn't subsided since Miren's bold invitation. He paced back and forth in his room, past the large, four-poster bed, past his man-high cabinet.

He found himself wondering what to wear. She liked his white shirt. He changed his trousers in favor of a tighter cut,

183

black. Well suited to piracy. He fished around in his personal case and found something else to please her. A silver hoop earring. Small enough not to be noticed, but pirate-like enough to engage a young woman's imagination.

He opened another button on his shirt and aimed for the door. He walked quietly, more to avoid waking Simon than disturbing Lady MacCallum or her son. The old Scotsman had turned protective, glowering whenever Nathan spoke to Miren. If Simon knew what Nathan intended for this night, Nathan felt sure he'd never make it to the cottage alive.

He escaped the house unnoticed, and was greeted with torrential rain. It wasn't cold or windy, a weak comfort as he slogged down the road to the cottage.

The sheep startled in the pasture, calling out in alarm. Nathan wondered what disturbed them, but with sheep it could be anything. Flip barked, and Nathan hesitated. Something was wrong. The sheep settled down, and Flip quieted.

Nathan walked on, but his disquiet grew. Movement caught his eye, near the pasture gate. He stopped, but saw nothing. It could have been a sheep, or Flip checking their welfare. Maybe Earnest had met Blossom and was making a break toward freedom.

Nathan smiled to himself. He was beginning to think like Miren. The sheep took on personalities other than wool and mutton. He was beginning to find their lives interesting. "Which shows how low I've sunk."

Maybe they'd had personalities all along, and it took Miren to show them to him. Nathan's heart warmed with affection, when he had expected lust. He was driven by desire, after all, to satisfy her, and himself. Simon was right about him. He lived for himself, and took what he wanted. Tonight, he wanted Miren.

Miren lay in her bed, drumming her fingers on her chest. She'd washed her hair and brushed it two hundred times. She'd gone outside in the rain to locate rose petals, then

crushed them on her wrist and throat. She'd picked wet bluebells to decorate her tin cup.

And Nathan still hadn't come. She felt sure he'd understood
her veiled message. She wanted to see him tonight. She'd
invited him to share her bed, and her body. She would deny
him nothing.

And he was late. The sheep had been restless, so she
couldn't tell if their motion meant Nathan was in the pasture.
Flip barked a few times, and her heart sped with excitement,
but Nathan hadn't come.

She'd been sure that someone passed by the back of the
cottage, through the conifers, but no one came to her door.
Miren got up again and paced. She looked out her window.
True, it was raining hard, but that wouldn't keep him away.

Miren sat on her bed again. She'd spent the last hour positioning herself around the cottage, trying to decide where
she should be sitting when he entered. Then she remembered
he would probably knock, and she'd be at the door. In which
case she would have her tartan blanket wrapped casually over
her shoulders, with just enough of her chemise showing . . .

"Where is he?"

Molly seemed restless, too. She didn't stay on the bed, but
moved around the cottage. She lay down, then got up, then
went to the door. She whined and scratched. "You've already
done your business, Molly."

Molly scratched with more urgency. Her whine elevated to
an impatient bark. Miren sighed and opened the door. Molly
barked and raced into the night. Miren heard her growling.

A cold, fearful sensation drenched Miren's heart. She
stepped outside and looked around. "Molly . . ."

Someone grabbed her from behind. A cold hand clamped
over her mouth before she could scream. Miren twisted and
fought, but her attacker wrenched her neck backwards.

"Don't fight me." His voice came muffled, shaking with
aggression as he flashed a long, thin knife. "I'll use it if I
have to. . . . Move!" He hauled her farther from the door, to-

185

ward the road. He shoved her in front of him, grasping her hair to keep her still.

Miren refused to surrender. She went limp, but he didn't stop. He dragged her forward, though it slowed his progress. She tried to see his face, but it was covered with a scarf.

Molly growled and tore at his trousers. Flip barked and bit at the man's front feet. Herding. Miren's eyes flooded with tears. The dogs were trying to help her, but her attacker wore high boots, and their bites couldn't reach his skin.

They reached the pasture gate, and he yanked Miren's head back, pinning her against his shoulder. He fumbled with the latch, then shoved the gate open. A horse stood on the other side of the fence, saddled and ready. Her attacker wrapped a rope around her neck, then pushed her toward the horse.

"We're going for a ride, vixen." His words were slurred, as if on purpose. As if he didn't want her to recognize his voice.

"Who are you?"

"An old friend." He chuckled, then started to lift her toward the saddle. Miren relaxed her body as if in compliance. He lifted her off the ground, and she kicked. He grunted and stumbled back. She jumped aside, but he still held the rope around her neck.

He jerked her toward him, and Miren fell to her knees. The rope tightened as he stepped toward her, a menacing black shadow drenched in rain, illuminated by shrouded moonlight.

I will die rather than go.

Nathan sprang from the shadows of the stone wall, knocking her assailant aside. The rope tugged and snapped as he dropped it, and Miren scrambled away. The man didn't flee. He rolled, then sprang to his feet.

"Nathan! He has a knife!"

The knife flashed as her attacker leapt toward Nathan. Nathan twisted aside, but Miren heard his sharp gasp of pain. The rain fell in sheets, obscuring her vision, veiling the two men as they fought. Nathan had the man's wrist, they grappled for the knife.

The attacker twisted the knife, aiming at Nathan's face. Miren fumbled in the dark road for a rock. If she could hit the right man . . . She found a jagged stone, seized it, and aimed toward the attacker's head.

Nathan pulled back suddenly, yanked the man's arm down and onto his knee. The knife sprang loose, but the man jerked aside. Nathan leapt after him, but the man vaulted onto the horse's back and wheeled it violently aside. The horse jumped forward with an angry grunt, then galloped into the night.

Molly and Flip barked wildly, charging after the fleeing animal, but they were no match for its speed. Both stopped, barking in unison. Just as he disappeared from vision, Miren's assailant turned his horse from the road. It jumped the hedge and headed for the pasture.

"Why would he leave the road?"

Nathan took her into his arms. "Miren, are you all right? Did he hurt you?"

"No. He threatened me, but he wanted to take me from here, not kill me."

Nathan eased her head to his chest and stroked her hair. "You're safe now. Do you know who it was?"

Miren shook so violently that her teeth chattered. Until now, she'd been stunned by the attack, too stunned to surrender to fear. "He said he was an 'old friend,' but I didn't recognize his voice. It must have been muffled by his scarf."

"We'll go back to the cottage and talk. I don't think he'll be back tonight, but I'm not leaving you alone."

They returned to the cottage with the dogs, where Flip remained outside like a small guard. Molly stuck by Miren's feet, whining and trembling. "I'm all right, Molly. You were a very good dog."

Miren's hands shook as she turned up the lamplight. "I thought it was you . . ."

"I was on my way. Too late."

"Not too late, Nathan." Miren turned around and saw blood drenching Nathan's white shirt. "You're hurt!"

"It's nothing. His knife caught my arm, that's all."

Miren seized her medical kit and extracted bandages. "Sit."

Nathan laughed, but he sounded weak. "You're certainly prepared."

Tears stung her eyes as she withdrew her shears. "I had to fix Molly from Muffin's bite, and then Blossom. Nathan . . ."

"I'm all right."

She forced control over her shaking nerves and cut his sleeve open. Blood soaked down his arm. "We must find a doctor at once."

"It's not as bad as it looks."

"You are so stubborn!" Her nerves stretched to their limits. "I'm sorry. Hold still and I'll see for myself how deep it is."

Nathan complied. He didn't wince as she carefully cleansed the wound, but he looked pale. "You've lost a lot of blood."

"I've got plenty."

Miren set her jaw hard as her cleaning uncovered his wound. "It isn't deep, perhaps, but it's long."

"It will heal."

Miren padded the long cut, then bandaged his arm thoroughly. "There. That should stop the bleeding, and protect you while you recuperate."

Nathan lifted his arm. "It might as well be in a cast. Half these wraps would have been enough."

Miren elevated her chin. "You complain too much."

He reached to touch her cheek. Their eyes met, and Miren's tears fell to his hand. "You're the one I'm worried about. Miren, this is my fault. I had no idea he'd go after you."

"What are you talking about? Do you know who it was?"

"I didn't see him, but I could wager a guess."

"You think it was Brent Edgington, don't you? Because

he left the manor for 'hunting.' I suppose you think that's not where he went at all. That he lurked here and waited to come after me. Why?''

''I don't know. But his voice—was it Scottish or English?''

''I'm not sure. It happened so fast, and I was so frightened. Molly and Flip were barking, it was raining. I'm not sure.'' Miren strained to remember, to hear the echo of her attacker's muffled voice. ''I think . . . I think it was English. But it sounded muffled. False, as if he disguised his voice on purpose.''

''Which makes sense if he is indeed 'an old friend.' ''

''Why would he tell me that if it was Brent?''

Nathan shrugged. ''He expected to get away with it, Miren.''

''He seemed . . . amused. Arrogant. That doesn't sound like Brent, somehow. Also, why would he say 'old' friend? I haven't known Brent long. I suppose his choice of words isn't important.''

''It might be, though I don't see its significance yet. What matters is that he went after you. Miren, I should have known. I should never have placed you in this kind of danger.''

Miren touched Nathan's hair. ''You couldn't have known. I will be careful. I shall purchase a revolver and keep it loaded.''

''That's not good enough. I'll arrange passage on a ship to America at once.''

Miren thumped down into her seat. ''I don't want to leave . . .'' *you*—Miren stopped herself and bit her lip hard— ''Scotland. I'm not ready. My sheep aren't ready. I haven't contacted Uncle Robert.''

Nathan held her gaze evenly. ''You don't want to leave me.''

Miren looked at her hands. ''You have nothing to do with it.''

He touched her chin and forced her to face him. Miren averted her gaze, but he waited until she glanced at him. ''A casual affair isn't worth your life, Miren. And that's all I've offered you. I was thinking of myself, my needs, but I won't have your blood on my hands."

He sounded cold, distant. Miren's shaken nerves gave way to a low ache deep within. He reminded her of reality, because she'd drifted so far on her own. She'd allowed herself to dream, and before she realized it, she was imagining a life at his side. When all he wanted was a temporary, engaging diversion.

"I see." Miren eyed his blood-stained shirt. "Yet I have your blood on my own hands, it seems. You were injured rescuing me."

"And if I'd been a minute later, you would be gone!" His voice came harsh, angry. Miren sat back, contemplating his dark mood.

"I'm not ready to leave, and it has nothing to do with you. I haven't earned enough money to go to America."

"I'll pay your expenses."

Miren braced. "You will not! Charity is out of the question. I intend to earn money from my sheep."

Nathan threw up his hands, winced, then banged his good arm onto her table. "When? Next spring? Perhaps two years from now? Earnest has barely met Blossom, woman. And if I'm any judge, it may take a good long while before he dares approach her."

A tiny smile grew on Miren's face. "You know their names."

Nathan rolled his eyes, looking impatient. "What of it?"

"When I met you, you didn't know your own horse's name. But you know my sheep."

He glowered. "They've made an impression."

"You know my dog."

"All of Scotland knows your dog."

"Not so. Most people ignore her. I'm sure Lady Mac-Callum doesn't know her name. She just calls her 'that vicious hound.' Simon calls her a little slackabout. Even Queen Victoria, who cares very much for dogs, kept referring to her as 'the noble collie.' She didn't know Molly's name. But you do.''

Nathan clenched his teeth. A muscle in his jaw flexed. ''There is no significance—''

''You care.''

''I care enough to know you can't stay here. And to tell you I can't offer you anything more than I've given already.''

''I haven't asked for anything.''

''Not in words, no. But you look at me, and I know you're seeing something more than a roll between your sheets. Miren, when I look at you, that's all I see. Do you understand?''

She felt foolish. All of a sudden, she remembered who she was and where she came from. She drew a long breath, then nodded. ''I understand.'' Miren looked up, but not at Nathan. Her gaze fixed on her small window.

Rivulets streamed down the pane, creating a mesmerizing rhythm. The light of her lamp reflected on the wet glass, and cast reality back into her little room. The longer she stayed with him, the more it would hurt when she lost him.

''I understand, Nathan.'' Her gaze shifted back to him. He waited, looking tired and tense, and still angry. ''I was unwise to deny your kind offer. If you still agree, I will accept passage to America at your expense. I will leave my sheep with you as payment, although I know it's not equal to the cost of transporting me.''

Miren rose from her chair and replaced her medical gear to the basket, then closed the lid. ''I have tried to be honorable in my financial dealings, but maybe I've been foolish not to seize what's offered.''

Nathan bowed his head, his face drawn and weary. ''I'll contact your uncle in America to be sure you have a situation established there.''

''That's not necessary. I'll find my way once I arrive.''

Nathan glanced up at her. He looked irritated. ''America is

191

a big country, Miren. You don't just land on its shores and ask directions to Robert Lindsay's house.''

He remembered Uncle Robert's name, too, but Miren made no comment. ''I'll inquire, and find him.''

''For all you know, he's dead. Miren, a week or so won't matter. I'll contact him, and your position will be safer.''

Miren puffed an annoyed breath. If she had to leave, she wanted to go now. A lot could happen in a week. She might surrender her pride, and offer what he asked for, to become his mistress for as little a time as he wanted. She might surrender everything to taste again the magic of his embrace, to find the place his lovemaking promised yet eluded her still.

She wouldn't find it with a husband, because Miren knew no other man would fill her heart this way. She had pride, and little else. Her dreams of America faded, leaving a dull certainty that life would go on, and she would grow old alone.

Simon told her that fate was within. Until this night, Miren had believed that with all the power of her soul. But now, looking at Nathan, seeing the distance in his brown eyes, she knew it wasn't always true. Fate resided in dreams. When they were shattered, it left little of value.

She would learn to be content. ''You are right, of course. A week or so won't matter at all.''

Flip is outside. We are safe. Molly curled up by the cottage door, knowing Flip lay on the other side, watchful. Brave. He'd done well to slow the young mistress's attacker so that Nathan could bring him down. Nothing would enter the pasture without Flip alerting them.

Still, Molly couldn't settle into sleep. More had gone wrong than the attack warranted. Obviously, a competitor for the young mistress had arisen, and tried a flawed tactic in securing her. As should be, Nathan defended her, and laid his claim instead. But now, when they should be together, secure, the young mistress and Nathan drifted apart.

Not in body, but in something deeper. They lay together

on Miren's bed, both sleeping. There had been awkwardness before they set down for the night. Molly felt it as unspoken tension. Nathan couldn't leave—he had to protect her. Miren had nowhere else to sleep, so they slept together. Neither undressed.

Their voices had changed. Rather than lean toward each other, both recoiled, as if touching might injure them in some way.

The mansion never looked farther away.

Molly got up and tried a different position. It wasn't merely that she felt the role of house pet slipping away. Sorrow filled the cottage, the slow beating of hearts, disappointment. All dogs were sensitive to such things, but many, like Flip, chose to focus their attention on sheep. Probably because sheep didn't hurt inside the way humans do.

Or if they did, Molly never cared to find out. Humans hurt for reasons Molly didn't fully understand. They cried, something she found distressing in the extreme. Nathan didn't cry, but Molly had sensed his discomfort, too. It was more than his injury. His life force remained strong despite the smell of blood. He would recover.

If she understood what separated them, she could work to settle the matter. Not knowing—that was hard.

Molly tried lying on her side. She tried lying on her back, with her feet up. That was generally her favored posture. It didn't work. Her own body seemed changed. Her smell altered, her senses became more acute. She felt restless. Something was coming, and she didn't know what it was. She felt like running, searching . . . or at least checking on what Flip was doing.

Molly sniffed at the door. Flip was resting, a light sleep. She whined, very softly, careful not to wake the humans. After a moment's silence, Flip whined back. He understood. He was there. He wouldn't leave, and she was safe for the night. Molly rested her nose on her front paws and went to sleep.

* * *

"Boy, you've got explaining to do!" Simon shouted through the window, then banged loudly. Molly barked, hopping up and down in excitement.

Miren opened one eye and groaned. She'd spent the night in restless dreams, tossed between sweet promises and bitter loss. She didn't want to wake. She wanted to forget. Nathan lay beside her, still sleeping despite Simon's racket. She'd woken several times to check on him, but his breathing remained steady, and his color had improved by morning.

Simon rapped again, and the window rattled on the verge of shattering. Miren crawled out of bed, pulled her tartan blanket over her shoulders, and went to the door. "Come in, Simon."

Molly darted outside to join Flip, and Miren sat at her small table, her head in her hands. Simon took one horrified look at Nathan, puffed his chest, and issued a loud moan. "What did you let that black-hearted—"

Miren held up her hand. "Please, not so loud, Simon. Nathan is sleeping."

"Is he?" Simon's voice boomed even louder. "I'll be waking him right enough!" Simon stomped to the bedside and yanked off Nathan's cover, exposing his bloodied shirt. Nathan opened his eyes, groaned, and pulled his covers back over his body.

Simon looked between them as if he'd walked into a situation he'd never seen before. "What did you two do to each other?" He sounded squeamish and eased back toward the door. "Not that I'm wanting the full story here."

Miren couldn't resist a smile. "It's not what you think, Simon."

"I'm hoping that's true. But, lass, as for what I think—my imagination don't stretch that far."

"A man attacked me last night. Nathan stopped him, but got knifed in the process. He's not terribly injured."

"What?" Simon's voice radiated through the cottage. "Attacked?"

Nathan sat up in bed. He raked his long fingers through his dark hair, then looked at Simon as if it pained him. "You are so loud. You belong at sea, MacTavish."

"What're you doing in this child's bed?"

Nathan rose reluctantly from the bed and seated himself beside Miren. "She's not a child, and as for why I'm in her bed . . . Sleeping, until you barged in. Someone attacked her last night. I stayed with her so he would not succeed on a second attempt."

"Noble." Simon sneered, though his face softened as he studied Nathan's bandaged arm. "Suppose you're too laid up to do much damage."

Simon seated himself across from Miren, looking back and forth between them like an eager puppy. "So, what happened? Who was it as came after you?"

Miren tried to elevate her spirits, to engage in conversation. She felt empty, as if nothing really mattered. Nathan hadn't touched her all night. She hadn't expected him to, but it still disappointed her. He just lay down beside her and went to sleep. And the ache inside her grew until it hurt.

"We don't know who the man was, Simon. It was dark and raining, and he wore a cloth over his face."

"What'd he want?"

"I'm not sure about that, either. He wanted me to go with him. He was trying to put me on his horse when Nathan arrived."

"Then he weren't after killing you. Just trying to make off with you."

Nathan looked around, then found Miren's pitcher of water. "Where's a glass, Miren? I've got a thirst like death."

Miren eyed her tin cup, filled with bluebells and lilies. Tears started in her eyes. She snatched up the cup and tossed the flowers out the door. She turned back to see Nathan watching her, his expression strange. He looked . . . sorry. Pity was intolerable. "They were old."

Simon's brow puckered. "Looked fresh to me."

Miren's gaze remained fixed on Nathan. "They were old."

He didn't argue. He knew the flowers were fresh, but he wouldn't challenge her now. His zest for teasing had left last night. Miren's pulse slowed until it seemed a struggle to go on. She sank into her seat and closed her eyes.

"Girl, you're needing sleep. I'll check the flock for you, and keep an eye on your door. And you, Nathaniel, ought to be seeing a doctor."

"There's no need. The cut isn't deep."

Simon nodded thoughtfully. "Knifed you, did he? Get a look at the weapon?"

Nathan looked under Miren's table, bent, and retrieved a long, thin knife. "This is it. He gave it up during our struggle."

"Can't have been a strapping fellow, then."

"He wasn't particularly strong, no. Probably as tall as I am, but small-boned."

Simon took the knife and examined it thoroughly. "Any chance it was Brent?"

"I can't say for sure. It could have been. But it could have been almost any man under fifty."

"Aye, but it's a bit suspicious, young Brent being off 'hunting' the very night trouble starts brewing."

Miren studied the knife in Simon's hand. "Can I see that, please?"

Simon cocked a brow. "What for?"

"Please."

He set it on the table, and Miren turned it from one side to the other. She positioned it to lie straight, then angled the handle up. She stood up to view it from another angle, then nodded triumphantly. "I was right. My assailant was, in fact, an Englishman."

Simon and Nathan exchanged doubtful glances. Nathan cleared his throat. "You can tell that an Englishman wielded this blade just by looking at it?"

Miren met his patronizing gaze evenly. "Yes, I can. Because, you see, this is the knife missing from the cutlery merchant's chest.''

"How do you know that?"

"I have a perfect memory for shapes. Also for words written on a page and for pictures I have seen . . . and eye color, of course. This knife is the same shape as the pattern left by the knife he'd sold that very morning''—Miren paused, allowing the moment to build—''to an English gentleman.''

Neither Simon nor Nathan had a response. Miren felt smug. Simon shifted his weight from foot to foot. "You don't say?"

"I do." Miren waited for Nathan's response. He looked uncomfortable.

"You're observant, Miss Lindsay. I'm impressed."

He didn't meet her eyes. He'd only looked at her once—when he realized she'd picked flowers for his arrival. Her pride deflated toward the dull ache again. "I suppose that points further still toward Brent."

"So it seems." Nathan picked up the knife. It glinted in the morning light, but dark blood stained its point. Nathan's blood. "It shouldn't be hard to verify. We'll locate the merchant, ask him a few questions. If necessary, we'll invite him to the manor and let him get a firsthand look at Brent."

Simon smacked his hand on Miren's table. The tin cup overturned, spilling Nathan's water. "Good going, lass! Finally we're onto something! I'll trot myself up to the manor, catch a slab of breakfast with the old hag, and find out when her mealy-mouthed lad is expected back."

Simon didn't wait for approval. He stormed from the cottage, disrupting the sheep and startling Molly, who barked. Miren watched him go, then shook her head. "I thought he was going to stand guard." She felt uncomfortable alone with Nathan, especially since he didn't speak right away to ease the situation.

"I'm sorry, Miren."

She grit her teeth, forced herself to smile formally, and faced him. "Sorry? About what?"

"Those flowers . . . You picked them for me."

Miren closed her eyes, fighting not embarrassment but pure fury. He had to mention it. Couldn't leave it alone. Oh, no . . . he had to rub salt in the wound. Pry until she fell apart. "I picked them to decorate my room."

"What have I done to you?" Startled by his quiet words, Miren wondered if his wound was worse than it appeared. "Changing is so much harder than I thought."

"What are you talking about?"

"When my father was driven from his land, I vowed to take better care of my family. So I sent my army salary to my mother and sisters, and I thought it was enough. When the war was over, I took to the sea, and I forgot my vow. We went to the Caribbean, to South America. I never thought of them, Miren. I enjoyed myself, made myself rich buying and selling exotic wares, and I never looked back."

Miren fidgeted. Pain echoed in Nathan's voice, deep pain. "I see nothing wrong with that—all men assume careers. Yours sounds rather enjoyable. There's no shame in that."

"Isn't there?" His gaze held hers, but she saw self-loathing in the black depths. A loathing that chilled her blood. "While I 'enjoyed myself,' my brother suffered in poverty. His wife died in childbirth, a dry summer left him with no harvest. He needed me, and I wasn't there. Because of that, he's dead. His son is fatherless, and I haven't done a thing to secure his inheritance."

"You're here."

"And what have I done? I've spent my energy trying to seduce a pretty girl. And I found out too late that the pretty girl has a heart, and hope, and all the things I lack. Miren, I found out that you matter, far more than I'm worth. I've placed you in danger, because I thought you might please me in bed. I vowed when my brother died to protect those who needed me. Instead . . ."

Nathan rose to his feet and went to her door. "I'm sorry."

She wanted to go to him, to tell him he wasn't responsible

for her fate. But such pain filled his eyes that she couldn't speak.

"Miren, I'm not sure what good my word is today, but I swear to you now, I'll never hurt you again. I will protect you, and see that you're safe with your family in America. No matter what happens, no matter what threatens you, I will find a way to save you."

Nathan didn't wait for her response. He turned and left the cottage. Miren watched him through the window. He took a position at the far end of the field, standing guard in place of Simon.

She hadn't fully understood his demons, how deeply he blamed himself for his brother's death. He carried his father's loss as bitterly, and cursed himself for what he couldn't change. He had a child's life to secure. And now he considered himself responsible for her, too.

But you're wrong, my friend. I'll protect myself from now on, and you'll see. When you need me, I'll be there. And one day, I may be the one to save you.

Chapter Eleven

Even the best-laid plans can go astray. I was so close. I could feel the comfortable carpet beneath my paws. Almost recline on my new, soft cushion. Taste the specially prepared table offerings. But no. Everything is going in the most peculiar direction. And not in favor of a house pet.

Nathan, who was supposed to be my hero, has fallen on hard times. At this moment, he is doing the worst task imaginable. He is—and it strains me to admit this—guarding sheep. My worst fears are realized. Rather than ensconce the young mistress and her house pet in the manor, Nathan has turned to herding sheep.

Who would have thought? A fine young man, well dressed, clean. A man with his own coach, a servant. He hasn't moved all morning. He just stares at the sheep. I don't know what he thinks they're going to do. Rampage the manor again, perhaps.

From what I've seen so far, Earnest isn't likely to rampage anything. I'd hoped at least for a good battle between the rams. Pawing the earth, charging each other, head-butting. But old Huntley wasn't up for it. I don't think he's even noticed his usurper's arrival.

Not only am I depressed, but bored. Bored enough to find myself tagging along after Flip. He doesn't do much. He likes to keep the ewes away from the gate, remembering how they broke free the last time. Flip seems bored, too. He's paying more attention to me than usual. Seems to find my enhanced smell intriguing.

Which is convenient, since I'm beginning to find him intriguing, too.

Sheep are the most boring creatures in all existence. Nathan began to understand Molly's reluctance to obey her age-old instincts. No wonder she favored following Miren. Nathan sat on a flat rock, staring across the pasture. The sheep barely moved. Every head was down, grazing. Beyond the pasture, the loch was still.

He was a man of action. Not tedium. But maybe it was the price paid for the havoc he had wreaked. Penalty. In hell. *In Scotland.* His honorable intentions didn't lessen the sexual pressure wrought from hours of desire. He ached. He'd spent a night in bed beside the woman he wanted most, and hadn't touched her.

The temptation had been strong. Nearly intolerable. She sighed in her sleep. She rolled over, and her leg brushed his. She rolled again, and her small, firm bottom touched his hip. Agony. Even the pain in his arm didn't diminish desire's force.

Hell.

His father had warned him of this fate. Nathan glared across the green pasture, but he saw himself at sixteen, defiant. Determined to join a war that Taregan, his father, said could only hurt their people's cause. Taregan had been right. The Seneca were divided, some sent to Kansas, a few remaining in New York.

Taregan defied the government's orders and built a farm on the old Seneca territory. The government took everything away, and sent Taregan and his daughters to Kansas. Glenna had remained behind, as the only person able to help David raise his baby son.

All the while, Nathan branded himself a war hero, and lived his own life without care about those he left behind. The war hadn't been horrible for him. He spent its final year at sea, apart from the nation's bloodiest battles. He'd spent it with salt spray in his face, adored by his crew, admired by women. He'd spent it making money and improving his ship.

When he returned after the war to the Seneca lands, he arranged for his father and sisters to be sent back to New York, but it was too late. His father's land had been lost, his pride shattered.

Taregan looked Nathan in the eye, and the bitter words still echoed. "*I have no son.*" The proud, dark face became imbedded in Nathan's mind as Taregan turned away.

Glenna wept, and begged Nathan to go after his father, to beg forgiveness. But Nathan's pride equaled his father's. He left the reservation, and returned to his ship, to the sea, and made himself renowned for his skill and ingenuity at trade.

When he returned, ready to make peace with his father, David was dead. And even Glenna turned her back.

"I've failed everyone who mattered."

Molly seated herself at his feet, then placed her paw on his knee. Nathan patted her. She lifted one ear for scratching. He complied. "I can't fail your mistress, Molly. I can't let her depend on me."

Nathan caught himself and groaned. "I'm talking to a dog." He peered down at her. She peered up at him. "You understand, don't you? I think I'm talking aloud to myself, but you're keeping tabs in your head. You *know.* I suppose you'll report back to her." The thought didn't seem impossible. "Well, you can tell her that I'm not doubting my decision. I'm sending her to America as soon as I can. Tell her

. . . tell her I'm not a man capable of love.''

"Boy, you've lost what you had of your mind.''

Nathan jumped, he gasped. His arm ached from the shock. Simon clambered over the stone wall and circled around Nathan as if his disease might be catching. "You can't resist, can you? Tell me, is it typical of the Scots to flay wounded men?''

"Aye.'' Simon's face twisted to one side. "Only if they're English.'' He seated himself beside Nathan, then crossed one short, stocky leg over the other. He rubbed his ankle as if it pained him. "Old lady expects her cherished bairn back in three days. We'll have at him then, and find out if he's the one wielding a blade, trying to make off with your girl.''

"She's not 'my girl,' Simon. Our engagement is a ruse, for the purpose of drawing Brent Edgington out. It appears it worked. Too well.''

Simon snorted and laughed. Not the response Nathan expected. "You're a fool if you think I'm believing you.''

Nathan looked to the side, confused. "It's true.''

"You got down on your knees—I know, because I fished it out of old Irene—and begged that lass to marry you. Promised her any number of things, just to get her wee 'yes.' ''

"It was necessary.''

Simon shook his head and clucked his tongue. "It's a shame when a man stoops that low. To crawl''—he issued another long series of disapproving clucks—"*begging*, lad. That puts every man worth his salt down a peg.''

"The little weasel wouldn't comply unless I agreed to certain demands. It was done for practical reasons.''

"Name one. Besides drawing out Edgington. I can think of a lot better ways of egging him on besides marriage.''

"The queen's entourage was brought solely as marriage material. That could get in the way of my plans.''

Simon cocked a brow. "And little Miren couldn't?''

Nathan felt tense. Cornered. "Since she'd already involved herself, I thought no further harm could be done. I was wrong, true, but I didn't know it then.''

''Weak. Try again.''

Nathan sucked in an angered breath. ''Most significantly, my engagement was viewed as both Scottish in nature and romantic by the queen. Which garnered her approval, which is necessary if I'm to secure David's inheritance and pass it to Nathaniel, which is my intention here.''

''Good little speech. Not that I'm believing even a scrap of it . . .''

Nathan set his jaw hard, his teeth grinding together as he repressed violence. ''Why not?''

''You couldn't know the old queen would take to our lass. Like as not, she'd pitch her up and to Inverness. You got lucky, boy. And not for the first time.''

Nathan closed his eyes, fighting for patience. ''What is your point, Simon?'' Amazing, how well he controlled his voice. The old Scotsman wouldn't pierce his armor, no matter what he tried.

''You proposed to that girl because you're as smitten and foolish as they come. I've seen men in bad ways before, lad, but you're the worst. Falling all over yourself to please her, to spend time in her company. Following her to market . . . Lad, you'd be carrying her skirt train if she asked it, and no mistake.''

No response seemed adequate. Simon was an old man. Probably dotard. Nathan could strike him down easily, kill him without effort. No trouble at all. Nathan exhaled a long, miserable breath instead. ''I know.''

Simon patted his knee. It occurred to Nathan in his numbed state of shattered pride that Simon had called him ''lad'' rather than ''boy.'' An improvement, albeit still condescending. ''Glad I am you're not up to denying it. Man does best when he faces his weakness head on.''

''I suppose you've 'faced' your weaknesses?''

''I only had one, lad, and that were long, long ago.'' Simon drew a long breath, gazing out over the quiet loch. ''Comes a time a man sees himself as hero, and that's dangerous. Most dangerous thing there is. A man gets a chance to protect the thing he loves most, and gets ideas as to how it's going to pan out.''

The old Scotsman was speaking of Nathan's mother. At another time, Nathan might have taken pleasure in pointing that out, but instead, he remained silent. Perhaps because Simon's words resonated deep. Too deep.

''This man, he has every reason to keep his hands to himself. Knows what's right and what's not. He puts her safety first. Respects her, and doesn't ply her when she's in need. Waits, figuring maybe a day will come when the time is right. Maybe when her husband forgets all about her and takes another wife.''

A strange and curiously moving admission. Nathan knew what had happened, he'd guessed Simon's motives, but to hear that low, rolling burr as it released its sorrow . . . Nathan's heart beat heavy and slow.

''He goes back when he's got some coins tucked away. Maybe he's lost a bit off his waist, trimmed his beard to best advantage . . .''

Nathan smiled at this, but he didn't speak. Simon had charm. His heart was full and kind. And broken.

''He comes into the village where he left her. He's aiming to take her away and see to her happiness himself, now that he's made his way enough to provide for her. And lad, when he sees her, she's like the sun. Prettiest girl a man ever saw. Black hair, blue eyes. Maybe she looks a bit like your little Miren, only not quite so practical. Maybe not quite so crazy, either.''

Nathan frowned on Miren's behalf. ''Miren isn't crazy.'' He clapped his hand to his forehead. ''What am I saying?''

''You're defending your lass, as you ought. When I say the girl's crazy, I'm not meaning she's got no sense. I mean she don't think like the rest of us. She thinks on her own, like maybe she's got connections to the Wee Folk.''

"That doesn't seem unlikely."

"As I were saying afore you interrupted . . . This man, he stands and he watches her as she's laughing with some other women. He don't see them. Only her. He takes off his cap and puts it over his heart, as a gentleman ought when he's speaking up. And he takes one step. Just one step, heart a'pounding. And as he's stepping, another man comes up behind her."

Simon paused as if the memory still grieved him. Nathan waited for the story to unfold, tense, though he knew the outcome.

"This other man, he puts his arm around her middle and he kisses her neck. Something this man I'm speaking of never imagined doing in his fondest dreams. He's thinking maybe he should shoot the young fellow. But she turns around and she sees him standing there, even as he's reaching for his gun. And she smiles, that God-sent smile that shows itself in his every dream. She waves, happy as a skylark to see him. Calls his name like a long-lost friend."

Simon fell silent for a long while. Blossom issued a perfunctory "baa," then sidled closer to Earnest, who responded with surprising fervor. Flip edged in closer, as if hoping for trouble.

"Tells him not to be shocked, not to hate her for a sin. But this young man, him wearing next to nothing besides skin breeches and a sawed-off tunic, a pair of leggings strapped over moccasins. A headband wrapped over way too much black hair . . ."

Nathan smiled at the detail of Simon's recollection. "Not quite 'nothing,' Simon."

Simon angled his stubborn chin. "It weren't decent."

"No . . . probably not."

Simon nodded, satisfied with Nathan's agreement. "She tells him this half-naked man is her husband. And she, with her eyes shining like stars, she tells him she's to have another bairn. And then . . . and then she thanks him for setting her free to find her heart's desire, for giving her boy a new father, one he can trust.''

Nathan stared at Simon, but Simon's eyes never left the loch. "He used to think she carried Scotland in her eyes. Blue and green, they were. Never saw such a shade." Simon coughed and cleared his throat, containing emotion.

"He didn't think of going back, not for a long while. But he wondered, this man, if that half-naked boy could do right by such a fair lass. So he finds himself heading back to the village. Maybe, even if he don't admit it to himself, he's hoping the boy turned tail and left her. Hoping she needs him again. But when he gets back to her, the boy is a man, prouder than a laird. And there, trotting along at his heels, smacking at shrubs with his little tomahawk, comes the most annoying, black-eyed brat the world ever produced—"

"Me."

Simon turned his gaze from the loch to Nathan and nodded. "You."

They looked at each other for a long while. A slight smile twitched beneath Simon's beard, then began to grow. Nathan smiled, too. The smile became a laugh, and they laughed until their eyes watered.

Simon dried his eyes with an old handkerchief, then stuffed it back into his pocket. "You made my life hell, boy. Every time I saw you, I thought I'd gone a little deeper into the fiery pits."

"Do you know, I couldn't wait for your visits? Every summer, I spent long nights planning."

"That ain't a surprise. Some of those tricks of yours must have taken months."

"A few."

"Young David, he were a good lad. So good as to be a sliver on the boring side. I'll tell you this once and never again. It was you as carried the Scots' blood, that which comes down from the Ancient Ones, from the Picts. Glenna, her line goes back beyond the dawn of Scotland. Whereas

Kenneth, his branch of the MacCallums don't go farther than the Normans."

"You kept coming back. Why?"

"When I first came, I came to see Glenna, to gut myself with what I couldn't have. But after a time, I came just to be among people who lived like those first Scots."

"The Iroquois aren't as primitive as the ancient Scots."

"Maybe not, but they weren't so far off as we're seeing up at the manor."

Nathan couldn't argue. "You could have a point there."

"Aye. Indians even take to painting themselves, *tattooing*. Which is how the Picts got their name. 'Painted ones.' It takes a blind man not to see the likeness."

"Then I have been blind. I've never seen so peculiar a land as this."

"It'll come, lad. It'll come. Maybe when you hear the pipes echoing in the Highland hills, and something in the far back of your mind remembers battles raging. Maybe when you wake early and the mist is on the glen. Maybe when you look in a pair of dark blue eyes and see a Highland loch."

Nathan sighed. "I was wrong. I've been there, after all."

Nathan and Simon took shifts guarding the cottage, but Miren's attacker didn't return. Miren began to feel restless. Nathan spent hours in her field, among her sheep, but he never talked to her beyond perfunctory greetings. She thought she'd seen him speaking to Molly, but she couldn't be sure.

He did tell her that he'd sent a message to her uncle, but that encouraged her very little. He slept in her cottage at night, on the floor, but he didn't eat with her. Simon shared her meals instead.

Nathan seemed to have made his peace with Simon, which gave her a small amount of pleasure. They spoke sometimes, as they switched shifts. Sometimes their conversations lasted well into the afternoon.

They'd spent most of the afternoon deep in conversation

GET YOUR 4 FREE BOOKS NOW — A \$21.96 Value!

Mail the Free Book Certificate Today!

Get Four Books Totally FREE – A $21.96 Value!

▼ Tear Here and Mail Your FREE Book Card Today! ▼

PLEASE RUSH
MY FOUR FREE
BOOKS TO ME
RIGHT AWAY!

Leisure Romance Book Club
P.O. Box 6613
Edison, NJ 08818-6613

AFFIX
STAMP
HERE

today. Simon had gone into Inveraray to interview the cutlery merchant, and learned that the Englishman who bought the knife was light-haired and fairly tall. He said he'd probably recognize the man again—despite the fact that all Englishmen looked alike.

His only doubt was about the man's age. He could be anywhere from twenty-five to his late forties. Not much help. He wore a mustache, like Brent, but he couldn't recall whether it was trimmed or long.

Nathan had retired to the cottage to sleep, and Simon stood guard alone. Miren's restlessness grew. She'd spent several days going nowhere beyond her field. Beyond the manor, a large meadow spread out like an invitation. She eyed it wistfully.

Maybe she would visit the monks. She could pick flowers, take Molly for a walk. Flip might even come, too. He'd shown a sudden interest in Molly's scent that threatened to distract him from sheep.

Miren positioned her Lindsay tartan over her shoulders and approached Simon. He didn't notice. "Excuse me, Simon."

Simon stood up and doffed his cap respectfully. "Lass."

"I want to go for a walk in that meadow." Miren pointed to the lush field. Simon frowned and shook his head, and Miren puffed an impatient breath. "You can see me from there. You'd certainly see if a rider approached. I want to go." She paused. With men, one had to be firm. "I will go. I will call out if I'm in need. I'll take Molly with me, and Flip, if he'll come."

Flip greeted Molly eagerly, his tail high, his neck arched. Molly seemed coy, spinning away and running in circles as she invited him to play. Flip complied, without his usual dignity and reticence. "Dogs are so odd. . . . If you have no objections, I shall go."

Simon opened his mouth to speak, but Miren held up her hand. "Thank you."

"You'd best take Nathaniel with you. I'll wake him."

Miren's eyes shifted to the cottage. "That won't be necessary. Molly and Flip are enough. I'll keep the loch in sight at all times, I promise."

"Not sure Nathaniel will approve."

"I don't require his approval." Miren decided to end any further argument. She hurried across the field to the gate, then headed to the meadow beyond.

Molly and Flip raced in circles. Flip seemed like a puppy. Miren's spirits rose as she watched the dogs play. Molly bounded through the bluebells, and Flip bounded after her. Molly was faster, but Miren noticed with wry approval that Molly let Flip catch up before daunting his pride.

Miren glanced back to be sure the loch was in sight. Simon stood alone, watching her. She held up her hand and waved. He waved back. Miren turned back to the dogs. They bounded over the crest of the meadow and down the other side. Miren made her way to the top and looked down.

Molly and Flip dashed around, spinning one way, then the other. Miren sighed. The walk did her good. The afternoon sun shone in her eyes, and she held up her hand as shade. Far across the meadow, just north of the abbey, someone moved. A man emerged from the forest, then walked along the edge of the pasture, keeping close to the trees.

It wasn't a monk. Miren's heart held its beat, her breath caught. He couldn't reach her before she got back to the cottage. She lingered a moment to see who it was. Blond hair glinted in the sunlight. His gait was unmistakable. *Brent.*

He hadn't seen her. Miren eased back until the crest obscured her presence from his view. She walked casually closer to the road. Simon wasn't looking. In fact, he seemed to have fallen asleep beneath the willow's shade. Miren relaxed. Brent wasn't prowling the west side of the meadow for her. But why? He wasn't carrying a gun, so he couldn't be hunting.

Miren's nerves calmed and she considered the matter. Maybe he hid his mask and black cloak in the trees. If she found them, Nathan's search would be over. Miren hesitated.

Better to let Nathan or Simon handle it.

"Miren!" Brent called to her, and Miren jumped. He laughed, then came toward her, smiling. He didn't look dangerous, but the blood drained from Miren's face as he approached.

"Brent . . ." Miren gulped. She couldn't let on that she suspected him. She had to remain calm. "I didn't realize you were back from your hunting trip. Did you have a good time?"

"I'm afraid most of our trip was fogged out. Didn't bag a thing."

Because he hadn't been hunting. That was obvious.

"What a shame."

Brent laid his hand on her shoulder. Miren tensed, and his eyes narrowed. "Are you all right?"

"Just a little tired."

Brent removed his hand. "Mother tells me that Nathan's been spending a good deal of time in the sheep pasture. Anything wrong?"

Dear God. Fishing for information. Miren swallowed hard. "Wolves. Well, not wolves. Some kind of predator." She gulped. "It frightened the sheep once or twice, so we're keeping a closer eye. That's all."

"That's a shame." Rather than leering or threatening, Brent just looked confused. "Hope you get it driven off." Brent paused. "Did this creature come after the sheep at night or in the morning?"

Miren hesitated, having no idea why he asked. "At night."

"Good, good." He actually seemed relieved. Miren exhaled a shuddering breath. Brent eyed her doubtfully.

"Have to get back to the manor, I'm afraid." Brent sighed and gazed heavenward. "Mother has guests for tea. Insists I be there. Guess I've put it off as long as possible."

"It was good speaking with you, Brent."

Miren watched him head for the manor. Irene met him at the door and drew him in, accompanied by two older women.

211

Brent wasn't lying. He was stuck for the afternoon.

Miren glanced back at Simon. Still sleeping. Brent was accounted for. A quick check might provide the necessary evidence. And she was still bored. "Molly, Flip! Come!"

Nothing. Absolutely nothing. Miren found the path Brent had taken, even into the trees. She'd taken too much time already. Simon might wake and find her missing. Molly and Flip weren't much as bloodhounds. They ran through the trees, chasing squirrels. They went deeper into the woods, but Miren aimed for the meadow again.

Something square caught her eye. Her heart jumped, her nerves tingled. "A trunk!" She'd found it. She wasn't sure what it contained, but evidence, surely. Miren clasped her skirt and hurried toward the trunk. Branches cracked as she stepped on them, but she didn't care.

It was a good-sized trunk, wooden. Well made, with iron trim. And a lock. A solid, large lock. Miren kicked the trunk. "Curses!"

She refused to surrender. She fiddled with the lock, but it didn't yield. Molly and Flip ran through the trees up ahead, then into the meadow. "Oh, hell! How will I open this?"

"You won't."

Miren screamed. She jumped, and tripped headlong over the trunk. A firm hand clasped her skirt just above her bottom, pulled her back, and righted her. She scrambled away, whirled, but he grabbed her again. He wasn't gentle as he turned her to face him.

"Nathan!" Miren's knees gave way and she sank back onto the trunk. "What are you doing here?"

"What am *I* doing here?" He'd never looked so angry. His brown eyes darkened to black, he loomed over her. His shirt was only half buttoned, as if he'd been woken abruptly. His hair looked tangled. "*What am I doing here?*" He moved closer, towering over her. Miren shrank back and gripped the trunk.

"That's what I said." Her voice came as a small squeak. He looked as if he wanted to strangle her.

"I think the better question is—"

"Oh. You're probably wondering why I'm here, it being a risk and all."

"An astute guess."

Miren gazed up through the trees casually. "Molly and Flip are here to protect me."

Nathan looked around. A calculated effort. "Are they? So they would race to your aid if I should, for instance, attempt to . . . oh, say . . . *wrap my fingers around your neck and squeeze until you turn blue*—"

"Nathan! There's no need to be vile. And, of course, if I were *truly* in danger, Molly and Flip would defend me. They know you, so they're not alarmed."

"They're not in sight! They're frolicking off in the meadow. While you"—his voice trembled with rage—"while you . . . What are you doing?"

"Don't shout. I refuse to answer if you're shouting."

"I won't shout. I wouldn't *think* of shouting. What are you doing, you crazy . . . Scottish female."

"I'm . . . Well, I'm sitting on evidence."

"Of what?"

"This is a trunk." Despite Nathan's fury, Miren felt proud. "Brent's trunk. He keeps it hidden out here. I expect he keeps his mask and other devices here, so we won't find them in the manor."

Nathan eyed the trunk. "Maybe. Or maybe he keeps . . ." Nathan paused. Miren's brow arched into a knowing posture.

"You can't think of any other explanation, either." Miren eased off the trunk and stood with it between herself and Nathan. "I know you're alarmed."

"Oh? Why would I be alarmed?"

"Don't be coy, Nathan. You're annoyed. You have every right to be. You see, I had a bit of trouble finding this, or I'd have been back earlier, before anyone noticed." She paused.

213

"Am I correct in assuming that Simon noticed I wasn't quite where I promised to be?"

Nathan nodded.

"And I'm sorry . . . Except that, of course, I *did* find this trunk, and it *is* evidence—"

"Of what?"

"Of . . . I don't know. Open it and find out."

"How?"

"Break it open! You're a man."

"And I consider myself a fairly strong man. But not strong enough to open a cast-iron lock." His voice had become a growl. No, his anger wasn't abating. It had altered slightly. It had become curiously compelling, but it wasn't gone.

For a reason Miren didn't understand, she liked his anger. In fact, she longed to provoke it further. "I'm perfectly safe here, you understand."

"You're sure, are you? What led you to this conclusion?"

Miren straightened, triumphant. "Brent is in the manor, having tea with his mother."

Nathan nodded again. "I see. And if, by chance, Brent *wasn't* your assailant? If another man has been lurking in wait to get you alone?"

He had her there. "Brent has a trunk hidden in the woods. He was just here this afternoon. I saw him, which is why I felt I had to—"

"Risk your neck?"

Miren elevated her chin. "I didn't consider it as such."

He started around the trunk. Miren moved to the other end. "So, what are you going to do about this?"

"I'm going to tie you to your bedpost and . . ." Nathan's words trailed off. His eyes flashed something akin to fire.

"I meant about the trunk!"

"Simon and I will find a way to break it open tomorrow."

"That sounds good."

Miren stepped back from the trunk, bumped into a tree, then aimed for the meadow. He was right behind her. Her thoughts twirled. She slowed, spotted him from the corner of her eye, then picked up her skirts and bolted for the open pasture.

She'd caught him off guard. Miren ran until her lungs hurt. She sped through the bluebells as if borne by fairy wings. Molly and Flip barked in excitement, then raced along ahead. Nathan came up behind her. She heard him, fast and skilled, like a hunter.

He caught her by the shoulders, still running, and lifted her off her feet. They fell, but her body didn't touch the ground. He lay above her, braced on his strong arms as his hair fell around his face. His black eyes burned, but he was smiling.

Miren's heart raced from running, from him. She stared up at him wide-eyed as the blue sky framed his beautiful head. Her heart ached with such suddenness . . . She squeezed her eyes shut to blot out the sight.

His body aligned with hers, meeting near her hips. She felt his strong thighs straddling her, holding her down. He lowered, slightly, and she felt his desire. "Nathan . . ."

She looked up at him, but he sat back abruptly, releasing her. Miren sighed. "I suppose we should go back to the cottage. Simon will be worried."

"Yes." His voice sounded thick, hoarse. Miren's nerves tingled. From desire. No matter what he said, he still wanted her.

Nathan rose to his feet and offered his hand. She took it and stood up, but he released her and walked on ahead. Miren stood a moment, watching his broad, strong back, his dark hair splayed across his shoulders. He walked looking down, fighting for control.

Miren stood motionless. A light breeze from the loch crossed the meadow, bending the bluebells, weaving through the tall grass. It cooled her face and softened her hair. He walked away, and Miren knew why she couldn't release him, why her imaginings kept coming back despite her defiance.

"I love you."

The breeze stole her whisper and passed it to the forest beyond. Yet her soft vow lingered in the air, surrounding her, filling her heart with a strength she'd never known before.

I am in love with you. She knew that pain would follow, but at this moment Miren didn't care. She knew her life would go on without him. Maybe she would even marry another, one day. But no one, not in all the world, would touch her heart so deeply.

She couldn't risk her heart further. It was already in his possession.

Chapter Twelve

This has been the most blissful day in my life. Flip is fun. I don't know how I misjudged him so.

The young mistress never allows me privacy. She hovers. I'd never noticed it before, but it's true. "Come, Molly." "Sit, Molly." She's overprotective. No question. If only a dog could issue the command "stay" to a human!

Molly lagged behind Miren, hoping to be forgotten. It didn't seem likely. Miren never overlooked her actions. Miren and Nathan were bickering. He was still displeased that the young mistress had frolicked without him. At least, Molly guessed that explained his fury.

Miren's stomping gait indicated that she, too, was enraged. Their argument escalated as they approached the pasture gate. Nathan reached to open it, but Miren shoved him aside and yanked it open herself. Molly wasn't sure if she meant to slam the gate into Nathan's stomach or not.

Apparently, he thought so, because he shook his fist at Miren's back as she whisked through the open gate and headed for the cottage. Nathan jammed the latch shut and stormed after her. Molly sat beside Flip, watching as Miren hurried to the cottage, opened the door quickly, and slammed it shut in Nathan's face.

Even the sheep took note of their peculiar behavior and stopped grazing to watch.

Nathan tried to open the door. It didn't work. Perhaps the young mistress stood on the other side holding it shut. His fists clenched. Molly and Flip exchanged a doubtful glance, then looked back at Nathan. He paused, collecting himself, then knocked.

Molly heard Miren's voice. She sounded pert. "No."

Nathan knocked again, harder this time. Molly felt sure she heard humming from inside the cottage. Nathan rattled the door knob. His effort escalated, but the door didn't open. "Woman, open this door!"

Molly heard it again. "No."

Nathan growled like a dog. He stepped back from the door as if he intended to find other sleeping arrangements. With a low roar, he turned back again, braced his shoulder, and rammed full force into the door. It popped open and he burst inside. Molly heard a sharp squeak from within, which must have come from Miren.

The squeak was followed by a crash. Then another, louder crash. Like a chair slamming against a wall. A tin cup banged on the window. Something shattered. Pottery, perhaps. Molly heard Miren's voice, taunting. Nathan cursed.

And then there was silence.

Molly and Flip looked at each other, then at the empty byre. *Alone at last.*

Miren held a dinner bowl poised and aimed at Nathan's head. Nathan gripped another chair. They stared at each other, mouths open, eyes burning. Miren dampened her lips with a quick dart of her tongue. Her heart slammed in her breast.

The dinner bowl slipped from her fingers and cracked on the floor. Nathan dropped the chair. They met in the middle of the room, caught each other in a fierce embrace, and kissed with a fury that soared past their previous battle.

She couldn't tell where he began or she ended. She couldn't tell if he pulled her closer or she pulled him. She grasped his hair, his fingers entwined in hers. They met in wild, feverish abandon—kissing, breath mingling. Nathan's heart pounded against hers, his pulse raged in the same rhythm as her own.

Miren gasped for air, then molded her mouth against his. He kissed her face, her eyelids. She tipped her head back and he kissed her throat. Miren's hands shook as she pulled open his collar. Buttons snapped and dropped to the floor as she parted his shirt. Her soul was on fire. Nothing mattered but burrowing deep within him.

Miren pushed his shirt from his strong, smooth shoulders and pulled it down to his wrists. She burned, so far beyond control that she thought never to return. Her fiery gaze swept across his wide chest, her fingers clenched as she pressed her mouth against his flesh.

His head angled back and he groaned, a low, masculine surrender as Miren licked and nipped, tasting him. Her lips blazed a warm trail over his muscled chest to his neck. She seized his hair and drew his face to hers. His arms clasped around her, he took her mouth in a demanding, deep kiss.

She pulled his shirt free and tossed it aside. Their eyes met, and they faced each other like two storms on a turbulent sea. Miren felt a power and magic she'd never known, a rage to challenge, and battle, and seek victory. It wasn't gentle nor passive nor peaceful. It was a storm between them.

Nathan showed no signs of surrender. The same lust to conquer glittered in his dark eyes. He caught her face in his hands, kissing her. His hands slid from her face to her neck, then over her shoulders. His quick fingers found the small buttons that ran down her back. Miren held her breath as the buttons came loose, cool air touching her back as he pulled her bodice forward and down. It fell to her waist, revealing her breasts squeezed upward beneath her corset, covered only by her thin chemise.

Her dress slithered to her feet. She had no idea how he removed so easily what challenged her every night. She stood, heart raging, her chest rising and falling beneath shallow breaths. His eyes didn't leave hers as he ran his finger along the line of her corset. He bent and pressed his mouth over her concealed flesh, then drew away.

He unfastened her corset, freeing her breasts to his touch. Miren felt dizzy. Her passion spiraled beyond control, beyond reason. She didn't think of stopping him. He cupped her breast in his hand, then bent to graze its tip with his tongue. The light fabric concealed nothing. Her nipple hardened into a taut peak as he sucked and teased. Her whole body tightened, she leaned against him.

He moved his attention to her other breast, then cupped both in his hands. He looked into her eyes, holding her gaze as he teased the little buds with his thumbs. She shuddered, her eyes closed, and he bent her back to kiss her neck. His hips moved against hers. He was hot and full, hard against her stomach.

Her inner depths burned molten, such a craving as she never imagined. He had brought her here before, sweet and slow. But now they spiraled toward the same destination, charging headlong toward such rapture . . . He grasped her waist and lifted her, holding her body full against his. She felt his male length poised against her woman's mound. She squirmed against him to fuel his desire further still.

He kissed her face as he carried her across the cottage. He sat her on the edge of her bed and knelt to unlace her low boots. The boots came off, and he slid his hands up her legs to remove her stockings. Miren trembled as they came off and slid to the floor.

He rose, and she fixed her gaze on his, a slight smile curving her lips. She pulled her chemise from her body and tossed it aside. His eyes burned black, his face seemed swollen with desire. He wouldn't deny her now. He wouldn't gain control of his senses until he found relief. She wouldn't allow it until she found her own.

"You want me. I want you, too." Her gravelly voice sounded to her like another woman's, a woman possessed by desire. A woman who longed to give all she possessed to the man she loved. No matter what happened between them, no matter how she hurt in the end.

His dark eyes took in her body, and she knew the sight pleased him. He didn't look away as he unfastened his trousers and kicked off his boots. His trousers lowered, revealing his strong hips, the hard cords of his stomach. He bent to pull them off, and Miren caught a glimpse of his firm buttocks. When he stood, his male organ stood poised from his body, engorged and dark. More than she had imagined.

Miren puffed a quick breath. It couldn't all be meant to fit inside her. Perhaps only the tip. She met his eyes, and he smiled. Not gentle or reassuring, but with a promise of something she couldn't know.

He took her hand and placed it over his staff, closing her fingers around its width. It felt hot, its pulse surged. Miren went weak with need. She didn't care how large it was. She would accommodate him somehow. Her fingers squeezed, and he caught his breath.

"This is what you've done to me, this is what I've endured . . . day after day, hour by hour."

Miren peeked up at him. "Does it hurt?"

"It aches, Miren. I ache."

She recognized this feeling. "I ache, too."

He smiled. "We will search out relief together."

Relief. That was what she wanted. Miren moved her hand up and down around him. His hard flesh seemed to grow, to burn hotter as she caressed him. His muscles drew taut, as if a great surge of energy and power were imminent. She ran

221

her palm over the swollen tip, and his breath caught on a harsh gasp.

Nathan seized her shoulders and pressed her back against the bed. Her grip loosened, and she wrapped her arms around his neck instead. He eased her body up, lengthwise along the bed, so that the pillows supported her head. He sat beside her, but he didn't touch her.

She lay naked, her heart pounding, her body ripe and tingling. But still he didn't touch her. For a brief flash, she feared he had come to his senses. That he would remember his purpose and turn away. She arched her back slightly, provocative.

"You know when I'm weak, don't you? You know what you do." His voice came like a growl, hoarse and deep. "You are beautiful, Miren. So perfect and so sweet."

She didn't feel sweet. She felt wanton. Wanton enough to ask anything, and see it delivered in full. "Please me." She liked the rich, commanding tone of her voice, though she wasn't sure where it came from. It worked admirably. He seemed to turn into flame before her eyes.

"Please you? Is that what you want? Not my heart or my soul or my life spent at your side?"

Miren smiled. She wanted all those things, but freely given. Not demanded. "I want satisfaction."

He looked incapable of answering, but he moved, took her legs in his hands, and knelt between her thighs. It felt odd. Awkward and odd, to lie back, to have her legs spread. To have him there, between. She hadn't been entirely sure of the position a couple took in lovemaking. She pictured them lying side by side, legs straight.

This seemed far more shocking. A woman concealed nothing this way.

She expected him to take her. His male length stood ready, poised. Her body seemed ready, too. But he just smiled. With one finger, he traced a line down over her feminine curls, then between her thighs. She was slippery and wet, perhaps in preparation for his entrance.

She clasped her lower lip between her teeth to keep herself still. She knew what he would do, tease her and torment her until she writhed. She knew it, but his touch still came like a fiery shock. He delved beneath her woman's fold, inward, then back to the small peak that crowned her desire. The small peak came wantonly to life, commanding all her being as it rose against his finger.

His eyes never left her face. He seemed to cherish her reactions, and she could hide nothing from his sight. His finger moved in slow, torturous circles, one way, then the other. It slipped up and down, barely grazing, then with increased pressure. She twisted beneath him, her back arched of its own accord.

He moved closer, then wrapped her legs around his waist. He held his staff in his hand and positioned it over her woman's mound. Its heat caressed her, smooth and hard, as he angled his hips against her. His staff rubbed against her small peak, and she cried out with fierce pleasure.

It pleased him, too. His hips moved in greater abandon. He sank down over her, bracing his arms on either side of her body. His new position afforded better contact, and the friction between their bodies increased.

Miren's legs tightened around him. She arched and squirmed, seeking. He seemed to understand, because he moved harder against her. Still not within. She wanted him within. She felt sure of it now. He would fit. She would make him fit.

"Nathan . . . More, please."

He chuckled, probably because she was politely asking, rather than issuing a fierce demand. He rested his forehead on hers, then sat up. Miren puffed an exasperated breath. "Don't you dare!"

He smiled. He gripped his length and moved it purposefully against her. Dizzying waves of pleasure coursed through her. "You can play, Miren. This is for you."

She wasn't sure what he meant, but she decided the matter

223

herself. She seized his staff and held it against her entrance, then pleasured herself as she saw fit. He allowed her control, he even clasped her hips in his hands to support her activity. It proved such wanton delight, Miren couldn't stop. Her pace quickened. Her hips twisted and circled and sought mindless release. Her senses spiraled, congealing and aiming toward greater heights.

Her control fragmented. He wrapped his hand over hers and positioned himself at her entrance. She cried out his name, she arched beneath him, and his swollen tip delved inside her. He filled her entrance, and it triggered a shattering response. Waves and waves of rapture coursed through her, sparkling through her loins, surging even into her toes. Her legs clamped tight around him as her ecstasy shuddered through her body, around his.

He should be deep within her. Instead he withdrew suddenly, even as she arched to draw him inside. A hot, liquid pulse met her sensitive flesh, spilling against her thighs as he groaned and murmured her name.

Miren watched his face. His eyes were closed, his whole face strained as his body quivered above her. His rapture lingered, then abated, and he lowered above her, his breath so swift and shallow that Miren thought he might faint.

She trembled violently beneath him, shocked by the suddenness of her release, of its power to surround her, and own her, and send her to some limitless plain she didn't know existed until now. Nathan seemed shocked, too. Miren softened his hair and drew him down to her. She kissed his face, and held him against her body. She wanted his full weight, but he braced himself on his elbows instead.

They lay together, silent, breath mingling as their hearts pounded an even descent. He rolled off her and gathered her into his arms. Miren kissed his shoulder, but she didn't know what to say. Her whole body tingled in the aftermath. She felt weak, but satisfied. Almost satisfied. A tiny frown crept to her lips.

"There is a place deep inside me that you missed."

Strange, how practical she sounded even now. Nathan twisted his head to look at her. He looked . . . amazed. "Is there?"

She nodded. "I believe so."

"I didn't 'miss.' Despite what we've just done here, you remain a virgin. There's little chance you bear my child. I protected you, woman."

Miren eyed him doubtfully. "I don't recall asking for your protection."

"You were well past issuing requests."

Miren fell silent a moment, pondering his restraint. She didn't want him to have restraint. She'd abandoned hers, after all. "The satisfaction is not complete."

"You are a demanding wench. You look satisfied to me."

"I am pleased, that is true. I am tingling in all parts of myself. My toes even feel the sensation. But there is somewhere, as I said, quite deep—"

"Quiet, woman. I protected you. Sexual release covers your whole body."

"Yes. Yes, so it does. I shall be content. For a while. I can't help thinking, though, that deeper penetration on your part might be enjoyable."

"It might." Nathan cleared his throat. "Miren, nothing has changed. We lost control. Maybe it had to happen. We've been headed for this since we met. But I won't put you at further risk. Your virginity remains intact. I haven't really damaged you."

Nathan's proclamation grated, but Miren restrained her annoyance. "No, you haven't. If I have a husband in the future, he will be the first to attain that deep portion which you successfully avoided."

Nathan's jaw set hard, but he didn't comment.

"I can present myself as a virgin." Miren paused. "I won't, of course, because that would be dishonest. I shall tell him what you and I did here, before he marries me. That is only fair." She peeked up. Nathan glowered, his lips looked tight. "Do you think it will bother him, despite the fact I remain a virgin?"

"I don't know."

"You sound sullen. It was your idea."

"I cannot believe that you are planning your wedding only *moments* after we made love."

"Almost made love."

Nathan twisted in bed to face her. "Making love isn't determined by whether or not there was deep penetration, woman."

"I stand corrected."

"You are a torment."

Her eyelids lowered. "It pleases me. Almost as much as you do."

Nathan sank back in the bed and exhaled a long, shuddering breath. He folded his hands on his chest and sighed again. "You please me, too."

Miren woke with a start and sat up in bed. "Nathan!"

He sat up, too. Ready to fight and defend her. He fumbled with the sheets. "What is it? Did you hear something? Is someone outside?" His words slurred as he fought against sleep. Miren patted his shoulder.

"Calm yourself, Indian. There's no one out there."

"Then why"—he paused to control himself—"why did you wake me as if the cottage was on fire?"

"Molly. I forgot all about her."

Nathan flopped back down in bed. "What of it?"

"I've never forgotten her before. I left her outside. She must be so hurt." Tears started in Miren's eyes.

Nathan yawned and closed his eyes. "Give her an extra cookie in the morning."

"You have to check on her."

Nathan opened one eye. "*I* have to check on her?"

"I'm naked."

"So am I."

"Yes, but you're a man."

"What does that have to do with anything?"

Miren wasn't entirely sure. Also, the room was cold. A light patter on the thatched roof indicated rain had begun again. "Men can be naked. Women can't."

He looked as if he wanted to argue but suspected he might lose. Miren kept her expression straight, as if her request was perfectly normal. Nathan sighed heavily, fueled by self-pity, then rose with undue labor. He groaned as he left the bed, hissed when he opened the door and rainy wind blew in, then stuck his head out the door.

"Molly! Get in here."

No response. Miren tensed with worry. "Where's Flip? He always sleeps by the door."

"It's pouring, woman. They're probably in the byre."

"You'd better check."

He closed the door, stumbled over something and swore. A chair. He set it right, then seized Miren's lantern. He went to the byre and looked in. Miren waited impatiently. "Well? Are they in there?"

He returned, closed the door, and crawled back in bed. "They're in there."

"You should have let her in."

"I don't think she's interested tonight, Miren. They're . . . occupied."

"What do you mean, 'occupied'?"

"I mean you can probably expect a litter of half-slackabout, half-sheepdog in the near future."

Miren beamed and clasped her hands like a grandmother. "Truly? Puppies! Nathan, are you sure?"

"Some things, my sweet, are mistakable. This isn't one."

Miren nodded and lay back down beside him. "How romantic!"

Nathan rolled his eyes. "Go to sleep."

His arm flopped over her, and he kissed her forehead.

227

Miren snuggled closer against him. She felt safe, cared for. She wondered if his gentle treatment was typical of a man's actions toward his mistress. Miren listened to his slow, even heartbeat as he drifted back to sleep. The rain fell in gentle tandem, and for this night, she abandoned all doubt. She might not have him forever, but tonight, to lie safe in his arms was enough.

"Trouble's brewing, lad! Get yourself out here!"

Nathan woke and swore. "He can't stand to let me rest . . ."

Miren rolled over and snuggled close to him. "Tell him to go away." She pressed a soft, leisurely kiss on his shoulder. Nathan's pulse quickened.

"Can't it wait, Simon?"

"No, it can't wait." Simon's voice mocked Nathan's. "Get out here!"

Nathan forced himself from Miren's side. She lay on her back, arms casually over her head, smiling. Her light brown hair spread out across the pillow. He wanted her. He had to restrain himself, as much for her sake as his own. Another night of passion might see his control shattered beyond recall.

Nathan dressed, then went to the door. He stood on the threshold, barring Simon entrance. "Miren isn't ready for visitors."

"Ain't a visitor, lad." Simon turned and gestured to another man. Nathan recognized the cutlery merchant from Inveraray Market. The merchant nodded, and Nathan offered a weak smile.

"Good morning, sir. Thank you for agreeing to assist us."

"Pleased to oblige, laird. 'Specially if we're sticking trouble to an Englishman."

"That remains to be seen."

The merchant looked around, seeming eager. "Where's this fellow? I'll be needing a good look at him."

Miren emerged from the cottage, doing up her long hair in

a loose bun. The merchant doffed his cap, although Simon eyed her suspiciously. "You're looking spry this morning, lass."

Miren sighed. "I had a good sleep."

Nathan's face felt warm. He cleared his throat and eased her to his side. "We're going up to the manor to pay a call on Brent. Join us."

He couldn't leave her alone, but this meeting required both himself and Simon. Nathan held out his arm, and she took it. "Proceed."

Lady MacCallum was breakfasting alone. "Dear Brent left early this morning on another of his hunting trips. He won't be back for at least a week, although he has promised to meet us at the Highland Games in Oban. He encouraged me to stay here, but of course, that is impossible. Her Majesty will be expecting my presence. I shall travel with the duke and his wife, however. You may use the coach."

Nathan sighed. Brent Edgington remained one step ahead. Nathan invented an excuse for the merchant's presence as Lady MacCallum set aside her tea. She fixed her gaze on the merchant, who looked uncomfortable. "Have we guests?"

"Mr. Shaw is here to view our collection of dirks and swords. And he's brought some wares of his own."

Irene angled her thin brow. "Indeed."

The merchant bowed, twice. "That I am, Your Ladyship. Figuring I might make an offer on a few pieces."

"Nothing in our collection is for sale."

Nathan placed his hand on the merchant's back. "Actually, I'm considering a purchase myself. I understood each MacCallum laird has added something to the collection."

The merchant brightened and clapped his hands. "I have just the thing!"

Nathan spent enough on one small sgian-dhu to purchase a race horse. He stood at the manor entrance, glaring as the merchant departed. Miren stood beside him, chuckling.

"You're quite a haggler. Perhaps you should go into business."

"The man is a pirate."

Miren hummed. "You should know."

Lady MacCallum stood on the bottom step with Muffin, awaiting the coach. "I shall be spending the day at Inveraray Castle, as a special guest at a private tea hosted by the duke." She cast a cold glance Miren's way. "I'm sorry they didn't think to invite you, Miren."

Miren nodded. "I shall endure the disgrace." She seemed pert. Happy. Lady MacCallum fumed. Nathan chuckled.

Grainger brought the coach around, then assisted Lady MacCallum to her seat. She clutched Muffin on her lap, but her eyes were still fixed on Miren. The vengeful look seemed unwarranted by the situation. Nathan found himself taking Miren's hand and squeezing reassurance.

Miren didn't appear troubled. She angled her head as the coach departed and issued a derisive snort. "What a crone! If she were just a speck bigger, I'd be sure she's the one who attacked me."

Simon joined them on the steps and raised a crowbar. "Since the old hag's on her way, we'll check on this trunk you found. Lass, you come with us, and we'll see what young Brent is hiding."

"It's gone!" Miren stomped around through the woods. "It was here. Nathan, you saw it. Wasn't it here?"

Nathan looked around, gauging the distance from the meadow. He'd been so frantic, terrified that something had happened to her, he hadn't noticed their exact position. He'd seen her kick the trunk, he'd heard her curse as she struggled to open it. And his heart had beat with such fury and relief that his knees had threatened to give way.

"My memory isn't exact."

"Well, mine is." She stood with her hands on her hips, a tight frown knitting her small, lovely face. She kicked at a stump, then waved her arms. Something caught her eye, and she marched through the trees. "There! It was right here."

Miren pointed to a flat, square spot on the ground where leaves had been crushed beneath a heavy weight. Nathan knelt to study the surface. "It was here."

"Damn! He moved it!"

Simon clucked his tongue. "Language, lass. Don't be forgetting, they're keeping tabs up in the Beyond."

Miren rolled her eyes. "I hope they're 'keeping tabs' on Brent Edgington. We'll never know what he's keeping in that trunk. It's my fault. He must have seen me, after all, and guessed we were on to him."

Simon nodded. "Took off in a hurry, didn't he? And he's not coming back 'til after the Games. That boy ain't no more off hunting than I am a sparrow."

Nathan looked toward the meadow. "Brent had this trip planned before Miren found his trunk." Nathan ran his fingers along the crushed earth. "Does Brent Edgington strike either of you as a powerful man?"

Simon grimaced and snorted. Miren looked thoughtful, then sympathetic. "I wouldn't describe him as powerful, no. Why do you mention it?"

"Whoever moved this trunk was strong enough to lift it and carry it out of here. See . . ." Nathan pointed around the vicinity. "No signs of dragging. That trunk wasn't small. It had iron trim. For one man to move it at all—"

Miren brightened. "Two men!"

Nathan stood up. "That seems reasonable."

Simon kicked at the flattened dirt and dried leaves. "Fellow like young Brent's likely to have an accomplice. Someone he's paying to do the dirty work. Just as he paid Patterson to do in the old laird."

Miren's face twisted to one side as she considered this. "Dr. Patterson was fond of money, it's true. He liked the prestige and power. What I find odd is that he'd make a mistake, such as dying in the fire."

231

"Smoke catches up to a man, lass. Probably thought he'd get out easier."

"If he escaped, why didn't Laird MacCallum or Nathan's brother?"

Simon hesitated. "That's a fair question, lass, and one I asked myself at the time. Looked to me like two of the dead men hadn't put up a fight nor tried to escape at all."

"Could he have shot them first?"

"Didn't find no sign of it. Bullets, they'd last through the blaze and show up in the aftermath. What I'm thinking is he poisoned them. He was a doctor, maybe he put them into a sleep first."

"Then how did he get caught in the fire himself?"

Nathan resisted the memory, but he had returned to the site with Simon. "There were three bodies. One lay beneath a charred door. It appears that the door caved in when Patterson tried to leave."

"Odd that he'd wait that long."

Nathan sighed. "No other explanation seemed likely. If you have one, I'd be happy to hear it."

Miren turned to Simon. She looked like a detective, eyes narrow, practical brain at work. "Was there anyone else around?"

Simon puffed an impatient, perturbed breath. "No, there weren't, lass. Had a young fellow guide us into David's farm, but he took off the first day."

"Then you're right. It had to be Patterson."

Simon snorted. "Thank you for telling us what we already knew."

"It still seems strange." Miren considered the matter a while. "How do you know it was Dr. Patterson who instigated their deaths?"

"Two of the charred bodies were piled together in a heap with kindling. That fire were started a'purpose, and on men who were already dead, or near to it."

Miren grimaced. "I don't require the full details, Simon. Was there anything else?"

"I found a campsite tucked back in the woods, where he'd hidden all sorts of gear, kerosene, tools. That's where I found the MacCallum badge pinched in his fingers. Figuring he stole it to prove to his accomplice back here that he'd gotten the job done."

"I see. Disgusting, but plausible." Miren eyed Nathan. "And you think Brent was behind this?"

Nathan ran over the evidence in his mind. He'd heard the story from Simon, but basing his investigation on the high-strung Scotsman's word still seemed tenuous. But David was dead, and the most likely reason was that his inheritance proved a threat to someone. "It points to Brent Edgington, yes."

Miren's lip curled at one side. "Why would he want to kidnap me?"

Nathan frowned. "We have no idea what he, or anyone, wanted that night, Miren."

"The logical speculation is that he wanted me to use against you, because of your inheritance. But that doesn't make sense."

"Girl has a point. If he was after killing her, he'd have done it, and hightailed himself out of there. He took her a'purpose."

"If only I'd questioned him a bit more!"

Nathan fought for patience. "He wasn't likely to spew his secrets to you, woman."

"If I'd played along—"

"No!" Nathan seized Miren's arm. She looked determined. "You are to restrain any impulse to go off on your own, is that understood?"

"I suppose so."

"These Games . . . They're in Oban, yes?"

Miren's eyes narrowed suspiciously. "They are. They'll be especially grand this year, because the queen is attending. Why do you ask?"

"We're supposed to attend. I'd thought to get out of it, but perhaps we'll go."

"Why?"

Nathan met her gaze. "My ship is in Oban. It might provide a good way to get you on board before suspicions are raised."

Her face paled, and she looked down to hide her disappointment. Nathan steeled himself against her sorrow. "I told you I would arrange your passage to America."

She didn't look up. "Yes, but we haven't heard from my uncle yet."

"He can be located after you arrive. I'll see that you have a place to stay until permanent arrangements can be made."

"I don't want to go." Her voice came small, but it drove like splinters into his heart. Nathan touched her chin, but she wouldn't meet his eyes.

"Miren, we agreed. Your safety is what matters. There's nothing for you here." He spoke as bluntly as he could with Simon standing beside him. He didn't want to hurt her, but he couldn't let her cling to false hope, either.

Miren twisted her chin from his grasp and turned away. "I know." She headed back toward the meadow, and she didn't look back.

Nathan drew a tight breath, then started after her. Simon caught his arm and held him back. "I warned you, lad. You're playing hero. And the only thing it'll get you is pain."

Chapter Thirteen

Flip expects me to stay at his side at all times. Which means I'm stuck watching the sheep. All day. It is a torment. And after such a night of bliss . . .

Males of all species are troublesome. The young mistress returned from her walk with Nathan and hasn't spoken to him since. He went to the manor, leaving Simon snoozing under the willow.

I fully understand the young mistress's grievance. The male provides his proper duty, which should be sufficient. But can he let it go at that? No. He feels he must take charge of the female's every action. Flip has tried to goad me into positioning the flock. He must be stopped.

For a few days, it was well worth the effort. My cycle is fading now, and it's time I return to what really matters. Securing my position as house pet.

Men are the most irritating creatures in all the world. Miren sat at her small table, fuming. Nathan had taken over her life. He'd taken her decisions and made them himself. As if they were his to make in the first place.

True, she had planned to emigrate to America. She had worked to secure passage on a ship. But he simply stepped in and took control, and insisted she go when he said, on the ship he chose, and not even by her own volition. She had intended to pay her own way. Instead, he was arranging everything.

He even sent word to her uncle in Maine. How rude! Miren had put off writing to her uncle because she feared if he learned of her destitute state, he would insist on paying her way. "Which is probably the case. He's a man."

Miren's frown deepened until her cheeks ached. Nathan was pushy. No question. He'd decided she was in danger. He'd decided it was his responsibility to protect her. "I never asked for his help." Except for the situation in jail. "And that wasn't a plea for help, either." No, she'd offered him a business proposition.

She'd allowed him to dictate her life because she cared for him. "Love doesn't make a person a slave." Miren rose from her seat. "And I will tell him so!"

She marched to the door. A soft breeze edged in from the loch. Miren studied her flock. Earnest was grazing close beside Blossom. Huntley was standing beside Simon, who slept beneath the willow. Two old men, resting in the afternoon. A pleasant sight.

And one she wasn't ready to abandon. "If I listen to *him*, I won't even see my first lambs."

Love wasn't meant to dominate a woman's common sense. Miren felt sure of that. Molly sat on her haunches beside Flip. Flip crouched as he watched the sheep. Molly looked bored. Maybe a little annoyed. Their eyes met. Miren sighed. She felt sure that Molly sighed, too.

Miren left the pasture and went to the manor. She let herself in. Muffin met her at the door, growling. "Drop!"

Muffin flinched at Miren's harsh tone, then slunk away.

"Nathaniel! I want a word with you. Now!"

Something dropped and shattered. It sounded like a teacup. Lady MacCallum whisked in from the sitting room, braced into full indignation. "Young woman . . . !"

"Where is my 'fiancé'?"

Lady MacCallum's eyes widened into pale blue pools of shocked offense. "The behavior you are exhibiting . . ."

"I'm here." Nathan came up behind her, but Miren didn't startle. She turned to face him, her hands on her hips. His eyes glittered, his lips twitched toward a smile.

"I wouldn't smile if I were you."

"What disturbs you, my precious angel?"

"I want to talk to you. *Alone.*"

Nathan glanced at Lady MacCallum. "If you'll excuse us . . ."

"That girl *must* be schooled in the arts of society at once. It isn't acceptable for you to marry . . ."

Miren seized Nathan's arm and yanked him toward the door. "Alone."

She didn't release him as she marched down the stairs. He wasn't resisting. She would have preferred some resistance. "Miren, my sweet . . . There's something I must know."

She stopped at the bottom of the stairs. "What?"

"Are we headed for another quarrel?"

Her chin elevated. "It seems likely."

His brown eyes shone with delight. A completely unsatisfying response. "In that case, we do need to be alone. You know where quarreling leads us."

A fierce, sputtering growl rose from her chest to her throat, then forced itself through clenched teeth. Miren twitched with fury. "The temptation to strike you is strong, but I will restrain myself."

She turned her back and marched toward the meadow. "Follow me."

She heard Nathan behind her. "The grass is tall, it could work." She knew what he meant. He wanted to make love

237

to her in the grass. Outside. In broad daylight. Maybe if they went over the crest a bit . . .

Miren clapped her hand to her forehead. "What am I thinking?"

Nathan caught up with her. "And if you'd share it with me—"

"I will not." Miren checked their position. "Far enough."

He was smiling. He looked sensual. She wanted to kiss him.

"There are a few things we need to set straight between us."

"Before or after?"

"Before!" She caught a quick breath. "There will be no 'after.' I have decided not to be the source of your idle time anymore. Meaning—"

"I know what you mean." His smile faded, but he didn't look angry. He looked resigned. "What do you want to talk about?"

"You are becoming, well, bossy." She didn't sound as sure of herself as she had when she left the cottage. Curses! He looked so rational.

"Bossy?"

"Yes. You have decided what I should do, and when, and you've taken over, despite the fact I'm quite capable of handling matters on my own. I didn't ask for your help. If you recall, I only offered a business proposition for your consideration. And a good percentage, too. Sixty percent was my original proposal, which was negotiable."

Nathan nodded, then scrunched his face as if straining his memory. "Sixty percent . . . of, what was it your fleece earned . . . twenty-five shillings?"

"That was only my initial income, sir. Much will follow, if I tend my flock to prime readiness."

"If you survive that long. . . . Miren, I understand—"

"You do not! You think you're responsible for me. Well, you're not. True, there was a slight problem with the man who attacked me, but I won't allow fear to dictate my actions. Or you, sir.''

'' 'Sir'? You're calling me 'sir'? You must be angry.''

She didn't answer, assuming that her expression revealed enough.

Nathan nodded again. ''The point of all this is that you don't want to leave Scotland. Is that it?''

Her eyes darted to the side, then back. ''Yes.''

''Why?''

''I'm not ready!''

''Because you want your sheep to prosper, or to stay near me?''

Her cheeks flushed with both embarrassment and anger. ''Your conceit—''

He touched her face, his hand softened a wayward curl. ''Miren, don't lie to me. And please, don't lie to yourself.''

She met his eyes. He looked sympathetic, tender. And he was right. ''I don't want to leave.''

''I know. But it's for your own good.''

''That's not for you to say.''

''It is if I'm the reason you're staying.'' He pulled an envelope from his coat pocket and handed it to her. ''Read it.''

She opened it and pulled out a letter. ''It's from my uncle.''

''It is. He sent word as soon as he received my message. He's been worried about you. In fact, he's been trying to find you. He wants you there, Miren. He says there's a position for you, as governess to his children. He mentions also that your social life should be greatly improved.'' Nathan paused. ''Apparently, his lumbering business attracts young men of means, probably bent on marriage.''

''What a comfort!'' Miren squashed the letter and hurled it at Nathan's head. He ducked, and it fell behind him. ''Tell me, have you selected a husband for me, too? Or do I get some say in the matter?''

''Please be reasonable—''

Miren poked his chest. ''You be reasonable! You don't

239

want me. Fine. I can accept that. You feel responsible, so you've arranged for my safety. Annoying, but also acceptable. But you will not decide how or with whom I spend my life.''

Miren whirled and started toward the cottage, leaving him speechless. She stopped, turned back, and pointed her finger at him. ''You want me gone. I will be gone. We'll carry this charade through to Oban, because I do think your scheme on behalf of your nephew is an honorable one. But when I board that ship, I leave you, and everything to do with you.''

Hot tears burned her eyes. Her chin quivered as she realized how final her words sounded. Nathan didn't argue. He didn't try to stop her. What she'd found in his arms had come and gone, and there could be no looking back.

No looking back. But for a single moment, she couldn't look away. He stood on the meadow crest, the loch breeze in his hair. He looked like a Highlander. Maybe he looked like an Indian, too. And within both, Miren saw something so stubborn, so strong, that she knew no plea would change his mind. He was doing what he thought right. She couldn't change him. She had no right to try.

Miren allowed his image to steal its place in her mind. She would remember him this way always. Tall and strong, and unyielding. So beautiful that her heart ached to look at him. And so distant that she could sooner reach the stars than touch his heart.

Miren turned away and started for the cottage. She didn't look back.

She didn't look back. Not once. She made her way through the bluebells, crossed the road, and swung open the pasture gate. She disappeared into her cottage, and never once looked back in his direction.

Nathan didn't move. He stood alone in the pasture, torn between following her and leaving her as she wished, alone. They had time yet. He hadn't fully acknowledged it to himself, but he had expected their affair to continue. He'd expected her in his arms this night, and every night until she left.

It wasn't fair. He knew that, but he reasoned that if she wanted it, too, their relationship harmed no one. It gave them both something to cherish when their time together passed.

Miren couldn't understand, not fully. Whether she believed it or not, her life was in his hands. He'd brought her into danger, he'd disrupted her life. If he didn't act to protect her, the same fate would befall Miren as befell David. She might one day look at him as his father had done, as a disappointment, as a man who failed her when she needed him. As hard as it had been to see her look at him in anger, disappointment would be worse.

Nathan looked toward the manor, then back at the cottage. He was trapped by his own failings, by what he couldn't be. If he could make her understand . . . He found himself walking toward her cottage, through the gate, and through her sheep.

Simon still slept beneath the willow, dozing past his allotted time. Nathan went to Miren's door and knocked. He heard a long, drawn-out sigh within. "Miren, please let me in."

He expected resistance. A firm, pert "no." He could argue, get mad, and break her door down again. It should be easier this time, weakened by his first blow, with the hinges only braced now. She'd be waiting for him, ready to fight. Assuming she had any pottery left.

And he would lose control and fight back, and they would surrender to the sweetest bliss he'd ever known . . .

The door opened, and Miren stood back for him to enter. The distance separating them widened, but she didn't look angry. She looked resigned.

"I don't want this between us, Miren."

"I know."

She walked to the bed and turned back. Tears glistened on her cheeks. Her hands worked quickly on her dress, and it came off. Nathan stared in amazement as she pulled off her shoes. She removed her corset, leaving only her chemise. She held out her arms to him, and a gentle smile curved her lips. "Come here."

Nathan hesitated. His body responded eagerly, but it felt like a dream. He crossed the room and stood before her, uncertain. Tears stained her cheeks, but she wasn't crying. He gazed down into her eyes and saw all her soul peering up at him. "I love you, Indian."

His throat caught, his chest tightened. He shook his head before he knew what he was doing. Miren placed her hand over his heart. "You're not beholden to me. I'm not asking anything of you." The rhythm of her soft Scottish burr soaked into him, mesmerizing and sweet. He would hear that voice forever after, echoing in his dreams.

"Miren, I never meant to hurt you."

She smiled. Chills coursed beneath his skin. He hadn't known, not fully, how strong she was, how much stronger than he could ever be. "You're not hurting me, Indian. You're giving me something I'd never have had without you." Her hand went to his face, and she ran her fingers to his mouth. "So I'm asking something, after all. I'm asking you to hold me, and do what you did before, and do it for each night to come, until I go on that ship."

Nathan kissed her fingers, but tears stung his eyes. "Will it be enough?" His voice came hoarse and strained, torn from deep inside him.

"Nathaniel . . ." Her smile was wider now, creating dimples in her cheeks. Yet her dark blue eyes still glistened with tears. Mist over a Highland loch. *He used to think she carried Scotland in her eyes . . .*

"Nathaniel, nothing will ever be enough between us. That's the way of it. There's nothing you and I can ever do that will take me deep enough inside you, or enough years to spend at your side. I have days. No, it's not enough. But it's all we have."

She transformed before his eyes. He wasn't sure how, but

242

the last vestiges of her childhood slipped away and left a woman in its place. A practical woman, a woman who knew her own heart, and knew what to ask of her lover.

He knew as he stared into her small, lovely face that this woman wouldn't die if he left her. Her life wouldn't end. She wouldn't hate him for what he couldn't be, or the things he couldn't give. She would go on. She would probably marry, and her husband would cherish her.

"I thought you and I hadn't said enough to each other. But I was wrong. I know what you are and what's inside you." Her hands slipped from his face to his shirt. She carefully unbuttoned his shirt, without popping any buttons this time, and left it hanging open. She placed her palm over his heart. "You're a good man, whether you think so or not. And when I'm gone, part of me stays with you."

It wasn't enough. He wanted all of her. He wanted her laughter, her soft whispers. He wanted her beside him, instructing him about sheep and dogs, and all the things he'd overlooked throughout his life.

And when she went to America, he wanted to be at her side, showing her a world she'd dreamt of. Showing her his father's homeland . . .

The man he saw beside her wasn't himself. Another man held her. A man she could depend on. A man he longed to be, and wasn't. He looked at Miren, but he saw his father at their last meeting. *"You think of your duties when it's too late. What you take into your hands you destroy, because you put yourself before everything"*.

It was true. He would live for himself, enjoying her. And a time would come when she needed him and he wouldn't be there. "Miren, I'll give you what I have, but you deserve more."

She pressed her mouth against his chest, over his heart. She rested her cheek against him for a moment, then looked up. "There is so much sorrow in you. Not for the world would I add to that, nor cause you any pain. I know you think you've

243

failed the people who mattered to you—your father, your brother. But I'm not them, Nathaniel. I want you, not for what you can do for me, but for what we can share. Do you understand?''

"You need me."

"And you're stubborn. That must be the Scots blood in you. Or maybe the Indians, they're stubborn, too?''

"They're stubborn, too."

"Then there's no getting around it. Aye, I need you. But not as my shield, Nathan. I need you''—her lips curved into a seductive smile, her eyes sparkled with sensual play—''as my sword.''

Her hand wormed its way down his chest, over his stomach, and beneath his waistband. Her small, seeking fingers found the tip of his staff and circled it with a light, teasing touch. Nathan's breath caught in his throat as she unbuckled his belt and pulled open his trousers.

"You need me, too." Her voice came low and raspy, altered by desire. She freed his erection, and he stood transfixed as she wrapped her hand tight around its base. She leaned toward him, face tilted up. She stroked him slow, and with such confidence that he thought his knees might buckle.

"I need you." Nathan took her in his arms and kissed her upturned face. He grazed her lips, then bent her back to kiss her throat. She didn't release him. Her caress tightened, turning greedy as she felt his surrender.

Miren backed away and ran her hand slowly from his base to his tip, then back to his chest. "I'll have all of you tonight, Indian. I'm warning you now, so you won't be surprised when it happens.''

As if it were her choice. As if she could decide how deep he penetrated her soft, warm body. Nathan's pulse surged. Maybe she could. "I won't leave you with my child, Miren. That's more important than your virginity." His voice shook. She smiled.

"It's too late for that. You won't impregnate me tonight, or any to come."

Nathan's eyes narrowed in suspicion. "How do you know?"

She looked practical. Sure. "Every female has a cycle. And in that cycle, a time when she's fertile. It's the same for sheep. Different cycles, but it's the same idea. My time has gone by, and by next month I'll be gone."

"You're not a ewe, woman."

She sat back on the edge of her bed, still smiling. She dampened her lips. Nathan felt sure she did it on purpose. Her gaze flicked to his erection, then back to his face. "You're sensitive there."

"Yes."

"To touch . . . to a kiss?"

"A kiss?" His voice came as a squeak. He'd never made such a sound before. Didn't know it was possible.

She took his staff in her hand, bent forward, and kissed its tip. She peered up at him. "A kiss."

His whole body trembled. He'd received a woman's attention this way before. He liked it. Because it was easy, because a distance remained. Miren brushed her lips over his flesh, and the distance shattered. She became part of his flesh. She gave to him because she loved him.

He felt her breath on his skin, swift and warm. "You've taught me much of kissing, Indian. Much that I didn't know. Perhaps there is more I might learn on my own?" She teased him, tantalized him with her intentions. Her fingers wrapped tight around his base, and she ran her tongue around his engorged tip, then brushed her lips softly down its length.

He went weak. His blood raged to fire, but he couldn't move. He just stared down at her, astonished at what she did that came from feminine exploration. She cast her gaze upward, peering at him beneath long, black lashes.

"You like it."

"Yes. I like it." His voice was shaking. His whole body quivered. "I like it."

"You are an agreeable man. I shall test your limits."

Nathan held his breath as she took his staff in her soft mouth. She touched her tongue to his taut flesh, tasting him. She murmured, then took him deeper. He felt dizzy, he sucked in air. She mimicked the rhythmic motion of lovemaking, first slow and gentle, then with more force.

Nathan clasped her head in his hands, his fingers in her hair. *Heaven*. Scotland was heaven. She suckled him fiercely, until his muscles tensed, until his hips moved with her skill. She held him at the brink of release, then withdrew. She looked up at him, eyes sparkling in triumph.

She moved back on the bed, her eyes fixed on his. She pulled off her thin chemise and held out her arms to him. "Deny me now."

A low, shuddering groan erupted from deep within him. Nathan sank onto the bed before her. Her legs parted, bent at the knees. She looked delicate, feminine, as she awaited him. She was smiling like a temptress, her breath rapid and shallow.

He caught her shoulders and she arched toward him, her arms braced on either side of her body. Her breasts jutted upward, firm and taut, strained with her own arousal. He bent to taste her. She tipped her head back and sighed, low and delirious. "Deny me now."

Fire filled him, his erection pulsed with such lust that he thought he might spill himself before he ever fulfilled her. Her nipple hardened into a pink, erect peak against his mouth, she murmured and gasped softly as he took it between his teeth. He laved it with his tongue until she arched still more and whimpered his name.

He knelt between her knees, cupping her breasts in his hands, teasing their peaks with his thumbs. She leaned back, her hair reaching the bed behind her. A long, waving strand coiled over her breast. "You're not what you seemed when

I met you, Miren. You're a goddess. I knew there was something . . .''

She lay back on the bed, waiting. ''This will be your last chance, if you wish to stop me.''

He smiled as he bent over her. ''I never stood a chance, woman, and you know it.''

She concealed nothing from him. No shyness infected her confidence, no fear. Only desire. She lay before him, her body open to his sight. He took in every angle, every sweet curve. Her beautiful face, her neck, her slender arms curved up at the elbows. Her round, firm breasts with small pink nipples. Her narrow ribcage, her waist, to the flare of her hips. Her long legs wrapped around him, but his vision trailed their length, to her trim ankles and narrow feet, to her small toes.

He turned his gaze back to her woman's core, to the soft triangle of dark curls. He touched her, just above, then down. He longed to bury himself deep inside her. She was ready. She wanted him with equal passion. Passion came easily to Miren Lindsay. Maybe he'd recognized that the first moment he saw her.

But he would take his time, please her, show her things she'd never dreamed. Slowly. That was his intention, to direct her pleasure. Miren reached for him, took his staff in her greedy little hand, and squirmed lower so that his tip met her damp curls.

Nathan's eyes grew wide. He realized where he'd gone wrong. He was . . . bossy. Making decisions for her, when she'd already made them for herself. He tried to lead, when she was already walking ahead of him.

''This gives such pleasure.'' She angled her hips so that the underside of his shaft met her sensitive core. She moved so that he rubbed against the small, tender bud. Pleasing herself, and fueling his desire beyond control.

She writhed and gasped, pleased, driving herself toward rapture. Nathan watched her, spellbound. Her bright eyes met his and she smiled, the temptress on the verge of perfect triumph. "Deny me now, Indian."

As she spoke, she maneuvered herself so that his staff pressed against her moist entrance, so that he felt her pulse where they met. She moved around him—restraint became torment. "Deny me."

His muscles quivered, his whole body raged. Desire blazed through him and clouded everything beyond her. "Never, my angel. Never."

Nathan clasped her hips in his hands and drove himself deep inside her. She tensed, shocked by his entrance. Nathan held himself still while she adjusted to his presence inside her. She bit her lip hard, her breath came short. Nathan bent and kissed her forehead, her cheek.

"Hold me, Miren."

She did. She wrapped her arms tight around his neck. "You found it."

Nathan swallowed, fighting to control his need. "What?"

"The spot . . ." She paused to gasp. "The spot you missed before."

Her inner depths softened around him, relaxing as she grew accustomed to his size. She squeezed tight around him, then relaxed again. Testing. She must have liked the sensation, because she did it again.

Nathan moved slightly. She caught her breath, and he paused. "Does this please you?"

"Aye. Verra moch."

"What?"

"I am pleased."

He moved deeper, withdrew, then entered again. She learned quickly. Her hips angled to meet his, she joined his rhythm with ease. She dug her heels into the mattress to increase the friction between them.

Nathan leaned back, opening the space between them so that he could watch her. He knelt between her legs, still deep inside her. She watched him, too. He took her hands as he thrust into her. They moved together, slow, then faster, over and over. He marveled that his restraint hadn't shattered, that he hadn't succumbed to release.

He wanted it to last, one more sweet joining before they finished. He wanted to see her face as her rapture built, as her breaths quickened. Her body quaked around his, she moaned and tensed, her legs clamped tight. She arched toward him, and her fingers gripped his as she twisted in sweet convulsions.

He felt her inner spasms, milking his own release. His pulse mingled with hers, and all the force of his desire poured into her, filling her. The rapture lingered, twitching with little pulses until it finally abated into a numb, contented heat.

Her arms sank to her sides, her legs relaxed on either side of him. She was smiling, taking long, deep breaths. Her eyes were closed. He had never seen anyone so perfectly satisfied.

"Now, my sweet temptress . . . Tell me, did I miss anything of importance this time?"

She opened one eye. She paused as if considering. Nathan frowned as he waited. "No, Indian. I think you found everything."

"Good." He bent to kiss her forehead, then withdrew from her body. She moved over, and he lay beside her. She didn't snuggle into his arms as she had the night before. She allowed him space, because she meant to keep to her word. She'd given him satisfaction, but she would ask for no more.

"Miren . . ." Something formed on his lips, in his mind, but he couldn't say it. *I love you, too*. It entered his head unbidden. She hadn't asked. She didn't expect such a vow. Nathan stopped himself. Cruel words, if he couldn't support them with his life.

He stared at the cubby ceiling. He loved her. It didn't seem possible. It seemed obvious, but not possible. He wanted to protect her from himself, because he loved her and he didn't believe he could fully protect someone he loved.

If he didn't love her, he would keep her with him.

This seemed . . . backwards. He knew it, but his inner voice told him it was true. He loved her, and for this reason he couldn't keep her.

Miren propped herself up on one elbow and kissed his cheek. "Sleep well, Indian."

She rolled over onto her side, cradled her head on her arm, and went promptly to sleep. Nathan stared at her back until his vision blurred. He eased her hair back, then kissed her shoulder. "Sleep well, my love."

He'd waited three years to go to her, knowing all the while it was his intention. He was ready now. For whatever she wanted—marriage, children, a home built together. He knew where she lived, in the rolling, low hills of central Maine. In a small village with white houses and tended lawns. He knew the house where she stayed with her uncle.

He rode his horse to a picket fence, dismounted, and tied it to a hitching post. He went through the low gate and walked to the door. He heard voices coming from behind the house, so he went around instead.

Miren stood with two other women, laughing. She was like the sun, more beautiful than he remembered. She wore a white dress with lace trim. She held a pretty bonnet in her hands, but her long hair fell loose. Nathan pulled off his own hat. Odd, because he never wore a hat . . .

He held it over his heart and started forward. A young man came from the back door of the white house and went to her side. He touched her shoulder, and she turned, smiling. The young man kissed her cheek and slipped his arm around her waist.

Nathan found himself withdrawing a gun. A full-sized rifle. Which was also odd, since he hadn't noticed a gun in his possession until now . . .

She turned to him, and her face lit. She didn't notice the rifle. He dropped it and stood, numb and shocked, as she waved. She came toward him, holding the young man's hand in hers. She was smiling, her eyes glittering like stars. He looked into those eyes, and he saw Scotland's heather-strewn hills, its waterfalls, its dark lochs.

She hugged him and kissed his cheek. She turned to the man at her side. Yes, he was young. He had a pleasant, reliable face, light hair. "Nathan, this is my husband Carl."

Carl? She said his last name, too, but Nathan couldn't make it out. "Trustworthy," perhaps.

The young man smiled, too, and shook Nathan's hand. "I'm so pleased to meet you, Nathaniel. Miren speaks highly . . ." His words drifted, Nathan didn't listen.

"I told Carl everything, of course. About how you were my first lover, how you got me out of jail, and helped me to America."

So casual! Carl just smiled, and Nathan realized with a cold shock that Miren's husband cherished her beyond jealousy, that he even accepted Nathan because he'd helped create what Miren became. Carl shared her life. Nathan was a visitor.

"We're expecting our second child." She looked so happy. Maybe he saw a little pity in her Scottish eyes.

"Second?" His voice seemed strained, as if he spoke from beneath a heavy, wet blanket.

A little boy toddled from the house and stood by his father. He waved what looked like . . . a tomahawk. Nathan took a closer look at the child's face. Simon!

Nathan shot up in bed, his breath as swift as if he'd been running. Miren stirred beside him and woke. She yawned, then glanced at the window. The sun's final light faded, which meant it must be near midnight. "What's the matter? I thought I heard you say something. 'Second,' was it?"

"Didn't waste much time, did you?"

Her eyes wandered to the side. "Hmm?"

"*Carl.*" Nathan spoke the word like a pronouncement of everlasting doom.

Miren squinted as if wondering if she still slept. "Carl who?"

"I didn't catch his last name. It sounded like Trustworthy."

Miren giggled. "Carl *Trustworthy*? Indian, you grow odder by the moment."

Nathan hesitated. A reluctant smile grew on his lips. "Never mind. It was only a dream."

She was fully awake now. Her brow angled. "You had a dream about someone named Carl Trustworthy? Who was he?"

Nathan felt foolish. "It's not important. Go back to sleep."

"I don't think so. And don't be thinking you'll get any sleep until I hear the full story."

"It's nothing. I dreamt you married a man . . . boy, really . . . named Carl . . ." Nathan cleared his throat. Fortunately, the light in the cottage dimmed, so she wouldn't notice if his face reddened. "Trustworthy."

"Oh." Nathan sensed Miren's repressed humor, but she nodded. "Go on."

"There's not much more to it. I was visiting you." He didn't tell her he had come for her, finally ready to make her his wife, only to find she'd married another. "You had a child, incidentally. Looked exactly like Simon, which is what startled me out of sleep. A child shouldn't look like Simon."

"Did he have a beard?"

Nathan laughed. "You know, I think he did."

"Oh, dear. Then I shall avoid all men named Carl Trustworthy."

Molly scratched at the door. Miren cast a pertinent glance at the door, then at Nathan. "Don't ask. I'm going." He got up and opened the door. Molly entered. Flip hesitated on the threshold, then entered, too.

Molly looked a little annoyed, but they curled up side by side at the foot of Miren's bed. Nathan knelt and patted Flip's head. "Love makes a fool of a man, doesn't it, old boy?"

He caught himself too late. *Love*. That remark revealed far more than he intended. He avoided Miren's eyes as he straightened, but she made no comment as he settled back on the bed.

He noticed a strange, sorrowful expression on her face, but he tried not to look at her. "This shouldn't surprise you, but it looks like rain out there."

"No, Indian. It doesn't surprise me at all."

Chapter Fourteen

*Not again . . . More wolves, of the human variety, are creep-
ing about outside the cottage. Several of them. By the scent,
I detect they've even brought their young. I wonder what the
young mistress has done to become a target of their vengeance?*

A low growl woke Miren from sleep. Molly crouched by
the cottage door, fur bristled. Miren's skin went cold with
sudden fright, but she didn't wake Nathan. Flip still slept beside the bed, but he might be too deaf to hear subtle movement outside.

Miren held her breath and listened. Distant thunder rum-
bled, and the rain beat harder on the thatched roof. A flash
of light illuminated the cottage, followed moments later by
another faraway boom. Miren relaxed. Molly never liked
thunderstorms. Generally, she sought position on or behind
Miren during a storm, but tonight she appeared ready to tackle
the enemy.

"It's all right, Molly. It's just rain." Miren kept her voice low to avoid waking Nathan. He reached for her in his sleep, placing his arm over her chest. He murmured softly, and Miren touched his hair.

Molly scratched at the door and whined. Miren sighed, then climbed carefully over Nathan. "If you wanted to go out, just ask. There's no need to be so dramatic." Miren slid her feet to the floor.

Molly whined again, but Miren shivered in the cold. She remembered the wet burst of air that had sent Nathan grumbling backwards the previous night. She seized her heavy nightdress and pulled it on, then wrapped her tartan over her shoulders. She started for the door, but someone knocked.

Miren froze. Molly positioned herself by Miren's feet and growled again. The knock came again. "Simon?" No one answered. "Is that you?"

Nathan sat up in bed. "What is it, Miren? What are you doing out of bed?"

"Someone's out there."

Nathan swung his legs off the bed and tugged on his trousers. "Are you sure?"

The knock repeated.

"Yes."

She trembled as Nathan crossed the room and went to the door. He waved her behind him. "Stay back."

Miren hesitated, then took Molly's collar, and they moved behind Nathan. "Be careful."

"A good suggestion."

Nathan found her corn broom and gripped it as he eased his hand to the door latch. He turned it slowly, then yanked the door open. A man stumbled in, fell to his knees, and swore. It wasn't Simon. His hooded cape fell back around his shoulders as he looked up.

Miren stared in astonishment. The man was completely black. His hair was black, his skin, his eyes. He even wore a black shirt, open at the throat, bound together only by loose

255

ties. He wore long black boots and snug black trousers. Trousers that resembled Nathan's pirate costume.

Nathan was laughing. He held out his hand and helped the black man to his feet. "Quite an entrance."

"You did it on purpose, you bastard." He slapped Nathan on the back, a friendly gesture despite his disgruntled words. "Left me standing in this damned rain until I'm soaked to the bone—"

"You're in now."

The black man turned his eyes to Miren. A slow, wily grin spread across his face. Miren shifted her weight nervously. He was a handsome man, with regal, chiseled features and bright, knowing eyes. "How do you do?"

"Not as well as Nathaniel."

Miren stiffened, then wrapped her tartan tighter around her shoulders. Nathan wasn't wearing a shirt, but he didn't seem embarrassed. "Daniel, this is Miss Lindsay. Miren, Daniel Hayes, my first mate."

"Oh." Miren relaxed, and her curiosity soared. "I'm pleased to meet you, Mr. Hayes."

"Daniel."

Nathan rolled his eyes. "What are you doing here? Did anyone see you?"

"I asked up at the house. Man in a uniform said you were spending your nights down here. On 'guard duty.' Some duty, man."

"Miss Lindsay is in danger."

"I see that . . . from you."

"Not from me."

Miren braced. "A man almost made off with me a few days ago. Nathaniel is here in a protective capacity."

"With his shirt off." Daniel scanned Nathan's disheveled appearance. "And no shoes."

Nathan cleared his throat. "I assume you're here for a reason other than to check on my personal life."

"Which is better by a long stretch than we were thinking."

Daniel turned to Miren. "Left us on the *Half-breed* with nothing to do, orders to stay put. And look what he's up to—"

"Daniel—"

"Get yourself dressed, Captain. You've got company." Daniel nodded toward the door, grinning.

"What's 'company'?"

"We had a little trouble on the ship. Nothing for sure. I'll let her tell you about it."

Nathan pulled on his white shirt, but he only buttoned it once. "Her?"

Daniel went to the door and whistled. Miren heard footsteps. Another man came to the door, stood back, and allowed a woman to enter. A small child clung to the woman's hand, holding a worn cloth rabbit in his other hand.

The woman pulled back her hood, and Miren's breath caught. She was older than Irene MacCallum, but she was far more beautiful. Black hair framed a delicate, lovely face, with clear blue eyes that glittered with intelligence. Chills coursed through Miren, as if she'd seen a ghost arise from the mists. The ghost of her own mother.

Nathan exhaled a breath of annoyance. "Mother, I told you to stay on the ship." His harsh tone surprised Miren. No greeting, no embrace. Instead, a tight frown curved his lips. The woman looked at him in silence, then sighed.

"Nathaniel . . . It couldn't be helped." She was Scottish, but her accent was mild, muted with another language. Miren guessed it was the Iroquois tongue.

The little boy peered up at Nathan as if facing a king. A king who might soon have him beheaded. Miren smiled gently. "How do you do, sir?"

He peeked at her, then Nathan again. "I'm good, miss."

Miren's smile widened. "So am I."

Nathan's mother turned to Miren, and one brow arched. Miren endured an excruciating wave of embarrassment. "Do tell?"

Nathan sighed. "Mother, this is Miren Lindsay." He hesitated. "She is posing as my fiancée."

His mother smiled. "And doing a fine interpretation." She held out her hand to Miren. Miren had no idea what to do with it. Men shook hands. Miren shrugged, then took the woman's hand. She shook. Miren fought the impulse to giggle. "Miren Lindsay? Not—"

"I am Cora Malcolm's daughter."

Glenna gazed long into Miren's eyes, then smiled. "Then our switch wasn't in vain." She glanced at Nathan. "And comes, it seems, full circle."

Nathan looked uncomfortable. "Miren is on her way to America, to join her uncle."

Glenna's face fell. "We shall see." She didn't wait for Nathan's response. She turned to the little boy and bent down to him. "Nat, this is Miren. Her mother and I were the best of friends when I was your age. So you and she are as good as cousins."

Nat looked hopeful. "I didn't think I had a cousin."

"Not until Nathan marries and makes some for you. Until then, Miren will suffice."

Nathan drew an impatient breath. "What are you doing here? If Lady MacCallum learns—"

"She won't. She doesn't know me, Nathan. I was thinking . . ."

Nathan groaned, but Glenna seated herself at Miren's table, looking at ease and as if she planned to stay. Miren decided she liked Nathan's mother. She thought for herself, and seemed sure of her own decisions. Which Nathan didn't seem to appreciate.

"You've placed yourself in danger, Mother."

Glenna's brow arched. "*I've* placed myself in danger? Who is here masquerading as a laird?" She glanced at Miren. "I'm assuming Miss Lindsay knows the circumstances of your arrival."

"I do. And I quite agree. Nathan has placed himself in

extreme danger, and to go fussing on about what those of us choose to do . . .''

Nathan sank into a chair and bowed his head. ''I had you hidden, Mother. You were to stay on my ship until I called for you.''

''Waiting grew tedious.''

Nathan just groaned. Nat bit his lip and buried his head in Glenna's arms. Miren realized the little boy was afraid of his uncle. And no wonder. Nathan hadn't greeted him, he'd barely looked at him. And he wasn't restraining either impatience or his temper.

''*Tedious? Tedious!*'' He started to rise, but Miren seized his arm.

''Nathan, behave. You're alarming Nat.''

Nathan nodded, controlling himself with effort. ''Tedious. That doesn't seem reason to disobey my instructions.''

''Perhaps not.'' Good, Glenna sounded chipper. Miren sat back, relishing the encounter. ''But it was necessary. For one thing—other than the fact that it's unreasonable to expect a small boy to exist on a small ship for an unlimited period of time—someone has made inquiries about your situation.''

Nathan looked to Daniel. ''Is this true?''

Glenna's expression turned fierce. ''I just said it, didn't I?''

Daniel hesitated, then shrugged. ''Near as I can figure, some Englishman was in Oban poking around, asking for 'Nathan MacCallum.' The troubling part is, this fellow seemed to know you left a ship in the harbor. Had a good idea when we arrived, too.''

''Did anyone see him?''

''None of our crew, no. Heard it on the docks. All we learned was he's a light-haired Englishman.''

Miren drummed her fingers on the tabletop. ''Could Brent have gone to Oban when he was supposedly off hunting?''

Nathan nodded. ''It's possible.''

Glenna straightened, victorious. ''There. As I said, we had

to inform you. Also, this is the last place they'd look for little Nat.''

Nathan cast a dark look his mother's way. ''Why do you say that? It seems obvious to me.''

''Nonsense. I have the situation well thought out. I haven't been in Scotland in thirty-one years. No one will recognize me here, so there's no reason—''

The door burst open and Simon charged in, gasping. ''Nathaniel, saw someone . . . lurking.'' His gaze fixed on Glenna, and his voice caught. Miren looked between them, remembering Nathan's claim that the old Scotsman had loved her always. From the utter devotion in his eyes, Miren knew it was true.

Simon's crumpled hat came off, and he held it to his heart. ''Your Ladyship.''

Glenna rose and embraced Simon fondly. She kissed his cheek, smiling as if meeting a long-lost friend. ''Simon. How good it is to see you!''

''What brings you from the ship, Lady?'' Simon's gruff voice altered in Glenna's presence. It softened so much that Miren could imagine him as a young man. Awkward, gentle— his heart in his eyes.

''Please don't be angry with me, Simon. I know you and Nathaniel meant to handle this on your own. But a situation arose that warranted action on my part.''

''Lass, you know I could ne'er be angry with you.''

Glenna cast a pertinent glance Nathan's way. ''If only we all felt that way. Some of us aren't quite so reasonable as yourself, Simon.''

''Lad giving you trouble, is he?''

Glenna sighed. ''And not for the first time.''

Miren chuckled and peeked over at Nathan. He glowered, refusing to meet her eyes. ''He is a troublesome individual at times. I think it's his penchant for *bossiness* that makes him difficult.''

His gaze shifted to her. His frown deepened. Miren

beamed. "How do you expect to keep hidden, Mother? Or do you expect me to explain your presence to Irene Mac-Callum?"

"Neither. Hiding seems . . . surreptitious. So it's necessary that my presence here seem natural."

Nathan groaned. "Mother, you're supposed to be dead. For convenience's sake."

"Of course, if I'm alive, Irene MacCallum's marriage could be proven invalid. But you're right. It is a nest I don't wish to stir."

Miren looked eagerly between them. "Are you going to stay in Scotland, Mrs . . ." She paused. "Lady . . ."

"Glenna. Your mother and I were friends, Miren. Let us be friends, also."

"I would like that." Obviously, Nathan inherited his stubbornness, coldness, and penchant for bossiness from his father. Glenna was a sensible, pleasant woman.

Glenna glanced down at Nat and stroked his soft brown hair from his forehead. "I'll stay, because Nat needs me. Nathan intends to return to his ship . . ." Her voice trailed, indicating she thought another course wiser for her son. "It's not for me to say."

Miren hesitated, but curiosity overcame her sense of propriety. "Where is Nathan's father? Did he come to Scotland, too?"

Glenna looked quickly at Nathan, then sighed. "Taregan remained in America. There is much unsaid between my husband and son."

Nathan frowned. "Too much said."

"Which should be unsaid, by both of you."

Nathan didn't respond, but his jaw set in a stubborn posture. Miren and Glenna sighed at the same time.

"You asked how I intend to conceal myself. Simple." Glenna paused, allowing Nathan's anticipation—or dread—to build. "I shall disguise myself as a housemaid. You will inform Lady MacCallum you've hired a new housekeeper,

which will both explain my presence at the manor and allow
me to fish out any information—"

"No." Nathan rose from the table and turned in a circle.
"No, no. You are not posing as a housekeeper. Madness."

Simon nodded. "I'm forced to agree, Lady. Placing yourself in danger, you are."

Glenna drew a patient breath, while Miren waited intently
to see how the older and wiser woman would handle a man's
difficulty.

"The matter is settled. Tomorrow I will appear as Nathan's
new servant."

Very good. Miren committed Glenna's response to memory. "*The matter is settled.*" She wished she had used that
remark sooner and more often with Nathan herself. "The matter is settled." She hadn't meant to speak aloud, but Nathan
caught her whisper. His eyes narrowed to slits.

"You're teaching my fiancée bad habits."

Glenna turned in her seat and assessed her son beneath a
penetrating gaze. "I thought she was only 'posing' as your
fiancée."

Nathan's face colored. Miren stared in astonishment. He
blushed. Even on his dark skin, it was obvious. Glenna noticed, too. "Well, well."

Nat crawled into his grandmother's lap and yawned. "Does
she belong to Uncle, Gran'mama?"

"A woman doesn't belong to a man, my dear. Two people
choose to spend their lives together because it makes their
lives fuller and happier than they would have been alone. . . .
Or with another person."

Miren sighed, and her eyes misted with tears. "I don't belong to anyone." Her throat tightened. "And no one belongs
to me."

She felt Nathan's gaze as he watched her. She wondered
what he was thinking. Molly sat at her feet, looking pert.
"Molly belongs to me."

Nat's attention diverted to the dog. "Dogs bite."

Miren shook her head vigorously. "Not Molly. She's very good. Like you."

Simon patted the little boy on the head. More of a friendly thump than a pat. Nat winced and hid his face against Glenna. "Help."

Simon didn't seem to notice the boy's fear. "You're safe with this one, lad. Flip won't notice you, but you can pat him if you want. But stay clear of that hairy fiend up at the manor. Take your legs off, it will."

Nat's eyes widened, he glanced at Miren for reassurance. "Hairy fiend?"

Miren hesitated. "Well, I don't think Muffin would take legs . . . at least, not yours. She did go after Blossom's . . ." Miren stopped and collected herself for the child's benefit. "I'd stay clear of her. She's a Pomeranian. Small." Miren held up her hands to approximate Muffin's size. Nat laughed and waved his cloth toy.

"Like my rabbit, Scruffy!"

"But meaner. We won't worry about Muffin. She stays on Lady MacCallum's lap most of the time."

Simon chuckled. " 'Cept when she's going after my shins . . . or your pup . . . or that fat ewe."

Glenna looked wistful. "I had a Pomeranian once. Dear little thing, he was. My grandmother gave him to me when I went to marry Kenneth. He died on the ship to America."

A chill of understanding coursed through Miren. She saw Glenna, terrified and abused, clinging to her tiny dog as her only comfort. To lose the dog . . . Miren's eyes puddled with tears. "I would be so lost without Molly."

Glenna reached across the table and patted Miren's hand. "For the love and friendship they give, we must endure their loss when the time comes."

Miren scratched Molly's ears. "That is true. Our time together has been good." She looked up at Nathan. He was watching her, a strange expression on his face. As if he'd just realized something, and it gave him both strength and sorrow.

As if he was thinking of the time when she would leave him . . .

He looked away, too casual, but Miren knew with a woman's certainty that she had seen into his heart. If he felt that, if he truly cared, why would he send her away? If for safety's sake, why not promise her a life together when the danger passed?

Nat reached his small hand to Molly's head, then withdrew it. Miren forced her attention from Nathan. "If you scratch here, behind her ears, she will be your friend forever."

Nat slid off Glenna's lap and approached Molly. Molly seemed to understand the child's hesitation and sat quietly. He touched her with one finger. "She's soft."

"I brush her coat daily, and she has many baths."

Nat tried a firm pat, which Molly accepted stoically. He scratched behind her ears, and she closed her eyes. Miren sniffed. "She likes children. She hasn't seen many, but I knew she would. Good dog."

Nathan looked impatient. "Daniel, I want you to take my mother and nephew back to Oban. Now, while it's still dark. I'll explain your presence somehow. I'm assuming you offered a reasonable explanation when you inquired at the manor?"

Daniel nodded. "Told 'em I was your brother."

Nathan slumped, but Glenna chuckled. "Daniel was wise in his actions, Nathaniel. He said he was a sailor on a transport ship, here for the purpose of delivering some of 'Laird MacCallum's' possessions from America."

"What 'possessions'?"

"Myself and my grandson, of course. Your housekeeper from America."

Nathan glared. "They know MacCallum's son was a farmer, Mother."

"He might have been a well-to-do farmer. Since we're supposed to be American, Nat's accent won't be a problem. As I said, we thought it out carefully. The matter is settled."

"Nothing is settled, Mother. Brent Edgington, or another man, is questioning my story. What if he learns that Kenneth's real son was David, and that he died? What if he learns David had a son of his own? Wouldn't it be convenient to learn the rightful heir is already in the manor, posing as the housekeeper's grandson?"

Miren winced at Nathan's blunt assessment. Nat peered up at Nathan with wide eyes. "Will he burn me, too?"

"No!" Miren took the boy's small hand. "Your uncle is . . . a worrywart. You should see what he's put me through. Afraid I'll be struck by lightning, fall into a pit, get lost in the forest. I don't know how he ever survived a war."

Nathan's mouth dropped, but Nat eyed her doubtfully. "Uncle won the war, cousin. He is brave. My father gave me his name so that I would be a hero, too."

Miren's eyes puddled with sudden tears. "Yes, I know. But all heroes and brave men are worrywarts. That is how they win wars."

Nat fell silent, considering Miren's interpretation of heroism. After a moment, he nodded. "I will be a worrywart, too."

Glenna met Miren's eyes and smiled gently. "All men are, my dear."

Simon set his hat to the table. "I'll keep a watch on them, Nathaniel. Put them in the servants' quarters next to mine." He paused and nodded respectfully to Glenna. "With your permission, of course, Lady."

Glenna took Simon's hand. "That sounds good, Simon. With you near, we will be safe. You've never let me down before, and I know you never will."

"Upon my life, Lady."

Nathan appeared both disgruntled and stubborn. "It won't work."

Miren and Glenna sighed at the same time. Miren adopted the other woman's assured manner. "It will. You may have forgotten, Nathan, but we're all traveling to the Highland

Games in a few days. Lady MacCallum is going with the duke, and Brent will meet us there. Your ship is in Oban. The Games are in Oban, too.''

Nathan looked as if he wanted to argue, but instead saw benefit in her words. "It could work, maybe. I'll put you on the ship . . . Daniel will take my mother and the boy to a port in England. Bristol, perhaps. Then escort Miss Lindsay to America."

Daniel folded his arms over his chest. "America? Do I drop her just anywhere, or did you have a specific port in mind?"

Miren kept her expression clear, but her heart flooded with unhappiness. He still meant to send her away. Why had she thought he could change his mind? "I am going to my uncle in Maine."

Daniel nodded. "We'll take her to Portland, then."

Nathan avoided Miren's eyes. "Go back to Oban and prepare the ship. I want it ready to leave at a moment's notice, but don't let anyone know you're about to set sail. In fact, make it look like you're doing repairs and can't set off for a few more weeks. Pass the word around Oban. I don't want Edgington a step ahead this time."

Nat rested his small elbow on Miren's knee. He liked her. Miren's heart warmed with a feeling she'd never known. *I want children, I want to be a mother.* She felt motherly, knowing that the little boy needed her, and that her instincts were strong.

She would go to America, because Nathan was stubborn, and because he didn't want her for a wife. Maybe she would meet another man. Maybe she would care for him, too. Enough to raise a family. As the thought formed, a dark pit opened inside her. No matter where she went, or how many years passed, Nathan would be inside her heart's core.

She wouldn't be like Glenna, because Glenna had overcome her tragic situation and found love beyond. No wonder she handled the men with such ease. She'd found her own strength, and lived her life as she wanted.

Glenna looked around the cottage. Her gaze fixed on Miren's bed. Miren's cheeks warmed with embarrassment. The sheets were tangled, the pillows close together. "Nathan sleeps on the floor!" Her voice came high and shrill. All eyes turned toward her. Miren bit her lip at the lie. "Most nights."

She wanted to die, to sink into the floor and disappear. Daniel coughed and cleared his throat, Simon issued a grumbling curse, and Nathan shook his head. Glenna took Miren's hand and squeezed it tight. "Then my son is an idiot."

A squeak came from Miren's parted lips, but she could muster no more.

Glenna eyed Daniel. "You gentlemen should be returning to Oban, shouldn't you?"

"Tonight?"

"That would seem wise."

Daniel looked disappointed, but he shrugged. "Suppose you're right. Sorry to miss it, Captain. Like to see you squirm." He doffed his sailor's cap, then went to the door. The other man who had come in with Glenna doffed his cap, too, but he didn't speak.

Nathan went to the door, too. "We'll reach Oban in a few days. Be sure everything is ready for a quick departure. But keep it quiet."

"You said that." Daniel cast a pertinent glance Miren's way. "You're right, miss. He is a worrywart."

The two sailors left, and Glenna stood up. "Daniel is charming, isn't he? Davidson is a mute, but quite a fine cook." She adjusted her skirt. "We shouldn't ascend to the manor until morning. Nathan must introduce me formally to Lady MacCallum."

Simon replaced his hat and bowed to Glenna. "I'll prepare your new room myself, Your Ladyship. I'm thinking you belong in the master's quarters, but—"

Glenna's face darkened. "I will never go in that room again." She caught herself, and her gentle smile returned. "Thank you, Simon. The servants' quarters will be more than enough. Living on the reservation has equipped me for small spaces.''

Simon bowed again. ''As you wish, Lady.'' He opened the door and paused, but he didn't look back. His shoulders straightened, and he went out into the rain.

Glenna watched him go. ''So good a man . . .'' She sighed and turned her sharp attention back to Nathan. ''We have only a few days before the Games. Incidentally, Nat and I will accompany you to the festivities. He will enjoy watching the caber tossing in particular.''

Nat peered up at his grandmother. ''What's caber . . . What is it?''

Glenna spread her arms wide. ''A huge man, like a giant, throws a tree to see how far it goes. Then other *huge* men try to beat him!''

''Men as big as Uncle?''

''Much bigger.'' Glenna puffed her chest and cheeks. ''Men with chests three times the size of Nathaniel's.''

Nathan frowned, insulted. ''Bulk doesn't make a man strong.''

Glenna eyed him playfully. ''Perhaps you'll try your hand, my dear. The Games, as I recall, are open to all.''

''A man's value isn't determined by how far he can pitch a tree, Mother.''

Miren tapped her fingers on the table thoughtfully. ''There's always haggis throwing.''

''What's that?''

''Tossing sheep entrails as far as you can. The winner earns great esteem.''

Nathan grimaced. ''For a Scottish pastime, it doesn't surprise me. I will attend these Games as a spectator, not a competitor.''

Miren clicked her tongue. ''A shame. When I was a small child, I won a medal for my rendition of the Highland fling.''

''A sight I'd enjoy watching.''

"I'm too old to take part now, Nathaniel. The costumes reveal too much, they say."

"Then you'll show me in private."

Tension coiled between them. They recognized it at the same time, and both averted their eyes from each other. Glenna watched them with a too-knowing smile. "Well, well."

"As for you, Mother, posing as a housekeeper is out of the question."

"Indeed? Where do you intend to store me until we depart for Oban?"

"I could hide you in the byre."

Glenna rose to her feet, ready to fight. She placed herself before her son and straightened her back. She wasn't a tall woman, but she held her own well. Miren studied Glenna's stance for future reference. Chin high, eyes narrow. Feet planted firmly apart.

Miren stood up, too. She copied Glenna's posture and faced Nathan, too. "You will resume your position on the floor, as will I. On the other side of the room, of course. Your mother and Nat can have the bed."

Nat hopped up and seized Miren's hand. "I want to sleep on the floor, too!"

"Very well. We'll make you a spot beside mine." She paused, keeping her face serious. "Molly likes to sleep beside me. She might like to use your legs as a pillow. Do you mind terribly?"

The little boy's eyes widened like saucers. "The floor, the floor! I'm a pillow!" He danced around, kicking.

Nathan rolled his eyes. "Just for tonight." He shook his head. "Madness."

Miren straightened. She kept her chin high, her eyes narrowed. She adjusted her feet farther apart. "The matter is settled."

Chapter Fifteen

I have a new playmate. A small human named Nat, who takes particular interest in scratching my ears, and even allowed me to sleep with my head on his feet. I like having young around. A small person to watch over, to keep out of trouble.

I learned from Flip how to keep one's charge in line. Herding a child isn't easy, but it can't be as bad as herding Blossom. Also, a small human is much more interesting.

Nathan has taken the new woman—whom I judged by scent to be his dam—to the manor. The young mistress and I have Nat in the pasture, where he is chasing sheep. Flip keeps herding them back into place. Blossom is thoroughly peeved, but Earnest stands his ground. He pawed the earth once in warning, and Nat took off after Huntley instead.

Huntley didn't have the energy to flee, so Nat is now brushing what's left of his wool. I may have to intervene. If anyone is brushed, it should be me.

*   *   *

"Lady MacCallum, may I present our new house-keeper . . ." Nathan stopped mid-sentence. He'd gone through with his mother's mad scheme and agreed to introduce her as his housekeeper. And neglected to think of a suitable name.

Glenna bowed twice and hopped to his side. "Call me Poppy, Your Ladyship."

Nathan cringed inwardly. Glenna looked ridiculous. She'd even blackened one tooth. Her hair was done up in an off-center bun, and she wore a dress several sizes too large for her body. He felt sure she'd padded her chest, too.

Irene MacCallum glared at her in disgust. "Poppy."

"Ain't my full name, you understand. I was born Poppen-such Frittater."

The word popped into her head and came out her mouth. Nathan wondered how he'd reached adulthood with a mother so bereft of good sense.

Glenna looked proud. "It's an American name."

Nathan repressed a groan. Irene looked pained. "A house-keeper must maintain certain standards, Laird MacCallum. Mrs. . . ."

Glenna nodded helpfully. "Frit-*tah*-ter, ma'am."

"Mrs. Frittater may have served adequately in America, but—"

"I did, at that, ma'am! Poor young Nathaniel, he didn't know squat about housekeeping. Had just enough money to bring in help. Even let me bring my grandson along. My daughter's boy. Don't have the slightest notion who his father was."

Nathan cleared his throat. "Mrs. . . ." He paused, glaring at his mother for choosing such a ridiculous name. "Poppy is surprisingly skilled at housekeeping or I wouldn't have sent for her. I'm *sure* you'll find her work of a high quality."

"I'll start right now! Where's the broom closet?" Glenna spun around, waved her arms, and took off toward the pantry. "Never you mind, Lady MacCallum. I'll hunt it up on my own. You just relax. Maybe I'll fetch you a cup of tea from the kitchen. I'll have your whole lovely home fixed up in a twitch. You won't recognize the place, I promise."

Lady MacCallum looked white and drawn. "This is unacceptable . . ."

Nathan couldn't argue. Glenna must have encountered Muffin in the pantry, because a fury of barks erupted. Something barked back. Nathan closed his eyes. Glenna. Muffin growled. Glenna growled, too.

"What is that woman doing to poor Muffin?"

Two barks mingled, then silence. Nathan held his breath. Glenna came around the corner, smiling. Carrying Muffin in her arms.

Lady MacCallum's mouth dropped in unison with Nathan's. For the first time, Muffin seemed relaxed. The little creature actually looked pretty when she wasn't snarling. Glenna patted her with a firm, long stroke. "Such a good dog!"

Irene seized the dog from Glenna's arms. "What have you done to her? All that growling and barking . . ."

"A Pomeranian needs to respect someone before they'll accept them."

"How"—Irene's voice lowered nearly to a growl—"how would you know?"

Glenna shrugged. "Seen a few in my time. Fat old lady up in Syracuse had a pair. Used to do housekeeping for her, and she taught me a thing or two."

Nathan stared at his mother in amazement. She'd never been to Syracuse. He had to admire the agility of her brain. Another thought struck him. He had to keep her away from Miren. Miren learned too quickly. After a few days in Glenna's company, they'd be staging an insurrection and demanding Scotland's sovereignty from England. He refused to allow himself to speculate on his own fate.

"If you're settled, Poppy . . ."

"You head on back to your fiancée, Laird. I'll turn your house upside-down and set it to rights. Don't you worry."

Nathan headed for the door. "I wouldn't *dream* of worrying." The footman held open the door, looking unusually happy. Nathan left, assuming the manor would be rubble by nightfall.

He headed for Miren's cottage. She seemed peaceful compared with his demonic mother. Until he remembered she'd called him a worrywart. And suggested he partake in haggis throwing.

Nathan stopped in the road. The more time he spent in her company, the more his wayward love deepened. She was playing with Nat in the pasture. The boy ran in circles with Molly. The ewes looked annoyed, but Huntley stood solemnly. Nat fed the old ram sprigs of grass as he passed.

Simon oversaw the procedure, chortling and slapping his thighs. Miren sat cross-legged on the grass, and Nat jumped into her lap. She wore her dark blue dress, her hair tied loosely at her neck, falling over one shoulder.

The sky was gray after the rain, but the day was warm. Tiny openings of blue fought the clouds, lost, and tried again. The sheep grazed at the far end of the pasture, avoiding the child.

David's child. Nathan hadn't returned for David's wedding, nor for the birth of his son. He'd been at sea. When given leave, he chose to spent it cavorting in Louisiana rather than visiting his family. The last time he saw David was when he left for the army. He was sixteen, David twenty.

David told him he was proposing to a girl he'd met at school. He wanted Nathan to wait for his wedding, but Nathan refused. David wrote often. Nathan answered once, and forgot to thank David for naming the baby after him. David's wife died miscarrying their second child. When Nathan returned to New York after the war, he'd intended to visit his brother, but his fight with Taregan drove it from his mind.

He'd brought David's son to Scotland, but he didn't know the boy. Apparently, the child had heard of him. David had built him up to heroic proportions. Proportions he didn't deserve.

Miren conversed easily with the child. Nathan had no idea what to say. On the ship from America, he'd avoided the boy, but the child followed him. He'd lost his temper, ordered the boy away, and scared him half to death in the process. It wasn't that he disliked children. He'd found himself caring too much, wanting to allow the boy the helm, to carry him around on his shoulders . . . And watching as Daniel and the other crewmen entertained the child instead.

He refused to get that close to anyone. Not a child whose need was so great. Nor a woman who hid her need, yet still declared her love.

They were playing together in the field. Nathan was alone. He was sending her away. He would secure the child's inheritance, then leave himself. He thought of his dream, of returning to Miren only to find she was lost to him forever.

It would be too late, even if she waited for him. He would never be the kind of man she deserved.

He wouldn't allow his nephew to grow dependent, either. He wouldn't play a father. He couldn't. It would be cruel, and if he failed a child . . .

He had a purpose in Scotland. To keep his family safe, to insure that his brother's child had a future. Brent Edgington seemed the most likely threat. Before they met again in Oban, Nathan wanted information. Brent's hunting trips needed to be scrutinized. Nathan considered who might know more.

Brent had mentioned hunting with the Duke of Argyll. A place to start. Nathan took a final look at Miren and the child, then headed for the stables.

"Where's Nathan going?" Miren saw him astride a large gray horse, heading down from the stables. "And should he be going alone?"

Simon tossed a makeshift ball to Nat and shrugged. "Lad knows what he's doing."

Miren hurried to the pasture gate, catching Nathan before he passed. "Nathan! Where are you going?"

He halted, but he didn't look eager for speech. Nat climbed the stone wall and ran to the horse. He patted its shoulder and looked up at Nathan. "That's a fine hoss, Uncle. My papa set me up on his saddle when he was riding. Can I ride with you?"

"No."

Miren shook her head. Nathan seemed to go out of his way to intimidate his nephew. The little boy shrank back, hurt. Nathan must have noticed. His face looked taut, he glanced down at the boy. Maybe he would soften his tone, apologize. Promise a ride later.

"Go back to the pasture before you get stepped on."

Or not. Miren sighed. Nat scurried back over the wall, tears in his eyes. Miren turned to glare at Nathan. He urged his horse forward.

"I'm going to Inveraray Castle. I'll be back late. The duke left me an open invitation. I intend to take him up on it."

"Why?"

Nathan's lip curved in annoyance. "He may have some relevant information about Brent."

"I don't see why it would take all day to find that out."

Nathan ignored her, probably because he had no good answer. "Simon, keep an eye on my mother." He started off, then slowed the horse again. "She's calling herself Poppensuch Frit-something."

Nathan rode away, leaving Miren confused and angry. "He pushes everyone away. Why?"

Simon came up beside her. "Don't have a speck of a notion, lass. Ask his mama. She'll be knowing."

Miren glanced at Simon. "Poppensuch Frit-something?"

Simon grinned. "She's got a Celt's brain and no mistake. Too much imagination and not enough fear. That's something that don't change over the years. I'm thinking she's got it more now than she did when she was a lass. Some women, they're born like flowers, and they fade. Poppensuch, she gets better every year.''

Nathan didn't return for dinner. Irene had informed Glenna that the workday was ended, and Glenna returned to Miren's cottage to eat. She brought a large shepherd's pie, which she doled out to Miren, Simon, and Nat in hefty portions. Miren noticed that Glenna didn't adhere to Lady MacCallum's strict manners, and all four dove into their pie with glee.

''Good pie, isn't it?'' Glenna wiped her mouth on her sleeve, then wiped Nat's with a napkin. ''The manor cook and I have become friendly. They're all eager for companionship up there. Old Irene doesn't allow for 'fraternizing.' ''

Miren frowned. ''Nathan should take over.''

Simon plunged his spoon into the pie and took another helping. ''The lad don't pay attention to the goings-on up there. Got his eye pegged on Brent and the old lady.''

''Which is why we have to pay attention for him.'' Glenna removed a turnip from her stew, shuddered, and set it aside. ''Turnips and I do not get along.''

Miren eyed the turnip favorably. ''I have an affection for turnips.''

Glenna passed her the turnip and explored the pie for other offensive items. She seized a piece of tough meat and gave it to Molly.

''I have learned several things from the cook. First, when Irene came to the manor, she fired all Kenneth's former staff. Even Hodge, who had been butler when Kenneth's father was laird.''

Miren's face puckered as she considered Irene's actions. ''Why would she do that?''

''She said the old staff 'couldn't be trusted.' Ridiculous, of course. What is also interesting is that she's fired the whole house staff several times since. No one has worked at the manor more than five years.''

"Except Grainger?"

"Grainger?"

"The coachman. He's been here since she married Laird MacCallum. He told me so himself."

Glenna leaned forward in her seat. "Interesting! Why would she fire the entire staff, for no reason but suspicion, yet keep the coachman?"

"Perhaps she has reason to trust him."

"She had no reason to distrust the others, according to the cook."

Simon sat back in his seat. "Grainger is a Yorkshireman, but that in itself don't make him untrustworthy. Yorkshire is a lot closer to Scotland than the rest of England. I'd be having more suspicions if he came from London."

Glenna took a sip of water. "Being from London isn't, in and of itself, suspicious." Miren noticed that Glenna didn't sound convinced. "Nor is being from Yorkshire. But there's something else I noticed today. Though she tries to disguise it, occasionally Irene's accent slips—when she's annoyed, such as when I broke one of Kenneth's priceless vases—indicating that she, too, is from Yorkshire."

"Is that significant?"

"It might be. What do you think of this Grainger, Simon?"

"Seems agreeable. Haven't had much to do with him since we got here. Drives us around, if he ain't driving Brent. He takes young Edgington off to his trips, but that ain't saying too much. Boy could be fooling him, too."

Miren ran over her conversation with Grainger, hoping to see new, possibly threatening meaning behind his words. Nothing came to light. "I spoke to him when he brought me from jail."

Glenna's brow angled doubtfully. "Jail?"

Simon shook his head and sighed. "Girl got herself in trouble after her sheep went rampaging over Garrison Campbell's lawn."

"I see." Glenna clucked her tongue in a commiserating

fashion. "Campbell was always difficult." She paused. "How did you meet Nathan?"

Miren hesitated. "My sheep stopped his coach, and later, he got me out of jail."

"You'll tell me more later. But now, what do you know about this Grainger?"

"I liked him well enough. He did say something odd, though. He said he was wild in his youth." Miren paused, straining her memory. "He said, 'A man's life gets stretched out of his control sometimes. But if he uses his head, he can get where he needs to be.' What do you make of that?"

Glenna tapped her lip. "He wanted to be here, working at the manor, obviously. Somehow he won Irene's confidence, and he's stayed on."

"I wonder why he'd want to. His quarters are in the stables, aren't they, Simon?"

Simon nodded. "It's just one room, with a rickety metal cot for sleeping. He invited me over for a nip of Scotch. I'll tell you, he ain't doing it for the money or the living space."

Glenna placed another portion of pie onto Nat's plate, which he quietly slipped to Molly. Glenna pretended not to notice, and Miren smiled. "How do Irene and her son treat him?"

"From what I've seen, Brent ignores him on the whole, but he's friendly enough. Irene, she just passes out orders. Ain't friendly or cold. Treats him like a servant—they ain't close."

Glenna considered the matter thoughtfully, then placed her plate on the floor for Molly to clean. "I can't imagine Irene being close to anyone, even her son. I noticed there aren't any paintings of him in the house, although a prominent cabinet displays his medals and trophies from croquet matches."

Miren sighed. "I noticed that, too. Lady MacCallum would boast about her achievements and who he socializes with, but she doesn't care about Brent himself. She's the same way about Muffin."

"Poor Muffin."

Miren and Molly looked at Glenna at the same time. "Have you met Muffin?"

"Dear little thing. She followed me all over the house, when Irene wasn't adjusting her bow or stuffing her onto that wretched cushion."

Miren and Simon exchanged a doubtful glance. Simon cleared his throat. "Didn't sink her fangs into you?"

"Of course not! Pomeranians are the sweetest dogs. They're very bright. When they're nervous or scared, they do tend to go on the attack. But if they're cared for properly, if they feel secure, they're good dogs. They sense their owner's emotions with great sensitivity, and act accordingly."

Glenna stopped and sighed. "My little Squire knew what I was feeling, and when I'd had a bad time of it, he'd come to me . . ." Her voice trailed. "That was long ago, but in those early years, knowing someone cared . . ."

Miren's eyes flooded with hot tears. "Like Molly."

"Like Molly. A girl needs a dog."

Nat held his cup for Molly to drink from. "A boy, too."

Nathan hadn't returned by midnight, and Miren's fear soared. She'd gone to the manor with Simon to settle Glenna and Nat into their room, then walked back expecting Nathan to be waiting for her.

He wasn't. Even Simon seemed worried. He stood out by the pasture gate, watching the road. Miren paced in her cottage, then joined Simon by the gate.

"Should we go looking for him?"

"If he ain't back by morning."

"Morning! Simon, that's too long."

"What do you suggest we do, girl? Head up to Inveraray Castle and ask the duke if someone's put a pinch on our Indian?"

Miren puffed an annoyed breath. "I wouldn't phrase it that way."

Hoofbeats silenced their conversation. Nathan appeared along the darkening road, his reins slack, humming. Miren's relief turned to suspicion. "What has he been up to?"

"Whiskey, by the look of it."

Nathan drew closer, and Miren's eyes narrowed to slits. His coat was unbuttoned, his cravat hung loose around his neck. "This is disgraceful."

Nathan swung his leg forward over the saddle and jumped to the ground. He didn't stumble, so Miren guessed the whiskey hadn't destroyed his agility. He led the horse to the gate, his dark gaze fixed on her eyes.

"I knew I couldn't leave you two alone." Nathan cackled to himself, then handed the reins to Simon. "Since you're headed in that direction anyway . . ."

His eyes never left Miren's face. Her heart beat too fast, her knees felt weak. "What have you been doing?" Her voice came higher than she intended.

"I'm not heading in any direction, boy!"

"The stables, Simon. If you don't mind."

"I mind! Oh, hell . . ."

"Thank you."

Simon grumbled incoherently, climbed the stone wall, and led the horse up the road.

Miren took a quick breath. "He's not your servant."

"And you're not my fiancée, but that doesn't stop us, does it?"

"You're speaking beneath the influence of whiskey."

"Only partly."

"I wouldn't have thought the duke was a drinking man."

"A drinking and pouring man, my dear." Nathan climbed the stone wall and took her arm. "When I left, he was sleeping soundly beneath his chair."

Miren grimaced, but Nathan bent and kissed her cheek. "And they say Indians can't drink. I am riding, walking—in complete control—while my erstwhile Scottish companion lies dreaming of bottles."

"Your head will be sore in the morning."

"I'm fine. Have you missed me?"

"Not at all." Miren stopped, slipped her arms around his waist, and kissed his chin. "Yes."

Nathan smiled and bent to kiss her. He stopped and glanced toward the cottage. "Are we alone?"

"Your mother and Nat are in the manor with Simon."

"Good."

Miren's heart took odd skips, her breath came shorter than usual. "Are we going to do what we did last night?"

"Over and over, until we can't move."

"Oh."

Nathan held open the cottage door. Molly abandoned Flip with the sheep and took position beside the bed. "After you, angel."

"Uncle." A small, tentative voice came from behind Nathan. He startled, and Nat clasped his cloth rabbit over his face.

"What are you doing here?"

Miren yanked Nathan aside and knelt, holding out her arms to the boy. "It's all right, Nat. You scared your poor uncle, that's all. Remember I told you, he's a worrywart. Jumpy."

Nat took a hesitant step toward Miren, watching Nathan as if he might bite. "I had a bad dream."

"Did you tell your grandmother you were leaving, Nat? She'd be scared to find you gone."

"Gran'mama was sleeping. I wanted you."

Molly positioned herself at the child's side. Miren took him in her arms and kissed his forehead. "What did you dream?"

Nathan stood in the doorway, impatient. "We'll take him back to his room, and he can tell you there."

Nat gripped Miren's sleeve. "I don't want to go back. There's a hairy fiend in the house."

"It's just Muffin. Simon was exaggerating."

Nat shook his head vigorously. "No, there's *another* hairy fiend." Nat paused and lowered his voice conspiratorially. "I think it's in the broom closet.''

Miren repressed a smile and nodded stoically. "I never liked the broom closet in my father's house, either.''

Nathan rolled his eyes. "There's nothing in the closet.''

Miren angled her brow. "Brooms.''

Glenna came hurrying down the road, her black hair loose around her shoulders. She saw Nat and clasped her hand over her heart. She didn't go through the gate. She climbed over the stone wall and raced across the pasture to the cottage.

"There you are! Nat, you scared me!''

Nat bowed his head, but Glenna didn't seem angry. "He'd taken his Scruffy, so I knew he'd gone off on his own.''

Nathan folded his arms over his chest. Miren considered his posture defensive, but why a child's presence disturbed him, she didn't know. "Take him back to your room, Mother. Keep a closer eye on him, too. We don't want him wandering—''

Nat started to cry. "There's a hairy fiend—''

"You can stay with us." Miren glanced over the boy's shoulder. "Can't he, *Uncle* Nathan?''

"No.''

Miren stood up, holding Nat's hand in hers. "The matter is settled.''

Nathan didn't argue, but he didn't look happy. Maybe he was disappointed because their night of passion had been disrupted. She was, too. But Miren sensed there was more to Nathan's reluctance than thwarted lust. Nat made him nervous, tense. Odd, because David's son was a likable, easygoing little boy.

Glenna touched Miren's arm. "Well done." She spoke quietly so Nathan wouldn't hear. Nat made a wide berth around Nathan and entered the cottage with Molly at his side. Nathan hesitated, then followed him in.

Miren sighed. "I would have thought he'd like children.''

"He does, Miren. And he's good with them, too. Or at least, he was. When he was sixteen, he rounded them up in our village and enlisted them in all sorts of trouble. Every child in the village worshiped him.''

"Then I don't understand. Why is he so abrupt with Nat?''

"Nat is a good boy. Very much like his father. David adored Nathaniel. Though David was older, Nathaniel was always leader. Always the one in control, who decided what they'd play . . . Into how much trouble they'd get. Do you understand, Miren? Nathan has always been strong. He thinks other people's lives are up to him.''

Miren frowned. "I've noticed that.''

Glenna laid her hand on Miren's shoulder. "It pleases me to see that he's found a good match.''

"He doesn't want a good match. He doesn't want anyone.''

"He is afraid to want. Maybe he's trying to punish himself for what he considers his failures. Sometimes I look at my son and I see a Scotsman, stubborn and ready to fight. That's what sent him into the American war. But in many ways, he is his father's son. He's too proud, and what he believes is deep. Taregan came from the Clan of the Wolf. They are hunters, Miren. To be successful, a hunter's vision is narrow and sharp.''

Miren looked at her feet. "Was Nathan's father so difficult?''

"They are much alike, but I had an advantage you lack. I was ten years older than my husband. And I used every year in my favor to hold my own with him.''

Miren's hopes deflated. She was twenty-four, Nathan twenty-seven. "Nathan has three years in his favor.''

"You'll have to find something else, then. My son has often been a mystery, even to me. And I know he is suffering. Go on as you see fit, Miren. He must come to his strength on his own. His heart must war with his pride, and win. It is a battle he must wage alone. His pride is strong. But a time may come, one day, when what he wants means as much.''

Nathan appeared in the doorway, frowning. "This was your idea, woman. Come here and tend this child.''

Miren sighed. "And I thought Simon was grumpy."

Glenna patted Miren's shoulder. "I wish you well, my dear. Good night, Nathaniel!"

"Mother."

Glenna headed back toward the manor, and Miren entered the cottage with Nathan. Glenna's words comforted her, but the hope offered seemed slim. She couldn't influence Nathan's decision. She couldn't make him want to keep her, nor could she soften his heart toward a small child who admired him.

Nat sat on Miren's bed with Molly. He clutched his cloth rabbit tighter when Nathan entered the room. "I will be good, Uncle."

Nathan nodded, but didn't answer. Miren tucked Nat into her bed and pulled her quilt over Scruffy. Molly adjusted her position on the boy's feet. Nathan left the cottage without speaking, but Miren sat on the edge of the bed.

"Do you feel better now, Nat?"

"Molly will protect me from the hairy fiend." Nat yawned. "And Uncle."

Miren wasn't sure if Nat meant Nathan would protect him, too, or if Molly would protect him from Nathan. She didn't dare ask. "Sleep well, Nat. We'll all protect you from hairy fiends, I promise. And in a few days we'll go in a coach to the Highland Games. They're such fun! When I was a little girl, I danced and won a medal. My father raced when he was a boy. He wasn't big enough for caber tossing or the hammer throw. And the bagpipes . . . they are so beautiful . . ."

Nat's eyes drifted shut, a smile on his small face. Miren watched him sleep, and her heart expanded with love. He was small. His nose was small, his hands were small. He looked so alone. He was a handsome little boy, with soft, light brown hair and green eyes. Miren wondered if he resembled his father or his American mother.

She wondered if he wanted to be in Scotland, to grow up

as a laird, or if he missed his home in America. What would he do with a house full of servants, and no parents? Glenna would stay with him, but he needed a father. Someone to teach him riding and fishing and all the things boys do.

Perhaps he would grow up on his own. She hoped he wouldn't be like Brent, desperate to please, to fit in. Maybe this desperation drove Brent to murder, because he feared the loss of his inheritance. Without his inheritance, Brent would be lost. A tragic reason for destroying another man's life.

Miren kissed Nat's forehead, then quietly left the cottage. Nathan was standing across the pasture, staring out over the loch. Miren picked her way between her grazing sheep and went to his side.

She touched his shoulder. "Are you angry?"

He didn't look at her. "No."

"I'm sorry our . . . plans were disrupted."

He nodded, but he didn't speak. Miren wanted to hold him, to comfort him. She knew he needed comfort, but she also sensed it wouldn't be welcome. "When do we leave for Oban?"

"The duke is leaving tomorrow. He's sending a coach for us, and he arranged accommodations in Oban."

"Molly, too?"

"Yes." Nathan glanced down at her. "I assume you want your dog with you in America."

"She has to come with me." Miren glanced toward Flip. "I hope they don't miss each other too much."

"They'll survive."

"And my sheep. Blossom . . ." Miren fought tears. "I won't see Earnest's first lambs. I suppose they'll do well enough without me." Miren looked toward the manor. "I hope you get everything worked out. So that Nat gets to live here. Are you going to stay with him until he's settled in?"

Nathan hesitated. "My mother will stay. I'll return to my ship once I've made the arrangements for his inheritance."

"What about the hairy fiend?"

A faint smile appeared on Nathan's lips. "I'll have it shot."

Miren tried to smile, but tears filled her eyes. "How will I know how it all turns out?"

He glanced at her. "Are we talking about the fate of the hairy fiend or something else?"

"About our . . . your investigation, Dr. Patterson, Brent."

"It's my intention to corner Brent at the Games, Miren. You'll know then."

Miren's mouth opened for a shocked gasp. "What do you mean 'corner him'?"

"I learned a few things from the duke that should force a confession. At the time my brother and Kenneth MacCallum were murdered, Brent was supposed to be on an extended hunting trip with the duke. As it happens, he left the first day, and wasn't accounted for until three weeks later. Ample time to pursue MacCallum to America, commit murder, and return to Scotland."

"You think Brent actually killed your brother himself? What about Dr. Patterson?"

"I don't know how Patterson fit in. It may be that he was just as he seemed, a concerned physician accompanying an ailing man."

"Then why were two bodies piled up, and one caught by mistake?"

"Maybe he woke too soon. A bitter end."

"So you're going to challenge Brent publicly? What if he denies it?"

"I've enlisted the duke's cooperation. Apparently, he's never trusted Brent Edgington, either. With his help, getting a confession shouldn't be too difficult."

"What about me?"

Nathan looked back across the loch. "What do you want to know?"

"If you secure a confession, I'm in no further danger. I don't have to leave Scotland quite yet."

He didn't answer, and she turned her gaze to her feet.

"Never mind." Miren looked up and across the dark loch. "It's time I went, after all."

Miren refused to cry, but she couldn't stay beside him, faced with all that might have been between them. He didn't want her enough. Maybe he didn't want her at all. Miren turned away, then looked back. "We'll have one more night together, in Oban. I want you, Nathaniel. Once before I go. If I never see you again, I'll have that memory."

He looked back at her, his dark face stricken with an emotion she couldn't read. "Miren—"

She held up her hand and smiled. "Nathaniel, the matter is settled."

Chapter Sixteen

No sheep anywhere in sight! My destiny bids welcome at last! Nathan has brought the young mistress and myself to a new place. A place of many houses set in the hills, and many people busy on the streets and docks. Coaches pass to and fro on well-kept roads, riders stop for ladies to cross the streets. Many of those ladies attend house pets.

A finer sight I've never seen.

We traveled in a huge coach with six horses at harness. All should be well, but the young mistress has been quiet since we left the small cottage. Perhaps because the chattering duke leaves no room for another to speak. He brought us to a tall building, where uniformed humans directed us to a collection of fine rooms.

It is my dream come real. Humans in full livery, hovering in dutiful attendance. Nat is with Glenna in one room. The young mistress and myself have another. Nathan and Simon each have rooms of their own.

When we arrived, large trunks of clothing waited by our

bed. The young mistress discovered several good dresses for herself, and a bow meant for me. I will wear the bow, because it is an occasion of merit.

I can't help wondering what Flip would think of my new bow, but he remained with the sheep. The young mistress said good-bye to him as if she thought never to see him again. She hugged Blossom, said reassuring words to Earnest—which he didn't require, because he was eating—and sat for a long while with Huntley, feeding him clover.

Her sorrow dampens my joy and makes me uneasy. Things are looking almost too good. I will keep myself alert for possible threats to my new station . . .

"You've got it on backwards." Miren stood in the doorway of Nathan's room, shaking her head. The Duke of Argyll had provided traditional Highland dress for Nathan's use, all in the blue and green MacCallum tartan plaid.

Nathan stood at the wide, arched window of his room, glaring over Oban to the harbor. He'd gotten as far as his kilt and, apparently, gave up. "I see no need . . ." He turned from the window, and his words trailed. His dark eyes widened as he scanned her new dress.

Miren felt shy. Glenna had helped her prepare and assemble her elaborate new gown, but it seemed so different from her usual dress. The bodice was snug over an even snugger corset, and her undergarments required a bustle, which seemed the equivalent of wearing a small coach.

Despite its cumbersome weight, she liked the dress. Her bodice was attached to a matching overskirt, which flared open to an ivory satin skirt beneath, both with green trim, an ivory fringe, and a wide, square neckline. Her hair was piled into a chignon, with tendrils left loose to frame her face.

"Miren . . . you're beautiful." Nathan's mouth remained open. Miren blushed.

"Thank you."

"Why aren't you stuffed into some ridiculous Highland costume?"

"Only the gentlemen assume the official dress, Nathan." She eyed the sorry state of his wardrobe. "But most of them have more success fitting it correctly."

Nathan glanced at his disheveled kilt and twisted plaid, then turned his gaze back to her. "You are beautiful."

Miren kept her eyes down. "You said that."

"It warrants saying."

Molly sat beside Miren's feet, looking proud. "Did you notice Molly's bow? It's the Lindsay plaid."

Nathan glanced down at Molly. "Majestic."

Molly looked even more proud.

"The queen sent me three trunks of dresses. Green ones as deep as the forest, ones the color of red wine and mead, and one the exact color of Loch Fyne. And Nathan, there's a whole trunk of plaids, both Lindsay and MacCallum." She paused. "I suppose she expects me to adopt your plaid when we marry."

"I'd thought to initiate you into the Clan of the Wolf."

Miren peered up at him. His smile faded when he realized what he'd said. Their engagement was a ruse to serve a greater purpose. Nothing more. Miren cleared her throat. "The sporran goes around your waist, not over your shoulder. You do not wear tight black trousers beneath a kilt . . ."

Nathan seemed relieved to have the subject changed. "I have to cover up these stockings with something."

"A shoulder plaid is not a cape." Miren went to the large black trunk and rummaged through the Highland dress.

She sorted through his clothing and laid it out on the bed. Molly hopped onto the bed and curled up on a large, soft pillow.

Miren held up a short black jacket with gold trim. "Here is your coat. You wear this over an ivory shirt." She found a loose shirt with full sleeves. "This will do." She placed it beside the jacket, then scrutinized Nathan's current appearance. "You can't wear your pirate shirt, Nathan. The collar is wrong."

Nathan turned back to the window, stubborn. Miren peered over his shoulder. The Oban port bustled with vessels, from small fishing boats to large cargo transports. "Can we see your ship from here?"

Nathan pointed to a ship with a black hull. It looked sleek and fast. "There. Simon is on board making sure it's ready. Daniel knows my ship better, but the old man wanted to check it for himself."

"Perhaps he misses the sea."

"Or he's found a good reason for avoiding this banquet." Nathan dropped his shoulder plaid, frowning. "I will wear my own clothes."

Miren turned her attention back to Nathan's new wardrobe. "Just for tonight, Nathaniel. We are attending a party. It was your idea to accept the duke's invitation, so you must dress accordingly."

Nathan eyed the articles of clothing and decoration strewn across his bed. "Not in that."

"You can't wear your pirate costume to a nobleman's party. You're supposed to be a laird now."

"It's impossible. I have no idea what to do with that . . . gear."

"I'll help you." Miren unbuttoned his shirt and pulled it off. She lingered a moment to view his chest. Nathan noticed her fixed gaze, and he smiled.

"Having you as my valet has its appeal."

Miren cleared her throat. "We don't have time. We *would* have had time, but you were off with the duke, and now you're being stubborn." Miren frowned. They hadn't been alone together once since Nat came to her cottage. Now they were in Oban, and she would be leaving. Unless he changed his mind at the last minute. Miren didn't want to hope, but she couldn't stop herself.

A practical woman keeps hope in its proper perspective.

Yes, she hoped he would decide to keep her. But she would assume they had one night together, and make the most of it. Unfortunately, they were to spend the evening at a banquet hosted by the duke, and for the benefit of the queen. "What were you doing so long with the duke?"

"It couldn't be helped, Miren. The duke has arranged support for the Games, in case Edgington gives us any trouble."

"Will Brent be at the party?"

"Ah, there is an interesting development. Lady MacCallum received a message from him when we arrived. He won't make it to the party, but he will join us at the Games."

"Why?"

"A good question. He may be planning something. Which is why the duke has arranged for several disguised guards to be on the premises."

Miren stood back. "Take off your trousers."

Nathan sighed, then removed his snug black trousers, exposing a fine pair of green and blue argyll socks. Miren nodded appreciatively. "They look good. You have good, strong legs." She bit her lip, thinking of his naked body stretched out before her. Nathan caught her expression and grinned.

"What do I wear beneath this . . . skirt, if not trousers?"

Miren hesitated. "What are you wearing now?"

"Nothing."

"That's it." She coughed to distract herself, then found a pair of low shoes with a silver buckle. "See if these fit."

Nathan put the shoes on, wiggled his toes as if looking for something to complain about, then shrugged. "They'll do. What next?"

"The coat, I think. Yes." Miren helped him with the coat, holding his sleeves. He grumbled through the whole procedure. Miren kissed his shoulder. "You are a trial, Indian."

"I see no point to any of these bits of cloth . . ."

Miren buttoned his coat and stood back to view her progress. "This is a Scottish chieftain's uniform, Nathaniel. Didn't you wear a uniform in the American war?"

"Yes. When I had to."

"What do Indians wear?"

"Practical clothing. It depends."

"For ceremony, they wear nothing of interest?"

"Tribal customs dictate certain . . . Wampum belts, perhaps."

"Earrings, feathers, and beads?" Miren chuckled. "And what do you call that pirate costume you wear? The leather vest, the big white shirt, the incredibly tight trousers. Those black boots." Her voice trailed, and Nathan's brow angled.

"A lure to women."

Miren's blush deepened. "You've worn many uniforms, Indian. One more won't hurt."

Nathan touched her cheek. "No, I suppose not."

Their eyes met, and Miren saw something she hadn't seen before. Confusion. He didn't know where he belonged, and he was afraid. Afraid he would choose the wrong path, afraid of what he didn't know.

Miren wanted to help him, but she remembered Glenna's words. *He'll find his strength on his own.* "Now, for the decorations . . ."

Miren seized the long plaid and wrapped it around his waist and up over his right shoulder. "Do you have a brooch? I didn't see one in the trunk."

Nathan gestured to his old coat. "In there."

Miren fished around in his pocket and found the Mac-Callum badge. She pinned the plaid over his shoulder, then seized the sporran. It was made from light fur, with Celtic designs lining the silver clasp and hung with black tassels. "Impressive."

"Is there anything else?"

"We have your badge, the sporran . . . You need a dirk and a sgian-dhu."

"What for?"

"Well"—Miren tapped her lip thoughtfully—"Lady Sarah is among the duke's guests. When she sees you looking like

293

this, knowing what you're wearing underneath . . . you may need a full arsenal.''

Nathan crossed his arms over his chest. "It's *your* intentions that concern me, woman.''

Miren peered up at him from beneath lowered lashes. "That remains to be seen.'' She hooked the sheathed dirk onto his belt, then picked up the small sgian-dhu. Three amber stones decorated its sheath and hilt. Miren fingered it with interest. "I've always wanted one of these.''

"I shudder to think why.''

Miren bent and tried to reach his legs. She puffed an impatient breath. "Tight corsets are an inconvenience. Place your right foot on the trunk, please.''

Nathan obliged, watching suspiciously as she stuffed the sgian-dhu into his stocking. Miren stood back to survey her handiwork. He stood before her, frowning, his foot still resting on the trunk.

His dark hair fell to his shoulders. Broad, strong shoulders that filled his black jacket to its capacity, offering good evidence of musculature. Miren swallowed. Her gaze lowered to the crisp, pleated kilt. It was woven with both dark and light blue, squared with a deep, rich green. Strands of white thread and black crossed the fabric.

Miren's eyes filled with sudden tears. "You are so beautiful. You look . . .'' Her gaze lifted to his. He looked . . . surprised, and still confused. "You look like a laird. A real laird. Just as I've seen them in my dreams.''

One dark brow angled. "You've seen lairds in your dreams?''

"I have, many times. Leading battles, they are. They've got swords, which you don't. The basket hilt variety, naturally. In my dreams, I'm following''—she paused and coughed—"*herding* my sheep, and Molly is with me. Men are fighting, the way men often do. And just when I decide to pass by, a chieftain turns and sees me. He looks just like you.''

"Prophetic. Maybe you should have passed by, after all. Men at war are dangerous, Miren."

Miren's gaze shifted to her feet. "A life wandering is nothing compared to seeing my laird up close." She didn't dare look at him. He was too perfectly tall and handsome. All that filled her dreams. Dreams she'd forgotten, shoved aside in favor of reality. Nathan brought them to her in warm, strong flesh, in a sweet embrace.

Maybe it was enough to taste the dream, even if only for a little while.

Miren closed her eyes until the threat of tears passed, then turned back to the trunk.

"What are you looking for? There isn't any room left on me."

Miren found a small pin, strained to reach it without splitting her corset, then held it aloft. "This!"

"What is it?"

"A pin for your kilt. See, it looks like a wee claymore." Miren pointed to the bed. "You'll have to stand up there. I can't bend over to pin this on."

"Let me pin it, then."

"You won't get it right." Miren pointed. "Up."

Nathan drew a long, weary breath, then climbed up on the bed. Miren stole a quick glance at his thighs, and her nerves tingled. Amazing, how every muscle moved in accord, defined to perfection.

Nathan cleared his throat meaningfully. He stood on the bed, arms folded over his chest, legs apart. His lips curved in a smile, his dark eyes twinkled. "If you're ready . . ."

Miren's blush soaked from her neck to her cheeks. "I was simply checking to see if you had everything on correctly."

"And do I?"

She ignored his leading tone as best she could. "Yes." Miren fixed her attention on his kilt, pinned the tiny claymore on the fold, then backed away slowly. His beauty stole her breath. Molly rose from her soft pillow and positioned herself beside Nathan as if she intended to enhance his image.

"Do I pass your inspection, Highlander?"

Miren gazed up at him and sighed. "You do."

The banquet passed quickly, because the plates were removed as soon as Queen Victoria finished eating. The first course's early departure alerted Nathan to the necessity of eating first, talking later. It wasn't easy. He sat across from the Duke of Argyll, who talked and ate with no interference.

Miren sat beside him, but she didn't eat much. Maybe her corset was too tight. But it looked good. Nathan took a hurried bite of roast pheasant, then turned to watch her. Her fingers curved delicately around her fork, but she took only a small bite.

"Are you well, Miren? I've never seen you eat so little."

She peered up at him, her blue eyes soft. "I'm not so very hungry." She glanced at the table, then lowered her voice. "Which is good, because the footmen just removed your plate."

Nathan sighed as the footmen carted away the remainder of dinner. Queen Victoria was a hearty—and fast—eater. "I don't know how she tastes anything eating that way."

Miren elbowed his ribs. "There's always dessert. But I was thinking of a sweeter pleasure."

Nathan's heart slammed against his breast. He checked her expression to see if she meant what she seemed to mean. Her lips curved at one corner, her eyes darkened to the blue of midnight loch. She meant it. She dampened her lips, subtly and purposefully. Fortunately, his kilt was loose enough to conceal his reaction.

"What's next?"

He spoke too loud, from tension, and the duke overheard. "You won't be disappointed, Laird MacCallum. After dinner, there's a fine ball appointed for Her Majesty's enjoyment. Should keep us all enlivened until the wee hours of morn!"

Nathan tried to smile. "An enjoyable evening." He waited

until the duke directed his conversation to his dinner partner, then turned to Miren, keeping his voice low. "How soon can we leave?"

Miren bit her lip. "It's customary to wait until the queen departs, I believe."

Nathan glanced at the queen. She sat at the table's head, speaking with her daughter. "After what's she's eaten, she's bound to be tired. Good."

Miren eyed him reproachfully, but he knew she fought a smile. "*I'm* not tired."

She was teasing him, letting him know that whenever they reached his bedroom, or hers, she would be ready. Nathan drew a tight breath and forced his attention elsewhere. Lady MacCallum sat at the far end of the giant table, her face strained with a false smile as she listened to an old Scottish colonel discussing his venture to the South Seas. His voice rose and fell with the excitement of his tale.

"Ship went down near the isle of Java. Half the crew drowned or got eaten up by sharks!"

Nathan heard Lady MacCallum's tense reply. "How dreadful." No feeling revealed itself in her words.

"I, myself, only just survived. Ended up on a cargo ship. Whole thing stank of sheep—merinos bound for Australia, they were."

"Australia." Nathan caught Lady MacCallum's grimace. She even shuddered. "I can think of nowhere more loathsome than Australia."

"Well, it's bleak, I'll tell you. Hot and wet like a dog's tongue in one place, and dried up like roasting bones in another. The Australian outback . . . now, there's a place . . ."

Nathan turned his attention away from Lady MacCallum and her dinner companion. He guessed that the queen had chosen the seating placements and kept Irene MacCallum as far away from her as possible. Even the good-natured duke admitted—under the influence of shared whiskey—that he'd rather put her behind the coach than travel from Inveraray to Oban with Irene.

The footmen delivered large platters of pastries and creams to the guests. Queen Victoria abandoned her conversation and concentrated on her dessert. Nathan noticed that Miren seized a shortbread pastry and devoured it in good speed, despite her lack of appetite.

She caught his knowing glance and smiled. "I needed something to maintain my energy." She paused, and one brow lowered. "For later."

Miren licked her fingers, and her eyes sparkled. "I think you should have one, too, Nathaniel." The footman retrieved the plates, and Nathan sighed.

"Too late."

Nathan liked dancing. Simon had often said it was in his blood, from native rituals. His mother said it was Scottish. Miren liked dancing, too. They glided across the floor to sweet music, and their gaze never left each other. Nathan forgot who he was, where he came from. For this night, he was whatever Miren Lindsay wanted him to be.

He remembered when he first saw her, picking her way through her sheep, wedging Blossom aside as she came to face him. Wearing a sackcloth dress, a small pack slung over her shoulder. He'd thought her lovely then. The loveliest thing he'd ever seen. He wondered if he'd told her then how much he admired her.

They spun through the other dancers as if floating on air. He remembered her pacing back and forth in the Inveraray Jail exercise pen. Her dog at her heels, her hair slick from the rain. She moved his heart then, too. And he'd said nothing.

She was dressed like a queen. Nathan caught a vision of Queen Victoria from the corner of his eye. She wore black, as always, with a white lace cap covering her hair. No, Miren wasn't a queen. She was as beautiful in burlap as satin, and as much at ease in either. She was happy, because she was with him. He realized with a cool shock that he was happy, too.

I can't lose you.

The music stopped too soon. Ladies applauded with soft claps, the men went to fetch cups of punch for the women, and Nathan decided the evening had gone on long enough.

He eyed the queen as she sat in a corner, her daughter beside her. "She doesn't look eager to leave."

Miren sighed. "No."

"Would you like some punch?"

"No."

Miren looked thoughtful. Her small, flushed face was scrunched to one side as if plotting. "Nathan . . ." She spoke his name slowly.

"I'm almost afraid to ask . . . What?"

She watched Lady Sarah, who held demurely to an older man's arm. The marquess, her future husband. Nathan caught a surreptitious glance his way, directed at his legs.

Miren tapped his shoulder. "I warned you. I hope you have the sgian-dhu ready."

"I'll slice her to quarters if she comes near me."

Miren chuckled. Not a delicate woman's giggle, but a solid, devious cackle. "Good." She tapped her lip with one finger. "Still . . . one might learn from Lady Sarah, I should think."

"Learn what?"

Miren turned to him, looking practical. Her most dangerous expression. "You said she intended to 'pleasure you' at Lady MacCallum's garden party."

"Keep your voice down, woman."

Miren glanced around. "No one is listening. Now, I was thinking . . ."

Nathan held his breath. If this was leading where he thought it was leading . . . He swallowed hard. "What did you have in mind?"

"She must have intended to take you someplace relatively private, quickly accessible, yet with just enough room for . . .

pleasuring.'' Miren moved a little closer to him, snapped up a fan he hadn't noticed she possessed, and spoke behind it. "I noticed a closet which I believe houses linen and tools for housemaids."

"When did you—"

"When I excused myself earlier." Miren puffed a quick breath. "I was hunting a wee bit for a suitable spot. And I found it. There's room enough for two . . ."

Nathan stared down at her, mouth agape. He tried to speak, and failed.

Miren closed her fan and slipped her hand onto his arm. "I have noticed that couples take walks. Beyond the ballroom is a balcony. I'm sure it's very pleasant—it looks down over Oban and the harbor. Let's go that way."

Nathan placed his hand over hers. "Why that way?"

"Because just beyond, easily reached, is the housemaids' closet."

His sporran fell in the right spot to conceal his burgeoning arousal. "There's a use to these clothes, after all." Nathan led Miren from the ballroom, along a narrow walkway lined with white columns, to a wide balcony.

Several other couples gazed out over Oban toward the sea. Lady Sarah sipped punch as her marquess pointed out important homes along the hillside. She looked bored and cast a hungry look toward Nathan.

Miren placed her small gloved hands on the balcony and leaned forward, breathing in the sweet evening air. The sun cast its final light over the harbor, glinting a pale light on her lovely face. A soft breeze released a tendril of her hair to blow across her cheek. Nathan fingered the loose strand and tucked it behind her ear. He trailed his fingers to the back of her neck, and she closed her eyes.

Tonight he felt sure of success. Tomorrow, with the duke's help, his brother's murder would be resolved. His nephew's inheritance would be assured. If the danger to Miren passed . . . *I love you.* He couldn't let her leave. He wasn't sure when he'd realized this, but since they'd stood by the loch together, the direction of his thoughts had changed.

He hadn't told her, because he hadn't been sure his plan would work. Tonight nothing seemed difficult. He would expose Brent as a murderer, install his nephew as MacCallum's heir, and tell Miren he wanted her with him. Always.

Miren turned around and leaned against the balcony. She reached up and fingered his hair, just enough to see that he still wore his earring. "You wore this for me, didn't you?"

"What do you think?"

She rested her hand on his chest. "It has the most curious effect. It reminds me I'm making love with a pirate"— Miren's hand slid to his belt, and she fingered his sporran— "and a Scottish laird."

"All at once?" His voice came raw and strained. Miren smiled.

"All at once."

She took his hand and led him casually along the balcony. Nathan's heart beat so fast he felt dizzy. Lady Sarah ignored her marquess as they passed by, watching suspiciously as Miren gestured to the far hall. "That way."

Miren smiled politely at Lady Sarah and the marquess. "Pleasant evening, isn't it?" She didn't wait for a response as she led Nathan from the balcony. "This way." She led him down the dark hall, then stopped by a small door. She looked both ways, then shoved it open. "In there."

"As you wish." Nathan entered the linen closet, and Miren followed.

"It's too dark. I can't see a thing." She bumped into what sounded like a bucket and sighed. "This is unacceptable. Wait here!"

Before he could respond, Miren darted from the closet and scurried down the hall. He wondered what he'd do if someone cornered her for conversation, but she returned holding aloft a lantern. "I took it from the balcony."

Nathan stood back as she entered the closet and closed the

door. She hung the lamp on a hook, then turned to face him. "I've planned this, you know."

"I can see that."

She bit her lip. "I'm sorry about the bucket. I expect Lady Sarah wouldn't knock over a bucket." She looked down and winced. "Oh, dear. It looks like ashes from a fireplace. All over your shoes."

"Easily cleaned, beloved."

Miren squeezed around him. Something clattered and fell to the floor. "Oh. Mops." She sounded pained. "I expect Lady Sarah would have chosen a better closet."

Nathan watched her as she fumbled around, her bustle knocking mops and brushes from hooks. "Now, what's that?" Miren bent with effort and picked up a large, feathered duster. She swung it around into Nathan's face. He sneezed.

"It's all right . . ." He paused to sneeze again. Several times. Miren clasped her hands at her waist, fighting tears.

"I'm sorry." She spotted something on his cheek and brushed it away. "A feather."

Nathan seized the feather and stuck it in his hair. "A pirate, a laird . . . and an Indian chief . . ."

A tiny smile grew on her lips, then widened until she burst forth in laughter. "All at once."

Nathan eased her into his arms. "I love you."

Her eyes widened in shock, but Nathan didn't wait for a response. He bent and kissed her. Not a kiss of lust in a dark closet, but tender, with his full heart in her hands. Miren wrapped her arms around his neck and pressed close against him. She drew back and kissed his cheek, the corner of his mouth, his neck.

"You are so beautiful, Indian. Do you know, I've begun dreaming of this?"

"I thought you were dreaming of Highlanders."

"Ah, but the dreams take a new turn." Miren backed away, her eyes shining. She pushed him against the door and ran her hands down his hips. "I dreamt I took you prisoner, and whatever I asked, you gave."

She opened his wee claymore pin and stuck it in the back of a brush. She kept her eyes on his as she parted the kilt and slipped her hand beneath. The soft lantern-glow lit her beautiful, eager face as her small fingers met his hardened staff. Her eyelids lowered and her lips parted as her hand closed around him.

Nathan gripped her shoulders and brushed his mouth over hers. He tasted her lower lip, then the upper, then dipped his tongue between her teeth. Her hand moved with greater urgency as he explored her sweet mouth. He felt her wild pulse, he knew she trembled with anticipation.

"Nathan . . ." She paused to gasp for air. "What do we do now?"

"What's expected in a closet, my love. I pleasure you to the limits of your endurance."

"Oh!"

He sank to one knee, took her hand, and kissed it gently. She waited for him to rise, but Nathan knelt before her instead. Her skirts were convenient for his purposes. The overskirt parted, leaving less fabric between them. He lifted her underskirt and petticoat, but his breath caught when he realized that she, too, abandoned drawers.

"You did plan this, didn't you?"

She took a quick breath. "Not exactly this."

He bunched the front of her underskirt with the petticoat in one hand, then ran his other hand up along her legs. He trailed his fingers over the rim of her stocking, to the soft curls hidden between her legs. Very gently, he kissed the soft inner flesh of her thighs.

"Nathan, I'm not sure this is what's done in closets . . . Do you think . . . ?"

He looked up at her. Her face was flushed, her lips puffy and parted for shallow gasps. "Miren . . . the matter is settled."

She leaned back against the wall. Something fell. A dust-pan. Miren edged it aside with her foot, as if hoping he wouldn't notice. His heart filled with such power that he thought he might fly and carry her with him.

He ran his finger up one thigh, down the other, grazing her soft curls without pressure. He bent closer and allowed her to feel his breath on her tender flesh. She must have, because a muted gasp escaped her lips. He glanced up to see her biting her lip.

"To the limits of your endurance, my sweet, precious angel. Hold still."

Miren was obedient. She didn't move, but her slender calf muscles tensed, her toes curled beneath her soft leather slippers. He brushed his mouth across her woman's mound, then dipped his tongue inward to her sensitized core. He found the small bud within, and a tiny squeak came from her throat.

"What are . . . oh . . . settled." She gulped and maintained silence. He tasted her, sweet like light honey. He teased her and her whole body tensed. The tiny bud came erect, fierce and willing, and he sucked gently, then harder when she whimpered his name.

He swirled his tongue in intricate patterns until she moaned and pushed back against the wall. Her knees quivered, her fingers clasped in his hair. His name came on every breath. "Pirate . . ." He lightened his touch and stroked gently. "Indian." He grazed her sensitive peak with his teeth. "My laird, och, my laird." Her words trailed into something he didn't understand. Low, rhythmic Gaelic words, driven with intensity.

He didn't know what she said, but he knew what it meant. All her Highlander blood, with its fire and determination, and the Lowlander, with its stubborn practicality, soared to fullness as he made love to her. He licked and sucked and teased until she cried out, oblivious to their surroundings. One leg arched and wrapped around his back. Her whole body quivered. Her small peak throbbed, and she twisted and writhed as ecstasy swept through her.

Nathan's blood burned, his body ached for fulfillment, but he waited until she reached her first peak of rapture. She tugged his hair, and he rose to his feet, pressing her against the wall as he pulled back his kilt.

He was beyond readiness, filled to his limits. He grasped her leg and pulled it up to his hip, then drove himself deep inside her. Her pleasure surged and doubled with his entry. Her inner depths squeezed around his shaft, tiny spasms rippled through her where their pulses mingled.

He lifted her from her feet, and she wrapped her legs tight around his waist. He thrust upward and she tipped her head back, lost in pleasure. His release came with shuddering force, over and over, until he had nothing left. Every nerve ending vibrated in the aftermath.

Miren's legs slid down beside his and she balanced on her toes. He withdrew from her body and held her. She buried her head on his chest. When she looked up, she was smiling, but her cheeks were wet with tears. All they were had met in passion. Nothing stood between them now.

He started to speak, but she pressed her fingers against his mouth. "There's no need. This is perfect between us. I will never, never forget."

Never forget? A cold wash sank over Nathan's heart. She believed he would send her away, that they'd never see each other again.

"Nathan! Laird MacCallum! Are you about?"

Miren caught her breath. "That's the duke!"

Nathan groaned. "I hope he's not in the mood for talking."

Miren giggled. "He's always in the mood for a chat."

Nathan adjusted his kilt, and Miren hurriedly replaced his pin. She straightened her dress and ran her hand over her hair. "Do I look . . . ravaged?"

Nathan took the lantern and held it near her face. "You look . . . satisfied."

"Oh, dear." Miren lowered the lamp and it went out, leaving them in darkness.

"Laird MacCallum?" The duke's voice came from farther down the hall. They heard him walk back toward the balcony, and Nathan eased open the door.

"There are stairs at this end of the balcony. If we can get there, we'll say we went for a walk."

Miren nodded, and they slipped from the closet. They reached the stairs unnoticed, and Nathan positioned himself as if they'd just come up.

"Your Grace! Did I hear you calling me?"

The duke turned, beaming with his usual pleasure. "There you are! I've been searching you out all over!"

"My fiancée and I went for a walk. Miren especially enjoyed the gardens."

"Ah, the rhododendrons! Brought over from northeastern America, you know. Your own part of the world . . ."

"You were looking for me, Your Grace?"

"Quite. I'm afraid I have to drag you away from your lovely bride-to-be, Nathaniel. Matter of"—the duke paused and smacked his lips as if broaching a delicate subject—"import. I'll have my coachman drive her back to your inn. She'll be safe. You have my word."

Nathan turned to Miren and took her hand, then kissed it. "I'm sorry, Miren. I may be late."

Miren nodded, but he saw her disappointment. "I had a lovely evening."

Nathan smiled. "As did I."

Lady Sarah and the marquess were seated at the far end of the balcony. They rose and joined the duke. Lady Sarah scanned Nathan's appearance thoroughly, her lips parted in recognition of his most recent activity.

"Your kilt pin, Laird MacCallum, is asunder."

Miren gazed down at Nathan's kilt, disingenuous wonder on her small, flushed face. "That's odd. I could have sworn it was on straight when we went for our walk."

Chapter Seventeen

The young mistress returned alone to our room last night. She seemed happy, but once she lay on the bed awhile, she began to cry. I offered comfort by licking her face, and she hugged me, but she didn't stop crying.

Something is wrong, and I don't know what it is. She woke early, at dawn. I am not pleased with rising from one's cushion early, but this morning I went to her side. She was staring out the window, with special attention to the water coaches. I am becoming suspicious of that sort of coach, that which floats on water. I am not a water dog, for one thing. Also, viewing them makes my mistress sad. I must keep her away from them.

Still, the situation here is favorable to my needs. I have a fine cushion, with tassels that are adequate for chewing purposes. Excitement fills the air. People are in a festive mood.

From our window I spotted the huge, lavish coach that bore the queen back at the estate. Through its windows, which have fine curtains, I saw two of her house pets. The smaller terrier *had a bow. I am still not entirely sanguine on that bow. I must assess its desirability at a later point in time.*

Miren woke early, but Nathan hadn't returned to the inn. Her new trunks contained a fashionable outdoor dress with a plumed bonnet and matching gloves. She put on the dress and checked herself in the looking glass. The black velvet coat fit snugly over her bodice and flared over her bustle. Fortunately, the bustle used beneath a day dress was less bulky than evening wear.

"I can sit in the coach. Good." Her burgundy outer skirt was tied back, revealing an inner skirt of black satin. Three burgundy bows tied the skirt behind her feet. Miren removed one and tied it around Molly's neck.

"You're very beautiful, Molly." Molly looked proud. Miren patted her head and went to look out the window. Coaches were already heading south through town on their way to the Games.

A knock startled her from the window, but it was Glenna who entered, Nat close beside her. "I've brung yer breakfast, miss." Glenna cackled and set the tray on a polished table. "I thought you'd want to avoid breakfasting with Her Ladyship in the dining room, so here's a good kipper and toast."

Nat pointed at a pot. "Tea, too. I like tea." He eyed the cups with longing. Miren smiled and poured three cups, one very low. She filled Nat's with milk, and they seated themselves around the table.

Miren eyed the kipper, but her appetite had dwindled to nothing. Glenna shook her head. "Are you sure, dear? You must eat."

"I'm not very hungry, thank you." Miren took a dutiful sip of tea, but her stomach felt tight and uneasy.

"Very well." Glenna seized the kipper and divided it between herself and Nat. "The Iroquois do wonderful things with squash and beans, but they know next to nothing about salted fish."

Nat tasted his kipper, grimaced, and turned to the toast, loading it high with red currant preserves. "Where's Uncle?"

"I don't know. He had to go with the duke."

Glenna set aside her kipper and drank her tea. "Simon was here this morning. He says Nathan and the duke are staging their men, readying themselves to corner Mr. Edgington. Men can be so high-strung."

Miren sighed. "I wonder if Brent's really coming to the Games at all."

"According to Simon, he arrived last night. Late. He is dining with Lady MacCallum now. Another reason for you to eat up here."

"Is Nathan coming to take us to the Games?"

Glenna hesitated. "Simon is accompanying us, but Nathaniel will meet us there. Lady MacCallum is going early, to situate herself near the queen. There will be a large crowd, naturally."

"If she knew Brent's fate, she'd head home now."

Glenna chuckled. "I only met the lad briefly. He seemed ineffectual, but it will please me to see Irene set back a peg. Do you know, this morning she instructed me to keep my lips together?" Glenna opened her mouth and pointed to her blackened tooth. "It *offends* her." Glenna clucked her tongue. "And after all the work I took getting it to look this way."

Miren's spirits rose with Glenna's presence. "I will miss you, Glenna. I don't remember my mother, but I think she was just like you."

"Cora and I used to pretend we were twins. Those were sweet days. You remind me of her quite closely, Miren. She was a practical girl, because she was a Lowlander. Yet she had such an imagination! We used to go on long expeditions in search of the Wee Folk. But I knew—I had a fairy with me all along. Cora carried their blood quite strongly. As do you."

"The Wee Folk have powers, they say. To make wishes come true."

"I called on them often. It takes a while, but wishes have power." Glenna gazed toward the window, up into the blue sky. "Before I married Kenneth, I had no fear. I thought I was lucky to become a laird's wife. I learned better soon."

"When he learned you and my mother had switched places?"

"Before our wedding, I confessed that Cora eloped with your father. I believed Kenneth would understand. Even laugh."

Miren eyed her doubtfully. "Laugh?"

"Aye . . . When Kenneth first came to visit your mother, she paid no attention to him, but I was impressed by his humor. I thought I would like him for a husband."

"Kenneth MacCallum was . . . funny?"

"When he wasn't drinking, yes. It is the one thing he passed to Nat. It skipped David, unfortunately. David was so serious."

"Was Laird MacCallum angered because of the switch?"

"Oh, Miren, his fury knew no bounds. I didn't understand. He'd only met Cora once, when she was fourteen. He paid no attention to her, other than to learn her parentage. Her parents, like mine, were dead, but her father had been Stephen Malcolm."

Miren considered this. "Was he wealthy or prominent?"

"Not to my knowledge. Rumor said he was descended from a Jacobite chieftain, one who fought and died in the war against the English. Some say he hid away a great sum of money before his death—in the form of jeweled weapons, crowns, and gold. I wondered if Kenneth had learned of this rumored fortune and thought to claim it for himself, through Cora."

"It seems a great deal of effort for the sake of a rumor."

"Aye, as I thought myself. Unless he knew something I didn't."

"I wish it were true." Miren chuckled. "Those dirks and crowns would be mine. I have an affection for dirks and sgian-dhus. But the treasure is, no doubt, exaggerated by time and imagination.''

''I expect so. Still, Kenneth never felt his estate was enough. Even a wee promise of such fortune would have meant much to him. It might have been enough to assuage his anger—which he directed through drink to me.''

Glenna spoke without emotion, and Miren marveled at her even temper. ''You speak of him with amazing forgiveness. I think I would want him dead.''

Glenna sighed heavily. ''I hated him, make no mistake. When a man lays a hand of violence upon a woman, there is no return to trust. Yet the effect of such abuse is strange. I feared myself more than Kenneth. I didn't trust my own body, because I couldn't protect it. I wished and wished, but no fairy came.''

Glenna paused. ''Maybe I'm wrong. Simon came. I wouldn't be at all surprised to find a pixie in Simon's ancestry.''

''He cares for you.''

''I know. It grieved me once, to know he cared and that I couldn't return his feelings. But Simon's first love is the sea. It always was, and it always will be.''

''And for you?''

''My love . . .'' Glenna closed her eyes softly. ''I had lived with the Seneca for almost a year. David had just started walking. I thought nothing could surprise me anymore. But one evening a young man entered the village, the chief's son. When I first saw him, I thought the sun rose and set at his feet. He'd returned from a long quest into Canada, and his father asked him to choose a bride. Every beautiful young woman wished to marry him. I sat with the elders, shucking corn, wishing with all my heart I were young and beautiful and innocent again.''

Miren's eyes puddled with tears. ''You are beautiful.''

''I didn't think so. When I envisioned myself, I saw a bruised woman, an old woman. A woman who lost innocence beneath her husband's fist. Miren, when I looked at that perfect, strong young man, I saw all the things I couldn't be. I ran into my adopted clan's longhall and I wept. I hadn't cried in years, but I cried that day.''

Miren couldn't speak. Nat looked up at his grandmother, an attentive expression on his small face. He took her hand, but he said nothing.

''While I was crying, someone touched my shoulder and knelt beside me. It was that beautiful young man. He asked me if I was crying because of his choice. I didn't know what to say, so I just shook my head. He said if it caused me pain, he would choose another, but he promised to be a good husband. He said he would treat my son as his own.''

''Oh!'' Miren shoved tears from her cheeks, but more came. ''He chose you.''

''He did. I've never understood why. When I ask him, he says he looked around and picked the woman he liked best.''

Miren sniffed. ''That sounds reasonable. That's the way I picked . . .'' She caught herself and bit her lip.

''The way you picked Nathaniel?''

Miren rose from her chair. ''I suppose it wasn't quite like that.''

''No. Each lover's story is different. That is the beauty, and why the stories are told over and over, and each one is new.''

Miren looked into Glenna's eyes. ''I am suppose to leave Scotland today, after the Games. I do not want to go.''

''Fate unfolds beyond our control, Miren. But don't fear. Sometimes it sees clearer than we do.''

The Highland Games were in full swing by the time Miren and Glenna arrived. Nat held Miren's hand, but seemed eager to sample the table offerings of shortbread and whiskey. ''Not just yet, Nat.'' Miren edged him away from the whiskey, but Glenna purchased a round cake of shortbread and gave him a sample.

Nathan was waiting, looking anxious. Miren saw him near

a large white tent, pacing. He spotted her, and she felt his relief across the field. Glenna waved, then took another bite of her shortbread. "The Iroquois don't know much about shortbread, either."

Nathan strode across the field, and Miren's heart quickened. Today was their last together. Tonight, she would be on board a ship for America. She would never see him again. The milling crowd faded from her vision as she watched him. He wore his pirate shirt and snug black trousers with his high boots again. As he came toward her, the wind tousled his hair and the sun glinted off his earring.

Molly wagged her tail eagerly and pulled on her leash to greet him. Miren stepped forward and he took her hands. "Miren . . ." He seemed moved to see her. Maybe he'd changed his mind. Maybe his soft words of love meant he wanted her at his side.

"Have you caught Brent yet?"

"The duke's men are in position. Edgington's here, and he's jumpy as a cat."

"Do you think he knows you're on to him?"

"Maybe. But I greeted him and he didn't notice. Odd."

Simon came up beside Miren. "As I've said before, young Brent's an odd duck anyway."

Miren looked around. Lady MacCallum hovered near the queen and the Duchess of Argyll, but she didn't see Brent. "Where is he?"

"We're keeping an eye on him. He's got Grainger with him, which is interesting. He needed someone to help him cover his actions. Grainger seems likely."

Miren sighed. "He seemed kind to me."

Nathan kissed Miren's hand. "You stay with Simon and my mother. The queen asked that you join her. You and Nat will be safest there, Miren."

"Uncle?" Nat tugged at Nathan's sleeve. "Has the hairy fiend come to the Games?"

Nathan glanced down at his nephew, a faint smile on his

lips. "He wouldn't dare." He touched Nat's head, then drew his hand away as if his own affection frightened him. "Stay with Miren, Nat. She'll keep you safe."

Nathan left, and Nat positioned himself close to Miren. "The hairy fiend won't come. Uncle will scare him away." Nat sighed. "I'm sorry that the hairy fiend has to miss the Games, though. Looks fun."

Miren squeezed his hand. "Maybe hairy fiends have games of their own."

Nat nodded, serious. "Eating little children. I know."

Miren led Nat through the crowd, but reaching Queen Victoria wasn't easy. She was seated before a large tent, surrounded by noblemen, silent guards, and excited onlookers. Lady MacCallum stood stiffly by the queen's chair, but everyone else looked happy.

The queen noticed Miren and motioned to her guards, who escorted Miren into the group. "Miss Lindsay, Her Majesty is pleased you could attend. I see your fiance and the duke are busying themselves."

Miren curtsied, and Molly dropped. Nat bowed, surprising Miren. She lowered her voice to a whisper. "Well done."

He nodded. "You, too."

Glenna stood behind Miren, but Simon shoved his way through the crowd, smiling happily as his victims glared. "Pleased to see you, Your Extreme and Majestic Eminence."

"And you, Mr. MacTavish. I trust your sheep are attended in your absence?"

Simon shrugged. "They'll do fine."

"The caber toss has begun." Queen Victoria raised her hand and pointed as an immense man with blond wavy hair squatted in position. Two men carried a pine-tree trunk and placed it upright in his hands. He labored to his feet. With the caber balanced against his shoulder, he propelled himself forward, stopped, roared, and thrust the pole upward.

The end of the caber hit the ground, went end over end, and the crowd burst into applause.

The queen clapped, too. "The caber toss has a fascinating history. The mighty Scots Highlander had to throw felled trunks into rivers to get them to sawmills. They had to reach the middle of the river so as not to snag."

Lady MacCallum's face stretched into an unnatural smile. "Your knowledge of Highland customs is truly impressive, Your Majesty."

Queen Victoria chuckled. "Not as impressive as the size of that next competitor."

The sound of pipers warming up their instruments distracted the queen. "I must admit, as fascinating as the caber toss is to me, it is the bagpipe competition that most moves my heart."

Lady MacCallum's lip curled, then contorted into another smile. "It seems to please the Scots."

The solo piping contest was the highest honor awarded at the Games. As the caber toss continued, the pipers assembled to begin their competition.

Nathan made his way through the crowd and stood at Miren's side. She noticed Brent coming the other way. He was dressed in full regalia, with a black cap and feather, and white button boots. He looked pale and nervous, but his eyes were bright. She felt a little sorry for him, cornered this way. She looked down at Nat and remembered his father's cruel death. No, Brent deserved no pity, after all.

"Brent, dearest. Where have you been?" Lady MacCallum said.

"I'm . . . I've got some things to . . ." Brent stuttered, then silenced himself.

The Duke of Argyll made his way to Brent's side. "Brent . . . I'd like a word with you, if you've got a moment."

"Not just now."

Lady MacCallum gasped and went white. "Brent!" She turned to the duke, fanning herself violently. "Of course, he has time to speak with you. Don't you, dearest?"

"Not now."

Brent passed in front of the queen, who made a small chopping motion with her hand. Miren met her eyes, and the queen winked.

"Brent!"

Brent turned to his mother. "I'm sorry, Mother. There's something I have to do."

The duke stepped forward, apparently sensing that matters had come to a head. The guards stiffened, their hands went to their weapons. "We need to ask you a few questions, Brent."

"Later."

The duke nodded to Nathan, who placed himself in Brent's path. "Now, Edgington."

Brent looked . . . not frightened, but annoyed. "No."

Nathan caught him by the shoulder. Brent didn't freeze or reach for a weapon. Instead, he rolled his eyes. Miren glanced at Glenna. "Something's not right."

Glenna just sighed and shook her head.

"You weren't on a hunting trip last week, when Miren was attacked."

"By wolves, I know . . . If you'll excuse me . . ."

Brent edged past Nathan, aiming for the queen's tent. "Look, Nathan. I'd be happy to chat another time. *Not now.*"

Brent's response took Nathan off guard. He released his grip, and Brent headed for the tent. Nathan glanced at the duke, who shrugged. "Odd duck, he is."

Nathan started for the tent, but the sound of a bagpipe stopped him. Miren caught her breath as the bag filled and began the most haunting, beautiful music she'd ever heard—except once.

"Nathan, that's the music we heard . . ."

Nathan's mouth dropped as the music slowed, then began again. Grainger held open the tent flap, his eyes shining with pride. And Brent Edgington emerged carrying an old, worn bagpipe, his eyes fixed ahead as music filled the air.

The queen rose to her feet, and the guards stood back. The

other pipers ceased their own music to listen. A caber-tossing competitor slowed and set his tree trunk down. Brent continued through the crowd and into the field. His music rose and lifted over the crowd and pierced toward heaven.

Tears flooded Miren's eyes and dripped to her cheeks. A slender, self-conscious Englishman had taken up Miren's national instrument and poured all his soul into its music. She'd never heard anything so beautiful.

"Your Majesty, please forgive him. I don't know what's come over him. Brent!"

The queen held up her hand. "Silence!" She closed her eyes and a smile formed on her face.

Brent moved across the field, ignoring the crowd, stepping in sympathy with his heart-wrenching music. Grainger pushed his way past Lady MacCallum. "I'd be silent if I were you, Irene. The boy's got a gift."

Her mouth dropped, but she didn't argue. No one but Miren noticed the quiet exchange. "*Irene . . .*"

Brent's song wound to its end. The bagpipe groaned and left its final, ignominious gasp. Brent stopped and opened his eyes. He was in the center of the field, looking lost. *The odd man out*. The crowd was silent. No one moved. Then, all at once, as one, they erupted in cheers and applause.

Brent looked surprised. Then his face lit into a beaming smile. The crowd moved in around him, patting his back, declaring him the winner even before the other pipers began. The queen summoned her guards, who fetched Brent to stand before her.

He bowed, but he stood straight and proud, meeting her gaze without flinching. "Your Majesty."

"Mr. Edgington. You have done England proud. Your skill proves that Scotland is in the heart first, not the blood."

Brent bowed, then backed away. Several pipers were already inquiring about his joining a pipe band. To Miren's surprise and pleasure, he seemed interested. She glanced at his mother, looking for signs of emotion. Irene's face looked frozen, contorted with anger. Yet beside her, their coachman's eyes overflowed with tears of pride.

Nathan stood motionless beside Miren. "I was wrong."

"You were wrong."

They looked at each other. Miren shifted her weight from foot to foot. "Now what?"

He drew her apart from the crowd. "I was so eager to prove Brent guilty." Nathan clasped Miren's shoulders. "Do you understand? I wanted it over. So you and I . . ."

"So we could go our separate ways, or stay together?"

Brent came up behind Nathan, smiling. "Sorry, Nathan. Didn't mean to put you off. What was it you wanted to ask me?"

Nathan released Miren and placed his hand on Brent's shoulder. "It's not important now, Brent. I've never listened to bagpipe music before. But today, when you were playing, I knew what it meant to be Scottish, after all."

Brent beamed with pride. "You are Scottish, Nathan. A laird. You know, I envied you when Kenneth went hunting for you. I used to be his heir, but he wanted his own son. I was afraid I'd be nothing without that title." Brent patted his sunken bagpipe. "But titles don't mean as much as I thought." He glanced at his mother. "I hope she'll understand, one day."

Brent seized Nathan's hand and shook vigorously. "I've been invited to join the Edinburgh piping band, and I've agreed. I have you to thank, Nathan."

Nathan looked doubtful. "Why?"

"Something you said at dinner. '*A man must seize life in many places.*' You said bravery comes when you want something more than you fear its loss. I took those words to heart. I learned the bagpipe when I'd gotten lost hunting, you see." Brent lowered his voice. "Truth be told, I hate hunting. Blood, killing . . ." He grimaced, then resumed a more manly stance. "I ended up at an old crofter's hut. All he had to his name was a bagpipe."

Brent patted his instrument. "This is it."

Miren's eyes misted. "He gave you his bagpipe?"

"He was old. Couldn't play much, because he coughed. He didn't have a son, so he passed it to me. Said I had talent."

"That is obvious. We heard you play one morning . . ." Miren's mouth fell opened. "Your trunk, the one in the forest . . . You kept your bagpipe in it, didn't you?"

"Didn't know anyone had seen it. Grainger helped me cart it around." Brent glanced toward Grainger. "Old fellow caught on to me a few years ago. But he's stuck by me, and encouraged me when I thought I was crazy. He'd take me off for my hunting trips and see that I'd get to a peaceful spot to practice instead."

Miren's brow furrowed. "Are you the reason Lady MacCallum doesn't fire him?"

"Fire him?" Brent sighed. "I'd do my best to see the old fellow taken care of, but my word doesn't go far with Mother. Why do you ask?"

"No reason, really. I'd understood that Lady MacCallum doesn't keep staff long."

"No. She doesn't. Grainger must be charmed." Brent touched his cap and bowed, then headed back to his admirers.

Nathan watched Brent Edgington among the other pipers. The band major was examining Brent's instrument and nodding his approval. Brent had changed. He looked taller than usual, and Nathan realized that until this day, Brent held himself tense, his chest caved. Like a small boy.

Nathan turned his eyes reluctantly to his own nephew. Nat stood beside Glenna, looking small and tense. Nathan didn't want to see it, but the comparison rose before him as if held on a canvas by angel hands. Brent lost his father young, like Nat. Brent grew up insecure, desperate to cling to any importance he could find.

Brent had a mother, true, but Irene wasn't a warm woman. Her disgusted apology to the queen revealed everything her child endured. And Nathan was leaving Nat to grow up in a large, cold house, with servants, with a grandmother who longed for her far-off husband. Taregan was too stubborn to join her, so she had come without him. But Glenna would never be happy in Scotland.

Nat seemed to be a bright child. Nathan had avoided him, but he couldn't help observing the small boy's attentive manner. When they left New York harbor, Glenna had wept quietly. Nat sensed his grandmother's sorrow, and took her hand while she cried, but he didn't pester her.

He needed a father. He needed a mother. He needed brothers and sisters. Pets. He needed . . . Nathan.

Nathan snapped his gaze from the child, but Miren had noticed his expression. "He'll be all right. He's a strong little boy."

"He'll end up like Brent, Miren."

Miren squeezed Nathan's arm. "That's not so very bad. Brent found his own way, despite everything. Look . . . Lady MacCallum is fuming. She'll lecture him and try to shame him from following his dream. But it won't work, Nathan. Because he's found his courage."

"You're saying no matter how I fail my nephew, he'll turn out all right."

"That's not exactly what I was thinking, but, yes. You can't make a bad person. You can hurt a person, you can shatter their confidence until they act only out of fear. But you can't make them bad. What's real in their core will surface, one day. When what they want, value, is equal to, and stronger than, what they fear."

Nathan stared down at her. A slow smile grew on his face. "Those words apply to my own life, far more than I realized."

Miren smiled, too. "I know."

The duke approached Nathan, shaking his head. "Well, my friend, we made a pudding of the whole matter, didn't we?" He paused to whistle. "Young Brent, he's got a way with the pipes. Never heard a thing so fair in all my days! Misjudged him, I'm afraid.''

"Yet everything I learned pointed to Brent as my brother's killer.''

Miren's eyes widened, but Nathan patted her hand. "I explained my situation to the duke.''

"Oh.''

The duke grinned from ear to ear, pleased at the confidence. He leaned toward Miren, speaking conspiratorially. "Always wanted to meet an Indian.''

Miren sighed. "Me, too.''

The duke straightened and his smile faded. "Your troubles aren't over, Laird. If Brent Edgington isn't responsible, someone else is. And he's still walking free.''

Nathan drew a long, tight breath. "I know.''

The duke's brow furrowed and he gestured toward the end of the field. "It's the Oban guard. What are they doing here?''

Nathan turned. A regiment of armed soldiers crossed the runners' track, disrupting the competitors from their race. The duke frowned. "Those are Major MacDuff's soldiers. He handled a brigade in India—dreadful man . . . Rumors abound, but he's in control of this area . . .''

"Did you request his support?''

"Of course not! My guards were enough to subdue Brent Edgington. He's here on his own. I shall inquire . . .''

The spectators murmured and jostled forward to view the oncoming regiment. A dark red coach pulled up behind the queen's tent, waiting. A coachman stood by the door, but he didn't wear livery. He looked more like a hired brute than a footman.

Simon positioned himself beside Nathan. "What's going on?''

"I have no idea.''

The regiment major ordered his troops into a turn. A tall blond man walked behind the major. He came around the major and smiled.

"Saints defend us . . ." Simon's voice broke on a sharp hiss, but Nathan didn't recognize the man. He was older than Brent, probably in his late forties. Miren stepped forward, her eyes wide in shock.

Nathan took her arm. "Miren, what is it?"

She was shaking. "Nathan . . . That man, he's Dr. Patterson!"

"It can't be."

Simon seized Nathan's shoulder. "It is, lad. That's him as killed your brother and the laird."

Not Brent, but Drew Patterson himself. Nathan's heart beat with cold fury. He edged Miren behind him, then strode toward the regiment. Every soldier aimed his weapon . . . at Nathan. Patterson stepped forward, fearless. "That's far enough, 'Laird' MacCallum."

Simon groaned. Nathan heard Miren's small voice behind him. "Oh, no!"

The duke stomped to the regiment major. "What is the meaning of this?"

The major raised his chin, looking smug and important. "Forgive the intrusion, Your Grace. We're here under higher authority than your own, with orders to take this man into custody." He gestured at Nathan.

The duke frowned. "For what?" He didn't wait for an answer. "If it's for impersonating a nobleman, that matter is known to me, and for an established cause which I deemed honorable—"

"Got him for a lot worse than that, Your Grace." The major turned to Nathan. "He's wanted for murder in the United States of America." He paused for effect. "For the murder of Laird Kenneth MacCallum and his own brother, David MacCallum."

"What?" Simon's voice boomed over the crowd. "That's the devil as did the deed!" He pointed at Patterson. "I was there myself . . ."

Patterson shook his head in mock disapproval. "Simon, no

322

one can doubt your complicity in these horrible crimes.''

Patterson looked supremely confident. His tactic was well conceived. His gaze fixed on Miren and his smile broadened.

Glenna pushed her way through the crowd. ''Ridiculous!'' She released Nat's hand as she aimed for the doctor. Nat clung to Miren's skirt, his small face white.

Nathan fought for reason. Time was short. Patterson had attacked Miren. Why? It made sense if Brent was trying to keep her from marrying Nathan, but what could Patterson want? Why would he risk capture himself by returning to Scotland?

Miren shook her fist at Patterson, as if words came hard through her anger. ''Nathan didn't kill his brother. He was at sea! Ask his crew.''

Patterson's gaze moved slowly over Miren, mocking. ''My dear little Miren. What a welcome is this? You, my sweet betrothed, are defending another man?''

''I am *not* your betrothed!''

Patterson's gaze whisked to Nathan, then back to Miren. A studied gesture. ''Aren't you? Consider well before you answer, my dear. It so happens that I have proof of this half-breed's crime. Surely, you don't think the word of his ill-begotten crew is equal to my own?'' He paused, contemplating. ''Even if it were true, it would take time. Time is something he doesn't have.''

The threat came clearer this time. Miren recognized it, too. ''What do you want?''

''This Indian's fate is best handled in America. Let it be so. But . . .'' He took a step closer. Miren gripped Nathan's arm. ''How it grieved me to learn you thought me dead, my angel.''

''I am sorry it's not so!''

''You were promised to me, soon to be my lawful wife. When I returned, after securing evidence against this half-breed's crime, I was shocked to find you in his company. How I feared for you! Were I assured of your safety, knowing our betrothal resumed its rightful course . . ."

Miren's mouth dropped. "You want me to marry you? Why?"

"For your protection, my dear."

"That's crazy." Miren uttered a short, humorless laugh. "I won't marry you. It's obvious you killed Laird MacCallum and Nathan's brother."

Patterson's brow rose. "*I?* Why should I, a physician in good standing, commit such a crime?"

Miren glanced at Nathan. "I don't know, exactly. We thought . . . We thought someone put you up to it."

Patterson laughed. "I am no one's lackey, my dear. No, it is clear that this man has bewitched you. Your father begged me, with his dying words, to care for you. It is my intention to do just that." Patterson moved quickly toward them and grabbed Miren's arm. The crowd murmured in alarm, but Nathan shoved him aside.

"Touch her and you die."

The Englishman's cold, blue eyes shifted to Nathan, glittering with malice. "MacDuff, is it fit to leave an accused murderer to his own devices?" Patterson clucked his tongue in mockery. "The lax nature of the Scottish troops must be addressed at some point in time."

The guards came forward to surround Nathan, their weapons aimed to kill. Two men held him restrained as Patterson pulled Miren away. She kicked and struggled, but he held tight. Molly snarled and attacked.

Nathan stood helpless, his arms wrenched behind his back by the guards as Miren's dog flung herself at Patterson's legs. He kicked, his boot thudded into the small dog's side, but Molly didn't stop.

"Someone get rid of this dog!"

A soldier reached tentatively for Molly, but the duke took her collar. "Quiet, lass."

Patterson gripped Miren tight. He bent low to speak to her. Nathan's blood ran cold when he saw her expression. Her eyes closed tight, her lips moved in a silent prayer. She nodded, and her struggles ceased. He'd threatened her with something so evil that she bowed her head in compliance.

"Forgive me." Her voice shook, small and toneless. The sound pierced Nathan's heart. She looked to him, desperate. She bowed her head again, staring at her feet as she spoke. "Your Grace, it is my error that has caused this . . . misunderstanding. I am promised to Dr. Patterson. With your permission, I will go with him now."

Patterson smiled in dark shades of victory. "You have heard my fiancée's admission, Your Grace. Major MacDuff will take control of the prisoner from here. But I request Your Grace's presence at the MacCallum estate. Miren and I will say our vows at the old church on the MacCallum estate." He gazed down at Miren like a doting husband. "I've already made the necessary arrangements, my darling."

Patterson had made the arrangements before they left for Oban. Nathan began to make sense of Patterson's devices. He'd planned this marriage since he'd learned that Miren was living at the estate.

Nathan couldn't guess his motives, but that much was clear. He'd followed them to Oban, and possibly realized that Miren was bound for America, or marriage to Nathan. Whatever his reason, Patterson had to work fast. His actions revealed that much.

The duke frowned, his eyes narrow and suspicious. "Why do you require my presence at your wedding?"

"A small matter . . . I require your seal of approval once I am Miren's rightful husband."

The duke hesitated. "I would prefer to sort things out here."

"I'm afraid that's not possible. I require your signature in connection with my wedding."

Nathan jerked to free himself, but a guard wrapped a cord around his neck and yanked him back. He couldn't fight. He had to maintain reason to save Miren. Patterson had cornered her, and time was short. He closed his eyes, he shut out the crowd, his enemy, and his friends. Miren's face lingered, desperate, needing him.

Fear rose in his heart—fear that he couldn't protect her. She needed him, and by his pursuit of Brent Edgington, he'd failed her.

Another voice rose inside his mind. It spoke in the Iroquois tongue, but its accent was Scottish. *"If a man could fly, he would fly. If he has no wings, he will ride the swiftest horse. If his horse falters, he will run. And if his legs fail, he will crawl. And yes, my son, he may die before he reaches his goal. . . . But he will die fighting."*

Nathan opened his eyes and spat. He curled his lip in the most dangerous snarl he could muster. "Take the girl, Doctor. She means nothing to me. But you won't pin my brother's murder on me. I've got alibis!" Good. He sounded desperate. Selfish. "What's more, you'd have done better to check David MacCallum's will. Because, Doctor, he has an heir."

Miren's mouth dropped. For a fraction of a second, he saw her doubt. He would betray Nat to save himself. Beside him, bound also, Simon caught his breath. "No . . ." He heard not anger but shock in the Scotsman's voice. For all Simon's accusations, he couldn't believe Nathan capable of a selfish act.

A tiny smile appeared on Miren's lips as her doubt disappeared. "You think of yourself always. I should have known!" She sounded petulant, and she turned her head girlishly away, refusing to look at him. The woman was practical. Smart. She couldn't know his plan, or if he had a plan. But she trusted him with her life.

Nathan's heart filled with love, but he kept his expression straight. He struggled against the guards, then spat again. Lady MacCallum stepped forward, a keen light of victory in her eyes. "Kenneth, my dear late husband, had no other heir besides his son. You are an impostor, revealed thanks to the thoughtful work of Dr. Patterson."

"I am David's heir! He left a will, and I have it." Nathan paused. "Somewhere."

Patterson's eyes shifted to Irene, then fixed on Nathan. His dark smile returned. "More than enough reason for murder. You've always been an opportunist."

Patterson turned to the duke. "When Laird MacCallum and his son were murdered, I barely escaped the blaze alive. Simon had disappeared, this Indian with him. I guessed at once they were responsible for the heinous crime. I checked on David's Indian half-brother and learned much not fit to share in public."

The duke frowned. "Good. Spare us the details."

Major MacDuff stepped forward. "This impostor has nigh on to confessed. I'll take matters from here."

The duke started to argue, cast a forlorn look Nathan's way, and nodded. "I see no other way. I will follow you to Inveraray, Doctor. It is within your legal rights. As long as the girl agrees, I am bound."

Miren hesitated. Nathan met her eyes and saw her terror. Patterson had threatened her, probably with Nathan's own life. Yet there was something else. Patterson thought he had the upper hand. For the moment, it was true. Let him act on that. A man sure of success is sooner to fall. Nathan had learned that from his certainty over capturing Brent.

He wouldn't make that mistake again.

Patterson bowed to the duke. "I will see you at the estate, Your Grace." He cast a quick, almost patronizing glance at Irene MacCallum. "And you, Your Ladyship, I trust you will also join us?"

"That is my intention, of course."

Nathan watched Irene's expression closely. She held herself very stiff, as if something had happened she didn't expect and she wasn't sure how to react. Yet if Patterson and Irene were allies, why abduct Miren? Clearly, Irene hadn't expected this turn of events, either.

Nathan held Miren's desperate gaze. He didn't need to offer

reassurance, because he saw her trust. She knew he would find a way to save her. What she didn't know, because he hadn't told her, was that he wanted her, always. That he belonged to her, because he loved her. That he wanted their lives spent together, with children, with collies who preferred luxury to work. With sheep in the pasture, and probably on the front lawn, too.

He could lose her, and she would never know.

Patterson took her arm, and Miren didn't fight. She went with him toward the dark coach, and his grisly footman held open the door.

Molly charged after them, growling and snapping. She bit Patterson, and he shouted in pain. "Get rid of this dog!"

The footman pulled a revolver, and Miren screamed. "Molly, no!"

Molly charged the footman and latched onto his ankle. He kicked, hard, and the little dog collapsed. Nathan's heart quailed at Miren's sob. "No!"

A muted, plaintive cry came from Nat, and he darted from the crowd after Miren. Nathan yanked against his restraints. "Nat, stop . . ."

The footman tried to push the boy away, but Nat squirmed around his legs and evaded his grasp. He darted up the coach steps after Miren. The footman started after him, brandishing his driving whip. The whip cracked, Nat screamed, and Nathan's blood ran cold.

Nathan turned to Glenna. "Stop him!"

Glenna ran after the footman. She grabbed him by his thin hair, but he shoved her aside. Patterson turned, still calm, toward the crowd. "Contain this deranged woman, MacDuff."

A soldier seized Glenna and pulled her away from the coach. Nat grabbed Miren's skirt and held fast. An evil smile twitched Patterson's lips. "If the child wants to accompany us . . ."

Miren tried to pry Nat's fingers from her skirt. "No, Nat. You must stay with Glenna."

"She's going to jail!" The boy's high, shaking voice pierced Nathan's heart. He needed someone. He needed the person least able to help him. He needed Nathan.

Patterson shoved Miren inside, and the coach started forward. Nathan relaxed every muscle, then tensed all at once—an old Iroquois trick. He broke free from his guards and ran toward the coach.

"Hold your fire!" The duke's shrill voice rang over the crowd, but a shot rang out. Nathan dodged and kept running.

"By the order of Her Majesty . . ." This voice no one refused. The soldiers stopped shooting as Nathan ran toward the coach.

"You can't go with Miren now, Nat."

Nat buried his face in Miren's skirt, crying. He shook his head and backed farther into the coach. Nathan held out his hand and tried to gentle his voice despite his fear. "Come with me, Nat. I'll take care of you."

Nat peeked out from Miren's skirt, then shook his head again. "You don't want me, Uncle."

The tiny words shot through Nathan's heart like bitter arrows. "I want you, Nat."

Nat looked doubtful. He wanted more, he wanted words he could believe, because Nathan had given so little until now. Nathan fought for calm. He had to be honest. A child would accept nothing less.

"I was afraid of you. Afraid I wouldn't be able to help you when you needed me, because I couldn't help your father. I was more afraid of you than the hairy fiend. But I love you, Nat. Please come to me."

Nat hesitated. "Swear?"

"I swear." Nathan ignored Patterson's revolver. He sank to his knee, holding out his arms. "Please, come to me."

"What about Miren?"

"I'll be all right, Nat. I'm going for a ride." Miren's light

329

tone amazed Nathan. She was practical, still. Brave, because it was necessary. "Go to your uncle. He'll take care of you."

Nat shrugged, then nodded. He jumped from the coach and ran to Nathan's arms. Nathan held him tight, then kissed his small forehead. Nat drew back and looked into Nathan's eyes, and for an instant Nathan saw his own brother looking back.

"I love you, too, Uncle."

Miren looked back over her shoulder. Her hair fell around her face, tears stained her cheeks. Not of fear, but of love. Nathan met her eyes and a tiny smile grew on her face. She mouthed words. Words he couldn't hear, but felt. *I love you, Indian.*

Molly limped to Nathan's side, whining. She spotted Miren, and growled as she aimed again for the coach.

"Molly, no. Stay!"

Patterson yanked her back into the coach and slammed the door. The coachman lashed at the horses, and the coach lurched forward. Nathan started to rise, to follow her on foot, to save her no matter what stood in his way.

The muzzle of a musket jabbed his temple, and soldiers surrounded him. "Boy, you aren't going anywhere."

Chapter Eighteen

I have learned something I didn't know. When a human companion is gone, out of sight, the connection between dog and human remains. I have never been apart from my Miren before. But I will find my way back to her. At all costs.

"What do you want with me?" Miren sat close to the coach wall, her hands bound at the wrists lest she attempt escape. Dr. Patterson gazed out the window as the coach wound north from Oban. He shifted his gaze to her, and her skin crawled.

"I should think that obvious, Miren. I'm honoring our former agreement. You will become my wife."

"We never had such an agreement. I refused."

Dr. Patterson smiled, evil and cruel. "Your refusal was a petty attempt to garner a quicker proposal, my dear, and we both know it. My wife lingered on the brink of her tragic death. I had to wait, for propriety's sake." He turned back to the window and made a "tsk" noise. Miren's hands clenched into fists. "Where did you go? I've often wondered."

Miren sneered. "I went from the gates of hell to the mountains of heaven, and I never looked back."

Patterson glanced back at her, his soulless eyes narrow. "Maybe you should have glanced back, once or twice anyway. Hell was at your heels."

"Not until you returned from America, after you murdered Laird MacCallum and his son."

Patterson "tsk"-ed again. "Surely you don't believe I committed that ghastly crime? Not when your beloved savage had far more to gain." His mocking words left no doubt. He didn't care if she knew. He even seemed proud of his deeds.

"What I don't understand is what you had to gain by their deaths. It might have served Brent Edgington to remove his stepfather and the new heir, but not you."

"Brent had much to gain. Poor sap was too stupid to know it. I witnessed his pathetic display with the bagpipes. Dreadful noise, don't you agree?"

"I wouldn't expect a coward to appreciate Highland battle music. It must have put a shred of fear into you, Patterson. Just a wee shred."

Patterson's mocking smile turned toward a snarl, and Miren knew she'd guessed well. "There's nothing to fear from a bagpipe."

"Scots history is filled with surprises, Doctor. Every one heralded by the mystic call of the bagpipe."

"You forget, as do too many Celts, that England dominates this land now. As I dominate you."

Miren angled her chin. "And the Queen of England knows every Highland plaid. She makes her most beloved home at Balmoral. Have we become English, or have the English become Scottish in part? Isn't that what Brent Edgington proved today?"

"He proved himself a fool, and little more."

"Ah, but you're wrong, Doctor. He proved himself a man."

"By playing a bag of wind? Miren, my dear, you are a naïve and winsome lass, aren't you? Brent Edgington is nothing without his title, without money."

"You think money and position and favorable circumstances make a man's worth. I think the opposite is true. No circumstance on earth can alter what you've created by your deeds, Doctor. I fear you shall learn this truth the hard way."

Patterson's eyes darkened with suppressed anger. "You have changed, my dear. Tell me, does this new self-assurance come from having an Indian between your thighs?"

Miren smiled. A wave of pleasure like intoxication swept over her. "An Indian . . . a pirate . . . and a Scottish laird."

She sat back in her seat, pleased with his rage.

He twisted the rope around her neck tighter, but she refused to back down. "In a short time I'll be your husband, and everything I ever wanted from you you'll give."

"What is that, exactly? Besides lust." Miren kept her voice taunting, but fought a sick tide of disgust and fear. *I will not act on fear, but on what I want*. She shoved fear aside and allowed her practicality to take over. She ran through what she remembered of Dr. Patterson. He tended the old wealthy noble families, but not the young. Because he loathed childbirth and pregnancy . . .

"It should interest you to know, my *husband*, that I bear Nathaniel's child."

Patterson's eyes narrowed. His thin lips curled in disgust. "That's impossible. You can't have known him more than a month."

Miren patted her stomach. "My body has already begun to change. I haven't experienced my monthly flow in three weeks. Nathan and I made love at our first meeting, you see." It was a risky assertion. She couldn't be sure when Patterson had arrived in Scotland.

"You moved from frigid maid to whore with amazing speed, didn't you?"

She nodded. "Indians settle lots of things with kissing."

Miren crossed one leg over the other. "Perhaps our wedding isn't so desirable after all."

Patterson laughed, and her hopes dwindled. "As pleasurable as it might be to sample your delights, my purposes are far grander."

"What 'purpose' can marrying me serve? And what makes you think I'll agree?"

"You'll agree, because I hold your Indian's life in my hands."

"He was left with the authorities."

Patterson grinned. "Authority, my dear . . . but whose? Major MacDuff and I 'associated,' shall we say, during our tenure in India. I'm an observant man. I learned a few things about the good major that could send his career in a serious downward spiral."

"You're blackmailing him."

"Coarsely put. But whatever I want done with your Indian, the major will do—lest I reveal his propensity for men. Kept a lover for years in Ceylon. Wouldn't think it to look at him, would you?"

"The major's private life is none of my business. Nathan's life is."

"I have them both where I want them. Where I have you, Miren. At my mercy."

"You have no 'mercy.' "

Patterson folded his long, thin hands on his lap. "It would be wise for you to remember. You have a choice, my sweet. You'll marry me to save your Indian, or refuse and he'll die. Per my instructions, Major MacDuff will be forced to kill him 'escaping.' "

"Why?" Her voice came too rushed, desperate. "Why do you want to marry me at all?"

"For the same reason Kenneth MacCallum sought out your mother and arranged for her hand."

Miren remembered Glenna's story. "For some ancient Malcolm treasure? That's ridiculous. There's no such thing."

Patterson's pale blue eyes glimmered. "Isn't there? Kenneth said differently. He told me quite a lot in his drunken stupors, in fact. Interesting enough so that I checked on his story. What your fanciful Celtic imagination calls 'treasure,' I call a vast inheritance left sitting at a vault in Edinburgh. A vault only accessible to Malcolm's heir. Or to a husband who possesses the duke's seal of approval . . ."

"What?" Miren shook her head. "That's not possible. If my mother had some sort of inheritance, she would have shared it with my father. We were poor, Doctor. So poor you lent your services for free, if you remember . . ." Her voice trailed as her understanding grew. "You knew it then, didn't you? That's why you tended my father, because you wanted to force me to marry you. You didn't try to heal him at all, did you?"

Patterson chuckled. "I even helped him along, my dear. And in the meantime, arranged for him to pay for my services by selling me his cottage. My wife took longer. But then, she was healthier when I began administering poison, drop by precious drop, into her system."

Miren didn't respond. Hatred filled her heart, blinding rage coupled with fear. "You killed my father."

"Your father was ill anyway. I simply quickened his last hours. As an act of mercy." His voice took on a taunting quality that spurred Miren toward violence. "I never did care much for my profession."

"Yet you enjoy killing, don't you?"

"It's necessary. I enjoy crafting people, Miren. Manipulating them, controlling them. I enjoy using my superior wiles to defeat them. Your mother knew nothing of her inheritance, nor presumably did her father. Kenneth stumbled onto the information while researching the connection between the Malcolm and MacCallum clans."

"They were once the same clan, I know."

"And your grandfather's branch proved far more wealthy than Kenneth's. He wanted their power. And later, I wanted his." Patterson closed his eyes briefly, swollen with his twisted pride. He couldn't resist bragging. Miren listened attentively, searching for anything that might help.

"Poison is a doctor's tool, but I use it wisely. The day he went to meet his son, I dropped a half-pint of sleeping powder into Kenneth MacCallum's whiskey. I watched them drink, frown at its taste, and drink again. I held the cup to my own lips and said it was surely a rare form of the purest Scottish whiskey ever tasted."

Patterson leaned his head back against the padded coach wall. "They drank, and I watched them doze off into fool's slumber. I lay them together, piled wood on their bodies, and lit a fine, healthy blaze. Sucked up that little wooden cabin in minutes."

Miren closed her eyes. If he told her this, he meant to kill her, too. "There were three bodies."

"Ah, yes. I'd almost forgotten. A guide led us to David's pathetic little farm—he'd built it out in the middle of nowhere. I killed the guide the first day and left him in the woods. When the time came, I dragged him to the cabin. Almost made a mistake. The blaze had burned faster than I guessed. I had to throw his rotten body through the door." Patterson touched his mustache. "Singed my hair in the process."

Miren fought an intense wave of nausea. "Why did you kill them? How did that serve you?"

"Let's say it served another's interest. My hand is in many pots. At the time, my dearest, I thought I'd lost you for good. Rumors around Kilmartin said you'd committed suicide. I know now those dotard farmers were trying to protect you. They never liked me, I'm afraid."

"Farmers have good sense." Miren paused. "What do you mean, 'hand in many pots?' What other pot?"

"It seems wise to keep that from you, in case I require it as a fall-back plan. But if my plan to secure your inheritance fails, I'm not completely lost."

"Where are we going, if I might ask?"

"We're headed to a place you know well, my dear. The MacCallum estate."

"Why?"

"We'll marry there, at the stone church on the MacCallum estate. I've already arranged for a priest to perform the ceremony. The good duke will sign papers securing my rights to your inheritance, and I'll be on my way."

"You can't expect me to agree, when I know you'll kill me anyway."

"You'll agree, because I have your Indian under my control. Two things can happen, per my orders. He can be sent to America, or he can die. It's your choice."

"Nathan isn't here. You left him in Oban. How will I know what your henchman has done with him?"

"I don't have time to give personal instructions at this point, my dear. I have two letters, to be sent by a courier. One says the Indian dies, one says he goes free to America."

Miren considered this. "I do not trust you, but I have no choice."

"In case you come to your senses and realize the Indian's life is valueless . . . I have something to threaten your own life." Patterson drew a small dirk from his waistcoat and held it to the window.

"What happened to your butcher's knife?"

"A weapon for each task, my dear. The larger knife was necessary to insure your compliance when I attempted to remove you from your miserable little cottage."

Miren's lip curled in disgust. "So if I refuse to marry you, you'll stab me? I doubt a priest will take kindly to a proposal like that."

"The good father needn't know about our private . . . arrangement."

Patterson fingered the dirk's sharp blade. "If you don't care about your own life . . . When the duke's coach arrives, there

will be several people you care for present. Possibly ...
Glenna MacCallum?''

Miren tensed, and Patterson laughed. "Your Indian pre-
ceded me to Scotland by a few weeks, but I located his ship.
Once I realized he had you watched at all times, I focused
my attention on proving him a fraud ..."

"Why? If I'm the one you're after, why do you care who
inherits Kenneth MacCallum's estate?"

Patterson's smile faded. His lip curled in a sneer, and Miren
guessed she'd come close to unveiling another secret. "The
matter is of interest to me. I asked a few questions—didn't
learn anything besides his arrival date, and that Simon was
with him. I was about to leave when I spotted the woman and
child. That disturbed my plan. The brat wasn't an Indian.
David MacCallum's son, perhaps?"

Miren kept her expression straight. "The woman you refer
to is Nathan's housemaid. The boy is her grandson."

"Maybe. But she's hovering near you, Miren. She'll come
with the duke. And she'll bring her grandson. . . . Something
tells me their lives are of interest to you."

Miren's anger overflowed. It came like bile to her throat.
"Yes, their lives have value. All life has value."

"Such a simple-minded wench you are. I doubt you could
endure something so tragic as a child's death."

Miren's heart ran cold, but she kept her voice even.
"You'll stab a child? So much simpler ... How do you expect to get away with that?"

"Stabbing ..." Patterson clucked his tongue. "So dramatic. A small prick, like that of an insect, can be so much
more effective." He opened a small black case at his feet and
withdrew a narrow vial. He removed the vial and dipped the
dirk's point into the clear fluid.

"The tiniest drop—applied, say, to the blade of a knife—
can send a man, or child, to certain death. The only cure is
an immediate—and vulgar—response. A well-meaning individual nearby has to suck the poison from the wound before

it enters the blood stream. Spitting it out afterwards, of course. Even so, it should leave the victim weak and deranged for days, even weeks afterward.''

Patterson recapped the vial and placed it in his waistcoat. ''Unfortunately, the cure wouldn't work on a child. They're too weak. The beauty of this particular poison is that it doesn't show up immediately. One can attack, then withdraw. The symptoms aren't noticeable until it's too late for the cure. Person gets dizzy, stumbles. Throat gets dry . . .'' Patterson affected a false shudder. ''Grisly, isn't it?''

''You are truly evil.'' Miren spoke evenly, without emotion. Nathan would come for her. Somehow, he would free himself, and he would come. But if Patterson saw him . . . She had to let Patterson think he was winning, that nothing threatened his plan. ''I take it you've used this method before.''

''I spent years in India, where poison is common. It was my own dear late wife who showed me this tactic. She eased her father to an early grave when he thought to pass his fortune on to his mistress. Unfortunately, her 'fortune' passed too soon, and with it, her usefulness.''

''A shame you two didn't have children, Doctor. The world needs more of your kind.''

Miren's caustic reply disturbed Patterson's composure. ''How lighthearted you are, Miren! It will be a shame to become a widower again, so soon after our wedding.''

''You'll force me to marry you at the threat of another's life, then kill me? Won't that raise suspicions?''

''I'll bring you with me to Edinburgh, collect your inheritance . . . And then I'll have no further use for you. Oh, it will appear accidental, of course. There are limitless ways of removing you, without casting suspicion on myself. But even were the authorities to pursue me, I shall be long gone by then.''

''What about your ally?''

A slight frown twitched on Patterson's lips before he concealed it. "Allies are useful at certain times. When their usefulness passes... Assuming this person has secrets to conceal, I face no threat from that quarter."

Miren's throat tightened as she realized the hopelessness of her situation. "As soon as we're away from the people I love, I will fight you. All the way to Edinburgh. All the way to hell."

Patterson fingered the rope attached to her neck. He tugged her forward, and she felt his dank breath on her face. "I'll keep you busy, Miren. Did you think your story of pregnancy would save you from your 'husband's' attention? It won't. I would make use of you now, but I don't want you soiled for our wedding. Afterwards, I'll take my fill of you all the way to Edinburgh."

Miren met his eyes evenly. "I will die first."

He slackened his grip on the rope, knowing he controlled her with or without its force. "You'll die after. When *I* choose. In fact, if need be, you'll be weakened by this same poison, and I'll have you while you languish."

Patterson twisted the dirk, then flung it at the wall behind Miren's head. His wrist flicked with lightning speed, and the weapon lodged an inch away from her temple. Patterson sat back and laughed. "Learned that in India, too."

The men in uniforms are evil. Like a pack of dark wolves. They held my Nathan to the ground while their leader took Miren away. In a coach. A coach such as I once coveted. I covet them no more.

Molly sat in the middle of the field, lost in the crowd. The coach disappeared, taking Miren with it. She tried to follow, but a uniformed man held her back. "What do we do with the dog, Major?"

Four men surrounded Nathan, and clasped metal hoops over his wrists. Molly sensed they were not for decoration. "Shoot it."

Molly in the Middle

Nat screamed, and Glenna stepped forward. "You will not shoot my dog."

The major looked confused, but Glenna took Molly's collar. "I am the housekeeper of the MacCallum estate. This is my dog. Shoot her, and I will see you in court, Major."

The major shrugged. "Keep her quiet, then." He nodded to his servants. "Take the prisoner."

"Not so fast." The fat woman who resembled Blossom made her way through the crowd, trailed by her servants. Molly felt reassured. This woman had final say. Even over Muffin.

The queen ignored the major in favor of the duke. "Of what has he been accused?"

The major stepped forward. "Murder, Your Majesty. Also, impersonating the rightful heir—"

"That is known to Her Majesty."

Nathan caught his breath. Molly glanced up at him. His mouth was open. "It is?"

The queen looked down upon him, despite the fact he stood several heads taller than herself. Molly considered it an impressive tactic, and wondered if she could use it somehow on Blossom.

"All is known to Her Majesty."

The duke looked uncomfortable. "You don't keep secrets from the Queen of England, Nathan."

Nathan smiled. "Apparently you don't."

Queen Victoria looked silently into Nathan's eyes. He met her gaze. Molly approved the interaction. "I like you, young man. But who are you, that I should believe you innocent despite Dr. Patterson's claim?"

Nathan didn't have an answer ready. Molly tensed. He needed an answer. She squirmed free from Glenna and nudged his ankles. "The little collie knows."

Glenna came to face the queen. "He is my son."

A sharp hiss startled even the queen. Lady MacCallum pushed forward. "That is impossible."

The queen's brow rose. "She is certainly not a housekeeper, Lady MacCallum. Her Majesty recognized that at once."

Glenna glanced at Nathan, then back at the queen. "How did you know?"

"Housekeepers keep themselves cleaner than this."

Glenna nodded. "Quite so."

The queen looked down at Nat. "Then you . . ."

"This is my grandson, Nathaniel MacCallum."

"The real Nathaniel MacCallum, I presume."

Nat straightened. "Your Extreme Eminence, I am Nat." He bowed quickly.

"You have been taught protocol by Mr. MacTavish, I see."

"Yes, sir, Ma'am. Will you let my uncle go?"

The queen's gaze shifted to Nathan. "Where would he go, do you think?"

"He would save Miren, so she can become my mother. As of now, she is my cousin only. But I want her for a mother."

The queen's lip curved to one side. Something about Nat's declaration confused her. Molly wasn't sure why. "I see." She turned back to Glenna. "Then you are the real Lady MacCallum?"

Glenna didn't answer. She looked to Irene. "No, Your Majesty, I am not. I fled my husband's cruelty years ago. A woman who married him and stayed his wife despite his abuse surely has earned that title. I do not desire it. My husband is Nathan's father. I will sign whatever papers are necessary to insure that Irene's station remains unaltered."

The queen nodded, but Irene offered no thanks. "This matter is a disgrace. Brent! Summon our coach at once."

Brent rolled his eyes. "It's not 'our coach' anymore, Mother." He didn't sound constipated anymore. Molly decided he might be good, after all. "It belongs to Master MacCallum." Brent bowed cheerfully to Nat. "With your permission, sir . . ."

"Granted, sir!" Nat laughed, and Brent patted his head.

"You will be the one to slay the hairy fiend." Brent saluted. "Perhaps don't kill it, but teach it a good lesson."

Brent grinned. "I'll pin it in a corner and play the highest note I can reach on my pipes. How's that?"

"Good."

Brent turned around and waved to Grainger. "We're taking the coach on back to the estate, Grainger. After that, we'll have to find our own way to Edinburgh. At least, if you'll agree to leave your post and come along with me."

Grainger nodded. "It would be my honor, lad."

Brent turned, smiling, to his mother. "And you, Mother. Kenneth left you enough money to set up somewhere else. I'll be joining the Royal Pipers in Edinburgh. Maybe you'd like to come along?" He didn't sound enthusiastic.

Irene's face formed a snarl. "You fool . . . Certainly not! Pipers. Ha!" She snapped her fingers at him. "If you'd been a better man . . ."

The queen braced into royal, and perhaps motherly, indignation. "That will do, Lady MacCallum. Go to your coach. I have seen enough of you."

Irene clasped Muffin in her bony hands and whisked to the coach. Brent cast his gaze skyward. "Think I'll sit up with Grainger for the journey." He headed off, his bagpipe secure beneath his arm. "Nathan, I'm guessing we'll meet again." He headed off, stopped, then bowed to the queen. "Almost forgot." He chuckled as if his error caused him pleasure, then continued on without a formal dismissal.

The queen sighed. "I almost begin to like that young man." She turned her attention back to Glenna. "No one knows the child's heart like a mother. So I ask you, do you believe your son a murderer?"

Glenna watched Irene storm into the coach and slam the door. "Of course not. Nathan brought Nat here as Kenneth's rightful heir. Until he met Miren, he had no intention of staying."

The queen eyed Nathan. "Ah. Then you have changed your

mind. Her Majesty was, of course, right.''

Nathan's mouth opened a little wider. His reaction seemed to please the queen. ''Young men in love can be stubborn, and sometimes overlook the best thing in their lives. Especially when they stumbled on it, rather than seeking it out for themselves.''

Simon sighed. ''That's more true than you know, Your Extremeness. More true than you know.''

''Then I will overrule Major MacDuff's orders and will leave the matter in the Duke of Argyll's capable hands.''

Major MacDuff went white. ''I have orders . . .''

One brow arched, so high that Molly tilted her head to view the queen's face straight. ''Orders that supersede those of Her Majesty the Queen of the British Empire . . . and many other places too numerous to mention?'' Her voice rose to a satisfying finish. Molly approved, but apparently MacDuff feared something more than the queen.

The duke puffed an impatient breath. ''MacDuff, there's nothing the doctor can reveal about you that we don't know already. Now, back off.''

The queen eyed the duke suspiciously. ''Is this a matter of which Her Majesty should be aware?''

The duke hesitated. ''I'm thinking Her Majesty would be happier not knowing.''

''Her Majesty values happiness. Release the American, Major. Her Majesty is at this point weary, and intends to proceed to Balmoral Castle. These Games have been . . . eventful, but I trust you all will conclude the matter on your own.''

Everyone bowed, even Simon. Some with grace, some awkwardly. Molly cocked one ear, but no one noticed. The queen stepped forward, but stopped beside Molly. She tapped her knee over her great, cumbersome black dress, and Molly rose up and placed her paws on the designated spot. The queen scratched her ears.

''Such a fine collie you are. Don't worry, dear little one. Your mistress will return to you.''

The queen raised her chin and progressed through the crowd, her house pets in dutiful attendance. A good, solid woman. Molly liked her, but she could never be the companion Miren was. For the first time, Molly didn't envy the favored house pets. If she could have Miren back, she would stick to a small cottage and soft brushing. If only she could have Miren again . . .

MacDuff released Nathan and left the field with his soldiers. The duke clapped his hands once, half in pleasure, half in excitement. "Well, then! That's settled." He paused. "Now what? I'm assuming you have some sort of plan."

Nathan didn't hesitate. "Go to Inveraray as Patterson expects, Your Grace."

"What about you?"

"I'll need a horse. The fastest horse you can find." He didn't wait for an answer. Nathan turned to Simon. Molly's head shifted with the conversation, although she began to lose its trail.

"The others will follow in the duke's coach. Simon, I've got another plan for you. Take a small, fast boat around and up Loch Fyne . . ."

The Duke's brow furrowed tight. "I don't know, Nathan. If I follow through and do as he asked, Patterson will think he's got the upper hand."

Nathan smiled, his dark eyes glimmering. "I'm counting on it."

Chapter Nineteen

He wouldn't dare leave me behind. I will not obey! Not that I am an obedient dog anyway, of course. But I will not start now.

The queen has left. Lady MacCallum has also gone, with poor, wretched Muffin clasped on her lap. I felt pity for the miserable little creature. Muffin tried to follow Glenna into her coach, but Lady MacCallum, the shrew, grabbed Muffin by the neck and pinched until she squeaked.

I sense a strange tension in Lady MacCallum that wasn't there before. She has always been bitter and angry. But now her bitterness has grown so strong that even Muffin fears her.

The duke brought a huge, dark horse for my Nathan, and Nathan is about to leave. Without me. I will not be left behind! My Miren needs me. I must find her. I will hunt down the coach that stole her, and I will bite its wheels until it stops. The coach will steal her from me forever.

* * *

Nathan steadied his tall bay horse, and leaned down to squeeze Nat's hand. "You take care of Gran'mama, Nat. I'm counting on you."

"I will, Uncle. Don't worry." Nat released Nathan's hand and climbed into the duke's coach.

Glenna stuck her bandaged head out the coach window. "Nathan, it's got to be the rumored Malcolm treasure. It explains why Kenneth wanted to marry Cora Malcolm, and why Dr. Patterson wants Miren now. When Cora married another, Kenneth kept his knowledge to himself." She paused. "He must have told Dr. Patterson about it, probably in one of his drunken stupors. He was always grieving about an 'opportunity lost.' "

Simon nodded. "I heard that tired song more than a few times from the laird's tongue. I'd guess Patterson convinced him to remain silent."

Nathan nodded. The answer had been there all along, in Miren. And she didn't know it herself. "Because Patterson had found Miren. He had attempted to coerce her when her father died. It was then she took to herding sheep."

Glenna tapped her fingers on the coach molding. "I still don't understand why he'd go to the trouble of killing Kenneth, though."

"Much remains unclear, Mother. We will unravel the mystery in time. After I've saved Miren."

"Nathan, take care. Patterson thinks all goes his way. If he should suspect . . . he will kill her."

"Mother, if I don't reach Inveraray first, he'll kill her anyway."

"You will. If you remember who you are."

Nathan eyed her doubtfully. "Are you saying my heritage can help Miren?"

"I'm saying it can help you. You are what you want to be. Your heritage doesn't define you, Nathan. It serves you. Let it serve you now."

"Cryptic."

"Were you expecting a map and a planned strategy?"

A reluctant smile grew on Nathan's face. "It might have been helpful. I have a map. The strategy is molded to the events. I will carry your words in my heart."

"They're not my words, Nathaniel. They came from your father. Taregan gave them to me, on the chance you were ready to hear."

"I am ready, Mother. But too late to prevent Miren's abduction. As I was too late returning from the war, and too late for David." Nathan's throat tightened as he recognized the full force of his fear.

"What do you want?" Glenna's question was simple, but unexpected. A slow, cool thrill grew in Nathan's heart, until it turned to fire and filled his limbs with power.

"I want Miren. For my wife, forever."

"And what will you do to get her?"

Nathan smiled. "Whatever it takes."

"Then, yes. You are ready. Go."

Nathan urged his horse forward, but Molly caught his eye. She sat forlorn and small beside Simon, her round brown eyes plaintive as she gazed at Nathan. He wanted to help her. She was Miren's pet, Miren's friend.

"Get in the coach, Molly. As I remember, you favor coaches."

One ear drooped. Simon tapped the coach step. "Up, lass. Up you go!"

Molly slunk backwards, refusing. "Pick her up, Simon. We can't leave her here."

Simon picked the little collie up and stuffed her in the coach. He tried to shut the door, but Molly hopped out again. She positioned herself by Nathan's horse and barked.

"No, Molly. You go with Simon."

She barked again.

"It's too far. You can't walk the whole way. I'll be riding fast."

"Lad, you're arguing with a dog. And a slackabout dog, at that."

Molly issued one pert bark and nudged the horse's pastern.

Nathan sighed. Miren's dog was as stubborn as she was. "All right. You win . . . I can always carry you side-saddle . . ."

The route from Oban back to Inveraray was made longer by the necessity of circumventing the long, thin body of water, Loch Awe. Nathan judged the time he could save by a direct route, the route unexpected. The Iroquois didn't survive by doing the expected, and Nathan chose his own path.

He chose the Highland pass, cutting east over the hills between the Firth of Lorne and Loch Awe. Patterson had taken the longer route by necessity. The coach road went slightly north from Oban, then cut east between Loch Etive and Loch Awe. From Dalmally on the northern rim of Loch Awe, Patterson would head south to Inveraray.

Nathan chose a shorter route. He rode straight from Oban, aiming for the central band of Loch Awe. There, he would attempt something only an Indian would dare.

Man, horse, and dog would swim the loch, and take the shortcut to the MacCallum estate. It was a risk. If he lost the horse, his journey would continue on foot. And he might then arrive no sooner than Patterson.

It was a risk he had to take.

Nathan rode like the wind. The duke had found the finest, strongest horse in Oban, and Nathan pressed it to its limits. Molly ran tirelessly beside the horse, never lagging. They stopped an hour after darkness, then rose at the first glimmer of dawn to press onward.

Nathan reached the shores of Loch Awe sooner than he expected. His horse was exhausted, and showing signs of lameness. Nathan dismounted at the bank and gazed across the water. He judged the distance a long swim, but one he could manage.

He ran his hands over the horse's legs. He found a puffy, blistered swelling inside the left front cannon bone. "Damn." Nathan stroked the horse's neck. "You've gotten me this far, my friend. I've asked more than I should already."

He could press the animal forward. The horse was well trained and willing. He'd go on until he dropped. "I don't even know your name."

"Creatures deserve our respect, sir. Names are symbolic of that respect."

Nathan pulled off the saddle. "I name you Tionontoguen. It is an Iroquois name for 'valley between mountains.' I honor your service, and set you free."

Nathan removed the bridle, and Tionontoguen eyed him doubtfully. "Go."

The horse didn't move. Nathan sighed. "Graze?"

The horse seized a shrub and munched thoughtfully. Molly looked at Nathan, then at the horse. She barked once, loudly, and the horse startled. It trotted a few strides away, then resumed grazing.

Nathan patted Molly's head. "We honor Miren by respecting what she believes, Molly. And when I see her again, I'll tell her my life belongs to her."

Nathan removed his boots and tied them to his waist. "By the time we reach the other side, it will be dark. If we start now, we'll rest on the other side, and be dry by morning."

He climbed down the bank and tested the water. "Cold, but no colder than the Genesee River in New York." Nathan dove into the water, and emerged shuddering. "Remind me to tell Simon about this."

Molly lingered on the bank, reluctant to enter the cold water. "Molly, I've got to go. Miren needs me. She needs you, too."

Molly took mincing steps into the water, stopped, then jumped. She sank beneath the surface, popped up in terror, and sank again. Nathan dove and swam back to shore. He caught her by the scruff of the neck and pulled her to the bank.

"You can't swim. All dogs swim." Nathan bowed his head. He eyed the dark water. It was a long swim alone. Carrying a dog . . . "I'm sorry, Molly. You'll have to stay behind."

He started to the water again, but she followed him.

Nathan sat down on a flat rock, shivering, his hair hanging in his eyes. *"I look at Molly and I see goodness, something of value. So I can't allow you to say my dog is useless. She is the best thing in my life."*

Nathan picked Molly up and carried her to the water. It felt colder the second time. He gazed across the loch. It looked wider than it had before, but he trudged deeper, wincing when his foot hit sharp rocks. He sank into the icy depths, positioned the collie under one arm, and began to swim.

I am not a water dog. If possible, I am less a water dog than a herding dog. Never have I been so cold, so wet, and so miserable.

Nathan swims well. He managed to cross the wide, dark, and cold water submerging me only three times. I scratched violently to keep us both afloat. He spoke severely, but he didn't release me. I found much of the swim relaxing, actually. Once I realized he wouldn't let go, I was able to hang my body limp and float along.

The only explanation for our crossing is that the young mistress is on the other side. Yet when we finally reached the far bank, no one was in sight. Nathan hung his clothes over branches, his boots upside-down, and he lay down to sleep.

We woke at dawn. Actually, I woke before dawn and roused Nathan. He issued a torrent of complaints, but he rose and we started off again. We ran toward the sun. Nathan ran like a hunter, and I, a hunting dog.

Perhaps I was wrong. When the need arose, I was a water dog. Then I became a hunting dog. I am what I want to be.

So I will cling to the hope that we will find Miren, and I will at last become a house pet. There is only one thing I'll never be, of that I'm sure. I will never be a herding dog . . .

Miren woke with a start. The coach lurched over the rough road, then steadied again. It moved slowly because the horses were exhausted. The coachman had advised Patterson to rest them, but he insisted they move on. The coachman resorted to lashing their backs at every stride when they balked at the steep hills heading south from Dalmally.

Even Patterson's grisly hired prisoner had more sympathy than the doctor. Yet Patterson seemed so calm. Never maniacal, never insane. He plotted his actions with a cold, brutal logic. Miren studied him as he slept, not like a captive, but like a Renaissance scientist studying the stars—beyond comprehension, yet still fascinating.

Her hands and feet were bound, so she could pose no threat to him while he slept. She wondered if she could kill him, should the chance arise. She knew, with disappointment and acceptance, that she could not. Not in cold blood, while he slept. Yet to save Nathan . . . or perhaps anyone Patterson threatened . . . she wouldn't hesitate.

It is because I value life, even in its most elemental form. Patterson's soul was a speck, it bore no kindness within. Yet there was a chance, after eons of time perhaps, that that speck might grow and develop, and learn to value what it once shunned.

A cool, bright realization grew in Miren's thoughts. *It doesn't matter what he does to me, if I live or if I die.* As Patterson's soul was a speck, her own grew fuller and brighter as she acted in accord with what she held true. When she resisted the longing to kill him, just as she once resisted the fear that would have made her his mistress, her soul reached toward heaven, and heaven answered.

Heaven gave her Nathan. She loved him, and she'd seen inside his heart. That was forever, and death couldn't dim its power. Heaven gave her Molly, and she'd shared her life with a small, loving dog. She was, no matter what the new day brought, a fortunate woman.

Miren closed her eyes and rested her head against the coach wall. Nothing disturbed her peace as she sank back into sleep.

The first light of morning dawned over Argyll. Miren looked out her window and saw the spires of Inveraray Castle. The MacCallum estate was less than a mile away. Her stomach knotted in fear, but she forced a deep breath.

The duke wouldn't arrive before the wedding, but perhaps Patterson's haste would work against him. He would have to wait for full morning to secure the priest for the ceremony. By then, the duke would arrive, and perhaps something could be done. Maybe someone would help her.

The coach maneuvered along the narrow road that led to the MacCallum estate. Loch Fyne came into view, and her heart clenched. They rounded a corner, and she saw the manor house upon the hill, its three gables glinting in the morning light.

She didn't want to look. It hurt too much, but her gaze shifted to the small cottage Nathan had given her. Her breath caught when she saw her sheep. They grazed peacefully in their little pasture. She saw Huntley beneath the willow, and her eyes puddled with hot tears.

"Eager for your wedding, my dear?"

Miren refused to look at Patterson. "It is my funeral I anticipate."

"To think that all this time you could have been my wife!" Patterson leaned forward to see her sheep. "What time you've wasted with those beasts. A shame. But, my darling, don't be hasty. You might enjoy a life of power and luxury. Think of it, Miren. Your inheritance will keep us in such style as you've never dreamed."

Miren turned and met his eager gaze. "A life spent in discord with the integrity of one's soul is worth nothing."

Patterson sneered, and his gaze turned black. "The monks at the abbey would appreciate your sentiment, I'm sure."

The coach passed the sheep pasture and turned left up the narrow grass road to the abbey. Miren looked out her window to see the manor again, remembering the day when her sheep interrupted the garden party. When Nathan got down on one knee and begged her to be his wife.

She closed her eyes, and she remembered her anger, and how he came to her late in the night on the weak pretext that he thought she was troubled. When she knew it was Nathan who couldn't endure a quarrel between them.

She remembered lying in his arms, and knowing love.

The coach stopped, and Patterson shoved open the door. Miren hesitated, gathering her final courage. She was frightened. Not of death, but of becoming his wife. In a church, beneath God's eyes. She wondered if God would understand why she spoke vows that raged against her soul's voice. "Please forgive . . ."

Patterson caught her soft whisper and his lip curled in a snarl. "Pray when I'm lying atop you, Miren. Worse is to come."

Miren lifted her chin and met his evil gaze. "Where is the letter freeing Nathan? I will see it handed over to one of the brothers before I agree to sell my soul to you."

Patterson edged the hilt of his poisoned dirk from his waistcoat, but Miren didn't flinch. She allowed for a slight smile. "Death now or later? It matters not. Where is the letter?"

He didn't have one. Miren sat back in her seat. "I wouldn't take risks now if I were you."

His mustache twitched with fury, but he withdrew pen and ink from his black bag, then a sheet of paper. He scrawled quick words, but Miren wasn't satisfied. "Show me."

He handed her the letter, and she read. It was addressed to Major MacDuff, and instructed him to return Nathan to America. "How do I know it's not a code meant to kill him?"

"You'll have to trust me, my darling. You don't have any other choice."

"I suppose you have no reason to kill him, once I've agreed. I do not trust you, but I see no alternative."

Patterson held open the coach door as his footman lowered the steps. "Come, darling. Our wedding is at hand."

Patterson offered his arm, but she stepped down without help. The white light of morning spread across the meadow where Molly and Flip had played, where Nathan chased her ... Where they argued, and the tension spiraled until he crashed into her cabin. And they fell into each other's arms, because love was too strong to be denied.

Miren closed her eyes. Wherever he was, he must feel her heart beating in his own. She felt his.

The abbey door was closed. "We're too early. The priest will be asleep."

The footman knocked, but no one answered. Patterson pulled Miren to the door, and he rammed the iron knocker. Miren held her breath. No one would answer. To barge into a church was disrespectful ... She heard footsteps, and her heart fell.

The door opened slowly, into darkness. A hooded man stood in the doorway, his face shrouded by his thick cowl. He seemed bent with age and introspection. He didn't look up. "Too early." He started to close the door, but Patterson caught it and held it open.

"It's not too early . . ."

"Brother . . . I am to be addressed as Brother at all times."

A low snarl grew in Patterson's throat. "Brother. I have made arrangements with Father Davies. He is expecting me."

"Can't be."

Patterson's grip tightened on Miren's arm as his anger surged. "He will perform my wedding ceremonies at once—"

"Not before noon."

Patterson twitched. "The arrangements have been made. Summon him."

The monk turned back to the door and looked around. Another monk edged through the hall, holding a Bible and mumbling. The two monks spoke in low, rhythmic voices. Miren couldn't understand their words, but they spoke for a long time.

Patterson pulled Miren into the dark church. No candles lit the hall, and the small wooden doors on either side appeared locked. She hadn't been inside the little church until now, but it harkened back to forgotten times. It looked smaller than she expected, the walls were stone, and ancient tapestries hung on iron hooks.

It wasn't cheerful, but she felt the strength of its vocation. And she stood on its hallowed ground, and would commit sacrilege. God would have to understand. She did it for Nathan.

"What's going on? Where is Davies?"

The monk looked over his shoulder. Miren couldn't see his face, or the face of the other monk. But she felt his disdain. "*Father* Davies."

Patterson clenched with anger. "My time is short."

The monk shuffled toward him. "Our time on earth is short, my son. But in heaven—"

"Where is Davies?" Patterson's booming voice echoed in the cold hall. The monk just shook his head and sighed.

"Father Davies has gone to pay final respects to Milton Spry—the hog farmer? Parishioner Spry came every Sunday, always in his best waistcoat and—"

"I don't care what some damned farmer wore to church. This wedding is of utmost importance. It must be concluded. I will send my man to bring the father here at once."

"Could be on his way to Betsy Frittater's christening by now."

Patterson braced. The delay frightened him. Miren enjoyed his discomfort. "A baby? How nice."

The monk nodded. "Fine little baby girl." Miren couldn't see the monk's face, but she felt his eyes on her. "Sorry we are to delay your wedding, my child."

"There's no hurry."

Patterson's fingers dug into her arm. "My bride is gracious." He looked around, and Miren noted a faint sheen of perspiration on his brow. "One of you men will have to perform the rites."

The monk gasped. "That is out of the question. True, we have the legal authority, but as brothers of the abbey, it is beyond our personal ideals and righteousness to do such a presumptuous—"

"If it's legal, you'll do it."

The monk straightened somewhat. "Impossible. I haven't practiced. I don't know the entire service, front to back. No, no. You'll just have to wait, sir."

"I will not 'have to wait.' "

The monk's hooded head tilted to one side. "Have we tithed this month?"

"What?" Again, Patterson's voice expanded in the close quarters.

"Tithed. A token to the good work of the Lord. Keeps us in new robes, too."

"You want money." Here was something Patterson understood. Miren's heart sank. Even a monk could be bought off. "Of course." Patterson nodded to his footman, who produced a felt bag filled with coins.

The monk seized the bag and shook it as if weighing its worth. "I'll see what I can do."

He turned and disappeared into a side room. Miren heard low speech, rambling on. She waited, but the monk didn't return for several minutes. She began to hope his superior reminded him of the errors in accepting bribes, but the door opened, and the monk appeared with another, shorter monk, the one carrying the Bible. He held it open, still mumbling.

"Brother Xavier will perform the ceremony."

"Make it quick. I'm expecting the Duke of Argyll shortly. I want this job done by then."

"The work of the Lord cannot be rushed, my son." Something scratched at the private chambers' door. The monk tensed, then hurried to the arched doorway at the hall's end and swung it inward. "This way."

The hall opened into a small, square church assembly. Stone pews formed short rows leading toward the raised pulpit. Plaques of the former MacCallums lined the rough wall. The windows were high, shedding little light through the red and gold stained glass, but the faint, dusty illumination created a mystical atmosphere.

At another time, the setting would be solemn and reverent. Miren walked between Patterson and the monk. Her arm ached with bruises from Patterson's grip. She imagined herself walking on her Uncle Robert's arm while Nathan waited, dressed in his pirate costume but wearing a cravat. Everyone they loved would fill these empty pews. Flowers would warm the cold pews, and petals would carpet the rough stone floor.

Miren's vision clouded with tears, blurring the short monk waiting at the pulpit. The taller, crouched monk took his place beside her, his arms folded over his ribs, his hands concealed beneath his long, full sleeves. Miren glanced toward him, but his massive hood hid his face. He looked like a wraith of death, like a dark specter. Beneath his monk's habit would be only dried bones and the devil's breath.

Miren snapped her gaze to the monk on the podium. All she saw of his face was a pointed gray beard. He'd taken trouble to achieve that point—it looked recently trimmed, as if he took great pride in his beard's spike. Fitting, for a devil.

Two grim specters would marry her to their high master, and her soul would perish. Miren trembled, but the crouched, old monk's shoulder touched hers. Despite her loathing, his touch offered comfort. Miren closed her eyes to blot tears, and Brother Xavier began his sermon.

"Gathered we are . . ." Brother Xavier stopped and looked around. "Don't you have a witness?"

Miren heard Patterson's teeth grinding. "Get on with it."

"Can't without a witness."

Patterson exhaled a furious breath. "Gyvers! Get in here!"

Miren glanced over her shoulder as Patterson's footman entered the church. He stepped gingerly, then yanked off his cap. A strange and touching gesture from a man who lived his life in crime.

Brother Xavier nodded. "Take your place, Master Gyvers. Beside the groom."

Gyvers positioned himself beside Patterson, looking tense but respectful. Brother Xavier turned his attention to Patterson. "Forgive me, my son . . . Don't know your name, or that of your lovely bride."

"I am Dr. Patterson. My bride is Miss Miren Lindsay."

"A doctor, you are! What a fine profession it is! Holding life in your hands, easing the pain of the suffering elderly. Bringing new babes from their mother's wombs. Oh, sir, you do indeed follow the Lord's work—"

"Enough!" Patterson's lips formed a snarl beneath his mustache. "I don't have time for this chatter."

Brother Xavier nodded. "We shall proceed . . ." He launched into a low, sonorous sermon that dragged on and on and seemed to lead nowhere. His voice rose and fell as he urged Patterson to remember his sacred duties. Miren noticed that nothing in the monk's sermon mentioned her duties.

Patterson held himself tense, every muscle drawn. He was sweating now. Miren felt cool, and with each word her pulse moved slower. *I am drifting from my soul.* She closed her eyes and saw Nathan, bound and imprisoned, when he loved freedom more than anything.

I want you to be free, I want it more than my own life. She imagined him on a ship, returning to his wild, endless homeland, the salt wind in his hair as he crossed the ocean. She imagined him running across mountains and fields. He would remember her, and know she loved him. Maybe her spirit could hover near him as he lived his life. Maybe he would feel her love.

Miren lost track of the monk's sermon. It seemed to end then picked up speed again and rambled forward undaunted by Patterson's sighs of impatience. Miren didn't move, but she felt that each word drained her soul, and with it, her will to live.

"Brother . . . End the sermon and conclude the procedure. Now." Patterson's voice quavered with repressed violence.

Brother Xavier's pointed beard lowered as his jaw dropped. "I haven't begun the singing of the Psalms—"

"There will be no singing! Conclude the wedding."

"A rushed job—"

"Is it legal?"

"Yes . . . But it's not proper. Or poetic."

"Do it."

"Oh, very well. I now pronounce you man and wife."

"You haven't asked my bride and myself for our consent. That is necessary for legality's sake."

"So it is!" Brother Xavier chuckled. "I'm a little out of practice. Now, Father Davies never forgets even a wee portion of the ceremony. You should hear him, Doctor. Fine sermon he gives. Fills you with the Lord's fire, it does." The monk sighed. "Sorry you couldn't wait to hear him."

Patterson just growled.

"Quite. Quite. Now where were we? Ah, yes. Miss Lindsay, do you take this man to be your lawful, wedded husband, in sickness and in health, until the blackness shall swallow his—"

The monk beside Miren cleared his throat, and Brother Xavier nodded. "For as long as you both shall live?"

Miren hesitated. Patterson's fingers bit into her arm. She thought of Nathan, and the letter that would set him free. "I suppose so."

The monk accepted her reply and turned to Patterson. "And you?"

"I do." Patterson drew a narrow gold ring from his waistcoat and jammed it onto Miren's finger. "Now, sign the marriage certificate . . ."

Miren bowed her head and stared at her feet. Tears dripped to her cheeks, but she didn't wipe them away. A single drop fell to the stone floor. Dim light angled through the stained glass and illuminated her teardrop, as if shining on her fate.

Miren swayed against the crouched monk. He caught her and steadied her, but Patterson seized her arm and pulled her away. "The Duke of Argyll will arrive soon. I'll need you to assure him of this marriage's legality."

"The Duke of Argyll! Lord Lorne, of the Clan Campbell! Married the queen's daughter, Princess Louise. And he's coming here, to the abbey! Well, well." Brother Xavier paused. "I wonder if he's offered his tithing this month."

He swung open the doors to the front hall, then led them to the small, arched entrance. He seized Patterson's hands beneath the robe and shook vigorously. "This was my first wedding, if you can believe it. Never thought I'd get to do one." The monk stroked his pointed beard. "Getting on in years, and Father Davies never takes ill . . ."

Patterson opened the church doors, ignoring the monk. The sunlight stung Miren's eyes, as if she emerged from hell into a fire. The salt of her tears stung her cheeks.

The duke's coach turned up the roadway, followed closely by Brent's coach. They passed the sheep pasture and turned at the fork toward the abbey. "The duke is here now. You will submit my marriage certificate for his inspection, then provide official documents for him to sign."

Brother Xavier smacked his lips as he viewed the oncoming coach, probably plotting his new tithe. "What documents are those, Doctor?"

"My authority to make decisions on my wife's behalf. I require the duke's seal of approval."

"Quite."

Miren took a breath, then turned to Patterson. "There is

another document you may have forgotten. One you promised to give to the Brothers.''

Patterson's eyes cast daggers of anger, but he couldn't refuse. He withdrew the letter freeing Nathan. Miren seized it, examined it to be sure it was the same she'd read in the coach, then turned to the crouched monk. He kept his head bowed so she couldn't see his face, but he nodded when she held it out for him.

"Please be sure this reaches its destination. So much depends upon it.'' She was shaking, but she placed the letter beneath his robe and he took it.

The duke got out of his coach. Irene MacCallum left Brent's coach and followed. The end was near. Miren placed her hand on the monk's arm. It felt surprisingly solid and strong. Odd, because his bones should be thin and brittle.

"Brother, if a person acts from a heart of love, yet sacrifices their very soul in so doing, do you think . . .'' She swallowed hard and squeezed her eyes shut. "Will God understand?''

The monk didn't answer, and she looked up at him, her breath still as she waited for words of doom. He lifted his head and smiled. His warm, brown eyes sparkled with tears, but his smile deepened as her mouth dropped.

Nathan.

He kept his voice low, for her ears only. "He will.''

Life returned to her soul with such force that she felt dizzy with hope. He had come for her. She'd sought to free him, and he was already free. He'd guessed Patterson's plan, and he was ready.

One thing he couldn't know . . . the dagger . . .

Patterson laid his hand on her shoulder. His fingers clenched in warning. "My dear, the duke has arrived and wishes to express his good will. Come.''

Nathan bowed his head again, and Miren forced herself to turn. "Your Grace. How good of you to come!''

The duke seized her hand and kissed it gently. "We could

not leave you alone on your wedding, my dear.''

"Thank you."

Patterson grabbed her arm again. He didn't relax, despite his plan's apparent success. "I need your seal, Your Grace."

Brother Xavier handed the marriage certificate to the duke, who applied his seal. "Now, this grants Miren Lindsay's husband rights to her fortune. Didn't know she had any, but there you go, Doctor."

Patterson seized the certificate as Irene MacCallum entered the church. "What's going on here?"

Brother Xavier folded his hands over his stomach. "The most beautiful ceremony, Your Ladyship. Dr. Patterson has taken Miss Lindsay . . . *Mrs. Patterson*, to wife."

Blood drained from Irene's face. Her gaze shot to Miren, shocked, as if she knew something to be true that she had long feared. "No . . ."

Something scratched at the office door again. It whined, and it barked. Miren closed her eyes. *Molly.* Nathan opened the door quickly and Molly sprang out, tail wagging with glee. Patterson noticed her, and his eyes narrowed.

"Where did that dog come from?"

The duke patted Molly's head and laughed, tensely. "Came in our coach, Doctor."

Irene started to speak, but her jaw set hard. Her gaze fixed on Patterson, and such pure hatred sparkled in her pale eyes that Miren stepped back. "Allow me to pay my respects, Dr. Patterson, on your wedding. Such a surprise."

Patterson cast a quick glance Irene's way. He looked nervous, but he smiled. "It was necessary."

"Was it?"

He dampened his lips in a hurried lick. "So many surprises. Not all are welcome. Are they, Irene?"

He was threatening Irene, as if he knew something about her past that was enough to ensure her silence now. Miren didn't have time to wonder. Brother Xavier stumbled, separating Miren from Patterson. Patterson reeled back, but Nathan jumped forward and grabbed Patterson by the neck.

Brother Xavier pulled Miren back, but Patterson tore his dagger from his waistcoat and stabbed backwards. "No!"

Nathan caught Patterson's wrist and wrenched until the dagger dropped. Patterson laughed, and Miren's heart caught in her throat. "Nathan, did his dirk touch you?"

"It's nothing, Miren. Just a scratch."

"It's poisoned!"

Nathan refused to release the doctor. Brother Xavier yanked off his habit, revealing Simon's familiar face underneath. "You stay back, lass."

"There's no time!" Miren struggled free of Simon's grasp and ran to Nathan. She tore at his sleeve and found a small point where the dirk pierced his skin. "Miren, get back!"

Patterson twisted to free himself, but Miren grabbed Nathan's arm. She placed her mouth over the tiny spot and sucked. She shook violently, her tears fell to his skin. She spat, then sucked again.

"Such a brave girl! Did it work, I wonder? You won't know, Miren." Patterson grabbed her hair and yanked her back. He wrenched the butcher knife from his boot and held it to her throat. "Didn't think I'd left this behind, did you? Never know when it comes in handy. Let go, Indian, or I'll rip her throat."

Nathan backed away. "You're surrounded, Patterson. You'll never get away."

Patterson clutched Miren's hair, tipping her head back to his shoulder. "Won't I? Gyvers! Get my coach!"

Gyvers hesitated. He glanced at the cross above the pulpit, but Patterson sneered. "Don't turn heroic now, Gyvers. Unless you want my wife's blood on your guilty hands."

Nathan nodded to the decrepit coachman. "Do as he says."

Gyvers turned and raced from the church. Patterson laughed. "Thought you had the upper hand, didn't you, Indian? Know that I won't kill her until I've had my fill. Your ruse worked, but mine worked better. Poison flows in your savage blood even now. Maybe the wench got enough out by her tender sacrifice. Maybe she didn't. But you'll be on your knees within the hour, gasping and shuddering. Maybe you'll get enough air to live, maybe you won't. I'm sorry I won't be here to see it.''

Miren kicked and struggled, but Patterson pressed the knife against her throat until he drew blood. Miren felt its hot moisture running in a tiny stream down her neck.

"Uncle, Uncle!" She heard Nat running up the stairs.

"Nat, no!" Glenna charged up the stairs and caught the little boy.

Miren strained to see Nathan's face. "Please don't die. Please.''

Glenna gasped and started toward Patterson, but Simon caught her arm. "No, lass. He's gotten the upper hand back, and he's got his own survival at stake now. Fellow like that don't have much else.''

"Miren . . .''

Miren tried to see Glenna, but Patterson dug the knife deeper. "He cut Nathan with a poisoned dagger. Help him.''

Tears streamed down Glenna's face, but she backed away, allowing Patterson to pass. Grainger and Brent stood on the stairs, both shocked. "You won't get away with this, Doctor.''

Patterson twisted sideways, so that Miren saw both into the church and the road beyond. Nathan stood in the doorway, edging closer. Glenna clutched Nat, both crying. Irene walked from the church and stood on the steps. She dropped Muffin, and the little dog crept to Glenna's feet.

Molly growled and snapped, but Patterson ignored her. Miren looked at her dog. "I love you, Molly. Stay with Nathan. Good dog.'' Her voice choked on tears, but Molly obeyed. For the first time. She backed away, one ear cocked thoughtfully.

Miren had seen that look before, but she hadn't recognized it until now. Molly was scheming. She wasn't an innocent, soft, round puppy anymore. Maybe she never had been. Miren believed she had picked Molly. Suddenly she knew that it had been the other way around. And Molly didn't intend to lose her.

Molly bounded down the stairs and raced away. Miren couldn't see where she was going. Patterson laughed. "Finally got rid of your hound, darling. A shame. I'd thought of shooting her."

He dragged Miren down the stairs, but Brent blocked his escape. "Get out of my way, fool. Gyvers!"

Gyvers brought Patterson's coach to the bottom of the stairs. The lead horse held its foot aloft. "Ain't getting far with this team, Doctor."

Patterson twitched with fury. "Get MacCallum's then! Now!"

Gyvers ran to Brent's coach and directed the team to the stairs behind the other coach. Miren saw the two gray horses. One and Two. "*Miss Lindsay, I give you my word to use their names at every meeting, if you will remove your sheep from my path.*"

Miren twisted her head to see Nathan one last time. She froze his image in her mind as he stood with his monk's habit torn open, revealing his white shirt. The breeze from Loch Fyne caught his long, black hair, and she saw his silver hoop earring.

Despite her fear, despite the butcher's knife held against her throat, Miren smiled. "Indian. Pirate. Scottish laird. . . .

Chapter Twenty

Humans bungle everything. A good house pet knows when to take matters into her own control.

Molly raced toward the sheep pasture. She bounded over the stone wall and darted toward Flip. Flip wouldn't understand, but he might follow . . .

The cruel man had Miren again. He would take her away in his coach. Molly had smelled her mistress's blood. She couldn't stop Miren's attacker, because she was too small. She couldn't stop his coach, because wheels didn't obey. They didn't herd . . .

Sheep herd.

She had to get them through the gate. It had broken once beneath the weight of a fat ewe. The ewes were even fatter now than they had been the day of the garden party. The gate would break again.

If something scared them enough. Molly growled and charged, but the sheep paid no attention. She wasn't a threat. She needed something so vicious, so terrifying . . .

Molly leapt back over the stone wall and charged back toward the abbey. Patterson's dirty servant brought another team forward, and Patterson dragged Miren down the steps. Nathan followed, but Patterson cut Miren's flesh, and he stopped.

Molly considered another attack, but she'd learned that biting was useless when a human was insensitive and fixed on other matters. Molly barked, a taunting bark. A call to adventure. A call that would inspire a wolf to hunting.

Muffin responded with a torrent of fierce yips. She bounded down the stairs and tore after Molly. Molly took the lead, keeping enough distance to attract her tiny nemesis.

She bounded over the stone wall again, but Muffin wasn't big enough to jump over it. But she could go under. Molly ran to the gate and barked. Muffin followed.

Then Molly saw the sheep, and every portion of wolf blood came alive in its dormant system. It growled like a fiend and charged. The sheep responded. Blossom first, because she had a long memory.

They panicked. But not in the right direction. Flip was after Muffin. He would be no help.

Something deep, deeper than she ever had known, came alive in Molly. She wanted them through that gate. She wanted them fast enough not to allow a simple latch to stand in their way.

She darted left and turned their leader. Blossom spun right, circled, then galloped across the field. The other ewes followed. Earnest's chubby body plunged forward with greater speed than Molly had imagined he possessed.

She darted right, then tore in at Earnest, driving him toward the gate. She spun back and drove the rear sheep forward, crashing into the ewes in front.

They couldn't stop, they moved as a tight group. Flip abandoned Muffin and sensed Molly's goal. He took the left front, she the right rear. And Muffin stopped in the field, gauging their purpose. She abandoned her bloodthirsty attack and drove the sheep from behind.

The first ewe collided with the gate. It creaked, but it didn't break. Muffin barked, and the rear ewes shoved themselves forward. Earnest slammed sidelong into the gate. It creaked. The latch gave, and the gate swung open.

The flock stampeded through the open gate, but they weren't headed toward the stone building. They aimed for the meadow.

Molly slowed and looked for Miren. Patterson shoved his servant aside and took the reins himself. He pulled Miren into the seat beside him and wrapped the reins around her neck. He whipped the horses, and they jumped forward.

Nathan ran down the road after them, followed by Brent and the others. But the coach was pulling away.

Molly barked. She raced to the fore of the flock and hedged their progress. Flip couldn't know what she wanted. He waited, following her lead. Muffin stayed out of the way, for once.

Molly met Blossom head on. Blossom saw a field of flowers and tall grass. Molly saw Miren. Molly crouched. She aimed at Blossom's front leg. She nipped. Blossom stepped aside, more annoyed than subdued.

Molly had been praised by a queen, and Blossom had the nerve to ignore her instructions! A queen. A queen who knew how to boss. Molly bristled and looked down her long nose at Blossom, though the ewe was much larger. Blossom hesitated. Molly growled, then jumped.

And Blossom turned aside.

They went wherever Molly directed. It was heaven. She nudged them back onto the road, then to the high wall that lined the pasture and the road.

The coach had to pass here to escape. Sixty Blackface sheep mulled in its way. Flip kept them from going into the meadow. Muffin kept them from returning to their pasture.

And Molly in the middle kept them just where she wanted them to be.

Miren saw her sheep. She saw her little black collie's head peeking up from the middle of the flock. She saw Muffin poised by the gate, and Flip by the meadow.

Patterson swore, then screamed in fury, "Go!"

One and Two hesitated, but Patterson lashed viciously at their backs, drawing welts on their flanks. Miren grabbed his whip.

Patterson shoved her aside. He tightened the leather reins around her neck, then wrapped the end around the handle. He jumped down from the driver's seat and flailed his whip at the sheep.

Miren fought to untie the reins, to free herself. Earnest butted into Patterson's legs, knocking him off balance. Earnest pushed between the horses' legs and made a break for the meadow. Flip cornered him and directed him back to the road.

Patterson struggled to his feet. "Damned sheep!"

Miren snapped the reins free and pulled them off her neck. Someone jumped to the back of the coach, then to the roof. Miren looked up. Nathan bounded over the roof, his black hair flying. He looked pale, and fear clenched inside her. If he spent his energy fighting Patterson, saving her, the poison in his system might still take hold.

"Nathan . . . No!"

He met her eyes and smiled. "Whatever it takes, Miren." She didn't know what he meant, but he leapt from the coach and landed among the sheep, behind Patterson. Blossom moved aside and took position by the coach door. Flip drove Earnest back, and he bumped into the coach. It swayed, and the door popped open.

Patterson cracked his whip at Nathan. Nathan ducked, but Patterson swung again. Nathan caught the whip and yanked Patterson to his knees.

Patterson drew his butcher's knife and aimed toward Nathan. Miren held her breath. Patterson lurched forward, nudged by a ewe. Nathan dodged his blow, then kicked. A good, strong kick that met Patterson's chest dead center. Perhaps the way Iroquois fight.

Patterson lowered his head and rammed toward Nathan. Nathan jumped back, pressing the ewes in toward the coach. Blossom put her front hooves on the steps, tested them, then climbed in. Molly picked her way through the sheep and followed.

Miren swung down from the coach and looked for something to aid Nathan's battle. Brent tried to wedge through the sheep. Simon shouted and waved his habit.

"Hold him off, lad! We're coming."

The duke was more agile, and thinner, so he squeezed alongside the coach. "Give it up, Doctor! The sheep have you."

Nathan stumbled, but no sheep bumped him. Miren's blood ran cold. His face went white. He looked to her, and his lips were blue. She held up her dress and tried to climb over the sheep.

Patterson saw his chance. Not to flee, but to kill. He clutched his butcher's knife and shoved his way through the sheep.

Irene MacCallum passed the duke. She didn't push or shove, she just walked through their round, soft, sheared bodies, her eyes fixed on Patterson. Nathan sank to his knees, and Patterson moved toward him.

Miren tripped over Earnest, crying, "No! Run away, you fool! Leave him alone!"

Irene walked up behind Patterson. He noticed her and started to turn. She held up his dirk in her bony hands, smiled, then plunged it deep into the back of his shoulder. His face went white as Irene withdrew the weapon.

"You dropped this." She held up the dirk. "I couldn't help

noticing that the blade was still dampened . . . all the way to the hilt. With poison?''

''You bitch!'' Patterson whirled toward her, clutching at her neck, but she stepped back as he fell to his knees before her.

Simon called to Flip. ''That'll do, lad. That'll do, Muffin. Good dogs.''

The dogs relaxed, and the sheep scattered, heading for the meadow as an assumed reward. Miren ran to Nathan's side, weeping as she drew him into her arms. ''You're all right. He told me it will make you sick but it won't kill you. I got it in time.''

Nathan looked into Miren's eyes, ignoring Irene and Patterson. ''Miren, are you all right?''

Miren nodded, then kissed his forehead. ''I love you so.''

''The poison . . . you didn't get any . . . ?''

''I spit it out. Don't worry.''

Nathan relaxed and leaned his head against her chest. Molly jumped down from the coach and licked Nathan's face. Nathan touched her head and gently scratched her ears.

''Thank you, Molly. You're a good dog.''

Miren tore off Patterson's ring and flung it aside. ''You were with me, Nathan. I am so glad.''

''I know.'' He sounded weak, but he was smiling.

Irene stood over Patterson. ''Who will suck the poison from you, Drew? You've twisted and tortured people all your life. I think you were born liking to cause pain. You used people for what they could give. But who loves you enough to save you?''

''You're back to where you started.'' Patterson clutched at his throat as his breath came short, but his hatred and venom poured with his last effort. ''Tell the duke where you started, Irene. A cheap whore, a dance hall girl.''

''I came from hell, Drew. I married Colonel Edgington and I thought I'd escaped. But he died, and you paired me with the 'poor widower,' Kenneth MacCallum. Drunken, raging

Kenneth, cheated by one woman, deserted by another. And all that rage came out at me. I came to you, begging for help."

Irene kicked at Patterson's chest. "You told me to stay. You'd found a better way. So I stayed. I stayed while he beat me until I couldn't walk."

"You wanted him dead. You wanted his money."

"Yes, I wanted it all. I deserved it! You set off to kill him, but you couldn't even do that right. You left an heir, you fool. When you came back, you said you'd kill the Indian, but instead you set yourself up with this girl. And now it's your turn in hell."

Patterson tried to stand. He lifted his fist toward the sky. "Hell! Hell! All of you, go to hell! I am in control." His lips went white, his eyes glazed. His fingers clenched at his throat, and he fell forward, dead.

Irene knelt and poised the dagger to strike again. Grainger walked silently to the side, caught her wrist, and removed the weapon from her grasp. "It's over, Irene."

She looked up at him, her face white and drawn but still remorseless. She cast a quick glance at the duke. Already focused on her own survival. "It was Dr. Patterson's idea to murder Kenneth."

The duke turned away, but Grainger faced her solemnly. "You didn't have to do his bidding, Irene. You could have turned tail and run out on the old laird, but you didn't. You stayed, because you wanted the position of Her Ladyship. For what? What did it get you?" He paused, and his tone softened. "How different things would have been if you had become my wife instead of tricking Edgington into marrying you."

Brent gasped, then made his way to his mother's side. "Wife?"

Irene rose to her feet and straightened. She turned her back on Patterson's lifeless body and lifted her chin. "I sent you to the finest schools. You had every opportunity to become something important."

Brent gazed at his mother, then sighed. "You didn't do it for me, Mother. You did it for yourself. I was a reflection of you, something to make you look good. That is all I have ever been, until now."

"You're nothing now! You could have been a laird, had power. Yes, I deserve that, to have a son of worth. You carry your father's useless blood."

"My father . . ." Brent turned slowly to Grainger, and his eyes widened with the light of understanding. "You are my father."

Grainger stared at the earth, but he nodded. "Didn't want to shame you with the knowledge. I used a threat on your mother to get my position here, but I didn't mean no harm. Just wanted to see you grow up into a man."

Brent clasped Grainger's arm, his eyes filled with tears. "There must have been times you thought *that* would never happen."

Grainger met his son's eyes, and his expression changed from shame to pride. "No, Brent. I've been proud to know you were my boy every day of your life."

Miren stroked Nathan's hair from his brow. His breath came slow and shallow, but his eyes remained open.

The duke knelt beside Nathan. "I've sent for a doctor." He stopped and shuddered. "A real doctor. Hold on." He rose and faced Irene. "Lady MacCallum, I am forced to accuse you in collusion with Dr. Patterson of the murders of your husband and Nathan's brother. Yet the crime may be hard to prove, and I would spare Brent the embarrassment of a trial."

Simon stepped forward. "I've got a better idea for old Irene."

Brent and the duke listened, and Irene braced herself. Brent glanced at his mother and shrugged. "Let's have it, Simon."

"Farmer MacBain, fellow we got Earnest from, is headed off to Australia soon. He's looking for a housemaid. His wife,

Prudence, she's got a bad back. And no wonder, hefting that bulk of a body around.''

Irene blanched. "No!''

Simon smacked his lips thoughtfully. "She'd be a hard taskmaster and no mistake, but the MacBains are good, solid folk. Might do old Irene a world of good.''

Irene whirled to face Brent. "I will not!''

"Mother, the matter is settled. I know Farmer MacBain and his wife. Sensible, down-to-earth couple. Simon is right. Australia will do you good. Maybe get your head out of your illusions about wealth and power and back to reality.''

"Never! I will not become a servant.''

Brent folded his arms over his chest. "It's that or prison. You choose.''

Irene hissed, but she offered no further argument.

Miren wrapped her arms around Nathan's waist. "We have to get him back to the house.''

The duke eyed Patterson's body. "Brent, if you'd take your mother in hand, I'll have Patterson's remains removed. Simon and I will carry Nathan to the estate.''

A rider appeared on the road. He stopped, then directed his horse toward the gathering. Miren looked to see if it was a doctor, but as the man drew near, her breath caught in amazement. Long black hair fell below his shoulders. He wore leather rather than cloth breeches, and a beaded earring hung from one ear.

He dismounted, and Glenna cried out in shock. She left Nat with Miren and ran to him, weeping.

"Who is that man?" Miren asked.

Nathan didn't answer. His eyes closed, and Miren's heart held its beat. "Simon! Help!''

Simon checked Nathan's pulse. "He's all right, lass. Just passed out.'' He glanced toward the man with Glenna. "As for that young rapscallion yonder . . .'' Simon stopped and sighed. "That's Taregan Wolf.''

"Wolf? Is that Nathan's real surname?''

"That's the English rendition, lass. I ain't attempting the Iroquois version. It's the name of his clan—had to take on a surname to appease the Americans."

Miren brushed away her tears. "His father came?"

"More's the pity." Simon eyed Taregan as he strode toward Nathan. "But the young fellow, despite his lack of decent clothes, has a way with herbs."

"You mean he can help Nathan?"

Taregan approached and knelt at Nathan's side. He touched his son's pale forehead, then bent to kiss his brow.

"Can you help him?" Miren's voice quavered, but her heart filled with hope.

Taregan took Nathan from Miren's arms. "That remains to be seen."

Simon helped Taregan carry Nathan to the manor. Molly followed close behind. Miren stood a moment, frozen between fear and hope. Glenna laid her hand gently on Miren's shoulder. "Come, my dear. Nathaniel won't die. His real battle is over."

Nathan rose from layers and layers of heavy sleep. He'd drifted in and out for days. Endless days in which he couldn't tell dream from reality. Sometimes he saw Miren beside him, speaking softly, telling him she loved him more than anything. Sometimes her words disturbed him, because she said she understood his need for freedom and wouldn't stand in his way.

He'd tried to answer her, but his lips wouldn't move. He'd felt her gentle kisses, and he knew she cried. He'd listened to her conversations with him, with herself, and he realized she feared their ending. She feared he wouldn't have the heart to ask her to leave. How could anyone be so wrong? He hadn't the courage to ask her to stay, until it was almost too late.

And now he was frozen in a poisoned slumber, and listened while she told herself it would be better for him if she left Scotland . . .

Nathan hoped it had been dream. Miren wouldn't leave. He'd woken in the night, and she'd fed him soup. He'd thanked her, and she'd wept, overjoyed that he was well again. He'd almost mustered strength to talk to her, but she'd left him, and sleep stole over his mind again.

He felt sure that it truly happened, but so much else had been dream. Perhaps Miren's doubts were only dream, too. He'd dreamt that his father sat beside him, speaking in Iroquois, telling him how he'd been wrong, that Nathan was right. That surely was dream. He'd dreamt that his mother entered the room and reminded Taregan they'd conceived him beside a river, beneath the stars.

Yes. Dream. This was more of his parents' relationship than he required knowing.

Molly hopped on his bed, twice at least, and Miren had scolded her. That seemed plausible. But Muffin jumped up, too, and that didn't.

Someone's hand pressed to his forehead. A cool hand. Miren. Nathan opened his eyes, but the dark man looking down wasn't Miren. Nathan closed his eyes, opened them, and looked again. Taregan still bent over him. Nathan turned his head from side to side. He checked again. Taregan was smiling now.

Nathan tried to speak. His mouth felt thick, his lips numb. He moved his tongue. It worked, though it carried little moisture. "What . . . are you doing . . . here?"

Taregan's smile faded, his dark eyes filled with tears. "Tending my son."

Nathan stared up at him. "Your son."

"You are far more than that, Nathaniel."

Nathan stared to shake his head. "No."

"You are Iroquois. You are Scotsman." Taregan's smile returned. "You are pirate . . . And I'm sorry I missed it . . . A monk. But your woman told the story well. And often."

"Miren . . ." Nathan looked around. His limbs lightened. He needed to see her. If his father's presence wasn't a dream, then her doubts weren't imagined, either. "Where is she?"

Taregan hesitated. Nathan sat up. His senses reeled, but he refused to lie back down. "Where is she?"

"Scottish women . . . make no sense."

Nathan's heart stilled. "She's gone. She left." He tried to rise, but his head swam. Taregan caught his shoulder and steadied him.

"She left this morning, after we were certain you recovered."

"Where did she go?"

"With Simon." Taregan's brow tilted upward. "For some reason, he was eager to leave. He and I never did get along."

"Where?"

Taregan's brow angled still more. "Anywhere."

Nathan contained his impatience. "Not you and Simon . . . Where did he take Miren?"

"To Simon's new ship. He's naming it *The Monk*."

"He's renaming my ship?"

"Said you gave it to him 'fair and square.' "

"Perfect. And he's taking my woman with him."

"He was reluctant at first, but she convinced him. Your woman thought your life would be 'easier' if she didn't make you choose."

Nathan bowed his head. "Scottish women . . . make no sense."

Taregan nodded slowly. "But they settle many things with kissing."

It didn't seem possible. He was riding, at night, through a storm . . . on the shortest route he knew between Inveraray and Oban. It was harder the second time. He reached the shores of Loch Awe at dawn. Exhausted, weak . . . But the poison was gone from his system. He carried a flask of herbal water Taregan had prepared, and he drank it for the purpose of "cleansing."

It tasted like something used to cleanse the floor.

Molly in the Middle

Nathan stared out over Loch Awe. His horse was tired, but he had no choice. It wasn't lame. "You're tired. I'm tired, too. But if we don't go onward, I'll lose her. If I have to swim the Atlantic Ocean, I'll do it."

The horse sighed. Nathan dismounted, pulled off the saddle, and led the horse to the loch's edge. "Iroquois ride bareback anyway." He walked into the water. The days of rain and gray skies had cooled the water since his last swim. Nathan sighed and glanced heavenward.

"You're not making it easy, are you?"

The Great Spirit answers those who act before asking. Nathan pulled the horse deeper. It hesitated, then complied. Fortunately, the animal liked swimming. They reached a small island, where Nathan allowed the horse to rest. They continued on and reached the far bank. The horse plunged forward and scrambled up the bank as if it spotted a friend. It whinnied. Something whinnied back.

Tionontoguen appeared through the trees. Nathan's jaw dropped as he climbed up the bank. "Haven't you moved?"

The two horses sniffed each other, then resumed grazing. Nathan's eyes narrowed. "If you're still here . . ." He checked around and found his old saddle. "Iroquois ride bareback . . . but monks do not." He caught Tionontoguen and saddled him, leaving the other horse free.

"You're not meant to be a wild creature anyway. Only a domesticated bit of prey stays in one spot."

Miren paced back and forth along *The Monk's* deck. She already felt seasick, and they hadn't left the dock. When she arrived, the ship had been hooked to a mooring in the harbor. But Simon had directed the ship to the wharf, not for repairs but to have the new name painted on the hull.

Every hour in Scotland hurt. Maybe she should have stayed, in case Nathan changed his mind. No, she'd argued this with herself a thousand times. If he'd changed his mind, he would have told her. He'd had plenty of chances.

The last night, when he woke and she fed him soup, he could have asked her to stay then. He didn't. He'd thanked her for the soup, mumbled something about Blossom needing to lose weight, then fallen asleep.

So he was coherent. More or less. Miren's eyes filled with tears. Her eyes hadn't been dry since she left Inveraray. Simon wasn't making matters easy. He'd proceeded slowly, stopping at inns for breakfasts, lunches, late lunches, and then early dinners. Now, on board the ship, she expected to set sail. But no. After his ship's new name was painted on, he decided the hull needed patching. His cabin needed a new sink.

Molly paced beside Miren. She wasn't happy, either. She'd vomited twice, so Miren guessed they were both seasick. Simon had given her the captain's cabin, which was surprisingly luxurious, but it only lowered Miren's spirits more.

Nathan's cabin. Here he had been a sea captain, free and happy. She walked the decks and imagined him at the helm, the salty air blowing his long hair. She lay in his bed and imagined him beside her. Perhaps a pirate ravishing his captive lady.

Or the captive lady ravishing her pirate.

Miren turned her back to Oban and gazed off the starboard bow. The sun set slowly, casting rims of orange and purple over the horizon. She was leaving Scotland, her home. She was leaving Nathan, her heart. She'd been too afraid to face him, terrified he'd hesitate, tell her how much he cared . . . But perhaps it would be better for them both if she followed her old dream and emigrated to America. Alone.

Miren's breath caught in her throat. "I've been reacting to fear! After everything I've been through, I ran because I'm afraid!"

"Is that it?"

Miren screamed. Molly yipped. They whirled at once. Nathan stood behind her, his white shirt open at the throat, his dark hair rippling in the wind. He wore his snug pirate trousers and high boots. He looked healthy and strong, the color back in his dark skin, his eyes bright and shining in the sunset.

Her breath came as small, tense gasps. Her hands shook, her knees went weak. "Nathan. You're here."

"I'm here." He took a step closer to her, but they didn't touch. "I feared to be too late." A slight smile curved his lips. "It seems that fear has driven us both of late."

Miren's eyes puddled with tears. "I didn't want to force you to keep me . . . to choose."

"So you chose for me?"

Miren hesitated, then nodded. "Yes."

"Is it what you want?"

"What I want? Nathan . . ."

He took another step toward her, but still he didn't touch her. "What do you want?"

She trembled. Her chin quivered. She squeezed her eyes shut, then looked at him. "I want . . . I want to go home!"

Nathan's dark eyes burned. "What else, Miren?"

She drew a quick gulp of air. "I want to be with you, Nathan. I want to marry you, and live in the same house, in the same room, in the same bed. I want to be Nat's mother, and the mother of those seven babies you promised me. I want my sheep!"

Tears glittered on his high cheekbones. "What else?"

Miren looked down at Molly. "I want Molly to have Flip's puppies where he can help raise them to be good sheepdogs. Only maybe we'll keep one with us, with Molly, because not every sheepdog likes herding, you know."

"I've noticed that." Nathan held out his hand. Miren placed hers in his, and he knelt before her.

"Then I'll tell you what I want, Miren. I've kept it from you because of fear. Fear I'd fail you, that I couldn't keep you safe. But fear doesn't change the heart. I love you. I've said it before, but I didn't tell you how much, forever. I didn't tell you I belong to you, and whether I fail you or lose you, or the world ends, I still belong to you."

"Nathan—"

"I'm not finished. I have many wants, my love. I want you with me, every day and every night. I want you as my wife. I want a home, with you, with children. With dogs, and with sheep. And I swear to you, every one will have a name." Nathan paused. "I've given my new horse a name."

He looked both proud and shy. "What did you name him?"

"I named him Tionontoguen."

Miren's eyes widened. She nodded. "What?"

" 'De-yo-non-DO-gen.' It's Iroquois for 'between two mountains.' "

Miren hesitated. "Meaning 'glen'?"

Nathan considered this. "Valley, glen. Yes."

Miren fought to restrain laughter. "You named a horse Deyo-something when you could have named him Glen?"

Nathan shrugged. "Glen for short."

Miren ran her fingers through his hair. "I love you so."

"Then marry me. Here, on board a pirate ship. Which is, in reality, a fairly respectable merchant transport, but don't let that dampen your lust for pirates."

Miren nodded. "We'll keep it between ourselves."

"Simon is captain now. He didn't have much authority marrying you off to Patterson, but he's got the power now. Marry me."

"Tonight?"

"Tonight."

Miren bit her lip. "Does that mean we could spend our wedding night in your old cabin?"

"If you wish." Nathan grinned. "And we'll send Simon and his crew into town for the night. I'll pay for a night at the pubs. That should keep them occupied."

Daniel overheard his offer. "Simon, the captain's got the girl on the ropes! You were right, he's chased after her like a puppy, begged for her hand. Good thing you got yourself a license to do marriages."

Simon stomped across the deck, holding a Bible aloft.

"The lads and I are ready. Gathered we are—"

Nathan held up his hand. "My lady has not agreed."

Miren shoved away tears. "Haven't I?"

"No."

Miren sank to her knees before Nathan. "Then, yes, my Indian laird, my pirate monk, I will marry you." She rose and kissed his face on both sides, then his mouth. "I love you, I love you . . ."

Simon issued a series of "tsks." "After the sermon, lass."

Nathan kissed Miren's cheek. Simon stood at the rail, his back to the setting sun. "It's a solemn occasion to behold, the joining of lad to lass."

Nathan sighed and took Miren's hand. "I've got a feeling this is going to take a while."

Miren kissed his shoulder. "We can wait, my love."

Simon cast them a firm, reproachful glance. "Take your positions, please."

Nathan's old crew assembled behind them. From the hills of Oban a bagpipe rose in solemn praise of the night. The music wafted from the hills, out over the harbor, and surrounded them with the soul of Scotland.

"If we are ready to proceed—"

"Wait!" Miren looked around, then slapped her thigh. Molly scurried across the deck and took her place between Nathan and Miren. She sat proud, her new red ribbon fixed neatly around her neck, the bow to one side. She looked up, first to Nathan, then Miren. Her expression was clear. *"At last."*

Miren turned to Simon. "You may proceed."

383

Epilogue

Argyll, Scotland
Autumn, 1872

Good things come to those who wait. Assuming they take action to reach the desired end.

I am living a life of leisure. When my Miren and Nathan take a drive in their coach, I accompany them. At times I wear my red bow. Other times it is left by my cushion. Miren has made me a cushion of my own, with gold tassels, and soft fleece to pad it fully. It was on this cushion that seven small versions of Flip came forth from my rear end.

I was surprised at the first. The little creature was messy, so I cleaned it. It was a male, and he attached himself to my body. I found this strangely comforting, and decided he could stay. The second pup was also a surprise. That one was a female, and she likewise attached herself to my underside.

The next four weren't surprises. Nor was their subsequent beeline for my underside. I settled down then, allowing Miren to wipe a damp cloth over my face. She cried and laughed, and squeezed every puppy as it appeared.

Nathan sat beside her saying, ''Just how many more are there?''

There was one more. It came well after the others. At first it didn't move, and an odd, cold sensation filled me. I cleaned it, but it didn't move. Miren cried, but she gave the pup to Nathan's father, who shook it, spoke to it, then swung it back and forth.

It came to life with a squeak, and has been my most vigorous daughter ever since. Miren has named her Scottish Melody, and calls her Melly for short. Nathan gave my sons and other daughter strange names, of too many sounds to remember. Miren has shortened them to such words as Mo, Nav, Al, and Patch.

Muffin has been allowed to visit my litter twice now. She was surprisingly respectful, and even attempted to clean Melody when she squirmed from beneath me.

Nat plays with my puppies for much of the day. We all go outside into the meadow and relax in the sun. Flip attends me daily, but his main interest is instructing them in herding methods. It pains me to watch.

Mo is the worst. He aimed first at a butterfly, but as soon as he saw Blossom and the flock, his little eyes glimmered with that look I know all too well. A sheepdog's fixation. There's nothing to be done about it, once it's begun.

I have more important considerations. Miren is getting fat. Only in the stomach, so far, but there is no denying her waist has expanded. Nathan seems pleased, and pats her stomach often. Nat pats her stomach, too. Had I known that a bulkier female attracted males earlier, I could have saved much trouble by urging her to eat more.

Miren sat on the grass beside Molly and her puppies. Nathan led Nat on his new Shetland pony, Simon, but the pony balked in favor of grass. Father Davies and another monk

walked through the meadow, picking flowers for the abbey.
Nathan waved, and the monks waved back.

Nathan led Simon to the road, then back to Miren's position. "We shouldn't have given him Simon's name. He's got
the same stubbornness."

"I had to name him something in a hurry, Nathan. You
were thinking up another tribal name. Wampanoag, wasn't
it?"

"I see nothing wrong—"

"We'd have to call him Wamp for short."

Nathan picked through the rolling puppies as they tumbled
and played in the tall grass. "Algonquin, Navajo, Apache . . .
Where are Abenaki and Mahican?"

Two puppies sprang through the grass, and Nathan laughed.
"I see. Stalking me."

He looked around. "And the other one . . . The one you
named."

Miren pointed at her side. Melody lay on her back, feet in
the air, her round stomach exposed to the sun. Her eyes were
closed, her little mouth open. Nathan shook his head. "There
had to be one that took after its mother."

"Melody will take action when it's necessary."

"And not before." Nathan seated himself beside Miren.
He gazed into her eyes, and a slow smile grew on his face.
"What about us, my love? What will we name this one?" He
touched her stomach gently, his smile widening.

"If it's a girl, I thought Cora, for my mother, if that's all
right."

"It's beautiful. What if it's a boy?"

"You choose."

Nathan lay back in the grass, considering the matter. He
held Miren's hand over his heart. "Akwesane?"

"I don't think so, Nathan. I'd like to be able to pronounce
my son's name. And I don't want to call him Ak for short."

"Good point. Have you another suggestion?"

"David, for your brother."

Nathan's dark eyes filled with tears. "Yes."

Nat slid off his pony's back and flung himself among the puppies, laughing. "When I am king, you will be my pages."

Abenaki and Algonquin bounced on top of him, and Nat howled with laughter. "All right! I will be your page and you will be kings."

Nathan watched Nat playing with the puppies, and Miren kissed his shoulder. "He is happy. He needed you, and you're the best father any child could have. I needed you, though maybe I wouldn't admit it at first. And you are the best husband . . ." Miren's voice caught. He kissed her cheek, and she rested her head on his shoulder. "Especially at night."

Nathan nodded stoically. "And in the morning. And when we get a chance, in the afternoon." He paused. "And at tea."

Miren blushed, then cleared her throat. "Tea time is approaching, you know."

"I know."

Nathan cleared his throat, too, and watched as Molly's first puppy tumbled down the road toward the pasture. The puppy reached the stone wall, tried to climb over, and flopped backwards. It righted itself, then tried again.

Nathan shook his head. "Try the gate, Mohawk!"

The puppy backed up, faced the stone wall, then hurtled himself up the rocks, kicking and struggling until he reached the top. He bounded down, proud, and raced toward Flip.

"Mohawk has a good herding instinct, I see."

Miren smiled as the fat little puppy stalked after Flip. "He's a good dog."

Miren had invited the old farmer who once owned Flip to take up residence in her cottage. He stood among the sheep now, blowing his whistle, proud as Flip separated Blossom and her three lambs from the rest.

Mohawk followed Flip, imitating his actions. He'd already left the litter in favor of staying with Flip and the new shepherd.

Miren sighed happily. "Mr. Stobbe seems happy, doesn't he?"

Simon tugged on his lead rope, straining to reach new grass. Nathan gave up and allowed him to wander free. "When you asked him to move into the cottage, the old fellow lost a good twenty years off his age, Miren. It was well done."

"I'm worried about Blossom, though. Mr. Stobbe says her internals were damaged giving birth to those three lambs. He says she's too old to have more, but Earnest won't take that into account."

Nathan hesitated, started to speak, but Miren held up her hand. "We will *not* eat Blossom."

Miren cast a warning glance Molly's way. Molly's ear drooped and she sighed.

Nathan chuckled. "Then what do you suggest we do with an aged, worn-out ewe who still attracts Earnest's attention?"

"Her lambs are ready for weaning . . ." Miren's eyes narrowed.

Nathan shook his head. "No."

Molly braced, looking horrified.

Miren looked from Molly to Nathan, then nodded. "The matter is settled."

No . . . It is too hideous to comprehend. No!

Molly stood on the threshold of the manor door. Her puppies played on the grass, but Melody sat beside her, one ear cocked doubtfully. The worst thing Molly could imagine, beyond her most hideous dreams, came real before her eyes.

Nathan and Nat stood like doormen, while . . . No. Molly forced herself to look. While Miren led Blossom, on a fine new leash, from the pasture . . . up the road. A flash of hope died when Miren didn't stop at the fork. No, she wasn't taking the fat ewe to the monks for their dinner.

Blossom was coming . . . home. To Molly's home. She wore a thick red ribbon around her woolly neck. It was tied in a fat bow. Blossom had been bathed, her regrown wool looked whiter than usual. And she was looking straight at Molly.

Blossom ambled up the stairs, pulling Miren along behind, and Molly snarled. She braced, ready to defend her home against this outrage. Blossom aimed for the doorway, nudged Molly aside, then progressed into the manor.

It was too much. Molly sank to her belly, nose on her paws. Melody looked at her, then flopped to her stomach, too.

Nathan trudged up the stairs after Miren. He glanced down at Molly and bent to scratch her ears. "I know."

He followed Miren into the house. "You are not keeping that ewe in our house, woman. It's . . . unacceptable, foul, and . . . insane. Of course, you're Scottish, so I should have expected something like this."

Nat bounded up the stairs, skipping every other step as he raced after Blossom. "Can Blossom sleep in my room?"

Nathan just groaned. Molly eyed the stone building and saw the monks toiling in their garden. She might take up residence with them. But they'd taken Huntley, for the purpose of trimming their lawn. She couldn't go there, either. She closed her eyes and imagined her future.

Life with Blossom. No . . .

Miren emerged from the front hall, tugging at Blossom.

"Fetch a potted plant, Nathaniel. We need something to lure her around to her new pen."

Molly opened one eye, holding herself tense. Nathan seized a potted plant and held it in front of Blossom. Blossom rushed at it with fervor, and Nathan backed down the stairs.

They led Blossom around to the back lawn, and Molly followed. A small pen had been set up beneath the rowan tree, with a bucket of water ready . . . for Blossom. Molly gazed toward the blue sky in thanks.

Nathan sacrificed the potted plant to Blossom's pen, and Miren shut the gate. "She'll be happy here. We'll give her special potted plants." Miren eyed Molly, a devious smile on her lips. "Molly will visit her daily."

Stobie Piel

* * *

The strange thing, the thing I can't explain, is that the young mistress was right. I find myself visiting Blossom's pen every day, even in the rain. The old ewe expects me. Even manages to knock me over every now and again, when I take a drink from her water bucket. I have a water dish of my own, but sampling Blossom's has a certain appeal.

Winter came, and spring. In spring a small, naked boy came from Miren's body. Nathan's father and Glenna assisted the birth, while Miren gripped Nathan's hand. I sat at the foot of the bed, more tense than I have ever been. As tense as Flip when he tends the flock.

Now that I've seen the little fellow, I understand why. Soon he will walk, and then run. He could go anywhere. He will follow Nat, and they will get into trouble. More children will follow. I know, because Miren and her Nathan wasted no time starting on another.

It will be my job to keep them all in line. I realize now that it wasn't a life of leisure I wanted, so long ago when I followed my mistress and her sheep through valleys and hills. I wanted a task worthy of my abilities.

I am a herding dog, after all. But my flock is human.

BESTSELLING AUTHOR OF
LONGER THAN FOREVER!
FOUR WEDDINGS AND
A FAIRY GODMOTHER

Only a storybook affair like the marriage of Cindy Ella Jones and Princeton Chalmers could lead to three such tangled romances—and happily ever after endings:

BELINDA

Kidnapped from the wedding party, the lonely beauty will learn how a little love can tame a wild beast—even one as intimidating as Cain Dezlin, the handsome recluse.

LILITH

Thrown together with Frank Henson, a seemingly soft-spoken security guard, self-absorbed Lilith will have to learn that with love and respect, there's a prince waiting behind every toad.

ROBERTA

The shy redhead's heart has been broken by a wicked wolf once before—and now that Maximilian Wolfe has shown up at the wedding she is determined to get to her grandmother's before the big bad Frenchman can hurt her again.

_52114-8 $5.50 US/$6.50 CAN

Dorchester Publishing Co., Inc.
65 Commerce Road
Stamford, CT 06902

Please add $1.75 for shipping and handling for the first book and $.50 for each book thereafter. NY, NYC, PA and CT residents, please add appropriate sales tax. No cash, stamps, or C.O.D.s. All orders shipped within 6 weeks via postal service book rate. Canadian orders require $2.00 extra postage and must be paid in U.S. dollars through a U.S. banking facility.

Name _____

Address _____

City _____ State _____ Zip _____

I have enclosed $_____ in payment for the checked book(s).

Payment <u>must</u> accompany all orders.☐ Please send a free catalog.

An Angel's Touch

Longer Than Forever

BRONWYN WOLFE

"A wonderful, magical love story that transcends time and space. Definitely a keeper!"
—Madeline Baker

Patrick is in trouble, alone in turn-of-the-century Chicago, and unjustly jailed with little hope for survival. Then the honey-haired beauty comes to him, as if she has heard his prayers.

Lauren has all but given up on finding true love when she feels the green-eyed stranger's call—summoning her across boundaries of time and space to join him in a struggle against all odds; uniting them in a love that will last longer than forever.

_52042-7 $5.99 US/$7.99 CAN

FOR LOVE AND HONOR

FLORA SPEER

Bestselling Author Of *Love Just In Time*

Falsely accused of murder, Sir Alain vows to move heaven and earth to clear his name and claim the sweet rose named Joanna. But in a world of deception and intrigue, the virile knight faces enemies who will do anything to thwart his quest of the heart.

From the sceptered isle of England to the sun-drenched shores of Sicily, the star-crossed lovers will weather a winter of discontent. And before they can share a glorious summer of passion, they will have to risk their reputations, their happiness, and their lives for love and honor.

_3816-1 $4.99 US/$5.99 CAN

Bestselling Author Of *A Stolen Rose*

Sensible Julia Addison doesn't believe in fairy tales. Nor does she think she'll ever stumble from the modern world into an enchanted wood. Yet now she is in a Highland forest, held captive by seven lairds and their quick-tempered chief. Hardened by years of war with rival clans, Darach MacStruan acts more like Grumpy than Prince Charming. Still, Julia is convinced that behind the dark-eyed Scotsman's gruff demeanor beats the heart of a kind and gentle lover. But in a land full of cunning clansmen, furious feuds, and poisonous potions, she can only wonder if her kiss has magic enough to waken Darach to sweet ecstasy.

_52086-9 $5.99 US/$7.99 CAN

A Stolen Rose

CORAL SMITH SAXE

Bestselling Author Of *Enchantment*

Feared by all Englishmen and known only as the Blackbird, the infamous highwayman is really the stunning Morgana Bracewell. And though she is an aristocrat who has lost her name and family, nothing has prepared the well-bred thief for her most charming victim. Even as she robs Lord Phillip Greyfriars blind, she knows his roving eye has seen through her rogue's disguise—and into her heart. Now, the wickedly handsome peer will stop at nothing to possess her, and it will take all Morgana's cunning not to surrender to a man who will accept no ransom for her love.

_3843-9 $5.50 US/$7.50 CAN

Futuristic Romance

Love in another time, another place.

On Wings of Love — Saranne Dawson

"One of the brightest names in futuristic romance."
—*Romantic Times*

Jillian has the mind of a scientist, but the heart of a vulnerable woman. Wary of love, she had devoted herself to training the mysterious birds that serve her people as messengers. But her reunion with the one man she will ever desire opens her soul to a whole new field of hands-on research.

Dedicated to the ways of his ancient order, Connor is on the verge of receiving the brotherhood's highest honor: the gifts of magic and immortality. All will be lost, however, if he succumbs to his longing for Jillian. Torn by conflicting emotions, Connor has to choose between an eternity of unbounded power—and a single lifetime of endless passion.

___51953-4 $4.99 US/$5.99 CAN

Dorchester Publishing Co., Inc.
65 Commerce Road
Stamford, CT 06902

Please add $1.75 for shipping and handling for the first book and $.50 for each book thereafter. NY, NYC, PA and CT residents, please add appropriate sales tax. No cash, stamps, or C.O.D.s. All orders shipped within 6 weeks via postal service book rate. Canadian orders require $2.00 extra postage and must be paid in U.S. dollars through a U.S. banking facility.

Name _____

Address _____

City _____ State _____ Zip _____

I have enclosed $_____in payment for the checked book(s).
Payment <u>must</u> accompany all orders. ☐ Please send a free catalog.